The
PERPIGNON
EXCHANGE

The
PERPIGNON
EXCHANGE

by

Warren Kiefer

DONALD I. FINE, INC.

NEW YORK

Library of Congress Cataloging-in-Publication Data

Kiefer, Warren, 1929–
The perpignon exchange/by Warren Kiefer.
p.   cm.
ISBN 1–55611–227–0
I. Title.
PS3561.I34P47   1990
813'54—dc20   90–55338
                                                                    CIP

Manufactured in the United States of America

10 9 8 7 6 5 4 3 2 1

DESIGNED BY IRVING PERKINS ASSOCIATES

*For
Kathleen*

May all your teeth fall out but one.
And may that ache until you die.

May all your teeth fall out but one.
And may that ache until you die.

I

◇ I was born the illegitimate son of a Palestinian mother and a French father in a squalid little village on the West Bank of the Jordan River. Under my Arab name, Dahoud el Beida, I trained as a guerilla in the Beqaa Valley before I was eighteen. I have lived by my wits ever since. Not always in luxury, but I cope.

In some circles, my good sense earned me a reputation as a serious, circumspect citizen with some ambition. Elsewhere, such as the Army of Patriots for Palestinian Liberation, or APPL, to which I once belonged, I have been described in less flattering terms. APPL was not an army at all, but a collection of fanatics who dedicated themselves to indiscriminate murder and the kind of rash, suicidal missions which seemed daft to me. Although my belief in the cause was sincere, my commitment was precarious, so I dropped out. But my hardcore APPL comrades did not approve of dropouts, and I soon became a fugitive from their vengeful justice.

I was not alone. When Yasser Arafat and the mainstream Palestine Liberation Organization renounced terrorism and recognized Israel's right to exist in 1988, APPL went after the PLO as well, and declared its solidarity with the liberation lunatic fringe. This included terrorist extremists such as Abu Nidal's implacable Fatah Revolutionary Council and the United Palestinian Armed Resistance Front run by Khalil Malduum.

I stayed a few steps ahead of them until circumstances betrayed me, forcing me once more into a life of tension and violence, the two things I dislike most.

Call me what you want—traitor, coward, turncoat, knave—but don't ask me to throw stones at soldiers who shoot back. And don't ask me to take innocent hostages or hijack airliners. Better men than I will have to carry the torch of Palestinian freedom because every time I pick it up, I burn my fingers.

At last, thanks to my martyrdom, I'm free of all that. One might

1

ask how a martyr can still be around to talk about it, and I can tell you it isn't easy. First of all, the path to martyrdom is perilous in the extreme, and the actual transition is scary when all you're trying to do is stay alive in a hostile world.

My aged friend Aboubakir Jeballah once told me, "Deny everything even if they hang you, because there's always the chance the rope may break." That, in a figurative sense, is what happened to me, and although my apotheosis was as unexpected as it was premature, it was all the more welcome because nothing less than a martyr's death could have saved my life.

Old Jeballah liked to say that a man's only real obligations apart from his children were to enjoy good food in the company of his friends, and good times with beautiful women. The trouble is that good food is fattening, true friends are hard to find, and beautiful women can be a man's undoing.

Take Solange. I married her because she begged my protection, but once the ceremony was over, she behaved as if she was the one who had done me the favor. One might argue that all I had to do was end it then and there. But she had me by the shorthair, as they say, because she knew too much about me, and regularly threatened exposure if I did not play her game. I was easy prey, but blackmail can sully the best of relationships.

By profession . am a business consultant specializing in computers, although the police in some countries might dispute that. I speak a dozen languages and hold degrees from Baghdad University and from Cairo, as well as a doctorate in cybernetics from the Haroun el Raschid College of Computer Technology at Aleppo.

These sheepskins helped me find work at different times in different places, which is surprising because they are all forged. The seals are imperfectly reproduced and the best of the lettering was done by an apprentice calligrapher in Damascus.

Solange always said I was tempting fate by misrepresenting myself, but she did not understand that documents make the world go round, forged or otherwise. "Someday, Beida," she liked to tell me, "you will go too far and get what's coming to you."

"And what is that, my dear?"

Smiling sweetly and drawing one finger across her throat, she would say, "A cell, a knife, a hangman's rope."

"And you, my dear? Will you get what's coming to you?"

"A woman knows her limits."

"Ah, but you don't know mine or you wouldn't risk your pretty neck by testing them as often as you do."

"Don't threaten me, Beida."

"I was only defining our relationship, *habibi.*"

"A real man would beat a woman like me."

"It's what you want, isn't it?"

"A real man would hump me until I begged him to stop!"

"You're such a romantic, Solange."

"And you're a sleek, self-indulgent son of a bitch," she would say with spite. "But insults don't pass your elephant skin."

"Considering the source, you're quite right."

That kind of lively exchange seldom led us anywhere but to a fight, after which we usually wound up in bed. "I love an aggressive man, Beida," she would hiss into my ear as I rolled on top of her. "Hard! Hard! Har-der!"

Solange's demands for money never let up, even when she worked. I met her when she was performing in Cairo cabarets as a belly dancer—*ecdysiast* she called it—and took in a fair amount of cash. She usually denied giving it to her various lovers, however, and if I protested, we would quarrel and end up in bed again. And so continued the vicious circle of our stormy lives.

In Cairo things between us got worse due to an unfortunate misunderstanding. I had done a deal for three hundred Madsen submachine guns with some Eritrean guerillas she introduced me to. The 9 mm. Madsen is a Danish weapon, simple and sturdy, ideal for use by these uneducated tribesmen. The Eritreans advanced me eighty thousand dollars, the balance to be paid upon delivery.

The guns were to be sent to one of their desert bases in crates marked "Bathroom Fixtures." Unfortunately, that is what the boxes contained so the rebels complained to friends in the Egyptian police who stopped me at the airport.

I passed the next several weeks in a Cairo cell before I found a judge I could bribe to sign a deportation order. Solange meanwhile had run out on me with most of the money because the Eritreans threatened to cut off her nipples.

I caught up with her in Greece to find she had spent every penny on clothes and jewelry. If I were a violent man, I would have put paid to Solange then and there. But again she got the best of me in bed. She was beautiful and I am vain, and she knew how to get round the forgiving side of my nature. In addition, it was spring and we did some business fleecing rich Japanese tourists until the police started closing in.

At the same time, an Arab acquaintance tipped me off that APPL had traced me to Athens and was sending one of their men. I put Solange on a plane for Rome immediately and changed hotels. Most of APPL's energies these days are devoted to fighting rival groups or snuffing defectors like me, and although I had been away from them for years, I was still high on their blacklist.

Luckily, I also carry a valid French passport in the name of David Perpignon—the only legacy from my capricious father, the French vice-consul in Nablus who was drunk the night he selected my surname, and misread the label on a champagne bottle. David Perpignon has never been in trouble in his life.

When the APPL killer reached Athens he hit a dead end because there was no one named Dahoud el Beida registered anywhere. And when the Greek police came to my hotel looking for the same dodgy Arab, they found only an innocent Frenchman named Perpignon listed among the guests.

APPL was not aware of David Perpignon's existence any more than Solange was. It was my best kept secret. And before the hit man or the Greek police could make the connection, I decided to move on to Vienna where I keep a small apartment under my French name and look after a few modest investments, another side of me no one knew about. That was when Fate played its meanest trick.

⟨⟩ The morning began brightly enough. I settled my bill and walked out under the noses of three policemen. No one followed me to the airport where I picked up my ticket on Egyptair and took my place in the check-in line, ostentatiously reading *Le Monde.* The flight I would be taking originated in Cairo and passed through Athens and Belgrade to its final destination, Vienna. I chose the Egyptian airline deliberately because there would be fewer passengers and less scrutiny at the gate.

Directly ahead of me in line was a most attractive blonde. Not ravishingly beautiful like Solange, but interesting and with hair tied back in a ponytail, her stunning figure set off by tight jeans and a blue voile blouse. Eyeglasses perched on the end of a rather short nose gave her an impish look as she peered over them at the airline clerk.

Several expensive cameras hung from her shoulders, and she was weighed down with a cosmetics case and a shoulder bag in addition to two large suitcases. When she spoke English, it was with a charming German accent, but soft, almost lilting. She passed an Austrian passport across the counter with her ticket while I stepped forward quickly to put her bags on the scale. I was rewarded with a gracious smile.

We were both flying first-class, and I heard her ask for a window seat. After she had smiled at me again and left the counter, I got the aisle seat next to hers. No point in being bored on my way to Vienna.

Passing the police check gave me a few nervous moments as the solemn young officer stared at my French passport. "David Perpignon?" he finally said, frowning up at me.

"Correct," I said, smiling.

He flipped through the pages until he found the entry stamp, then looked from me to the passport photo and back again, until I wanted to jump out of my skin. They learn this trick of silent staring in police school, and it's effective, believe me.

"Is anything wrong?" I asked.

He held my passport up between two fingers and for a second I thought it was all over. Then he said, "This expires soon, M. Perpignon. Don't forget to renew it." He stamped it and handed it back with a smile. "Have a nice flight, *monsieur.* Next?"

I looked for the Austrian girl in the departure lounge, and did not see her. There was the usual collection of Arab transit passengers waiting around with no hand luggage, and a trickle of passengers like me who were joining the flight in Athens.

Two shifty-looking types skulked near the departure gate. They were the kind who looked as if they had stolen the money for their tickets, with a week's growth of beard and dressed in cheap, grease-spotted suits. Scrupulously avoiding them was a handsome Egyptian woman with three noisy children accompanied by a Swiss governess, several Arab businessmen, and a red-faced German lady with a figure like a Bavarian beer stein.

Near the departure gate a group of neatly dressed, clean-cut young Arabs were talking among themselves. I took them for university students, and like young people everywhere they wore those miniature headphones and little clip-on radios of the kind sold in airport free shops.

On the far side of the lounge, a tour guide handed out boarding passes to twenty couples with name badges and identical carry-on bags labeled "Iliad Tours." I did not have to hear them to know they were American. They were all middle-aged and older, the women with blue hair, white sweaters draped from their shoulders and sequinned eyeglasses on cords around their necks. Except for two or three tiny creatures who clung to their husbands like sparrows in a wind, the others were mostly rosy-cheeked old cows who filled their stretch culottes to overflowing.

The men were pale and freckled for the most part, their sagging bellies stuffed like sausage into wash-and-wear polo shirts, their brightly colored madras pants bulging with traveler's checks and credit cards. When one slumped into the chair next to me, I read on his name tag, "Hi, I'm RUSTY KIRSHBUAM, VIIth International Congress of Maxillary Surgery and Orthodontics, Athens."

Rusty acknowledged my presence with a friendly grin and said, "You American?"

"French."

"I'm American. We were supposed to fly TWA but there was a bomb scare on the jumbo so they put us on this Arab puddle-jumper. I didn't even know they used the 737s on international runs. What do you do for a living, Mr . . . ?"

"Perpignon. Computers."

"Bernie Cohn, you say? You going to Vienna, Bernie?"

"I live there when I'm not travelling."

"Oh? Then you really know it. We're booked into the Imperial Hotel. Pricey, but I heard it's all right."

"It's old and elegant. You will like it."

"The place in Athens was a rip-off even if it was included in the trip. But Vienna's extra. My wife Helen—that's her over there . . ." He indicated a broad-beamed woman in Bermuda shorts. ". . . she's nuts about Viennese pastry even if she should do without it, know what I mean?" He patted my arm familiarly as he added, "What the heck, Bernie, when they get to a certain age, you got to humor them. You married?"

Only a few days earlier I might have scored off people like Rusty Kirshbaum, relieving their bulging pockets while we talked. Shop clerks seldom look at passport photographs, and Rusty's credit cards would be good for a few thousand dollars worth of saleable merchandise before reports of their loss were circulated. But I had no wish to compromise David Perpignon's good reputation in the event I got caught. It was bad enough that Dahoud el Beida was on the run from the law.

To my great relief the Austrian girl appeared again, coming out of the ladies' room. She sat directly across from me at a right angle so that I could watch her watching the others, and she seemed as amused as I was by some of our fellow passengers.

While the Swiss governess flirted with one of the Arab businessmen, two of her young charges knocked over a sand-filled ashtray with a great clang. The mother looked up from her fashion magazine, saw the mess, cuffed the nearest child, and went back to her reading again without a word.

The young Arabs who looked like university students remained aloof from the other passengers, although their attention, like mine, was drawn to the two bearded dirty-looking fellows who loitered near the gate. They looked like the kind of sleazy lowlife one sees in the most disreputable quarter of Cairo. Or Paris or Marseilles too for that matter.

Although they must have passed the same check I did, no one frisked us, and the pockets of their ill-cut jackets sagged with God knows what. They could be thieves, murderers, hijackers, whatever. Actually, if I had not been compromised myself, so to speak, I would have called some security guard's attention to them.

I was glad when they announced the flight. In spite of my outward calm, I knew there was always a chance some bright cop would add two and two, and suddenly decide to put a hold on David Perpignon before he left the country.

Luckily, nothing of the sort happened. We lined up like sheep,

first-class passengers ahead of the rest, and I arrived at my seat after
the Austrian girl was in hers, looking out the window. When she
saw me, she smiled and said, "What an amazing coincidence. The
same man who was behind me in line."

"If you stop to think about it," I said, pretending to count heads,
"it boggles the mind. The mathematical probability must be at least
a hundred to one."

"In favor or against?"

"After I heard him give you your seat number, in favor."

"Are you always so blunt?"

"I try to make friends wherever I go. Am I succeeding?"

She answered with a shrug which could signify anything.

"You are obviously a woman who is honest with men."

"Does that surprise you?"

"In my experience, it is rare."

"What about men who are honest with women?"

"An endangered species."

"At least that passes for a straight answer."

"I am scrupulously honest about important things."

"Is meeting me important?"

"We haven't exactly met yet, have we?"

"That is begging the question. You should know what's important. Who makes the major decisions in your life?"

"I do, naturally. Are *you* always so blunt?"

She laughed. "*Touché*. I like to know where I stand."

"Of course, meeting you is important. I said to myself when I first
saw you in the check-in line, there goes an important young woman
I should absolutely like to meet, which is why, as you guessed, I
immediately asked for the seat next to yours."

"You don't lack confidence."

"Neither do you."

She said, "I believe I'm going to enjoy this trip after all. Have you
ever been to Vienna?"

"I have a small apartment there."

"Oh! Where?"

"Seilergasse. Behind St. Stephen's church."

"I don't believe it! Then we're neighbors! What number?" When
I told her, she said it was amazing we had not run into each other
there, in the shops or on the street.

"I travel a lot," I said.

"So do I. I'm a photographer."

"What do you photograph?"

"Anything that pays. This trip it was spring fashion collections on the steps of the Parthenon. What about you?"

"Also anything that pays. In my case, computers."

"Do you have a name?"

"Yes, do you?"

"My, my," she said. "Here we are exchanging names already. What will you want to do next if I'm not on my guard?"

"I guarantee nothing illicit, strapped in like this. I'm David Perpignon and I'm delighted to meet you at last."

"That's a nice name and thank you."

"Indeed. And you are?"

"Maria Valeria de los Angeles."

"Really?"

"No. But it's a grand name isn't it? From a television soap opera I loved as a child. My real-life name is Karen Koenig."

Usually my encounters with women were fairly pedestrian, even dull, but this girl was remarkable for her good humor and apparent candor. As the plane taxied toward the runway we continued sparring, taking each other's measure. I decided I liked the way she talked, the way she moved, and the way she crinkled her eyes when she laughed.

In a beauty contest, Solange would win and Karen Koenig would lose. But I was not judging a beauty contest. I was experiencing something quite extraordinary for the first time in my life, and I didn't yet know what it was.

Birds know it. Fish know it. Practically every creature on earth knows it. As the plane careened down the runway and lifted off into the polluted haze of Athens, I knew I had rarely felt so perfectly in tune with another human being, and that if I never saw her again after we landed, I would not soon forget her.

She gripped my arm hard. When I turned to look at her, she was biting her lower lip and trying to speak at the same time.

"What did you say?"

"Nothing. I was praying out loud."

"Well, you can stop now. We made it. We're airborne."

"Yes," she said, relaxing her grip a little. "Now all we have to do is get down again."

I patted her hand reassuringly, not realizing how difficult getting down again would be.

About fifteen minutes after takeoff the steward asked if we would like something to drink. Karen wanted champagne and I decided on the same. Why not? I had made it safely out of Athens and was on my way to my favorite city with a pretty girl beside me. It was cause to celebrate a little.

We toasted Vienna, and had just taken the first few sips when one of the university students came from behind and rudely jostled the steward. As Karen and I watched in stunned surprise, another student rammed the drink cart hard into the poor man's middle, knocking him sprawling, while the first one dived into the tiny galley area and began dumping food trays on the floor. My first thought was that he had lost his screws, as they say, and was desperately seeking something to eat. But then I turned to see the other students milling in the aisle as well. My second foolish thought was that either they were all starving or this was some kind of tasteless student joke. That idea died when the one in the galley stood up holding an automatic pistol. Then another of the group appeared with a submachine gun and two more pistols which he passed to his friends who had shoved the three terrified stewardesses into the laps of startled passengers. The weapons had been smuggled on board in a food cart.

The man from the galley kicked open the cockpit door and placed the muzzle of his gun at the captain's neck.

"Shut off your radios!" he ordered in Arabic.

"But we must monitor the frequency," the pilot said.

"Turn them off or I'll kill you!"

The captain removed his headphones, flicked some switches and announced with amazing calm, "They're off."

"Now tell the passengers we are going to Libya."

"We cannot go there. We have only fuel for Belgrade."

"You're lying!"

The copilot said, "It's true. We cannot make Tripoli without refueling. Nicosia, Cairo or perhaps Beirut, but there is fighting there and they may not let us land."

"Beirut then," the man with the gun shouted. "We will go to Beirut, refuel, then on to Tripoli."

The captain announced over the cabin loudspeaker, in both Arabic and English, in a voice as cool as a summer breeze, that the aircraft was being diverted to Beirut. "Please obey the people with the guns," he said, "and we shall all arrive safely."

The gunman complimented him and said, "Now make the correct turn right to course one-one-eight."

The two pilots exchanged a look indicating that the man with the gun was no fool. He had preselected the correct course for Lebanon and watched until it came up on the gyrocompass.

"You will maintain radio silence until I tell you," he warned both pilots, waving the pistol in their faces again.

The girl student, who of course was not a student at all, but an armed terrorist, came forward with one of the stewardesses who showed her how to work the cabin loudspeaker.

"Attention all passengers," she said in Arabic, "this machine and everyone in it are now under the protection of the United Palestinian Armed Resistance Front!" She was shrill and nervous, and her angry face glistened with perspiration in the cool comfort of the cabin. She added that she and her friends would now be collecting passports, and anyone who refused to comply with their orders would be shot.

I retrieved the bottle of champagne from the drink cart as Karen whispered, "I don't understand the words but did she say what I think she said?"

"The guns say it all," I replied, refilling our glasses, "but they want everybody's passport. Do you have yours handy?"

The Arab girl was standing over me, one hand outstretched and her gun pointed at Karen who dug in her purse and handed over the passport. "Austrian," the girl said. "Jew?"

"What business is it of yours," Karen said.

"She's with me," I said, passing her my Palestinian passport in the name of Dahoud el Beida.

When the hijacker saw the nationality, and checked the picture against my face, she spoke over her shoulder to the leader in the cockpit, "This gentleman is one of us. What do I do?"

"Give him back his passport," he told her in Arabic, and called out to me, "A thousand apologies, sir, for the inconvenience, but we must do what we must do."

I nodded at the Arab girl and said, "Don't be nervous. The passengers will cooperate because they are afraid."

She returned my passport and indicated Karen. "What about her. Is she your wife?"

"Wife-to-be," I said.

The girl shrugged, looking from me to Karen and back again, as if there was no accounting for taste.

The leader was watching us and called out to the girl to stop the socializing and get on with collecting the passports.

"I don't understand," Karen said to me. "What is going on? Why did she give us back our passports?"

"Because the one I showed them is Palestinian."

"You lied to me then? You are not French?"

"Not at the moment, no. It's a long story, but from now on, call me Dahoud el Beida."

She drained her glass and gave me a withering look. "The great honest man with women!"

I poured us both more champagne and said, "Be grateful for small blessings now that we're engaged."

"Are you mad?"

"No. They are. But as long as they think you're my fiancée, you're safe. So play along."

"Who are you? Why are you siding with them?"

"My dear, for the time being we are both siding with them because they have guns."

She was going to give me a flip answer, but when she saw the urgency in my expression and grasped the full dimensions of the disaster she looked at me with wide, frightened eyes.

"Good," I said. "I'm getting through. I was not lying to you. I am French and my name is David Perpignon, but . . ."

"I understand. You are with French secret intelligence."

"For God's sake, don't even think such a thing! That could really get us wasted. I speak Arabic and have a passport with my mother's Palestinian name. That's all. End of story. My Arab name is Dahoud, can you remember that? Dahoud el Beida."

"I am not a fool, Mr. el Beida."

"We're engaged, remember?"

"Dahoud, then."

"Splendid."

"What will they do to us?"

"Nothing if everyone stays calm. They usually want prisoners released from somewhere, that sort of thing, but I'm surprised they picked an Egyptian target. In the past they've always gone for European or American airlines."

"Who are they?"

"Very hard-line terrorists. The leader is a Syrian cutthroat named Khalil Malduum who was cashiered out of the Syrian army for murdering Israeli prisoners."

"Isn't he the one who bombed the jumbo in Lisbon?"

"He claimed the honor. The plane was supposed to be blown out of the air like the one over Scotland, but the bomb only tore a hole in the belly. It caught fire when the pilot tried to land."

"Awful! So many people burned to death." Karen watched the man in the cabin who still had his pistol trained on the captain's head. "Is that Malduum?" she whispered.

"Can't be. Too young."

The man saw her looking at him and smiled. I said under my breath, "Smile back," and to her credit, she was able to do it.

The plane droned on for an hour or so with no further disturbance. What I had mistaken for innocent Walkman radios were actually wireless intercoms which enabled the hijackers to communicate between different parts of the plane. The stewardesses were allowed to serve sandwiches, but few passengers had any appetite.

When all the passports were collected, the Palestinian girl spread them on the galley counter, telling the leader that there were seventy-one passengers on board. In first-class beside us were two Egyptian businessmen, the red-faced German lady, and the Egyptian woman with her children and their Swiss governess.

The remaining passengers in economy class included the "Iliad

Tour" group of orthodontists and their wives, and the two Arabs who looked like thieves or hijackers and were not.

After studying the passports for fifteen minutes and separating them into different piles, the girl told the terrorist leader, "There are thirty Jews, and some I'm not sure about. And two military."

"What military?" he said.

"American soldiers."

"Bring them here."

A few moments later, two muscular young men dressed in T-shirts and bluejeans were prodded forward. One wore glasses and the other had an eagle tatooed on his forearm. They were nervous and compliant, but not outwardly frightened, the kind who would certainly have resisted if guns were not pointing at their heads.

"Kneel down," the leader called from the cockpit and the one with the glasses sank to his knees. When the other did not immediately follow, the girl gave him a vicious clout with her pistol which opened a nasty cut behind his ear. He half-fell, half-knelt beside his companion in the aisle, and the girl taped their wrists tightly behind them.

Looking back down the aisle, I saw that the hijackers were paying more attention to what was going on with the American soldiers than to the other passengers. The hijacker with the machine gun lounged against the lavatory door in the rear of the plane while the two who had prodded the soldiers forward stood at the dividing panel between economy and first-class.

That's when all hell broke loose. In an enclosed space like an airplane cabin, a revolver makes a very loud noise, but a submachine gun sounds like the end of the world.

A single shot made me turn in time to see one of the dirty-looking Arabs shooting at the man who had the machine gun.

The other scruffy one had thrown himself to the floor and was also shooting in our direction. But he only got off two or three shots before being riddled by a burst of machine gun fire when the mortally wounded terrorist caught his finger in the trigger as he fell against the lavatory door.

Our champagne glasses rolled on the carpet and women screamed as bullets sprayed the plane. It was a miracle that dozens of people were not killed or injured. Only when the gunfire suddenly ceased, did I piece together what had happened.

The two grungey Arabs who had aroused my suspicions in the airport were cleverly disguised security guards. They showed more courage than sense and might have succeeded in overwhelming the hijackers but luck was not with them and their timing was poor.

Now, one sprawled dead a short distance from the dying terrorist by the lavatory door, while the other lay wounded in the aisle. Another hijacker was pressing the muzzle of his gun against the man's neck.

The two Americans had thrown themselves flat on the floor and were uninjured. But beyond them near the galley the Arab girl lay with the back of her head blown away, her life pouring out on the carpet. A stray round had also creased the captain's sleeve and smashed into the instrument panel.

A blue haze and the stench of cordite filled the cabin. I emptied the last drops of champagne into our glasses, and Karen took hers in a trembling hand.

I said, "They won't hurt us." But I was not at all sure.

The leader was uninjured, but hysterical with rage. He kicked the two Americans several times before he knelt by the dying girl. Then he seemed to focus on the far end of the cabin where his companion still had the security guard pinned to the floor.

"Kill him!" he shouted, forgetting his intercom. "What are you waiting for?" and the other one fired two shots point blank, making the man's head jump from the carpet before he lay still.

Some passengers screamed while others sobbed and whimpered, oblivious to the voice on the loudspeaker until he shouted, "Quiet, or we'll kill you all!" He waved his gun at them and grabbed the microphone. In good English he said, "Listen to me! We had hoped to avoid bloodshed! But . . ."

Husbands quieted their wives and the Egyptian woman hugged her children closer to her while the red-faced German lady watched the terrorist with undisguised loathing. The Swiss governess rocked back and forth, weeping silently into a handkerchief.

"You were warned!" he shouted, forgetting to press the microphone button. Then realizing his error, he said it again, and his voice reverberated through the cabin. "You want to defy us! I'll show you what happens to those who do that!"

I did not really believe he would do anything more, after what we had just seen. But I was wrong. He kicked the tatooed American soldier until he stood up, then grabbed his bound wrists and jerked him around to face the rear of the plane. He gave him a shove which sent him reeling past the first-class partition so that he was in full view of all the passengers.

When he put the pistol to the unlucky soldier's neck, I still thought he was only going to prod him further. Instead he cocked the hammer, pulled the trigger, and sent a bullet crashing into the poor man's brain. The soldier pitched forward, seemed to shrug his shoulders once or twice after he hit the floor and then lay still, bright arterial blood pulsing from the wound.

I don't know whether it was the unexpected shock of the act, or the gratuitous brutality of it, but the silence that now prevailed was absolute. The passengers seemed beyond screams, beyond weeping, as if there had been a collective decision to abandon all protest, all reaction, in return for the simple privilege of staying alive.

IV

◁▷ We had been flying less than two hours, and five bodies lay on the cabin floor, two of them terrorists. I wanted to believe that the worst was over, and that the hijackers' anger had at last subsided. But if things were suddenly less violent it was simply because their bloodlust was temporarily sated, and like terminal cancer, had only entered a state of brief spontaneous remission.

The leader, whom the others called Najeeb, sent his two surviving companions to make a weapons search of the male passengers which turned up pocket knives and nail clippers, but no guns. We were soon approaching Beirut, and Najeeb ordered the captain to turn on his radios. To my surprise the air pressure in the cabin had not yet been noticeably affected by the bullet holes. No oxygen masks had dropped and the pilot did not have to seek a lower altitude.

Najeeb held his gun to the captain's head and directed him to turn on the cockpit loudspeaker so he could hear both sides of the radio conversation. The pilot identified himself to Beirut Approach Control and informed them that his plane had been hijacked, and that he required immediate clearance to land and refuel.

Beirut told him to standby, and then after a very long wait, said, "Negative, Egyptair flight. You may not enter, repeat, *NOT ENTER* Lebanese airspace."

"I knew it," the copilot said.

"How many minutes to reach Beirut?" Najeeb asked them.

"Twenty," the captain replied.

"I will talk to them," Najeeb said.

The captain passed him an extra headphone and throat mike and showed him how to click the button to talk. "This is the United Palestinian Armed Resistance Front!" he shouted. "We are landing in twenty minutes! Have fuel ready and no police or soldiers!"

Beirut replied, "Repeat, negative, Egyptair. You are denied permission to land. You may *NOT* enter Lebanese airspace."

The captain spoke calmly into his microphone. "Beirut, this is Egyptair captain. Mayday, Beirut, mayday! This is an emergency. We have wounded on board. Our ETA Beirut is zero-nine-forty Zulu and our fuel is marginal. Request immediate clearance to land. Over."

"Standby, Egyptair." Another long wait ensued while Najeeb fidgeted behind the two pilots, looking down the aisle of the plane where the bodies lay, then back at the men in the cockpit.

"We land with or without clearance," Najeeb said.

"We can't if they block the runway," the copilot said.

"They will not do that."

The captain said, "They've done it before."

Finally the radio voice returned, "Egyptair, Beirut."

"Beirut, Egyptair," the captain said.

"Squawk seven, four, two, three, one, one, Egyptair. Cleared for direct visual approach runway three-six. Notify final. Do you require medical assistance?"

"Affirmative, Beirut," the captain said.

"No, we don't!" Najeeb shouted at the radio. "Don't anyone come near us when we land! Only petrol!"

For the next twenty minutes, most of my energy was concentrated in crossing my fingers. I hoped they would let us go when we landed, but I was not at all sure.

Najeeb continued to shout instructions at the tower as we lost altitude and crossed over the beach south of the ruined city. The captain made a gentle left turn before lowering the wheels and lined the Boeing up with the north-south runway. When we touched down two minutes later Karen uttered a very long sigh.

We were directed to the opposite side of the airport from the terminal where the pilot parked well away from any buildings. With the engines shut down it suddenly became stifling hot in the plane. Children began to whimper as women desperately fanned themselves and men tied knots in the corners of their handkerchiefs and wore them on their heads.

Najeeb allowed one stewardess to dole out water, but everyone's thirst was so great, it was unlikely to last. He paced the cabin, looking out one window after another. He had made it clear that only one fuel truck was to approach the plane, stop fifty meters short, and await instructions.

But no fuel truck appeared.

Instead, three truckloads of soldiers in full combat gear arrived, and quickly surrounded the plane. They remained about two hundred meters away, well out of pistol range, but comfortably close for their sharpshooters to pick off any careless hijacker.

Najeeb began screaming at them in Arabic to back off immediately or he would start killing the women and children.

The captain said to the tower, "Beirut, this is the captain speaking. Please remove the soldiers. In the name of God do as he says! You are gambling with all our lives!"

That seemed to calm Najeeb, and he even patted the pilot on the shoulder approvingly. But when the minutes ticked by and the soldiers remained in place, he began to fidget and then to pound one fist angrily into the other. Suddenly he bolted from the cockpit and grabbed the steward by the neck. "Open the door!"

The man was very frightened as he struggled with the handle but finally managed to swing the big door open. Najeeb himself hung back out of sight and shouted at me, "You! Palestinian! Give him a hand!" He wanted us to drag the dead American to the door. The steward took the corpse by the feet and I by the shoulders. Then, under Najeeb's direction, I half-sat the body in the doorway, its legs dangling out of the airplane.

In spite of the heat, I was in a cold sweat as I was doing this, aware of at least fifty rifles aimed at my head. I did not know that there were also long-lens cameras trained on me which would change my life.

Najeeb had taken the machine gun from his colleague and was screaming over the radio again, "Beirut, the man in the door is an American soldier spy! This is what we do to them!" He waved me away and put a burst of fire into the dead man's back. The corpse jumped as if alive, and pitched forward to fall fifteen feet to the tarmac.

"Now put her in the same place," he said to us, indicating the dead girl terrorist. After the soldier, she was light as a doll. I propped her in the doorway and quickly got out of the way. "This is a college student!" Najeeb shouted into the radio, and fired another short burst into the girl's back.

In death she was less cooperative than in life however, and did not fall out of the plane like the soldier, so Najeeb told the steward to push her out. This gutsy little man saw his opportunity and jumped with the body, becoming the only one of us to escape. At the time I wanted to applaud him and was glad he made it. I did not realize that he had heard the girl say I was one of them, and that he would soon become a damning witness against me.

The tower asked them to stop the killing and Najeeb shouted. "We have just begun! If the soldiers aren't gone in five minutes, we will kill all passengers!"

Five minutes later the soldiers were still in place, and Karen said, "Do you think he means it?"

"Probably. But I believe the military will pull back."

"Will he let us go then?"

"Don't count on it. I think he would have at the start, if they had just sent a gasoline truck."

Another ten minutes passed and nothing happened. Najeeb grabbed the microphone and shouted, "Beirut, time is up!"

The voice replied immediately, "Please have patience. There is no radio link with the military commander. They have been given orders to stand down but it takes time to communicate. We are very sorry, but please be patient. Give us time."

"You have five minutes! Where is the petrol?"

"It will arrive as soon as the soldiers withdraw."

For the next hour Najeeb's threats continued and nothing happened. Then, as suddenly as they had arrived, the soldiers filed back to their trucks and left us alone.

But still no fuel truck appeared. The voice on the radio said he would attempt to find out the reason for the delay, but another hour passed like this until the heat inside the plane was unbearable. What little water and soft drinks there were on board were soon gone. People began moaning and whimpering, and children were crying. Some one called out from the back. "Let the women and children go! You have enough hostages with the men!"

That was the wrong thing to say to a monster like Najeeb because his mind worked in other directions. He grabbed the nearest Egyptian child by her thin little wrist and flung her at me. "Take her to the door! Show her to them!"

"But she's a child!" I protested, putting my arms protectively around her tiny shoulders, frail as birds' bones.

"Precisely! Show her to them!" I did as he ordered, determined to keep myself between him and this helpless creature. I knew he would murder a child as easily as he had killed the soldier, but I rationalized that he would hesitate to shoot a fellow Palestinian in the back. I decided if that was what he was going to do, I would follow the steward's example and take the child with me.

Najeeb was on the radio again, telling them, "The girl is next, Beirut, if the petrol lorry is not here in five minutes!"

"Egyptair," the tower replied, "we have discovered the problem. There is no Egyptair employee here with authority to pay for the fuel. Shell will only deliver for cash."

"Are they all mad?" the captain said.

"You are stalling!" Najeeb shouted into the microphone. "Get the petrol lorry here now or we kill the child!"

While this was going on I held the trembling girl in the doorway telling her softly not to worry, that I would not let anything happen to her. And across the tarmac they were snapping pictures of me which would grace the front pages of every newspaper in the world the following day with captions like, "Arab terrorist takes child hostage!"

"Egyptair, we are trying to contact your West Beirut office to authorize payment," the tower said. "We are doing our best, sir."

"Collect it from the passengers," the captain said to Najeeb. "They must have enough cash to pay for the fuel."

"How much will we need?"

"Five thousand dollars will take us to Amman and back."

While I consoled the terrified child, Najeeb sent his two companions through the plane demanding two or three hundred dollars each from the passengers until they had enough. Meanwhile the pilot begged the tower to send the truck, saying he would pay cash when the fuel came aboard.

It was another half hour before the truck arrived and parked as instructed. Najeeb ordered a stewardess to extend the steps while I returned the little girl to her mother. At the same moment, one of the hijackers grabbed a woman passenger and marched her down the aisle at gun point. It was Mrs. Kirshbaum, the wife of the dentist who had spoken to me in the lounge.

She was weeping when she reached the door and now began to cry out "Don't kill me! Please don't kill me! I have children! Grandchildren!"

Najeeb struck her across the mouth to shut her up, but the blow only made her sob the harder. As the other man bound her hands behind her back, Najeeb told him, "If anything goes wrong, kill her and the driver before you come back aboard." The second terrorist took a black stocking from his pocket and pulled it over his head.

Mrs. Kirshbaum had to be pushed and almost carried down each step to the hot tarmac where she immediately collapsed when she saw the bloody bodies of the girl terrorist and the American soldier. The hijacker continued to kick her painfully until she staggered to her feet and lurched ahead of him to the shadow of the Shell fuel truck.

When Najeeb let me return to my seat, Karen was more concerned for me than for herself. "Are you all right?"

"Thirsty, that's all."

"This is a nightmare for all of us," she said, "but it must be worse for you. Your own people doing this."

"They're not my people," I said bitterly. "These are not the kids who throw stones in the *intifada* and fight for a better life. These are psychopaths who enjoy their work. Look at their faces. Killing is a high for them."

"You were going to jump with the child, weren't you?"

"I considered it."

"I saw you cuddling her and calculating the fall."

"A good thing our fanatical friend didn't see me too."

"I took some pictures," she said under her breath. "I have him shooting the bodies in the doorway."

"For God's sake don't take any more! If they see you doing that we're finished. My Palestinian passport won't help."

While the refueling was being carried out, the pilot asked the tower to send water, and another smaller truck came immediately. At first, Najeeb refused to allow the copilot to leave the plane to assist in bringing the water aboard, but finally his own thirst got the better of him and he gave permission.

In less than half an hour we were ready to take off, and everyone blessed the pilot when the engines spooled up and fresh, cool air began to circulate through the cabin again. We were allowed to drink our fill, and my spirits lifted as we became airborne, thinking that at least Karen and I would probably be turned loose in Amman even if the others were not.

I never guessed that this was only the first day of an odyssey of terror that would last days for Karen and me, and months for many of the others. We had hardly got used to the cool air when Amman refused us permission to land.

"We go to Damascus then," Najeeb said peevishly, but Damascus also refused to have us. His fury then returned and I think he actually might have started killing again, except the captain said, "We've got company."

Looking out to the left of the Boeing I saw a Mirage fighter practically touching our wingtip. It bore the hollow, six-pointed star of Israel and a number. Karen squeezed my arm and said, "Thank God! We're getting help."

"Not the kind we need."

She pointed across the cabin and I saw through the opposite window another Mirage on our right wingtip. Both aircraft were close enough for us to see the pilots' faces clearly.

A voice in Arabic came over the cockpit loudspeaker. "Egyptair, this is your neighbor speaking. Can we help you?"

Najeeb screamed into the microphone, "Go away! Back off! Leave immediately or we kill everybody!"

"Egyptair," the voice replied calmly, "you are cleared for landing Jerusalem. We will escort you. If you release the passengers, you may refuel and leave unharmed."

"Go away!" Najeeb shouted, "or we kill them. You hear this?" And he fired two shots through the roof of the cabin. "We start the killing now!"

Instantly the Israeli fighters veered off and turned in opposite directions away from us. "Now what?" Karen said to me.

"We go to Libya," Najeeb announced.

At this moment we were flying directly above the Sea of Galilee which isn't a sea at all, but rather a small inland lake. To the north we had Syria and Lebanon, to the southeast, Jordan, and directly off our right, Israel, or as I had been taught, Palestine.

"We're going to have a fuel problem again with Libya," the copilot said as he worked a small calculator in his lap. "We can make Benghazi okay, but not Tripoli."

"Then fly to Benghazi," Najeeb said.

The captain started to put the plane in a steep turn to the north and Najeeb shouted at him, waving the gun again, "Where are you taking us! Libya is to the west!"

"We have to detour north through Lebanon. We can't risk crossing Israeli airspace," the captain said.

"Fly straight west," Najeeb ordered. "They know we're here. They will not shoot us."

The pilots brought the plane around to a westerly heading, directly into the afternoon sun. I, too, doubted the Israelis would shoot, but one never knows. If they did, it wouldn't be the first time missiles had been fired at a defenseless airliner.

The last of the food was shared out and many people, Karen included, succumbed at last to tension-induced fatigue and fell sound asleep. We crossed Israel without incident and came out over the Mediterranean at an altitude of about twenty thousand feet. There was no cloud and I could see what I presumed was the port of Haifa shimmering in the afternoon sun.

I was dozing myself when I heard more radio talk coming from the cockpit. It was nearly sundown and when I looked to the left of the plane I saw what seemed to be the entire Egyptian air force flying abreast of us. Actually there were only about six planes but they were so close they filled the sky. Najeeb saw them too, and for a change he was not angry.

But the Egyptian pilots were less friendly than the Israelis. This was an Egyptian airliner and national pride was at stake. A dialogue of mutual ultimatums ensued between the flight leader and Najeeb which made my blood run cold. Egyptair was told to divert immediately to Cairo and land, or else, while Najeeb threatened to murder everyone on board if they did not disappear.

When Egyptair did not change course, the Egyptian air force opened fire. They did not shoot directly at us, thank God, but over our bow, so to speak. Cannon shells and tracer bullets streaked past the Boeing, converging at a point which seemed barely inches in front of our nose.

The captain swerved to avoid the flack, making a sudden evasive turn more suited to a warplane than an airliner, and we rocked and shuddered as the plane passed through the turbulence caused by the exploding shells. Passengers screamed and Najeeb sprawled cursing against the back of the captain's seat.

Then we entered a shallow dive and pulled up low over the water, lowering flaps and landing gear to slow us down. The jets streaked by above, unable to match our speed without stalling.

After fifteen minutes, the copilot said, "Our fuel burn is too high to make Benghazi. We'll have to backtrack to Cairo."

That rekindled Najeeb's rage, and he struck the captain from behind with his pistol, shouting, "You did it deliberately! I'll kill you! I'll kill you!"

V

Najeeb had given strict orders that no one was to leave his seat, but when Rusty Kirshbaum's wife returned safely from the fuel truck, the anxious dentist had rushed forward to embrace her. Although the woman ignored her husband's show of reckless ardor, it earned him a punch in the ear from one of the hijackers, and a fierce shove against the drinks cart. But Najeeb was in a hurry to take off so they let Rusty hug his wife and sit her down in the row directly across from us.

Mrs. Kirshbaum was virtually catatonic by then—between her

fright at being singled out from the other passengers and the heat on the tarmac—and she seemed totally unresponsive to her husband's fussy ministrations. She did not weep or whimper, but stared vacantly ahead, rocking back and forth as she hugged her pendulous breasts, keening to herself. Rusty Kirshbaum shook his head gravely at me, the way one does beside the bed of a desperately ill person.

When the Israeli planes overtook us, every passenger except Mrs. Kirshbaum expectantly watched the action outside the windows. And when the Egyptian fighters fired cannon in our path, the noise and turbulence terrified all but her. Her husband would pat her arm and whisper, "Helen, dearie, it will be all right," but shock had carried her beyond hearing.

After the copilot said we could not make it to Benghazi, and Najeeb in his fury began to pistol-whip the captain, Mrs. Kirshbaum seemed to come out of her trance. The unfortunate officer stumbled from the cockpit and fell on all fours at the head of the aisle, not far from where she sat, the blood dripping like sweat from his nose, speckling his impeccable white shirt.

When he tried to get to his feet, Najeeb went for him again, but a piercing scream stopped him in his tracks. Like an avenging fury Mrs. Kirshbaum launched herself at Najeeb. Fat, middle-aged ladies are not expected to offer resistance, and the hijacker could not have been more surprised if he had been attacked by a giant bat. The momentum of her charge carried Najeeb over backwards through the open doorway of the cockpit, and his gun flew from his hand to land inches from my feet. He tried to roll free as she scratched and pummeled him, but the dead weight and sheer mass of the woman made this difficult. I saw Fate mocking me as I picked up the gun, and Najeeb saw it too. The sight of the gun in my hands turned him very pale at first, and perhaps in those few seconds the possibility existed that I might have turned the tables. But I was as astonished as he was, and my reflexes were a good deal slower. So by the time I realized I had the advantage, I had lost it. A glance to my right showed one of the other hijackers with his machine gun pointed in my direction.

Even then, perhaps, I might have been able to put the gun to Najeeb's head and force the others to drop their weapons. But that only happens in films. In real life an exchange of glances had settled the issue.

When Najeeb finally squirmed away from the heroic Mrs. Kirshbaum and got to his feet, he merely put out his hand to have me give him back the gun. He wiped an arm across his badly scratched face, looked around him in amazement, and laughed. It was the one moment of humor in the entire hijacking episode, and only he saw it.

He was still smiling as he shook his finger at the woman the way one does with a naughty child. "Get out of your seat again, you old bag," he told her as he pointed the gun at her husband, "and I'll kill him."

The captain had struggled to his feet while this was going on, and now daubed at the cuts around his eyes with paper towels.

"You! Drive us to Libya!" Najeeb said in Arabic.

"We won't make it."

"Then back to Beirut."

The captain shook his head. "Our fuel won't take us that far either. Flying at this altitude was the only way to avoid an accident with the fighters, but it doubled our consumption."

"Then we crash into the sea," Najeeb said.

"We can still make Alexandria or Cairo if we turn back."

"Never!"

"The only alternative is Cyprus, then," the captain said wearily, "if they let us land."

When the captain returned to his seat and laid his hands on the control yoke, the copilot said, "Are you all right?"

"I've been better," he replied as he began a turn to the north. "Tune in the Nicosia VOR and let's get a radial."

They were speaking in Arabic.

"No radios!" Najeeb said.

"If you don't want to make a great splash in the sea, we must turn it on to find Cyprus."

"All right. But one trick and you're dead. I only need one of you to fly this machine."

"If we don't make Nicosia," the captain said, "you won't even need one of us."

After a moment the copilot said, "Nicosia ETA twenty-one minutes. Fuel thirty minutes."

"Nice," the captain said in English. "We have eight minutes and fifty-nine seconds to fool around."

The sun was setting, a red ball in the west whose rays glazed the surface of the Mediterranean with flecks of pink gold. Karen said, "Look!" and I thought she meant the spectacular sunset.

"It's very beautiful," I agreed, "but the circumstances leave a lot to be desired. I'd be happier looking at Viennese streetlights."

"I didn't mean that," she said, and then I saw the planes.

I counted six against the setting sun and for a moment thought the Egyptians had come back. But no. These were different, and in the shadowy twilight I could not at first make out the markings. They did not come as close as the Israelis and they did not fire ahead of us like the Egyptians. They simply enveloped us. One in front, one on either side, one above, and presumably one below and one behind, although I could not see the last two.

The one on the left was close enough finally for me to read "NAVY" on his tail and see a number and a five-pointed American star. These were Tomcat fighters from the Sixth Fleet. There was no radio talk now because Najeeb forbade it. But the fighters escorted us to the final approach for Nicosia airport before peeling off into the early night.

For awhile the island of Cyprus was a mountainous pink shadow on the northern horizon, its spine of rugged peaks rising over six thousand feet from the sea. Once we passed Cape Gata and the coast, the mountains grew darker and more sinister as we descended toward them. When it almost seemed that we would crash into the nearest one, the ridge line suddenly dropped away and we were on the other side of the island. Nicosia soon appeared in the distance like a profligate swath of jewels twinkling in the night.

"Three minutes," I heard the copilot say.

"Outer marker?" the captain asked him.

"Coming up."

The final approach was very bumpy, but a few minutes after sunset we touched down with a squeal of tires and braked to a stop.

All lights had been turned off inside the plane, except for the faint glow from the cockpit instrument panel.

A jeep with a chequered flag and a "FOLLOW ME" sign appeared on the runway ahead of us, its lights flashing. Najeeb had already delivered his standard sermon to the tower about no interference, and we were guided to the far side of the field as in Beirut, well away from the main terminal area.

As soon as he saw where they wanted us to park however, he

made a scandal with the tower. The captain had followed the jeep to a remote position shared only by a charred, derelict DC-8, and while he maneuvered our Boeing into a slot on the narrow hardstand, Najeeb shouted at the tower operator that they must find us a different place to park in the open.

"Standby, Egyptair and we'll see what we can do."

As we waited, one of our engines stopped, and then the other, and Najeeb vented his anger on the pilots again. "I did not tell you to shut down the engines!"

"We did not shut them down," the captain replied. "We've just run out of fuel."

"I don't believe you! It's another damn Egyptian trick!"

The copilot pointed at the instrument gauges and said, "It's no trick, sir. Look here and see for yourself."

They convinced Najeeb finally, but his frustration at being forced to stay in a place he disliked only fed his anger. "We cannot remain here!" he insisted. "We must refuel and move!"

Karen peered through the window at the dark, burnt-out DC-8 perched on the edge of the field, its paint and engines gone, its flaps drooping like the wings of an exhausted bird. "Why doesn't he want to stay here?" she asked me, sotto voce.

"Too close to that old airplane. Police or soldiers could use it for cover if they decided to come after the hijackers."

"My God!" she gasped. "Would anyone be that foolish?"

"Do you remember what the Egyptians did in Malta back in 1985?"

"Vaguely."

"They stormed another 737 of theirs that had been hijacked, and killed the hijackers."

"Good."

"They also killed fifty-seven passengers."

She wanted me to tell her they would not do something so ill-advised again, but I could only shrug and pat her hand. At that moment I felt as helpless and as foolish as Rusty Kirshbaum. I also felt as if I had betrayed them all, even though I knew it wasn't true. To have reacted in any other way than I did—with a machine gun pointed at me—would have been sheer suicide.

But the fact remained that while I gave Najeeb back his gun, it was fat old Mrs. Kirshbaum who gave us all back our dignity.

Observing her now clinging to her husband's arm, it was hard to believe the Joan of Arc I had seen emerge from that chrysalis of pink sagging flesh and stringy dyed hair.

While Najeeb argued once more about fuel deliveries and the need for an auxiliary power supply, one of the stewardesses said, "There is no food and people are hungry."

"All of Palestine is hungry," Najeeb replied angrily. "You will eat when we get where we're going."

There were other problems beside the lack of food. By the time we landed in Cyprus, we had been in the hands of the hijackers about twelve hours. The heat in Beirut and the tension since had taken its toll on all of us. Now, although Najeeb allowed a forward door to be opened, there was a growing stench of body odor, blood, lavatories and decay in the cabin.

Karen and I were lucky because we were next to the open door, so an occasional whiff of pine resin and charcoal cooking fires reached us on the evening air. But behind us in the cabin, people were fanning themselves again, not because of the heat—it was cool enough in the night at that altitude—but against the miasma generated by so much sweat, fear, and death on board.

One of the dentists in Rusty Kirshbaum's convention group had the temerity to say that the bodies should be taken off the plane for health reasons, but Najeeb ignored him. The two security guards were left as they fell for everyone to see, but the dead hijacker was granted an airline blanket over his face.

Najeeb showed no sign of fatigue, only an inexhaustible font of bile as he began to rant again at the people in the control tower. Nicosia was not cooperating, he said, and the consequences would fall heavily on the passengers. Like the Lebanese authorities, the Cypriots called for patience and said they were moving as quickly as possible to satisfy the hijackers' immediate demands. Water and food would soon be on the way, but there was a problem about jet fuel.

I thought Najeeb would have a stroke when he heard that. He began to scream incomprehensibly, cursing and threatening in Arabic and English, saying he did not believe their lies about delays. When he finally ran out of breath, the voice from the tower said it was not a question of a delay. The problem with the jet fuel was that they did not have any.

This news cut his hysteria as he struggled to comprehend what they had told him. If it was a lie, it was as outrageous as it was ingenious. And if it was the truth, it was a catastrophe.

For a moment he simply stared at the microphone in disbelief, his ringent mouth silent for once, the fingers of one hand stroking the butt of his pistol. I would not have been surprised then if he had begun to carry out his murderous threats because he was a man on the brink. But the time it took the tower to explain why they had no fuel somehow carried him past the worst part. He retreated from the madness I had seen in his eyes and gave way again to anger.

The tower was saying, ". . . because a lorry drivers' strike has interrupted regular deliveries . . ."

"Get the petrol!" he screamed. "Take it from other airplanes! But get it or the killing starts again!"

The tower replied, "We have been in touch with the military field at Akrotiri. They have jet fuel. We are trying to get clearance for you to land there."

"We are not flying to military fields!" Najeeb shouted. "We are staying here until you send us petrol! You have one hour!"

"Sir, I repeat, we do not have any at this moment."

"Get it!"

"Standby, please Egyptair."

In the afternoon a water van appeared and we all sat tensely while the water was poured into jerricans and brought aboard. Najeeb refused to allow anyone else near the plane although by then the lavatories were backing up and were barely usable.

At midnight, we were still standing by and nothing had been resolved about the fuel. There was no noticeable movement on the ground, no action of any sort. Except for the water van and the "FOLLOW ME" jeep which had led us to the hardstand when we arrived, no other vehicle had ventured near us. No planes had landed or taken off, and none had overflown the airport.

The other two hijackers were showing the same signs of fatigue as the passengers by then, and Najeeb allowed them each to sleep about four hours while he remained on his feet until dawn.

By that time we had been on the ground twelve hours, and in spite of constant assurances, only the water had arrived. Najeeb finally requested food as well, but again he was told to wait. Either the Cypriots were the most inefficient race in the entire Mediterranean or they were deliberately dragging their feet. But why? I had no idea and that worried me very much. Normally when a hijacked plane is transient, it is in a country's best interest to pass the buck, to service and refuel the aircraft as quickly as possible and get rid of it. But after a few more hours, there was no mistake about it. They were stalling, and Najeeb knew it. The word had gone out, and the place was obviously off limits now to all ground and air traffic, under quarantine to protect the rest of the world against the plague of terrorism we carried.

Each time Najeeb called the tower and repeated his demands, all he got was "Standby, Egyptair," or "We're doing everything possible, sir. Please have patience."

At ten o'clock on that second morning Najeeb suddenly picked up the microphone and told them, "Nicosia control, we will kill one passenger at eleven if the fuel is not here."

More official pleading followed, but he refused to acknowledge any transmission except to say, "You have one hour, Nicosia!"

When he ordered the dead guards dragged to the door I assumed he was planning a repeat performance of Beirut. But as soon as the corpses were propped in the doorway, he told the tower, "You are not to be trusted Nicosia! Here are two passengers to show we mean business!" And with that he blew both bodies out of the doorway with a short burst from the machine gun.

The charade at least prompted them to send baskets of sandwiches, which we all wolfed down as soon as they came aboard. But otherwise nothing had changed. As the day wore on the heat began to build again, and the stench from the remaining body in the rear of the airliner even reached us near the cockpit.

At noon the Cypriot Minister of the Interior came on the radio and explained that they would be bringing fuel by military truck from a United Nations depot at Limassol. He asked Najeeb to let the women and children go.

"No one leaves the plane."

"At least the children."

"No one!"

One woman collapsed from heatstroke and she was brought to the door for air just before sundown. Najeeb said if she did not recover, she would be the first one shot in the morning.

Our second night began with more shouted recriminations, but

Najeeb was finally running out of steam and would soon need sleep. No fuel had arrived in spite of all the promises. A new radio voice claiming to be a United Nations observer said the delay was due to strikers blocking the roads. But with luck, he assured Najeeb, the trucks should arrive during the night.

Probably the only thing worse than having someone like Najeeb for an enemy was to have him as a friend. Strung out and popping amphetamines now, he leaned over the seat in front of me and offered his hand. "Najeeb Hassan," he said, "and you are . . .?"

"Dahoud el Beida."

"Your help with that foolish woman was timely, Beida," he said in Arabic. "We have had some bad luck because we were careless and these pilots thought they were being clever. But the Greeks don't dare refuse us the petrol. They will deliver."

"I hope so," I said honestly.

He chatted on about himself as if we were two men who had just met in the bazaar, apologizing again for the inconvenience to me and my "fiancée." "But you will have a great story to tell your children one day," he said cheerfully, as if we had been witnessing some unusual sporting event instead of bloody murder.

In response to his questions about myself, I admitted I was born in Nablus and had once trained as a guerilla, but that I was now a business consultant and computer specialist.

"But you are Palestinian first, last and always," he assured me, yawning at last, "and that is all that matters." Leaving the other two on guard then, he finally succumbed to exhaustion, telling them to wake him a few minutes before midnight.

"What will happen?" Karen asked me.

I feared the worst and was trying to come up with an acceptable lie. But before I could the fuel trucks arrived.

VI

⟨⟩ Najeeb was on his feet again instantly, peering out the window. He ordered the two tankers to park directly in front of us, under the full glare of the landing lights, and sent one of his companions to check each truck carefully and search the drivers. While one truck waited, the other was allowed to park next to the wing where the copilot would do the actual refueling under the eyes of one of the terrorists.

Things were tense from the beginning. The trucks carried military markings and the drivers were soldiers, which Najeeb did not like at all. Only after more assurances from the United Nations representative did he allow the first truck to move into position near the wing. Meanwhile the other hijacker stood near the door, a gun to the head of the woman who had been suffering from heatstroke. "You see her clearly, Nicosia?" Najeeb called to the tower. "She will die if you try anything!"

Because of Najeeb's elaborate precautions, it took the first truck over half an hour to unload and move away before he allowed the second truck near the plane. While his attention was on the unreeling fuel hoses, I happened to glance out the opposite side of the plane and saw some movement through the dark windows of the abandoned DC-8. At first I thought my eyes were playing tricks, but then I saw it again.

There were men inside the hulk. How or when they got there, I didn't know. Probably the same moment the trucks arrived. It took no special imagination to assume that whoever was inside that old airplane was armed, and that their intentions were to free us from our captors. All I could think of was how the abortive Egyptian attempt at Malta had ended by killing most of the passengers. Apparently I was the only one who had noticed anything. While the one hijacker remained on the tarmac with his gun pointed at the copilot standing near the fuel hose, the other held the sobbing woman in the doorway, catching her by the hair whenever she seemed about to faint. Najeeb checked the passengers in the cabin from time to time, but mainly kept his eyes on the refueling. They

were nearly finished when we heard a sudden whine of turbo engines and saw the blinding glare of landing lights as a big military
transport thundered over us and touched down on the main runway.

Najeeb immediately began screaming at the tower again, demanding to know who the newcomer was. The controller replied that the
airport authorities themselves had not yet identified the strange
aircraft.

"Bloody Egyptians, that's what they are!" he muttered. "They
think they're cute! Start the engines!"

"The hose is not disconnected yet," the captain said.

Najeeb shouted out the door to remove the hose immediately and
get aboard. Then putting his gun to the pilot's head again, screamed,
"Start them, damn you!"

As the main electrical system came on and engines began to spool
up, I watched the huge transport slowly turn at the far end of the
runway and pull off, dousing its lights.

"Move!" Najeeb shouted. The copilot had reached the top of the
stairs with the hijacker behind him when the woman who had been
held in the doorway broke loose and threw herself headlong down
the steps. She fell at the bottom on all fours, like an animal awaiting
slaughter, and I thought they would certainly shoot her.

Instead, she was saved by the gun, as they say. In this case it was
the first shot fired by the team attacking the plane. While the
hijackers' attention had been entirely focused on the newly arrived
military transport, the derelict DC-8 behind us had disgorged fifteen
men in face paint and black sweaters, who dashed beneath our wings
before the stairs could be retracted.

Two of them made it, and two more came behind. While one held
the stair rail as the plane began to move, the other shoved the
woman out of his way and came up the steps shooting. The hijacker
at the door was cut in half by his bullets, and fell, blocking the
doorway.

Najeeb fired over him, killing the soldier who had nearly reached
the top step and taking out the commando behind him as well. A
stun grenade fired at the open doorway bounced harmlessly off the
fuselage to explode beneath the Boeing, blunting the assault and
ending any real chance of boarding the plane without further casual-
ties.

Those few precious seconds gave Najeeb all the time he needed. The plane had begun to gain speed by then, with the door still open and the stairs half extended. Najeeb shouted at me to help him with the door.

As we got it closed, a fusillade of shots ripped through the cabin, tearing away the upholstery of my seat and taking out the arm rest. Miraculously, Karen was unscathed although a bullet passed through her purse. If I had not risen from my seat when I did to help with the door, I would have been killed.

That reckless barrage nearly decapitated Najeeb's remaining companion, leaving him dead with a giant-size hole in his neck. But it also killed the other American soldier where he sat on the floor, and wounded three more passengers. Why a dozen others were not slaughtered I'll never understand because bullet holes seemed to be everywhere in the cabin wall, and some of the windows had been blown out as well.

We had pulled on to the runway by then and Najeeb was screaming, "Take off! Take off or you both die!"

"The stairway is still partially out," the pilot said, "and the port fuel cell is not properly closed. If we take off this way the fuel will siphon out of the tank in flight."

"Take off!"

Stray bullets still picked at the plane as we taxied the length of the runway before turning around and moving into position for takeoff. A powerful searchlight was trying to follow our movement but only now caught up with us, stabbing shafts of bright, blinding light through the windows. As we began our takeoff roll there was one large bump as if we'd gone into a hole, and then a continuous series of small ones as the plane canted to the right.

"They've shot out a tire!" the copilot called as the pilot slacked off on the throttles.

"Keep going!" Najeeb screamed in his ear.

"We may not be able to land," the pilot said.

Najeeb struck him with the pistol barrel and nearly knocked him unconscious. As he sagged in his seat, the copilot said, "All right! We go! But leave him alone," and he shoved the throttles full forward.

We lurched down the runway, gathering speed, and I could see that the copilot had his hands full trying to keep the lopsided airplane on a straight line. He was calling out speeds to himself and finally said, "Rotate," as the plane dutifully lifted off.

To my horror our momentum only kept us airborne for a second or two before we crashed back to the paving, bounced once or twice and veered crazily before flying again, this time straight out towards the dark mountains. I heard Rusty Kirshbaum say, "Jesus Christ, I can't take any more of this!"

Only then did I notice that Najeeb, the sole survivor of the five who had taken over the plane out of Athens, was wounded. He tried to hide it at first, but there was too much blood and his expression indicated he was in pain. From what I could see at first, a bullet had caught him in the right side of his chest. It had done damage to ribs and shoulder, and he had to hold the machine gun in his left hand.

Now was the moment, of course, for David Perpignon to become a hero. What could be easier than overpowering a seriously wounded hijacker who held his gun cradled in his left arm and considered me a friend? But a wounded Najeeb was less predictable and more lethal than when he was in one piece. Like many fanatics, he tended to be a little suicidal, and the idea of a bullet-riddled death meant nothing except glorious martyrdom for him. That is the terrorist's advantage, of course, over any normal person.

He saw me watching him and smiled. Did he suspect? No, because he beckoned me to him and asked me to make up a dressing for the wound. But he never dropped his guard, not even with me. I might have got the edge, God knows, I never stopped searching for it, but every time I glanced in his direction he was looking at me, as alert and trigger-happy as ever.

He made me prop him up in the flight engineer's seat directly behind the pilot who had come back to his senses by then.

"Tripoli," Najeeb said, lifting the lobe of the captain's ear roughly with the muzzle of his machine gun.

"Can't make it," the pilot said. "We're losing fuel too fast because we didn't get that port tank closed properly."

"What do you mean?"

"The pipe is open," the captain said, "and fuel is being sucked out by the action of the air over the airfoil."

"You will go to Tripoli!" Najeeb said.

"Look," the captain said, "I'm fed up with you and your whole damn crowd." He did not yet know that Najeeb was the only one left, and unfortunately I could not say a word without Najeeb overhearing. "I don't know how far we'll get, but Tripoli isn't in the cards unless you arrange for mid-air refueling."

"Benghazi, then."

"With luck, maybe," the pilot said.

"You get there or I kill you!"

"It we don't get there, you won't have to kill me." The captain laughed, more out of frustration and sheer incredulity than anything else. "In your next life," he said to Najeeb in Arabic, "study physics."

"Why?"

"Never mind," The captain returned his attention to the instrument panel. "Our pressurization system is out. This bird will not go higher than eight thousand feet."

"It doesn't matter," Najeeb said.

"It increases our fuel burn."

"We will make it."

"Enshallah," the pilot said.

Karen had not uttered a word since the attack began when I had told her to stay as low as possible. Crouched half in her seat, half on the floor, she looked up at me as the lights went on in the cabin. "I don't believe it," she said. "We're still alive."

"That's the good news."

"And the bad?"

It took a little longer to report as I relayed what I had overheard about the lack of cabin pressure, the lost tire and our fuel situation.

"Can you . . . ?" she asked me.

"If I see the chance without getting everyone slaughtered, I will. But so far he has surprised us all."

"You can beat him at his own game," she said.

I knew better than that, because I wanted nothing to do with Najeeb's game. I also knew that I was our only hope of liberating the plane before we reached Libya.

But his desperation made Najeeb more paranoid than ever, and the pills he swallowed had him wired. Sitting in the cockpit with the muzzle of his machine gun pressing the back of the pilot's skull, he was as dangerous as a cornered snake. He was not afraid to die. In fact, he almost expected to go out in a blaze of gunfire, while the rest of us wished very much to live.

The longer I studied the situation, the more hopeless it seemed. Unless he lost consciousness, I could not take him out without the pilot—and possibly the copilot, too—being killed.

The estimated flight time to Benghazi was about an hour and a half, and soon after we left Cyprus we had company again. At sunup they were clearly identifiable as the same group of American naval flyers as before. They stayed with us for an hour. Shortly after they left, a flight of three Libyan Mirages picked us up and escorted us the last leg of the trip. During the entire journey, the copilot periodically called out our fuel reserves. By the time we were a few minutes from Benghazi, our margin again was as narrow as it had been on our approach to Cyprus.

We were cleared for landing.

"Can they land with a broken tire?" Karen asked me.

Before replying, I looked ahead at the silhouettes of the men in the cockpit. The two pilots silently at their work, flipping an occasional switch, talking to the tower. Najeeb, weak as a kitten and occasionally letting his eyes droop. The sandy coast of Libya coming up ahead as the plane lost altitude.

The servo motors whirred and flaps were extended a little, then a little more. Then the wheels thumped down and we held our breath. "If anyone can do it, these fellows can," I said to Karen.

And they did.

VII

◇ In Benghazi, Libyan troops immediately surrounded the plane, and except for Najeeb who asked me to help him down the stairs, no one was allowed to leave. Only later did the Libyans remove the two dead terrorists and send an ambulance for the remaining wounded, including the much abused and battered pilot. Two polite young officers of the Libyan *mukhabarat,* or security police, took charge of the passports left on the galley counter by the dead terrorist girl.

By the time we had been on the ground an hour our tire had been changed and an auxiliary power supply connected so that the cabin remained comfortable in spite of the warm sun. The same ground crew managed to straighten the stairway so that it could be retracted and extended without jamming, and men even came aboard to clean up the mess in the cabin and empty the lavatories.

The mood of the passengers had changed dramatically with the attentions of the Libyans. Although no one was allowed off the plane, people were smiling and stretching, walking the aisles and saying things like, "It will soon be over" and "What nice fellows these Libyans are."

Their good opinions seemed confirmed when a food service van appeared and trays of sandwiches and cold soft drinks were served by the two stewardesses.

"Aren't you relieved?" Karen asked me.

"Yes, of course."

"You don't seem to be."

"Just waiting, I guess."

"For what?"

"The other shoe to drop."

"I don't understand."

"It doesn't make any sense."

"What doesn't?"

"Why does a group of Palestinian extremists hijack an Egyptian plane out of Athens and demand to be flown to Libya? Why this particular plane? And why haven't they asked for something? What do they want?"

Karen was thoughtful for a moment before she replied, "Yes, I see what you mean. I'm so glad to be alive and free of that awful man, I can't think of anything else."

"It isn't over yet," I said.

"Oh, God, I hope you're wrong."

"So do I. But I don't think so. They've made no demands that Israel free any Palestinian prisoners, nothing like that."

"Maybe they have and we don't know about it," she said. "Couldn't there be negotiations going on behind the scenes?"

"If there are, I hope they get what they want."

"That's probably why the Libyans have been so polite."

I gave her a skeptical smile.

"That could be the reason," she said firmly. Then she laughed. "I always try to see the bright side. And the darker the picture, the harder I try. What do you think will happen now?"

We did not have to wait long to find out. After the plane was refueled, two Libyan pilots came aboard to fly it. That meant we were not heading back to Egypt. The Egyptian copilot remained in the cockpit at first, but he was so exhausted he soon left the Libyan crew to review their check lists alone while he curled up to sleep on one of the first-class seats.

The two young *mukhabarat* officers returned just before the door closed. One of them announced that because of the plane's illegal entry into Libya, we had to proceed to Tripoli where all passengers would be processed. As the starters whined, the captain said we would fly at five thousand feet because the cabin pressure system was out of order, and our flight time would be an hour and ten minutes.

"What does he mean, 'processed,' " Rusty Kirshbaum asked me.

"I suppose they have to stamp our passports and make everything legal," I told him. "Arab governments are sticklers for visas and permits and all that."

"Think we'll make Vienna tomorrow?" Rusty Kirshbaum said.

I doubted it, but I did not say so. The more courteous the Libyan behavior, the more I was convinced that something disagreeable still lay ahead. If they had been willing to let everyone go immediately, they would have done it in Benghazi, and passengers could have taken the first flights back to Europe.

Or the Libyans could have notified the Egyptians to send another plane to take us all to Cairo while a fresh Egyptian crew flew the damaged Boeing home. Libya obviously intended to do neither if we were now being taken west to Tripoli.

Mrs. Kirshbaum fell asleep before takeoff, but her husband was once again cheerful and energetic, roaming the aisles to check on his friends, and reassuring everyone, most of all himself. "Do you think that fancy hotel in Vienna will charge us for the nights we didn't stay?" he asked me.

"Probably not," I said. "By now you're probably all celebrities, and they'll love the publicity."

"I hadn't thought of that," he said, pleased with the idea. "But it doesn't make up for what we went through, does it? What did you think of my little Helen?" His eyes were full of love as he looked down at his dozing wife. "Wasn't she something?"

I agreed that Helen Kirshbaum was indeed 'something,' the only one to stand up to the infamous Najeeb.

"It goes to show you," Rusty said. "You never know when you get out of bed what's going to happen before the day is over."

"But you don't expect to be hijacked. At least I don't."

"Kirshbaum's Law," he said. "If bad things can happen, they will."

I said I found Kirshbaum's Law incomplete.

He was amazed. "Is that right? In what way?"

"If bad things can happen, they will happen *to me.*"

Rusty laughed and said I had a great sense of humor for a Frenchman. He would remember to tell his friends what I said. ". . . happen *to me,*" he echoed. "How about that?"

When we touched down in Tripoli we were told to keep our seats and close all window shades until further instructions. The one on Karen's side had been shot away, however, so we were among the few passengers who could see what was happening outside the plane. There were no soldiers waiting, only more officers of the Libyan security police who stood around the bottom of the stairs.

No power was supplied for the air conditioning, and the heat inside began to build immediately. "What's going on?" Rusty Kirshbaum asked me irritably.

"I suppose they'll tell us soon."

Eventually a new *mukhabarat* officer came aboard and asked if anyone still retained his or her passport because there were more passengers than documents. When Karen and I both raised our hands he took our passports and left. A few minutes later, Karen called my attention to a scene on the tarmac where a long, gleaming Mercedes had arrived and parked near the plane, followed by two buses. The limousine obviously carried someone of importance, but the smoked glass windows made it impossible to see in. No one got out of the car, but a dozen dark-eyed young men in military khakis disembarked from the buses to stare at us. They all wore black berets and carried submachine guns.

"Soldiers?" Karen said.

I was not sure, but a certain arrogant casualness about them told me they were not soldiers from any regular unit. And I was right. They turned out to be from Najeeb's gang, Kahlil Malduum's elite personal bodyguard, the cutting edge of the United Palestinian Armed Resistance Front.

One of the security policemen came aboard to say that temporary accommodations had been arranged, and bus transport had arrived to take us to town.

He then read off a list of passengers who were to ride in the first bus, which included four French students, Rusty Kirshbaum and his wife, and most, but not all, of the dental congress group.

When one of the dentists whose name had not been on the list called out, "What about us?" the police officer said the rest would be going in the second bus.

"Where do we get our luggage?" someone else shouted.

"It will be delivered to you," the officer replied.

"See you later, Bernie," Rusty Kirshbaum called to me as he followed his wife gingerly down the stairs, carrying their hand luggage. "Damn, I'll be glad to get into a cold shower."

As soon as the first group had stumbled aboard the bus under the eyes of the armed black berets, the *mukhabarat* officer read from a second list which included the remaining Americans, an English couple, the copilot, stewardesses, and the other Egyptian nationals. They would take the second bus.

"I'm beginning to feel left out," Karen said nervously. We had not been on either list, but neither had the Yugoslav, German, Austrian, or other European passengers. "It's a funny way to divide people."

"Not so funny," I said, "if you know how they think."

"What do you mean?"

"If I'm not mistaken, the first busload was all Jews."

"Oh!"

When the second group had left the plane, the officer said, "The rest of you will go directly to the terminal where you may claim your passports and luggage, and make further travel arrangements. Do not leave the transit area except to board your flight out of Libya, or you will be arrested."

Karen heaved a great sigh and rose from her seat while I saw that the policeman was holding only my passport in his hand. He glanced at it and said, "Dahoud el Beida?"

"I am el Beida," I replied.

"You will come with me."

"But we are together," Karen protested, and then looked at me in surprise. "Aren't we?"

"Go with the others," I said, touched by her reaction. "I'll join you as soon as I can."

"But I'm worried about you."

"I'll be all right. I'm Palestinian, remember?"

"I don't like it," Karen said loyally.

"If I don't catch up with you before you leave, I'll call you in Vienna as soon as I get in."

"Do you promise?" I nodded and leaned down to kiss her. "Thank you, David," she whispered into my ear as I embraced her.

I followed the officer down the damaged stairway, squinting against the glare of the Libyan sun, noticing the bloodstains still marking each bright aluminum step. The policeman led me across the tarmac to the Mercedes, opening the rear door and motioning me inside, "Please."

A solitary figure in combat fatigues beckoned from the shadowy interior. He was gaunt and ugly with a large potato nose and dark scraggly beard, but it was the eyes one noticed most, like fiercely burning points of fire. They were the eyes of a mass murderer, mystic, and madman who now put his arms around me and hugged me close, reeking of some cloying sweet scent.

"Welcome, Beida, my dear," he said. "You're much more attractive than your pictures, but that is only fitting for a hero."

"I don't understand."

He indicated a stack of newspapers and told me to see for myself. Sorting through them I saw my image on the front pages of the *International Herald Tribune, Frankfurter Zeitung, Il Messagero, Daily Express,* and *Le Monde,* apparently terrorizing a child in the doorway of the hijacked plane.

"I am Khalil Malduum," he said, pausing dramatically to let the name sink in. "Our beloved Najeeb Hassan has reported your actions to me by telephone. He is recovering, you will be happy to know, and all of us in the Front are rejoicing."

The United Palestinian Armed Resistance Front, or UPARF, was not as well known as Abu Nidal's Fatah Revolutionary Council, and not on friendly terms with my old friends at APPL, but it was no

less violent. Like Nidal's organization the UPARF was also the bene-
ficiary of Qaddafi's hospitality.

Khalil Malduum had been publicly disavowed by Yassar Arafat
and every other moderate Palestinian. Arafat, in fact, had been the
target of at least three different attempts on his life by UPARF
assassins.

Prior to Najeeb's hijacking of the Egyptair flight, the most recent
UPARF outrage had been the spectacular in-flight bombing of the
American jumbo bound for New York from Rome.

Sitting beside this monster now, I did not have to read the newspaper articles about me to know what they contained. The picture
captions made me almost sick to my stomach, but even those were
unnecessary because the photographs alone told the whole revolting
story. In addition to the ones of me, there were others of the jet on
the ground in Beirut and Nicosia, with the dead bodies lying beneath the plane.

Luckily, the photographs were so grainy that I probably would not
be recognized if one did not already know who it was in the pictures.
But two of the newspapers had come up with something fairly close
to my name as well: Daub Beda said one, and Dawdle Baba, another.
It was only a small step for an observant policeman to put that
garbled information together with the pictures and the circumstances, and come up with Dahoud el Beida.

"Are you pleased?" Malduum said to me. When I did not reply
immediately, he said, "I am very pleased."

VIII

⟶ "I am not pleased," Najeeb Hassan told me a week later as he
settled next to me on the feather-soft rear seat of Kahlil Malduum's
car. He had just flown to Tripoli after being released from the
Benghazi hospital, and Malduum had sent me to fetch him from the

airport. His ribs and shoulder were swathed in bandages and his right arm rested in a sling.

"Does it matter?" I said.

"I ran the risk," he answered sullenly, "while you got all the attention in the press and television."

God knows, the publicity he coveted did me nothing but harm. The newspaper articles made me out to be the ringleader, rather than just another innocent passenger, but there was nothing I could do to correct that now. Not only had I not been able to leave Tripoli when I wished, I was being treated as a celebrity by both the Palestinian terrorists and the Libyans because of my so-called participation in the hijacking.

"I'll write to all the newspapers if you like," I told Najeeb, "and say they should publish your picture with a correction telling the world that Najeeb Hassan, and not Dahoud el Beida, murdered those people."

"I know you are joking, but I am serious," he said.

"I am not joking. Murder is murder, and if you think I'm happy about all that publicity, believe me I am not."

"I am not criticizing you," Najeeb said, "because you are older and have been fighting in our cause since I was a child."

He must have had me confused with someone else but I was not going to disabuse him of his belief as long as I was in Libya.

"It was my first mission in charge of others," Najeeb went on peevishly, "so naturally I wanted credit for its success."

"I'm surprised Malduum considered it successful with four of you dead."

"Why shouldn't he be satisfied? We accomplished our main objective. Partly thanks to you, but we did it."

"Oh? What was that?"

"Capturing the American Jew hostages."

"What about the Egyptians?"

"They are only to confuse the issue, to keep Egypt off balance and frustrate any peace talk with the Zionists. I admire you, Dahoud, I do, really, but you can't blame me for being a bit put out because none of the write-ups mentioned me."

Here was this cold-blooded killer pouting like an ingenue because he did not get top billing, as they say! I reassured him that fame was a fleeting matter, especially for a hijacker. I did not add that I counted on the public's short memory to forget they ever heard of me in connection with the whole sordid business.

When my picture and Arab name had hit the newspapers, the Greek police quickly identified me as Dahoud el Beida but mistakenly branded me as one of the terrorists and requested my extradition. So did the Egyptians, also to answer the old Eritrean charges. As usual Libyan relations with everybody including Greece and Egypt were so awful that the more the Greeks and Egyptians insisted, the more the Libyans were determined to protect me. They knew nothing of my French identity, of course, and reasoned correctly that Dahoud el Beida would probably be arrested if he were to return to Europe any time soon.

With the personal blessing of Colonel Qaddafi himself, I was offered asylum and a Libyan residence visa so I had no choice but to ride the wave of Palestinian popularity as long as they considered me a hero. Meanwhile, I planned to get away when I could. To that end, I enlisted the aid of the only friend I had in Libya, Aboubakir Jeballah, a colorful old scoundrel who always had a weakness for me. He owned the country's largest construction firm, but his interests extended to arms dealing, drugs, and smuggling.

Like the old Mafia dons, Aboubakir Jeballah divided people into three categories: enemies, friends, and victims. There were probably more victims than enemies, and more enemies than friends, but I was lucky to be considered a friend almost from the day we met.

I found him at a small farm he owned outside of Tripoli, playing backgammon with his bodyguard Mahmud, a legendary Tibu fighter and cutthroat who is said to have held his knife to Qaddafi's jugular on at least one occasion. Although Jeballah was Arab on his father's side, his mother was a Tibu princess, so he looked more African than anything else. Small, black, and birdlike, Aboubakir missed nothing as he embraced me like a son. He had read all the newspaper articles and was greatly amused at my sudden prominence in the Palestinian terrorist movement.

The last time we had met was in Egypt when I did the Eritrean machine gun deal. It was Jeballah who diverted the machine guns while the guerillas received sinks and tubs and toilet bowls.

When I explained my predicament, he smiled and told me not to be impatient. "Everything is opportunity," he liked to say, "if you know under what stone to look." He had made his first fortune gathering scrap iron from the desert battlefields of the Second World War, so he knew what he was talking about.

His counsel was always wise, and most of the time for me it had been profitable. "Don't be in too much of a hurry to leave this country," he said. "You are clever, and for a clever man, there are fortunes to be made in Libya."

"Not with the likes of Khalil Malduum," I said.

He smiled, then cracked some pistachio nuts and spat the shells out on the carpet. "Wait and see what they offer you."

"It is different for you," I said. "You have respect from them. They fear you and even Qaddafi does not dare touch you."

He smiled. "If that is true, why worry? You know you have my protection. But don't overestimate my reach. Qaddafi could crush me in an instant with his planes and missiles. He leaves me alone because he needs me."

"Needs you? You mean he is somehow involved . . . ?"

He raised one hand to silence me. "He is involved in nothing but his own delirium. But we have our arrangement. He prefers corruption organized by me to the old haphazard system. He allows my monopoly in black market goods for the same reasons. Everyone in Libya knows that Qaddafi's puritanical laws permit no vice and no excess. They also know where to find it."

"From you."

"Stay here and get rich."

"I can't go far as Dahoud el Beida."

"Here you can. A little patience is all you need."

Although the Libyans had let Karen and twenty other passengers leave the day we arrived, a spokesman for Qaddafi admitted that Libya was still holding the Egyptair crew as well as a number of other Egyptian nationals, four Americans and two English citizens who all faced serious charges. Asked what the charges were, he replied that they ranged from illegal entry to espionage. Not until each charge had been thoroughly investigated and the accused brought to trial, could a disposition be made of their cases.

In addition, the pilots were accused of intentionally violating Libyan airspace which Libya regarded as a hostile act. The Egyptair Boeing 737 would remain in Tripoli as evidence of this aggression until Libyan sensibilities were satisfied concerning the unauthorized use of its skies. The outraged Egyptian government immediately declared a state of emergency along its frontier with Libya, and according to the *International Herald Tribune*, Washington was considering among its options another bombing raid on Tripoli.

The Libyan spokesman at first denied any knowledge of an additional thirty-one missing Americans and four French passengers who were also said to have been on the plane. When pressed by Swiss and Italian diplomats about this group, however, a press officer representing the Libyan foreign ministry said there had been reports that some passengers had been taken off the plane by a Palestinian group. But he stressed that Libya had no record of who they were or how many except that he had been told they were no longer in the country.

So Rusty Kirshbaum and his colleagues had disappeared. But if they were no longer in Libya, then where were they? I did not have to ask because Malduum loved to brag to me about the secret deal he had arranged with Qaddafi. He laughed as he confided that they were being held in the dungeons beneath Tripoli's old Karamanli Fortress, where Barbary Coast pirates had imprisoned hostages for centuries.

The United Palestinian Armed Resistance Front had its headquarters in Malduum's luxury villa overlooking the sea on the outskirts of Tripoli, the former home of the Libyan crown prince. At the entrance Najeeb and I were both frisked and then ushered into a large shadowy room barren of furniture.

Khalil Malduum rose from the rug where he had been squatting and wafted toward us on a cloud of his sickening perfume. He put his arms around the wounded terrorist, saying, "So, Najeeb Hassan, my dear, you have come back to me in one piece."

"*Khaif haleq*," Najeeb greeted him. "I am in one piece thanks to el Beida," he added generously.

When Malduum smiled it was more of a sneer, revealing long feral teeth like chips of yellow bone. The effect was unpleasant to say the least, yet one had the feeling he considered himself attractive, even handsome. He took my arm in a familiar grip and said, "Our loyal Beida, the most photographed man in the movement."

"But they never catch my good side," I said.

"You see, Najeeb Hassan, what a wonderful sense of humor he has? This man who even laughs in the face of death."

I did?

"But now like us, he has a price on his head."

I responded as if it didn't matter, and cursed the day I met them. Considering Malduum's reputation and my vulnerability at the time of this audience, I had no choice but to play along. I had kept on the right side of his followers when they were waving guns around the airplane, and I now hoped to keep on his good side—if he had one—without getting any closer than necessary.

"Beida, my dear," Malduum said, "I would like you to think about joining the Front officially."

As if I wasn't in enough trouble! I had spent my life dodging the Palestinian cause, and especially avoiding madmen like him. "That would not be wise at this time," I replied.

His eyes narrowed. "Why not?"

"You said it yourself. I am the most photographed man in the movement. I am too visible. My picture is in every newspaper."

He considered this and nodded. "Perhaps it is enough that we can count on you without becoming part of my official command."

"They also serve who stand and wait," I said fatuously. When I saw that he missed the literary allusion completely, I added, "It is a line from English poetry."

His mouth pursed in disapproval. "It sounds like something the English would say. How do you feel about them?"

"I beg your pardon?"

"The English."

"I have no feelings about them one way or the other."

He appraised me for awhile like meat on a hook, the basilisk eyes unwavering. It was common knowledge that he had personally murdered several followers he suspected of treachery, and he thoroughly enjoyed the effect his reputation had on people.

Finally he smiled, although again it came off badly. "An excellent answer. Najeeb said you were fearless on the plane. Objective. Restrained. Cool all the way."

"It is true," Najeeb said.

Is that what it looked like? When I wasn't catatonic from heat and thirst aboard that ill-starred flight, I was certain I would die at the hands of Najeeb's fanatical band or that inept Egyptian SWAT team that muffed the assault on the Nicosia runway.

"I believe in first impressions," Malduum said. "What lurks behind the mild face you show the world, Beida? A lion?"

I allowed myself a shrug of modesty as he embraced me. "I am seldom wrong about people," he said, one arm still clutching my shoulder as he walked us toward the door, "and I feel we're very much alike, you and I."

He had his other arm around Najeeb. "You hear what I said, little tiger? This man is one of the clever ones."

If that Syrian psychopath interpreted my refusal to join him as a sign of intelligence, and my discreet replies as a mask for courage, I was not going to discourage him quite yet. I was used to sailing under false colors; one more masquerade would not mar my reputation. And quite frankly, during those eventful days even I couldn't always keep the real me in focus.

IX

⟨⟩ Shortly after my meeting with Malduum, I made the acquaintance of Captain Nagy of the Libyan *mukhabarat* who informed me that my future was in his hands. Disagreeable, bitter and suspicious, Nagy became a malignant presence in my life from the first day.

Fat, pockmarked, ugly as a toad, he suffered from an endocrine deficiency which left him practically a dwarf. "We are impressed with you as a freedom fighter," he said. "Make yourself useful and you won't wear out your welcome. Keep your nose clean and you have nothing to fear."

"I am in your debt."

"As a refugee from Zionist terror you are popular. As a pushy Palestinian you are not. Do we understand each other?"

"I'm sure we do."

"Excellent. Colonel Qaddafi supports your heroic struggle against Zionist imperialism. But we are not a charity organization for Palestinian refugees. Those who are not engaged in the actual fighting must do useful work. Khalil Malduum informs me that you are a computer specialist."

"That is correct.'

"You are lucky we have an opening at the Bank of Libya."

"I appreciate that," I said, not appreciating it at all. I had a grim vision of myself in some boring bank job, trapped in front of an IBM console for the rest of my stay.

As it turned out, the computer section of the Bank of Libya was a shambles, and the German managing director was desperate to find a competent person to take charge. Poor Herr Doktor Eidletraut was a dyspeptic, balding fellow who looked ten years older than he was, and perspired a lot as he peered through rimless, tinted eyeglasses at an indifferent Arab world.

Although I did not know it at the time, he was at the end of his tether, as they say, fed to the teeth with Libyan incompetence, terrified of Qaddafi, and overwhelmed by the immense responsibility he carried for so many billions of dollars. After a half-hour interview, he decided to take a chance on me.

Bankers love anything with seals and ribbons, and when he took me to meet with Mr. Bahamy, the Libyan chairman of the bank, my garish fake diplomas were accepted at face value. "Mr. Beida is by far the best qualified man we have seen," Eidletraut told Bahamy.

"One can see that." The Libyan admired my fancy degrees before handing them back. After a tour of the bank premises with these two, I was hired. Not to run a computer as I had expected, but to manage the entire section which included about twenty-five employees. The original computer system had been installed by Americans, modified by Germans (which was when Eidletraut joined the bank), fine-tuned by an English electronics company, and nearly trashed by some Polish specialists the Russians sent to help the Libyans.

I had to laugh. The salary was an astonishing twenty-four thousand dinar a month, or about eight thousand dollars, plus free rent on a five room flat with garden and garage, and the full-time use of a Volkswagen Rabbit.

It was the best employment I had ever had, and honest into the bargain! Leaving aside my ersatz degrees, no scam was necessary on my part. Although I was over my head and had to bone up on many computer functions and a lot of systems terminology, no one else at the bank knew half as much as I did, so I was in no danger of being caught out.

I started by throwing out much of their equipment and most of their software. Whatever was obsolete, unworkable or incompatible I discarded. I ordered all new American terminals, printers, and programs through an Austrian firm that brokered American hi-tech products to embargoed countries, and within a few weeks, I had a workable system installed in place of the disaster I had inherited.

For the first time in three or four years accurate daily balances were available to the key staff and directors of the bank, and to Qaddafi's auditors. Again I was something of a hero.

The fallout from the hijacking continued to be big news. After the first ten days Libya let all the Egyptian women and children go, but the remaining passengers and the two pilots were still detained to face charges. Egypt began to mass troops along its border with Libya, and the United States Sixth Fleet moved an aircraft carrier and three destroyers into the Sirte Gulf and parked them there in defiance of a threat by Qaddafi to attack the American ships.

Tunisia had been asked by both Washington and Paris to intervene and try to procure the release of the other thirty Americans and four Frenchmen the Libyan authorities claimed to know nothing about. But the Tunisian representative was kept cooling his heels by Qaddafi, and UPARF leader Khalil Malduum was not available.

In the United Nations General Assembly, the Greek delegate introduced a resolution which accused Libya of sanctioning air piracy, murder, kidnapping and theft by providing a base, and giving aid and comfort to the international criminals responsible for this latest outrage. When the text was being read, the Libyan representative removed his earphones, and when the vote went overwhelmingly against Libya, he walked out of the General Assembly muttering that they were all tools of the international Zionists.

A day or so later, the American president told the media after a tennis match, "Many American lives are at stake, so we're not rushing in half-cocked. You all saw what we did when Iraq committed outrageous and illegal acts. Although we're keeping our options open, we are prepared to deal with these modern Barbary Coast pirates just as harshly as we dealt with their forebears in the last century."

That sent reporters running to their reference shelves to discover that the American navy had bombarded Tripoli in 1804 in retaliation for repeated acts of piracy by Yusef Bey Karamanli, and that

Marines had been landed the following year. The American response then put an end to Yusef's piracy and to Yusef, although his
Karamanli descendants retained some power until the 1930s.

I began work at the bank eagerly enough because it gave me the
best excuse to see as little as possible of Khalil Malduum, Najeeb,
and others of the UPARF. It also kept me out of the limelight.
Reporters were always darting in and out of Tripoli, and I was fair
game if they could find me.

When I was a child and someone looked in my direction demanding to know who did something naughty, I would blush with guilt
even though I was innocent. Even today, if I am accused unjustly,
the heat of shame will rise to my cheeks, and I am apt to behave like
a guilty man. I mention this because there were moments when I
felt a twinge of conscience for not attempting to save those people
on the plane. I knew I would be dead if I had tried to intervene, yet
for reasons I cannot explain, I still felt guilty.

Without calling undue attention to myself, I asked around about
the American hostages, and discovered that after first being kept in
a camp on the coast, the men had been brought to Tripoli and shut
up in the Karamanli Castle Fortress while the women were moved
inland to Garian, and put in one of the huge troglodyte cave com-
plexes people there used to live in.

I had been right about what motivated the hijacking. Najeeb and
his gang had been monitoring airline offices in Athens for weeks
prior to the assault on the Egyptair flight.

Najeeb had selected Athens because airport security there was the
sloppiest in Europe. His group had originally planned to smuggle
their weapons aboard an American jumbo but after Malduum's
recent bombing, the American airline baggage inspections had
become more thorough. Malduum preferred American hostages because the United States, he believed, would cave in easily to save
the lives of its citizens. It could also put the heaviest pressure on
Israel.

Hardcore Palestinian terrorists hate Egyptians almost as much as
they hate Israelis and Americans, so when Rusty Kirshbaum's group
booked on the Egyptair flight, Najeeb got the bonus of an Egyptian
plane.

But the plan to barter the hostages for the release of the twelve
UPARF terrorists being held in Israeli jails was a serious miscalcula-

tion. Rumor and fact are indistinguishable in Arab countries, and people believe the most preposterous things. Over endless cups of tea Libyans speculated on whether the Americans would bomb Tripoli again as they had in 1986. Najeeb told me that even Qaddafi thought they might launch another air strike, and he was furious at Malduum for causing him such anxiety.

Meanwhile the Israelis flatly refused to deal, and while the Americans talked tough, they did nothing. Only the Egyptians reacted with spirit and continued to threaten Libya with everything including all-out war if they did not receive satisfaction.

Qaddafi did not take such threats seriously because of Libya's technological superiority over Egypt. Although outnumbered, the Libyan armed forces possessed the most modern and sophisticated arsenal in the Middle East, with the exception of Israel and Iraq. And Qaddafi was currently spending his country into serious debt acquiring new weapons systems.

But as the weeks became months, the whole business died down. The events in the Persian Gulf dominated the headlines, and it seemed that even Washington had decided there was not much they could do about the hostages, who were now lumped by the press with others being held in Lebanon. The American president no longer referred to piracy or the historic precedent of violent options. When questioned at all about the hostages, he parried weakly with, "We are still exploring all avenues in trying to secure their release, but these things take time."

It was an election year in America, though, and pressure was mounted for something to be done. Although the president was not a candidate, his party still wished to hold on to its majority in the Congress. Likewise the opposition was determined to gain ground, so there was a certain amount of political bickering over what was or was not being done to liberate the hostages.

For me things seemed to be working out well enough as I drew my extraordinary salary and awaited an opportunity to cross quietly into Tunisia and hop a plane for Vienna. Karen was frequently on my mind, and I very much wanted to pick up with her where we had left off when Najeeb Hassan so rudely interrupted our liaison.

I had no intention of seeing Solange again if I could help it. I liked her better as a faraway memory than a live-in nuisance. The only problem was she had made her way to Rome, read about me in the

Italian papers, convinced herself I was some kind of hero, and wanted in on the action. For months I stalled her while she threatened to join me. Then foolishly I sent her some money to keep her at bay and this only excited her greed. She assumed from my unfortunate press coverage that I had become a big shot in the Palestinian resistance movement and was holding out on her. I was in fact making an energetic effort to stay clear of the different factions headquartered in Tripoli, especially Khalil Malduum's murderous band. Unfortunately, they did not feel the same way about me.

Malduum himself regularly invited me to his lectures on the uses of terror, and I found it extremely awkward to decline. He was mad as a hatter, but diabolically cunning, lucid and articulate, a compelling speaker. He would tell his followers, "We may be too weak to destroy our enemy in battle, but nothing of his shall be safe! Not his women nor his children! Not his hospitals, schools, transport, restaurants, synagogues, cinemas or supermarkets! Wherever he goes, our gift of terror must go with him!"

He guessed correctly that people's fear of random violence outweighed any negative consequences for the individual terrorist. He also knew that while the value of hostages was relative, the payoff in pain and anguish from bloody mass murder was immediate. He spoke with feeling about humanitarian principles as applied to disenfranchised Arabs in the Occupied Territories, yet was callously indifferent to the hundred victims who burned to death on the American jet he had bombed. He often preached the value of "sleepers" who work quietly at their professions but stand ready to die for Palestine, and he singled me out as an example. The solemn respect I received from his young followers gave me heartburn as well as a bad conscience.

One evening after a particularly nauseating lecture on hi-tech torture in Iraq, Malduum asked me to stay behind. "At last I have a mission, Beida. For you and your wife."

"My wife?" Until that moment, Solange had been one of my better kept secrets, a part of my life I was willing to pay for with a little hush money, as they say, but would prefer to forget.

"Does that surprise you?"

"But she's in Rome at the moment . . ."

"We know where she is. She has been in touch with us."

I should have known.

"You are to fly to Rome."

"They'll arrest me as soon as I step off the plane."

"No they won't, because you will be using another name."

"I doubt I can take the time from my work . . ."

"Captain Nagy will arrange everything with the bank."

"That's very kind of him, I'm sure. But . . . what is it you want me to do?" I expected the worst. Bomb a schoolbus? Set fire to a hospital? *Shoot the Pope?*

"Your wife will be waiting when the plane stops in Malta, and she will continue to Rome with you. There you will both pass through Italian customs and check in to the Hotel Flora on the Via Veneto where my brother Ahmed will contact you with instructions. Then you'll proceed to Catania, before returning here."

"But I don't know if my wife wants to get mixed up . . ."

Khalil Malduum curled his lip in an attempt at a smile. "She will be waiting. And at Catania, Khalid Belqair will be waiting also."

"You mentioned Italian customs."

"You will be carrying important luggage but no one will inspect it because you'll have a Maltese diplomatic passport in the name of Sicara which is already prepared."

"Who is Khalid Belqair?"

"One of us."

"And what am I supposed to do for him?"

"Whatever he requires."

"Are you sure I'm the right man for this? Someone younger, in better condition, more tuned to the needs of . . ."

"You are the man I want. As always, you are too modest."

"Must my wife be involved?"

"She is good cover."

"Perhaps."

"Don't you trust her?"

"I wasn't thinking of that."

"You were thinking of your girlfriend, the Viennese photographer Najeeb told me about." Malduum was amused at my discomfort. His own taste ran to young men, but he was open minded. "It is in our interest that your Egyptian wife travel with you."

"I've gotten by here very well without her until now."

Again, a sneer of amusement. "Later, if you wish, I can have her sent away, and you are free to pick up with anyone you choose."

X

 Solange was not waiting for me at the airport gate when I arrived in Malta, but there was a squat, grungey-looking man about my age holding up a sign with my name written in Arabic. It was noon and our connecting flight to Rome did not leave until five.

"I am Beida," I said to this fellow. "Where is Solange?"

"At the hairdresser," he said. "She will meet you at the Phoenicia Hotel for lunch. I am Bashir, the publisher."

"Publisher?"

He named a clandestine left-wing magazine edited in Damascus that appeared sporadically in support of Malduum's brand of violence and terror. I was trying to place his accent when he said, "I am Iraqi exiled from my country."

"That's too bad."

"I don't mind. I am settling in Libya now."

"Thank you for bringing me Solange's message." I put out my hand. "Maybe we'll see each other again some time."

"Yes, in Rome tomorrow. We all serve the same cause."

"Is that so? Well, nice meeting you." But he was not to be shaken so easily. He insisted on getting me a taxi and riding with me to the Hotel Phoenicia. He was so shabby looking I doubted the doorman would let him pass, but we did not have to put it to the test because he finally left me just outside the main entrance.

Solange swept into the bar an hour later, exquisite as ever, causing eyes to turn and follow her, lingering hungrily on her extraordinary anatomy. In the months since I had last seen her, she had grown even more beautiful, if that was possible.

Solange is a bit nearsighted, and it was a moment before she discovered me in the shadows. Then she ran forward, threw her arms around me, hugging me with such force and returning my kiss with such passionate sincerity I almost forgot what a sly, greedy deceiver she was. Small-waisted with perfect breasts and strong dancer's legs, her slender figure could have decorated a Pharaoh's tomb. Fingers twined in mine as her mascara-darkened eyes beckoned. "I took a room," she said. "Unless you really want to eat."

"Do you have the key?"

She held it up, smiling, and darting her tongue in and out at me in a lewd and suggestive manner. Her hair which was normally black, at the moment seemed to be a kind of flecked white and gold. "Do you like it?" she asked me, and when I nodded, she added, "I just had it done."

The beds in the Phoenicia are old and hard and lumpy. But like most things left by the British they were built to outlast the Empire and are eminently serviceable. We were both out of our clothes in a minute as she said, "I want to hear all about the hijacking but not yet."

"There's not much to tell."

"Good, then we have more time for this." She was happily kneading my groin with both hands by then, and we coupled standing up before we reached the bed and fell upon it. For the next two hours we thrashed and pumped and plunged, coming up for air and an occasional kiss or caress, but mostly cavorting like reindeer in rut until I collapsed and fell asleep.

She shook me awake in time to catch our plane. I had left my luggage in deposit in order not to pass through Maltese customs. When I retrieved the large mysterious suitcase Malduum was sending with me, I checked the locks to make sure the bag had not been tampered with. We were travelling on forged Maltese diplomatic passports as Mr. and Mrs. Antoine Sicara. The Maltese immigration policeman waved us through with a salute.

On the plane Solange wanted to know all about the hijacking. When I told her I had been wrongly blamed for it, at first she refused to believe me. "I know you Beida. You're like an iceberg. Besides being cold, most of you is hidden. But I must say you had me fooled. I never would have picked you for a terrorist."

"I am not a terrorist."

"Then why did you take over that plane? I saw your picture, so don't lie to me. If the whole world knows, why shouldn't I?"

"Solange, for the last time. I was an innocent victim."

"Is that why you're working for Khalil now instead of sitting in some Libyan jail? To tell the truth, I didn't think you had that much courage, but I was wrong, so why not take the bows?"

"If you'll shut up about it, I will."

"It makes you more interesting. I thought I was married to a small-time hustler and I find out my husband is a fighter for freedom, a man of such mystery he couldn't even confide in me."

"You may think what you want, Solange. But before we land, you would be wise to practice being Mrs. Sicara."

"What do I have to do?"

"Think, which I know doesn't come naturally to you. We are Christians from Valetta. I am a diplomat specializing in ecclesiastical law and will be attending a Vatican conference."

"How boring!"

"It is supposed to be boring. If it's all the same to you, Solange, I've had enough excitement for one season."

When we arrived at Rome's Fiumicino Airport, I flashed my Maltese passport and the officer on duty snapped to attention. "Excellency, welcome to Italia. Right this way, please."

"I beg your pardon?"

"They are waiting for you in the VIP salon."

"But my luggage?"

He summoned another officer who saluted me and dutifully followed with the suitcases on a cart. A third officer appeared next to Solange and said, "Madame, will you follow me, please?"

"But I'm with my husband."

"You're sure you haven't made a mistake?" I asked the first man. "I am here for a Vatican conference."

"Yes, yes, excellency. The Archbishop is receiving you in the Papal lounge. But Madame Sicara, I'm afraid must be accomodated for the moment in one of the other VIP rooms reserved for ladies."

Khalil Malduum had said nothing about a reception committee, but it seemed the best thing was to play along. I said as much to Solange who only shrugged resignedly and followed me with resentful eyes as I went off with the officer. A gaggle of priests in their black cassocks clustered around the entrance to what I assumed was the Papal lounge, and I thought, God help me, they really do think I'm here to see people at the Vatican. They were looking in my direction so I smiled and nodded, wondering what the devil I was going to say. One tall fellow in his late forties wore a different magenta or purple skull cap and trimmings of the same color on his robe, and I assumed he must be the archbishop. He was the first to extend his hand and guide me toward the Papal lounge.

He said warmly in English, "How was your flight? We're so happy to have you join us." His accent was American, and up close he was very fit and hard looking, with close-cropped, salt-and-pepper hair, muscles like a boxer, and a grip on my arm that was almost impolite. He was not at all my idea of a high-ranking churchman. Yet he was making such an obvious effort to put me at ease, smiling broadly as he ushered me ahead of him, that I was determined to play my part as convincingly as possible.

"Now then," he said as we passed into the dimly lighted salon behind the man with my luggage, "what do you have for us?"

Before I could answer, the door banged closed and I saw directly in front of me two uniformed Carabinieri holding chained German shepherd dogs. I had barely registered this when the archbishop slammed me against the wall, spun me around and twisted my arm high against my back, saying, "All right, asshole, what's your real name!"

XI

◇ Another hand was on my neck pressing my face painfully against the wall. At the same instant I felt a sharp, cracking pain as someone belted me on the inside of my legs with a club and snarled in English, "Spread 'em!" and I was rudely frisked.

The archbishop sounded very much like an American giving orders. The other priests stood back as handcuffs were snapped on my wrists and I was jerked roughly away from the wall and spread-eagled over a chair.

"Again. What's your name?"

"Sicara."

Someone kicked me hard in the thigh. "Your name, shithead! We know what it says in the passport."

"I am a Maltese diplomat," I cried. "You have no right . . ."

Another blow, higher up on the tender inside of my thigh.

The officers with the dogs were dragging the large suitcase across the room. The archbishop called out, "Check for wires! It could be booby-trapped."

The dogs sniffed and panted excitedly around the bag, and it took all the officers' strength to pull them off. "Like it, boy?" one of them said. "Smell pay dirt?"

"Let Mister diplomat open it," the archbishop said, jacking me to my feet and spinning me toward the suitcase.

"I don't have a key," I muttered.

"Not good enough!" The archbishop's face was lean and tanned, with little crosshatched wrinkles around eyes like chips of blue ice. The grip of his fingers really hurt my arm.

I made the mistake of saying, "What do you want from me?"

His answer was a vicious openhanded blow to my cheek which sent me into the arms of one of the officers, a bear of a man with a baby face, a beatific smile and bad breath. He caught me like a ballerina and flung me back at the archbishop who hoisted me by the knot of my tie. "Once more, with feeling! Now where's the key?"

"I don't know."

The open hand again, striking the side of my head like a bell clapper.

"I . ."

Slap!

". . don't . . ."

Crack!

". . . . know."

Slap!

I looked around, groggy, expecting another blow. Instead the archbishop brandished what looked like a policeman's billy club under my nose. "Now try again! What's your name?"

"I told you. I am a Maltese . . ."

"Wrong answer." He drove the club into my midriff, knocking all the wind out of me. I fell against a sofa, gasping.

"Please!"

The tip of the club dug under my chin. "What's your name?"

"Dahoud el Beida."

"What was it yesterday?"

I shook my head, expecting another assault, but to my surprise he backed off suddenly and tucked the club under one arm while he riffled the pages of my Maltese passport. In a calm voice he said, "Malduum's forgeries are improving."

He tossed the passport to the baby-faced officer who said, "Don't let the costumes fool you, Beida. We're not real priests."

As if he had to tell me that. "So entertain us," the archbishop said. "What felonies were you planning to commit this trip?"

"Who are you?"

"An avenging angel, asshole. Authorized to send you back to the States where good people want to try you and execute you for kidnapping, arson, hijacking, and murder, among other crimes."

"But I've done nothing!"

"Except take over an airliner, kill two American servicemen, and kidnap thirty-one other Americans."

"I was only a passenger myself, a hostage like the others."

"Not according to the Libyans, not according to our intelligence reports, and not according to our pictures. We've got you live and on camera, buster."

Meanwhile, two Italian officers were jimmying the suitcase. The big baby-faced officer waved them back the minute the lid of the suitcase was raised, and reached into the bag with both hands. I saw only dirty laundry before he exclaimed loudly, *"Eccolo!"* and came up with a small paper-wrapped parcel.

The others gingerly removed a series of similar packages, one of which the archbishop held out for me to see more closely. "So you're innocent, are you? Well, well, well!"

"I was asked to bring that luggage. No one told me what was in it. I had no choice. I swear I'm not a drug smuggler."

For some reason he thought my remark was extremely funny. "No," he said, laughing. "No one thought you were. You're not a Maltese diplomat either. So what are you?"

"Semtex," the big Italian announced, hefting more of the parcels. He counted twelve in all, each weighing about two pounds, in factory wrapping with Cyrillic as well as Latin lettering.

I was horror-struck. Semtex is a powerful plastic explosive manufactured in Czechoslovakia which was used by Malduum in the jumbo jet bombing. It is easy to mold, resistant to heat, safe to handle, and difficult to detect.

So how had they known what I was carrying? A routine check by those bomb-sniffing dogs? No. These men knew about me long before I landed, probably before I left Tripoli.

"Beida," the archbishop said, "We could snuff you right now, and nobody would know or care. Save the state the cost of a trial. You don't exist in Italy, you know. You never arrived."

The baby-faced officer leaned close, overpowering me with garlic. "You're dead unless we bring you back to life. But we can't do that unless you tell the truth. *Capisce?*"

"Look, there were witnesses on that plane who could tell you I had nothing to do with the hijacking."

"We've talked to a few," the archbishop said. "The steward who jumped for his life said the terrorists took orders from you."

"That's preposterous," I told him. "The man's lying."

"Why would he lie?"

"Then he's confused. How should I know? He's Egyptian. I'm Palestinian. Maybe that's enough reason. Anyway, he is mistaken. All I did was keep people from being killed. Talk to Karen Koenig in Vienna. She was there and she knows the truth."

"We've talked to enough people, Beida, and most of them give you low marks." The blue eyes raked me like lasers as he leaned forward and said, "We know you are working with Malduum. What we don't know is how dedicated you are."

"Anything I've done has been under duress."

"Sure. Innocent bystanders like you travel around all the time with plastique explosive in their baggage. The next thing you'll want us to believe is you didn't know it was there."

When I said nothing, he smiled as if he understood perfectly. "You *do* want me to believe that, don't you?"

"It's true," I mumbled.

"Don't insult my intelligence!" he roared, placing his nose so close to mine, I felt his hot breath and the spray of saliva. He paced angrily in front of me before telling the baby-faced officer, "This is a waste of time. He may wear a tailor-made suit, but he's just another raghead. They're all fanatics or stupid or both."

Baby-face agreed. "You're right. The only way is to lock them up or kill them—straight away."

"Wait," I pleaded. "Everything I told you is the truth."

"But you haven't told us anything," the archbishop said.

I was not going to be anyone's fall guy, and I said so. Least of all for a gang of madmen like Khalil Malduum and his followers. I told the archbishop my instructions were to check into the Hotel Flora where Malduum's brother would call.

"Can you reach him if you have to?"

"No. I don't know where he is."

"What about your wife?"

"What about her?"

"Is she involved?"

"Hardly at all, really."

"Cut the bullshit, Beida. She left Rome only yesterday, and today she returns with you on a fake Maltese passport."

"But she knows nothing."

"She knows Malduum. She telephoned him in Tripoli."

"That was only to find me."

"How touching."

"She read all those lies about me in the newspapers. She wanted to be part of the excitement and contacted Khalil. He decided she could be useful cover, so here we are."

"Aren't you lucky."

"That's what you think. After what came out in the press, I couldn't leave Libya. I am Palestinian. The Armed Resistance Front thinks it owns me."

"Poor fellow," the archbishop said.

"All I want is to go my own way without interference."

"And now you're going to tell me that's what you were planning to do when we caught up with you."

"Correct."

"You were tired of being a terrorist celebrity."

"I told you it was all a mistake."

The question is, what do we believe? You understand our dilemma, don't you?"

"It's the truth. All of it."

"Where are the remaining hostages being kept?"

"They are still in Libya."

"We know that, asshole. We want to know where."

"They were taken to Zavia first, a little town on the coast west of Tripoli. Khalil's main training facility is there. But he was nervous about security so close to the sea, so he moved the men to the old Karamanli Fortress in Tripoli. It's right on the water, overlooking the harbor, next to—"

"We know where it is," the archbishop said.

"It is also the headquarters of the *mukhabarat*—security police. The dungeons there were used for centuries as a prison by the Turks, then closed until Qaddafi came to power. That is where the men are being held."

"You're sure."

"Malduum himself told me."

The archbishop and Baby-face exchanged glances but they did not interrupt or make any further comments. I had the feeling I was confirming information they already had.

"Go on. What about the women?"

"The American women and the French hostages were taken inland to the town of Garian. Then there are also two others who were injured when the plane was attacked in Nicosia and are still hospitalized in Benghazi."

"Clumsy fucking Egyptians," the archbishop said. "We asked them to hold off. Go on. Tell me about Garian. Does Khalil Malduum have a training camp there too?"

"No. I heard that he's holding the hostages in the old troglodyte caves. It makes sense."

"What are they?"

"The ancient part of Garian consists of man-made holes in the ground like huge bomb craters. They are fifty feet or more in diameter and as deep as seventy-five feet. All around the inner faces of these holes, rooms have been carved out of the sandstone, and people still live in some of them. Other families use them for livestock and chickens, or for grain storage."

"How do the people get in and out?"

"Ladders that reach the cave rooms. But from outside an underground passage runs to the floor of the hole. It is the only way in. The passages are narrow, hundreds of feet long and could easily be defended by a handful of men."

"Continue."

"That's all."

"That's not all!" He demanded to know who else I was ordered to make contact with beside Malduum's brother.

"A man in Catania whose name is Khalid Belqair. I have no idea who he is and no way to reach him until he contacts me."

"That's more like it." The archbishop paced the floor, glancing at me from time to time as if I was some curious flotsam. "I have two options," he said finally, "Put you on a plane to New York in an hour to stand trial." He stared at me for a long moment. "Or send you to carry out your instructions."

"You want me to deliver the explosives?"

"Not quite."

"How do I explain that to Malduum?"

"You won't have to."

"They'll kill me if I try to foist off an empty bag."

"You'll be under surveillance the whole time. Play your part well and I'll see that you get what you deserve."

God knows what he thought I deserved, twenty years to life probably, but I really had no choice except to go along. As the baby-faced Italian officer also pointed out, Italy could offer me a third option in their maximum security prison at Gaeta just for bringing in the Semtex.

"The minute Malduum's brother opens that bag . . ."

"Beida?"

"Yes."

"The bag is bait."

My experience with the archbishop lasted less than an hour, and toward the last, he became quite friendly. Why not? I was only telling the truth, and anyone with the slightest feel for the whole depressing affair could see I was not a terrorist.

"Maybe," he said when I protested my innocence for the tenth time, "but no jury would ever believe it."

While I waited, they filled the suitcase with packages like those they had removed, and refastened the hinges so that the scratches barely showed.

"You can reach me day or night at one of these numbers," the archbishop said. "Ask for Dick Diamond."

"You're American. FBI? CIA?"

"It doesn't matter. Work with us, Beida, and I'll back you. Let me down just once and you're history."

"How do I know you won't dump me?"

"You are safe as long as our interests coincide."

"But I don't know what your interests are."

"Simple. I only want those hostages released unharmed."

"Malduum will let them go only when his men are freed."

"That's not going to happen, Beida."

"Then you're in a no-win situation. He won't back down."

"That's not going to happen either."

As I rearranged my tie, Dick Diamond offered me an ice-cold vodka from the VIP bar. Although I seldom take anything stronger than wine, I knocked it back. I felt better.

"When you leave here, do exactly what Malduum told you to do. We'll be watching you, so you're safe if you follow orders."

"Suppose they see you watching me?"

"You better hope they don't. And Beida?"

"Yes?"

"Your command performance here this evening was videotaped in living color. In the event we are not satisfied with the rest of your show, we'll make sure the Palestinians see the tape."

By the time they turned me loose, I had recovered my poise sufficiently to face Solange. She was angry at being left out of what she had been told was a Vatican reception for diplomats.

"You would have been bored to death with all those priests, Solange. I got away as fast as I could."

"Some of them were good-looking," she said. "Who was the one who greeted you?"

"Who cares. They have nothing to do with us." But she did not shut up, and as soon as we were waved through immigration, we had our first fight. By the time we reached the hotel, I was ready to throttle her, which is what she intended. So the evening ended with a spirited roll around the big bed in our $400-a-day room, paid for by the United Palestinian Armed Resistance Front.

For two days I waited in vain for Khalil's brother, Ahmed Malduum. When Solange was out each morning I called Karen's flat in Vienna and got her voice on the same recorded message saying she was in Paris and would return in a week. My disappointment was profound, but I left long messages, saying I was all right, but not yet free to return to Vienna. I would explain in more detail when we met or when I called her again.

On the third day Solange's Iraqi "publisher" friend appeared in the Hotel Flora lobby. He did not look quite as disreputable as he had in Malta, but he still attracted suspicious glances from the concierge. To my surprise he invited us to lunch at a very pricey restaurant on the Pincio. I almost began to believe I had misjudged him until he stuck me with the check.

At least he got Solange out of my hair by accompanying her on a shopping outing. After trying to reach Karen one more time without success, I was leaving the room when the telephone rang.

"Beida?" A man's voice, high-pitched and uncertain.

"Speaking."

"You have something for me."

"It depends on who you are."

"I am Ahmed, the brother of Khalil," he said in Arabic. "I have been away and could not call sooner." He told me to check the bag at the *Stazione Termini,* Rome's main railroad station, and leave the baggage stub for him with the hotel concierge.

"Will it be safe?"

"Quite."

"That's all?"

"Do it within the hour."

"Yes, of course."

I called Dick Diamond's number and he told me to follow Ahmed's instructions to the letter, then take a boat for Tripoli.

"What boat? I hate boats. I was planning to fly back."

"You leave Naples tomorrow evening with your wife. Pick up your reservations in the port."

"Then what?"

"Enjoy the trip."

"You mean I'm free to go back where Khalil can kill me?"

"You don't trust us, do you?"

"Give me one reason why I should."

"If it makes you feel better, we're not too keen about you either. But you're all we could find on such short notice."

"Look, Mr. Diamond, the Hezbollah in Lebanon have been holding some Americans for more than five years. In case you haven't noticed, Khalil Malduum is just as patient as they are, and twice as violent."

"If I didn't believe you could help us get those hostages back, I would not have let you go. And that's your best guarantee."

"You're dreaming."

"For your sake and theirs, I hope not."

"Has it occurred to you that when I get back to Libya I'll be out on a very dangerous limb?"

"It's the same limb you were on before, my friend."

"Only before I didn't have you waiting to hand me a saw."

XII

I left the Hotel Flora in a taxi and spent fifteen minutes in traffic jammed up around the Largo Susanna. Then another fifteen minutes trying to cross the Piazza della Repubblica while a helmeted policeman pleaded futilely with drivers blocking each other in all directions. In forty minutes we covered a distance I could have walked in ten, and pulled up in front of the *Stazione Termini* where the driver said cheerfully, "You should see it at rush hour."

The suitcase was heavy with whatever Dick Diamond's men had put in it. Bricks probably. I lugged it to the check room and was waiting in line when a natty-looking Arab in an expensive silk suit touched my arm lightly and said, "Beida?"

I nodded. "Ahmed?"

He raised one hand to silence me. Behind him a porter waited with a hand truck.

It was a sudden shift in the arrangement, but I should have been ready for it. Last-minute changes in plans are what keep terrorists alive. Unfortunately, Dick Diamond would be staking out the hotel, expecting the man to pick up a baggage check at the concierge's desk, and now there would be no baggage check.

"You've done well," Ahmed Malduum said, one arm on my shoulder. "I will say as much to my brother. When do you return?"

"Tomorrow."

"Good luck, then."

"You, too."

He followed the porter through the departure gate to the platform where the Rapido for Milan was leaving in five minutes. If he opened the suitcase on the train and discovered he'd been had, he would get off at the first stop and send people after me, and he would call Khalil Malduum in Tripoli. Here or there my life wouldn't be worth a plugged piaster, as they say, thanks to the careless planning of Mr. Dick Diamond.

Okay, I told myself, it's time to look out for Number One. I would return to the hotel, collect my personal belongings, settle the bill, and take the first plane out for Frankfurt or Zurich, then get a train to Vienna where David Perpignon could surface unmolested while

Dahoud el Beida vanished forever. Solange could cope. She had her friend Bashir, and there was no way Malduum could blame her for my defection.

At the hotel, the concierge had a message for me to call Mr. Diamond as soon as I arrived. The two numbers Diamond had given me at the airport were again included for my convenience. Wonderful. But I had made my decision. He could save his own chestnuts from the frying pan. If he was clumsy enough to lose Malduum's brother as a negotiating piece for the hostages, that wasn't my fault. At least the terrorists did not get the explosives this time, and he would have to be satisfied with that.

But in a week or a month, Khalil Malduum would send another courier with another suitcase full of death. Libya had imported over a thousand tons of Semtex from communist Czechoslovakia before the democratic government took over and President Havel stopped the exports. If one calculates that only 200 grams are needed to blow up a jumbo-jet, the Libyans still had enough Semtex plastique to wipe out all the world's airlines and supply other terrorist operations for a hundred and fifty years!

I was checking out of the Flora when a telephone call came for me. Dick Diamond again probably, double checking that I had the luggage check. I told the concierge to tell the caller that I had already checked out.

He delivered the message, then held the telephone against his lapel and said, "Sir, it's your wife and she says you could not possibly have checked out."

I should have known. Every time I thought I had my life organized, I could count on Solange to appear as an unnecessary complication. Love her or leave her, that was the question. It was easily answered.

Leave her.

"Sir?" The concierge waited expectantly, holding the telephone.

But I have a sentimental heart, and although I was about to abandon Solange forever, the least I could do was say goodbye.

"Beida, what is this idiot saying about you checking out of the hotel? What's going on?"

"Nothing, my dear. A mistake. How was your shopping?"

"Bashir found the cutest dog. A dachshund."

"Lucky Bashir."

"Oh, it's not for him, Beida. He bought it as a present."

"Very kind of him."

"For me."

Bashir couldn't pick up a lunch check, but he could buy her a dog, and Arabs hate dogs. Good luck to them, I thought. "Make sure it has all its shots," I said, "in case it bites somebody."

"You don't mind?"

"Not at all. I hope you'll be very happy together."

"You're jealous. I always wanted a little furry friend."

"Bashir is certainly that," I said, checking my watch. There was a Swissair flight at five-fifteen for Zurich. I wanted to be on it.

"I meant the dog. Will I have to sneak it in the hotel?"

"I wouldn't know about that, Solange."

As we spoke, I became aware of someone behind me, waiting, presumably, to use the telephones. I moved to let him by, but when he remained where he was, I turned to see the baby-faced *carabinieri* officer from the airport. He wore a gray suit instead of his uniform, and watched me with an expression of benign patience.

When I hung up, he said, "I've told them you changed your mind and will be keeping the room for another night."

"That's very considerate."

"We do our best, Beida."

"I delivered the bag," I said.

"We know all about the bag."

"I see."

"And Beida?"

"Yes?"

"No more sudden changes in plans. Unless you want trouble with the wrong people, be on that boat tomorrow. *Capisce?*"

"*Ho capito.*"

I ordered tea in the bar after he left, my life again reduced to wreckage and all my plans awry when Solange arrived carrying this sausage dog in her arms. Don't misunderstand me. I like animals. But this was a truly ill-tempered creature, growling and snapping at everything that came within a few meters of it.

Solange was delighted when I told her we were leaving the following day by boat, and immediately sent Bashir to reserve a berth so he could join us on the trip. I gathered that apart from his so-called publishing business, he also represented some extremist Arab political organization that was looking for a handout from Qaddafi. His most outstanding quality, however, was his ability to avoid spending money. He was such an accomplished sponger I thought of him as the Thief of Baghdad.

On the train to Naples the next day I had to put up with three hours of his pretentiously boring political claptrap while Solange "oh'd" and "ah'd" over each specious pronouncement. That and her dog's penchant for pissing against every vertical surface in the railroad car made the trip pure torture. By the time we arrived at the offices of the steamship line, I had also heard enough of Solange's inane chatter to last me a dozen marriages.

A curious thing happened that evening just before we left Naples on the ancient Italian liner, *Città di Tunisi.* Solange had already boarded with Bashir and the dog, and I was lingering behind on the mole watching the preparations for sea, still trying to concoct a feasible escape plan. A young, flashily dressed man in a white suit and purple shirt accosted me. His movements were jerky, and he looked around furtively as if expecting someone to strike him from behind at any moment.

I had noticed him watching us earlier in the steamship office, but assumed his interest was in Solange. Now, close up under the shadowy light of the quay, I could see that one side of his face bore an ugly red burn scar.

"Act as if I'm seeing you off," he said in Arabic. He took my elbow and propelled me rapidly up the gangplank.

"Look, I don't know who you are, but if you're in some kind of trouble, you've come to the wrong person."

"Trouble?" he sneered. "You're the one's in trouble."

"Who are you?"

He was silent as I handed over my ticket and passport to the fat old purser who passed us aboard with a wave of his hand, grumbling, "Five minutes only for visitors."

The man steered me to the far side of the ship, out of sight of the other passengers. He was breathing heavily, his eyes darting right and left, checking to see if anyone had followed.

"What's this all about?" I demanded. "Who are you?"

He did not answer, but when I saw his hand move inside his jacket and a knife blade flash, I threw myself at him and we both crashed into the ship's steel bulkhead. That much I remembered from my APPL training. In close quarters, when hand-to-hand fighting is unavoidable, if the other fellow has a knife or bayonet, the two safest places to be are far away or pressed against him.

Lucky for me, he was not an expert or he could have killed me easily. He was the kind of bird who is used to relying on guns, and probably only chose a knife because he thought it was quiet. I was stronger than he, but I could not get a clear blow in until I managed to pin his wrist against a stanchion with one hand while I punched with the other until the knife flew over the side. Then we grappled for a minute or two with nothing more than the sound of our breathing until I realized I was winning. He apparently reached the same conclusion because he struggled away from me, tearing his jacket as I tried to hold him and hit him again. Then I slipped on the wet deck, he writhed out of my grip, and I wound up with the torn jacket in my hands.

He rushed quickly past the startled purser and down the gangplank. Once ashore he dashed along the shadowy quay, away from the brightly illuminated ship, almost breaking into a run.

I did not know who he was, but I knew where he came from. APPL still had a contract out on me, as they say, for quitting them, but I really had to laugh if this was the kind of cut-rate assassin they were using to carry it out.

I could still see him hurrying along the edge of the breakwater, passing decrepit warehouses served by a row of ancient towering cranes. Then, two other figures emerged from between the silhouetted buildings and blocked his way. When he bolted back toward the ship along the path he had come, another man appeared behind him. What followed then was so blurred and improbable that I almost convinced myself I had imagined it.

For an instant I thought it was just a mugging, a common enough event along the Neapolitan waterfront. Then I saw the flashes and heard the faint popping of revolvers, barely audible against the other noises of the port. The man dropped to the pavement, then got up and ran again as the others closed in.

When they overtook him, there was a scuffle and they seemed to be searching him, but he broke free once more and dashed between the warehouses. The others followed and I heard four or five more dull pops, then silence.

XIII

As far as I could tell, no one else had observed any of this. I thought of summoning the police or calling Dick Diamond in Rome, but I did neither. Although I did not actually see him go down, I imagined my would-be killer bleeding to death on the cobblestones, and wondered who in the devil had ambushed him.

In case anyone wished to question me about it, I decided to get rid of the jacket. Next to me was a ship's lifeboat, covered by a weathered tarpaulin. I raised one corner of the rotting canvas, rolled the jacket in a ball, and dropped it inside. Later I would see what was in the pockets.

As the ship got underway and we passed out of the harbor, I was still a little shaken so I wandered up to the bar and ordered myself a dry martini to settle my nerves. Unfortunately, Solange followed immediately with the dog under one arm.

Two men standing at the bar took special notice of her entrance and immediately made room. She rewarded them with a gracious smile as she perched seductively on a stool with the dog growling in her lap. Bashir came in a minute later and elbowed his way to a place on the other side of her.

The man nearest me was a tall, friendly fellow about forty who introduced himself as Alan Preston, head of a firm that installed plants for turning sea water into fresh water. With him was a brutish German engineer with white blonde hair and small, cruel-looking blue eyes. They were seeking a large contract in Libya, Preston said, and he asked me about my work.

"Computers," I replied. "With the Bank of Libya."

"You're probably just the man I should talk to. Do you think I'll have problems bringing in machinery and supplies?"

"There aren't many Americans working in Libya anymore," I said, "and you could very well encounter some prejudice."

"I'm not American. I'm Canadian."

"That might make a difference," I said, doubting it.

The German, whose name was Heinz Hueblen, seemed to be wrestling with some private anxiety the way he ordered drinks, but his interest sparked when I talked about the Bank of Libya.

Having such an attentive audience I warmed to my theme. But Solange cannot shut up for long so she eventually interrupted with a typical non sequitur. "My Pupi was seasick in the cabin," she crooned, stroking the dog. "He threw up his biscuit."

When I reached over to pet him, the little beast curled his lip and snapped at me. This pleased Solange so much, she laughed and said to Preston, "Never trust a man your dog doesn't like."

I suppose she realized how little I appreciated her humor because a few moments later, in her own inappropriate way, she tried to make up for it. Preston was very curious to know if I was acquainted with any high officials in Libya, and especially if I had ever met Colonel Qaddafi.

Solange said brightly, "Qaddafi received him personally the first day he arrived." I could have throttled her, but under the circumstances I could only go along with the lie and give her a look that conveyed my annoyance. She responded with a little shrug of apology, as if to say, "What's the harm in trying to impress these guys? Who knows, they may do you some good."

Solange can be enchanting with men when she first meets them. She also can talk them to death in several languages. She rattled on to Preston now about women's treatment in Arab countries, saying that although she had never been to Libya she was looking forward to a colorful and erotic experience.

I thought she meant "exotic," and corrected her. But she batted her eyes at us, saying, "Why not both?" which made him smile.

Hueblen had meanwhile put away four drinks to our two, and when he ordered another, Preston gave him a warning glance. The German's attention was on a swarthy, pockmarked man who had entered the lounge and ordered tea. The fellow was tieless and wore his shirt buttoned to the collar, Muslim style, with a week's growth of grubby black beard. His suit had the gray, shapeless look of cheap Egyptian tailoring, and his movements were furtive and clumsy, with that self-conscious awkwardness some people show in unaccustomed surroundings. As I spoke, he kept glancing in my direction with obvious interest.

Preston was the first to notice it and comment in an undertone to me. "Any idea who that is?"

"None whatever."

"He acts like he knows you."

The stranger looked directly at me, although he could not hear what we were saying. I have noticed the phenomenon of people suddenly doing this when they feel they are being talked about.

"If someone was staring at me like that," the German said, "I'd damn soon find out his business."

I did not relish the idea of challenging the man, but my own curiosity got the better of me. When I approached him, the stranger seemed embarrassed, even a little angry as he looked away, pretending to be interested in something beyond the window. But when I asked him politely in Arabic why he had been staring at me, a sudden smile appeared. He said he was nearsighted and thought I was an old friend from Nablus.

"You are Palestinian?" I asked him.

"Oh, yes," he lied. "And you?"

"Libyan," I lied back.

His inflection sounded Syrian and had nothing to do with Palestine. So what the devil was he trying to put over on me?

"I hope you find your friend from Nablus," I said.

"You see, I was under the impression . . ." He waited uncertainly, then said, "I thought this friend would be able to do a favor for me. But it seems I was mistaken."

Was he Belqair? I had no idea. But after what happened on the Naples docks, I was wary of all strangers.

I rejoined Preston, saying, "Mistaken identity."

"Odd," was all he said.

Hueblen gulped his last drink and drummed his fingers on the bar as he watched the stranger finish his tea and leave. For awhile the German glowered at his empty glass, then suddenly strode across the room and out the door without a word.

When a new round of drinks came, Solange raised her pink lady and said, "Chin-chin," while Bashir asked me in Arabic, "Why are you sucking up to this American shit?"

Preston inquired if what he said was an Arab toast. To cover up, I replied that it was an old one, and hard to translate.

"Well, cheers," Preston told Bashir.

"Up yours," Bashir replied in Arabic.

"Good health." I translated, telling Bashir to shut up. Solange thought it was very amusing, but the Iraqi's yellow eyes narrowed with suspicion that he was the butt of a joke. Solange reassured him, then said to me, "Be a dear, Beida, and take Pupili for some air. That will make him feel better."

The conversation had palled anyway and I was pleased to take advantage of the opportunity to examine the jacket I had left in the lifeboat. I dragged the reluctant little animal up the stairs to the boat deck where the wind nearly blew us both away. Since we had passed out of the Bay of Naples, the sea had risen alarmingly and the old boat pitched and rolled like a log in a sluiceway. It was typical of the season in that part of the Mediterranean. The storms seldom lasted more than a day or two, but they were known for their violence. The worsening weather guaranteed my privacy and after making certain no one else was around, I retrieved the jacket from its hiding place.

There was light from a porthole under which I found a sheltered space and checked the label. A men's shop in Beirut. Synthetic wash-and-wear material of the kind made only in Damascus or Baghdad.

In one pocket was a roll of low denomination Italian lire notes, perhaps a hundred dollars worth. Nothing else, no wallet or passport. But the inside breast pocket yielded a slip of Rome hotel stationery which I studied in the dim light while the dog trembled and whined at my feet. Scrawled in heavy marker ink were the words "Dahoud el Beida, Hotel Flora, *Città di Tunisi*, APPL" which told me all I wanted to know. I let the wind take both paper and jacket.

When I retreated indoors, the dog got away from me and went tearing down the stairwell in the direction of our cabin. Good riddance, I thought, but then I decided I'd better go after it rather than risk a hassle with Solange. As I reached the bottom of the stairs, I saw my cabin door ajar and heard the dachshund barking hysterically. I assumed Solange was there, but when I entered the stateroom to tell her the beast was making too much racket, I came upon someone else. Lying half in, half out of the shower stall was the Arab I had spoken to in the bar, his bulging eyes open and unblinking, tongue protruding, and a pair of Solange's sheerest pantyhose twisted about his neck.

<><

XIV

◁▷ I am no stranger to death. What Arab ever is? But I would have bolted from that cabin in a flash, except it occurred to me that a casual person finding a body there might assume I had something to do with it. Solange was nowhere to be seen. The incriminating stocking had to be removed somehow, and the man himself got out of the stateroom.

But who was he? A cursory search for identification yielded nothing except an envelope containing two keys which I dropped into my pocket. As I was contemplating the best way to get him out of there I heard Alan Preston's voice call out, "Ready for dinner, Dahoud?"

"No. I'm not hungry."

"Something wrong?"

"No, nothing! Go away!"

But it was too late. He was already by my side.

"Good lord! What have you done?"

Why is it that when something bad happens around me, people always assume *I* had something to do with it? At that moment, my nervous state was so precarious I barely reached the sink before my dry martinis came up, and I wasn't seasick. Preston approached the man in the shower and said, "What happened?"

"How would I know?" We both looked at the corpse.

"Did you kill him?"

"Of course not."

"I see."

"You don't believe me, do you?" I said angrily.

"Calm down, my friend. If I have trouble piecing your story together, the police will be even more skeptical."

"I can't report this."

"If it was self-defense, you have nothing to fear."

"I didn't kill anyone and I have everything to fear! They will want to know why he died in my stateroom. *I* want to know why!"

"Whatever happened," Preston said, "you can't just leave him there."

"Look," I said. "I have had some misunderstandings with the law which could make this awkward."

"What are you trying to tell me?"

"Let's say I might have trouble proving my innocence."

Hueblen appeared then, eyes red and puffy from drinking. His bleary gaze shifted from me to the body, but he did not seem at all surprised and said nothing. I had the very definite feeling they were play-acting for my benefit. Why did they both show up so suddenly? Were they friends or enemies? Although Preston was the kind of man one trusts instinctively, Hueblen was not. A cold-eyed, vulgar sort of fellow, he seemed capable of anything.

Hueblen knelt and searched the dead man's pockets with a casual efficiency that chilled me. He found some dollars, a few thousand Italian lire, and a snub-nosed revolver.

Preston frowned impatiently. "Anything else?"

Hueblen continued the search, even running his fingers expertly around the waistband of the corpse's trousers. "Nothing."

"Passport? Credit cards?"

Hueblen shook his head. "Not even a key to his cabin."

"He had to have a passport to get on the ship," I said.

"Not if he slipped aboard," Hueblen answered.

"Mr. Anonymous," Preston said. "What was he doing here?"

"We spoke Arabic in the lounge," I told them. "He had a Syrian accent, but pretended to be Palestinian. Why?"

Preston rattled the door lock. "It was forced," he said.

"Do you think he was a thief?"

"Hard to say."

"He claimed he mistook me for a friend of his." I was tempted to mention the incident on the quay in Naples, but thought better of it.

I might have trusted Preston even though I half-suspected he knew more than he admitted. But Hueblen's role confused me, and some sixth sense of survival warned me not to bet on either of them until I knew a good deal more than I did at that moment.

Preston shrugged and said, "In for a penny, in for a pound," as he approached the body and motioned to Hueblen to give him a hand. Hueblen dragged the corpse out of the shower and lifted it to his shoulders as I tripped over one of those cursed ship's doorjambs which rise above a man's ankle. Preston said, "Never mind, Da-houd. Let me handle this."

I stood aside gratefully as Hueblen staggered past with his terrible burden, and I heard the metal door to the outside deck clang shut. In the silence that followed I imagined the luckless Syrian's last plunge toward the ink-dark sea, vanishing in the ship's wake to share his secret with the fishes.

I heard the door slam again and felt Preston's hand on my arm. "All right. It's over," he assured me, "but let's go back before people start asking questions. Heinz, you stay here and see if you can fix that door."

"I appreciate your help," I told Preston.

"Let's hope I've done the right thing. I'd hate to think we were accessories to a murder."

"But you must believe me . . ."

"Relax," Preston said, "If I didn't accept your story I would not have lifted a finger to help you."

After we left the German, I said, "He knows what happened, Alan. He was as anxious as I was to be rid of the body."

"He was only trying to be helpful. You don't really think he had anything to do with the man's death, do you?"

"You saw how he behaved in the bar. Nervous as the devil before he followed the fellow out and didn't come back."

"Are you accusing him, Dahoud?"

"No, of course not, but . . ."

"I'm relieved to hear that. I'll join you in the dining room. Try to put the whole unpleasant business from your mind." He gave my arm a gentle pat and looked me straight in the eye. "Don't look so worried, old boy. You're in the clear. It's over. Don't look back." He excused himself to wash his hands, and said he would catch up with me in a few minutes.

Solange was at the entrance to the dining salon, and as soon as she saw me she said, "Bashir's seasick. Where's Pupi?"

It took me a few seconds to realize she was asking about her dog. "Isn't he with you?"

"Beida, you took him out for air and never brought him back!" Her voice grew shrill as her eyes searched frantically beyond me toward the passageway. "What have you done with my baby?"

"I haven't done anything with him, Solange. He's got to be around here somewhere."

"Why did you let him off his lead?" She flounced out angrily, calling, "Pupi! Here, my sweetheart! If he fell off the boat, Beida, you'll regret it!" And everyone in the dining room looked up.

After a few minutes Preston joined me. "I passed your wife in the passageway. She seemed upset about her dog. What happened to it?"

"Unfortunately, nothing."

I barely had time to order the wine when Solange returned. The barman had found the dog wandering around, fed it olives and potato chips, and kept it in the bar. She was calmer once the animal settled down under the table.

Because of the shuddering, disconcerting movements of the boat, there were few people in the dining salon. But eating relaxes me in any kind of weather, and although the cuisine aboard the *"Città di Tunisi"* was not extraordinary, it helped settle my nerves. Second helpings of *tortellini alla panna* and chicken *cacciatore* restored my strength.

We were finishing our main course when Hueblen entered the salon. He seemed drunker than he had been earlier, unsteady on his feet as he came toward our table. Other passengers eyed him warily as the *maître d'* hastened to attend him before he made trouble. He muttered something in German to Solange as he sat down next to her, bumping the table. I did not hear what he said, but he kept looking at her foolishly, grinning as if he expected an answer.

After it became obvious that this drunken lout was making a play for Solange, Preston tried to distract me with conversation. I paid no attention to Hueblen's leering looks or Solange's exasperated glances. If anyone could defend herself in that kind of situation it was Solange. She thrived on flattery and attention, but not heavy-handed passes. The German was as subtle as a Tiger tank and just as determined. His hands had been beneath the table for some minutes when she suddenly erupted with a slap across his face.

I had seen it coming and rather enjoyed the little scene. But I was unprepared for what happened next.

Her hand is small and his cheek is hard, so the tiny slap she dealt him did little more than focus his bleary attention. He laughed and then, to my astonishment, he hit her back. The slap cracked like a rifle shot as her chair toppled and she went sprawling. The other diners froze, food halfway to their mouths, and the dog came yapping out from under the table. Instinctively I jumped to my feet and seized Hueblen by the shoulder. I don't know who was more surprised, he or I. In spite of his drinking, his reflexes were quicker than mine, and he threw a bone-jarring right to my jaw, sending me reeling into the *maître d*'s arms. As I shook stars from my eyes, Preston angrily ordered Hueblen to leave the room, giving him a shove to send him on his way. He helped Solange to her feet and asked if she was all right.

She was so shaken, she could hardly speak, but she nodded, fighting tears. A red welt had appeared where he had slapped her, and after awhile she took a tiny compact from her purse to repair her make-up.

She whimpered, "Poor Beida. Did he hurt you too much?"

"It was nothing," I lied, passing my tongue over two or three loose teeth. "But the man is crazy."

"He's drunk," Preston said. "I'll deal with him later."

"It was probably my fault anyway," Solange said.

"Your fault!" I was outraged. "The man is a coward and a bully! How could it possibly be your fault if he attacks you?"

She put her compact away and shrugged. "Who knows what goes through a man's mind? Maybe he thought I was playing. You know that funny dance Germans do where they slap each other to the beat of the music?"

I poured her some wine, but she shook her head. "If you don't mind . . ." She rose finally to leave.

"Lock your door," Preston warned her.

She touched my arm again in apology and left us.

"A word to the wise," Preston said when we were alone.

"I know. I was a fool, but I cannot stand to see . . ."

"That isn't what I meant."

"I beg your pardon?"

"Don't."

"Don't what?"

"Carry it any further."

"I had no such intention."

"When he drinks he loses all sense of proportion."

Before we left the table, I thanked Preston again and offered to help him any way I could in Libya.

"Dahoud, I'm going to need an Arab-speaking associate with good connections in Tripoli. Interested?"

The offer, if such it was, caught me by surprise. "But I told you I'm a computer specialist," I said.

"Perfect."

". . . With a background in corporate finance."

"Ideal."

"At the moment, I'm very well placed in the bank."

"You could still retain your bank position. In fact, any arrangement between us could remain confidential if you prefer."

I don't recall exactly what I said, but I must have hesitated, or my answer worried Preston because he immediately said, "I would make it worth your while."

"That's very generous, but . . . I'd have to clear it with . . ."

"Of, course, of course. But in principle?"

I liked Preston. He was patient and seemed to have a sense of humor about the pitfalls and delays of doing business in the Arab world. I thought he was a man of some taste as well as good sense.

After we adjourned to the bar he was very supportive, as they say. Although nothing could erase my suspicions of Hueblen or make me forget the killing, Preston now behaved as if nothing had happened. When I speculated anew why anyone would strangle a man in my cabin, he became annoyed.

"Drop it," he said.

"But there's bound to be an investigation. Someone must know he was on this boat."

"We agreed it has nothing to do with you, so forget it."

"How can I if Hueblen's loose?"

"With fifty passengers on board this vessel, it could have been anyone."

Reluctantly, I agreed.

"That's more like it," Preston said amiably. "It shows some common sense instead of hysteria."

"Don't be fooled for a moment by my tranquil facade," I told him. "I am hysterical."

He laughed in a way that was meant to be reassuring. "Don't worry. The worst is over."

"What do you mean by that?"

"Nothing. Just relax."

After the bar closed at midnight and we were returning to our separate staterooms, he said, "Stay clear of Hueblen the rest of the trip, and don't expect an apology. He's the kind of drinker who won't even recall the incident tomorrow."

In the passageway outside my stateroom, I paused under the dim light to study the contents of the envelope I had taken from the dead man.

The two keys were wrapped in a piece of notepaper with the number "620 A" written on it. The larger key was flat, of quality steel, bearing the name "Chubb, London" on one side, and "B of L" on the other. Unless I was mistaken, it was a safe deposit key from the Bank of Libya. The other key was from an ordinary padlock, probably fitting the inside tray. And presumably the number written on the paper was that of the box.

When I opened the door and turned on the light, the dog went for my ankles, but a good kick sent him whining into Solange's bed. I saw that everything was as I had left it except for her lingerie strewn about. I don't know what I expected. Certainly not another corpse in the shower, but the dog going for me like that set my teeth on edge. Solange did not even wake up.

XV

⟨⟩ In the morning, loud voices and the rattle of the gangplank marked our arrival in Catania. Looking out the porthole, I saw several police cars on the quay with their lights flashing. A dozen uniformed *carabinieri* waited to come aboard, and my first thought was, they have found the body and are after me.

I was having breakfast with Solange when they entered the dining room. She noticed my discomfort and asked some snide question about what I'd been up to.

"Nothing. I'm clean."

"Then stop squirming. You have guilt written all over your face. As if you'd strangled somebody."

I nearly choked on my coffee. But the officers were not interested in me. One of the stewards told me later that they were after an Arab terrorist thought to be hiding on board.

As soon as I could, I left Solange to her second cup of tea and found the ship's sole telephone where I dialled Dick Diamond's numbers in Rome. Although he or his men were supposed to be watching over me, I hadn't seen any sign of them since the airport. And after lying awake half the night, I had decided that with one dead body, and probably two, between Naples and Catania, I should at least let him know the dangers I faced.

The first number rang and rang without an answer. The second was picked up immediately.

"Dick Diamond, please."

A woman said in Italian, "Who is calling?"

"Beida."

"Who?"

"Mr. Beida from Catania. I'm calling from Catania."

"One moment please." After a lengthy silence, a man came on the line. "Who did you wish to speak to?"

"Mr. Dick Diamond."

"Your name, please?"

"Dahoud."

"One moment, please, Mr. Dowd. I'll see if he's in."

I was aware of odd electronic noises on the line as I waited, and wondered if they were trying to trace the call. No need, I had already told the girl where I was calling from.

She returned. "Sorry. There's no one here by that name."

"But someone else is looking for him. I was just told that he . . . Look, is this . . . ?" and I read her the number.

"Yes, but there is no one by that name at this number."

"I spoke with him there the day before yesterday!"

"I'm sorry. I cannot help you."

"Do you know where I can reach him?"

"I'm sorry, we have no information on such a person."

"Who am I talking to?"

The line went dead.

The ship was scheduled to lay beside the quay the entire day, loading oranges, lemons and canned tomatoes for Libya. In the distance, like a painted backdrop to the port, Mount Etna frowned on the parched countryside. Near her crest at ten thousand feet was a slender collar of snow beyond the faint haze of volcanic smoke that drifted down over the city.

Colorful horse-drawn carts dodged nimbly between railroad cars being shunted back and forth on the busy mole. Ancient cranes swung cargo nets above the heads of waiting stevedores, their muscled arms raised expectantly, like communicants at mass.

Excited by the bustle of the port, Solange went ashore with Bashir shortly after breakfast. Preston followed a little later, inviting me to lunch. I declined, really not daring to leave the ship because Khalid Belqair was supposed to contact me. If he actually existed and did appear, I hoped he might throw a little light on the events of the last two days.

In Tripoli when I asked who Belqair was, Khalil had merely said, "one of us." I assumed he meant another terrorist, but being Syrian himself, he might have meant the man was Syrian. If that were the case, then the fellow killed in my cabin *could* have been Belqair. Although Malduum said he would appear in Catania, he might have boarded the ship sooner, and perhaps it was he the police were searching for this morning.

Such permutations left me dizzy. It is a bitter business to be a terrorist suspect when one is an innocent victim. On the other hand, I am lucky Dick Diamond and the Italian police saved me from becoming an unwitting accessory to mass murder. Thanks to them there would be no bombing on my conscience. But the solution to one problem only seemed to create so many others.

Why had Diamond befriended me and then deserted me just when I needed some answers? He knew I could not return to Tripoli without reporting to Malduum, yet he made no move to coach me on what I was to tell him. Everything? Nothing? What?

I was standing alone on deck, pondering these questions, when a taxi arrived on the quay bearing a frail, elderly gentleman in a white linen suit and floppy Panama hat. He gestured with a cane at a sullen, fat boy in a bottle green jacket who helped with his luggage as one of the ship's officers pointed me out and waved them aboard. If these were messengers from Khalid Belqair, they were certainly an odd pair.

"*Buon giorno,*" the old fellow said with a slight bow. "Is Mr. Preston about?"

"Not at the moment."

He had come up the entire gangplank unaided and now stood panting on the deck, daubing at his brow with a huge silk foulard.

He said in perfect English, "What a pity," then followed me into the bar where he fanned himself with his hat until he got his wheezy breath back. He had thick, wavy white hair and pale blue eyes. His face was gaunt, with high cheekbones and a nose that only a thousand years of breeding could have made.

"I am Luciano, *Principe di Pozzogallo.*" He waved his young assistant away, saying "See to the luggage before you go," then looked around admiringly at the tacky ship's lounge, studying the fly-specked ceilings, running his gnarled fingers over the ancient cracked varnish. "And you are . . . ?"

"Dahoud El Beida."

The old man squinted at me through a pince-nez he held to the monumental bridge of his nose. "I am trying to place your accent."

"I am Palestinian."

"Of course! Why didn't I see that?" In flawless Arabic, he added, "What brings you to this godforsaken island of Sicily?"

"I'm passing through en route to Tripoli. I live there."

"Well, you are the lucky man. I spent some happy years there myself and I am looking forward to seeing it again."

"I am amazed at your Arabic," I said.

"As good as your Italian?" The old eyes glinted with good humor and mischief.

"Preston won't be back 'til after lunch, I'm afraid."

"No matter. He and I can catch up on the voyage."

The pince-nez lent him an air of distinction few people can boast these days, while his great floppy hat gave him the appearance of a man dressed to appear in a costume film. The fat boy returned after depositing the prince's luggage. "Good trip, Excellency," he muttered.

"Yes, yes," the old man said impatiently. "Did you unpack my things? Lay out my dressing gown and *'nécessaires'?*"

"Everything as always, sir."

"Then you may go."

He remained where he was. "My money, Excellency."

"But I paid you."

"Not lately."

The prince said to me, "They're like children, always trying to cadge a little something extra." He checked his pockets, fished a much-crumpled five thousand lire bill and squinted at it.

Seeing it, the boy made a sour face. "Eighteen thousand five hundred. I paid the taxi from my pocket."

"Rubbish. The taxi couldn't cost that much. Anyway, my wallet's in my baggage, so you'll just have to wait 'til I come back."

"You aren't going any place until I get paid," the boy said rudely, snapping his fingers and holding what I presumed was the prince's passport under the old man's great beak of a nose.

"Give me that, you thief!" The prince brandished his cane but the boy jumped just out of range, saying, "First, my money."

The old man wasn't the least embarrassed, and looked around in exasperation until an idea struck him. He said to me. "Perhaps you'd be kind enough to advance it until I go to my cabin?"

When I held out two ten thousand lire notes, the boy snatched them from my hand, tossed the prince's passport in the old man's lap, and scampered off the ship, amazingly agile for one so fat.

"Once it was considered a matter of pride to serve a Pozzogallo," the prince said. "Now, nobody wants the job."

"The world is changing," I said. "Old customs die out."

"Just save me from amateurs," Pozzogallo replied wearily.

No one came looking for me after all; no Khalid Belqair or his ghost, while this charming old mountebank entertained me over lunch with stories about Italian colonial days in Libya where he had served with the army. He treated the *maître d'* with royal disdain which only caused that personage to fawn over him and ignore me.

Hueblen looked in on the dining salon around one o'clock and glanced in our direction, but left without a word. Old Prince Pozzogallo showed no sign of tiring as he spun out tales of trekking the great Sahara, of daring prewar raids against the Tibu in the south and the Senussi rebels in Cyrenaica.

"What takes you back to Libya now, sir? Nostalgia?"

"Money," the old boy said. "I'm broke."

"I'm sorry to hear that," I said, wondering how on earth he expected to make any money in Libya, and surprised the Libyans even gave him a visa. But he was so obviously unemployable probably no one cared.

"With Preston, all that will change," he said happily.

"What will you be doing with him, exactly?"

He paused before answering. "I am an archaeologist. His company has agreed to subsidize a new edition of my book about the Roman ruins in Libya."

I said sincerely that it sounded like interesting work.

"It used to be. Under Mussolini, we had money to dig, but foundation grants are frugal these days. I was lucky with Preston."

Preston appeared behind him at that moment, in time to hear this last bit of conversation. He smiled. "What an unexpected pleasure, your Excellency."

"Couldn't telephone, so I came straight to the boat."

"Glad you did. Any progress on your visa?"

"Got it yesterday. I'm coming with you."

"That's wonderful news," Preston said. "Dahoud, Prince Pozzogallo is the doyen of Italian archaeologists. He has supervised excavations all over the Roman empire."

"And the Persian too," the old man said.

Preston said, "Are you sure the work won't prove too strenuous?"

"Strenuous? At my age, everything is strenuous."

After an extra coffee with Preston and the prince, I retired to my cabin for a siesta. I was awakened by Solange clumping in, laden with packages. God knows what she could find to buy in a place like Catania, but she managed.

"Did Belqair show up?" she asked me.

"No one showed up."

"Khalil will be furious."

"That's not my problem."

"What do you suppose happened?"

"In this kind of business anything is possible."

"How would you know?"

XVI

◇ The storm had blown itself out, and Malta was cold and sunny when we arrived. But fast-scudding gray clouds dappled the sky, and a stiff breeze raised spindrift on Grand Harbor. Preston invited Solange, the old prince and me to lunch with him at the Hotel Phoenicia. Hueblen was obviously *persona non grata* since the previous evening, and Preston had not included him. Preston hired one of the ancient, creaking *carrozze* on the quay and we were about to leave when that damned Bashir insinuated himself into the carriage, muttering some insult as usual aimed at our host.

"Is that another one of your wonderful Arabic sayings?" Preston asked in all innocence, and I was caught in the middle. But old Pozzogallo saved the day by saying, "Yes indeed: 'Love is the wine of old men, but sex is the vinegar.' "

"Your friend has the true wisdom of the desert," Preston said to me. He suggested Bashir write down the brilliant words Pozzogallo had put in his mouth, which made Solange break up, and nearly gave the old prince a stroke from laughing.

The Hotel Phoenicia terrace was sheltered from a wind that raised whitecaps on Grand Harbor, but it was cold where the sun did not reach. The tables near us were occupied by elderly English couples, rosy-cheeked and cheerful, whose talk made it clear that the sun had not yet set on their geriatric empire.

Somehow we all got through the lunch, and after picking at her floating island, Solange announced she wanted to walk it off in the picturesque streets of Valetta. Old Prince Pozzogallo offered to be her guide, and although that was not what she had in mind, she accepted. To my relief, Bashir decided to accompany them, probably to keep her from the old man's clutches, and the Iraqi's departure left the atmosphere at our table decidedly lighter.

Over coffee, Preston again began to quiz me about what he could or could not bring in to Tripoli. I reminded him of the American trade embargo. Washington prohibits anything made in the States from being exported to Libya.

"There are ways around that," he pointed out, "if we deal with European intermediaries. What I worry about is that the terrorist organizations there will give us trouble."

I hesitated before answering because I really did not know, but I wanted to reassure him. "The different terrorist groups have an understanding with Qaddafi that gives them sanctuary as long as all their moves are made outside of Libya."

"What about the Al Fatah gang?" he said. "Is it true Abu Nidal liquidated two hundred of his own men?"

"That's what they say, but now he's dying of cancer."

"It couldn't happen to a nicer guy," Preston said.

"He never bothered foreigners in the country as far as I know," I told him. "Neither did Khalil Malduum."

"I like him the best," Preston said facetiously. "He only hits safe, easy targets, like airliners with children and cruise ships full of elderly couples. And he's never present personally."

"In Palestine," I said, "they call him an evil genius."

"He's evil enough," Preston said, "but I don't know how much of a genius he is."

"He's clever," I told him, "and fanatically committed."

"What always puzzled me is he's not even Palestinian."

"That never bothered him. He believes in terror the way other people believe in love or money or kindness. He's very thorough and professional. No pity, no sentiment, no interest in anything beyond the best way to inspire fear and sustain suffering."

"Is he popular? I mean among Arabs?"

"I would doubt it. Except with a few madmen like himself. Malduum is a sadistic killer who loves his work. If Qaddafi ever abandoned him, he'd hire on with the ETA Basques or the Irish Provos or the Sikhs. He'd find the first cause that liked violence for its own sake, and the nastier the better."

"Have you ever met him?"

"I have."

"What is he like personally? I mean I've heard Nidal could be quite charming when he wished to be."

"Driven. Possessed. I would not want to be his enemy."

"The only pictures of him are years old," Preston said. "Just think. No up-to-date photograph and he's probably the most wanted fugitive in the world."

"I read that Greece is offering a reward for his capture."

"So is the United States," Preston informed me, "as well as the U.K., Israel, Spain, Saudi Arabia, Kuwait, Germany and Holland. For a grand total of over five million dollars."

"Is he worth it?"

Preston laughed. "Those governments seem to think so."

I was not anxious to be drawn into further discussion of my relationship with Khalil Malduum, so I gradually turned the conversation back to Libya itself. Preston's curiosity about the government and its peculiar policies made this easy, and he began to question me again about many of them.

"What must we do to get our machinery out after we finish

construction?" he said. "I heard the Tripoli port captain will expe-
dite anything for a small honorarium? But suppose I want to move
things by land. Would there be difficulty at the frontier?"

"The frontier posts are small, the honorariums smaller."

"And if I wished to avoid them entirely?"

"What could you possibly want to smuggle *out* of Libya?"

All he said was, "When you're dependent on strangers, it helps
to know more than one way to skin a cat."

Preston regularly looked at his watch as if expecting someone, and
glanced around the terrace. The aged Englishmen and their wives
clustered around the *buffet froid*, their plates at the ready, chatting
and joking as the chef served up slices of ham and turkey. How I
envied their peace of mind! The men were old soldiers for the most
part, ramrod straight or paunchy and red-faced, with a hard drinker
here and there being elaborately courteous to the ladies. The women
were pale and mostly skinny, wrinkled as turtles, gossiping about
bridge, flowers, and distant grandchildren.

Suddenly against this tame domestic background with its air of
stuffy gentility, a different sort of man appeared. A handsome figure
with dark intelligent eyes, the easy walk of the natural athlete, and
a brooding Byronic gaze. Immaculate in blazer and gray slacks, he
wore his hair a trifle long, giving him the careless, civilized look of
a college professor. But his arrival disrupted the tranquility of the
scene as surely as a shark swimming off a bathing beach. Old soldiers
made way resentfully and their wives stopped in mid-sentence because they all sensed the menace beneath the civilized veneer of this
man. No one could have pinpointed what it was, but I knew. He
walked without moving his arms in a sinister glide that reminded
me of Khalil Malduum.

Preston was facing away from him when the man laid a hand on
his shoulder. Without turning or looking up he merely said, "Hello,
Duff. Dahoud, this is Duff Elliot." It was uncanny, and later I asked
him how he knew who was there behind him.

"The footsteps. I'd know them anywhere."

Duff Elliot was some years older than I had first guessed. Although he had no gray in his hair, fine creases were evident around
the throat and eyes, and his large, powerful hands were veined and
liver-spotted. A man of contrasts, he was muscular and hard beneath
his polished, urbane exterior. I learned later that he kept the years

at bay through daily workouts, lifting weights, running, mountain climbing and God knows what else. He was a champion in two or three martial arts, a swimmer and a gymnast. He was also a considerable intellectual, something he was at pains to conceal. But Preston told me he loved a good debate on any esoteric issue—teenage abortion, the ozone layer or the authorship of Shakespearean sonnets—and would seek it with the same aggressive enthusiasm he brought to his physical activities.

Elliot could sit motionless as a cat for long minutes while listening, then suddenly erupt in a flurry of questions demanding sensible answers. I found him an odd mixture of avid curiosity and bored indifference; at one moment capable of the most penetrating insight; at the next, filled with snobbish arrogance.

At that point I knew nothing about Elliot's background but gathered that he and Preston shared some military connection from the past and were now involved in this Desal business to make fresh water in Libya.

"Everything is on," he told Preston as he drew up a chair.

"I'm glad it's settled."

"Will you be on schedule?"

"If we aren't, we'll lose the shot."

"The time frame worries me. Sure you can do it?"

"I'll hack it on my end," Preston said. "What about you?"

"Have I ever let you down?" And both men laughed.

XVII

 We arrived in Tripoli early the following morning, and as we waited to leave the ship, Preston took me aside. "Dahoud, I hope you'll decide to come with us."

I did not tell him that I was not free to choose without first consulting Captain Nagy. I simply said how much I appreciated his offer and would let him know within a day or two.

Rather than wait to be sent for, I went directly to Khalil Malduum's villa and was not surprised to find Bashir already there
asking Najeeb Hassan for an audience. Hassan showed me in first,
saying, "Be careful what you say, Beida. He's in a murderous mood."

The blinds were closed against the sunlight, and the stuffy room
reeked of stale sweat and camphor oil. Malduum was propped up in
bed, dressed in a long striped *djabalah* and dictating into a small
tape recorder. He seemed to be suffering from a head cold, and kept
daubing at his watery eyes and runny nose with a "Ramada Inn"
hand towel. The eyes followed me to where I waited at the foot of
the bed as he continued to speak into the machine. An AK-47
assault rifle lay on the coverlet beside him.

On the way to the villa, I had decided that the safest way to deal
with an unpredictable lunatic like him was to tell the truth, leaving
out certain details. I would tell him I left the valise as instructed by
his brother, without mentioning the police intervention at the airport.

I would not tell him that a stranger in Naples had been sent by
APPL to kill me, nor would I tell him that another man, who might
have been Khalid Belqair, was strangled in my shower on the ship.
As it turned out, I did not get past my initial greeting before he put
down his little recording machine and fixed his eyes on me. I prayed
that he knew nothing.

"My trip was not a success," I said. "I am sorry."

"You think I don't know that! What do you take me for?" He
swung his legs off the bed and seized the weapon, and for a few
seconds I thought it was all over for me. But he was only shoving
the gun out of his way. "Why am I always the first to hear bad
news?" he rasped. "Do you know what that bag was worth to us?"

I shook my head.

His eyes narrowed suspiciously as he asked me in a level voice,
"Do you know what it contained?"

"Clothing? Personal effects? I don't know."

He held my gaze, searching for the lie but unable to find it. "No
matter," he said finally. "It was critical material my brother needed.
But now Ahmed is in the hands of the *carabinieri!*"

"No!"

His voice grew shrill as he started to rail about how the police must have been watching me, probably had my hotel telephone tapped, had men waiting when his brother picked up the suitcase, followed him and arrested him.

"If they knew," I said, "then someone told them."

"Who! You?"

I tried not to panic as his eyes bored into me. "Khalil," I answered calmly, "first of all, I am Palestinian and I know that whatever I carried was needed by the cause. Second, I am not suicidal. Would I have come directly here this morning if I had betrayed your brother? When Ahmed called and told me to check the bag at the train station, I thought that if the bag was valuable, it was a foolish thing for him to do, but I followed orders. Then I went to Catania and waited for a man who never showed up."

He careened around the room like a caged animal, slamming into furniture, banging his fists against a bedside table, sending the tape recorder flying. "I am surrounded by liars and traitors! Incompetents! Cowards!" He seized the assault rifle from the bed again and really looked as if he might use it. "It was him! I know it was him!"

"Who?"

"That snake Belqair, who else? I should have killed him in Beirut! I will do it yet! I'll find him and cut him to pieces." Panting like a runner, he levelled the gun at me, finger on the trigger, eyes bright, spittle spraying from his lips.

"But you can't be sure," I said.

"No? If he is innocent, why isn't he here! Why!"

"Naturally, I . . ."

"I ask you that! Why?" His anger seemed to abate for a moment and his expression became almost melancholy. "If he had not betrayed me, he would be here like you! He would face me and say, 'Khalil, my dear, I am back!' You're too forgiving, Beida. I loved him but I shall kill him yet. Do you hear what I say?"

"I'm sure you will . . ."

"I owe you an apology, Dahoud el Beida."

"Not at all . . ."

"I was not sure of you at first. But your presence is indeed proof of your innocence. You say, 'Khalil, my friend, my beloved leader, I did my best and I regret things did not go as you planned.' That is loyalty! That is devotion!"

His mad, feverish eyes sought mine again as he put the assault rifle aside and threw his arms around me in a sudden crushing embrace, breaking down entirely. Warm, fat tears rolled over his cheeks and stained my jacket, and I could feel the hard butt of a pistol under his nightshirt.

As he sobbed his evil heart out, I knew there was no way I would ever tell him about the man in Naples, the keys in my pocket or anything else to do with that ill-fated trip.

He calmed down finally and ordered tea brought in. "It is a heavy loss but one must be prepared."

"I'm sorry about your brother."

"I was speaking of the suitcase."

"Bad luck, I suppose."

"Ahmed was careless. He wanted to be clever like me. But the Italians too, are clever. Yet . . ." He raised both hands in a gesture indicating it was all in God's hands. ". . . they are always willing to negotiate with a gun at their head."

"Will they release him?"

"Oh, yes. You'll see."

"Still . . ."

"There are thirty left now, and not all of them Jews. Something for everybody. English, Christian, Jew, whatever. The women have lost weight in Garian, and the men here in the Karamanli Fortress have aged a hundred years. Of course they were old to begin with, but they have lost their rosy cheeks." He laughed.

"I understand there have been protests. This morning's paper showed demonstrators in Washington demanding that the American president do something about their release."

Malduum gave me his half-smile, half-sneer. "It's working well enough. Wait for them to start protesting in Tel Aviv!"

"Do you really think they will trade?"

"I may have to step up the pressure, but that is easy."

"How?"

"There is a Chinese saying, 'Kill one, frighten ten thousand.' Well, one already died of a heart attack and I decided to take the credit for killing her."

"I see."

"Do you remember that wonderful video of the American Colonel Higgins hanged in Lebanon by the Hezbollah?"

I remembered it only too well. The revolting tape had been widely shown on world television. The Marine had been a United Nations observer kidnapped and held hostage before they hanged him.

"We hanged the woman," Malduum said, wiping his runny nose and choking back his laughter, "and it is quite realistic. A heart attack was no use to us, but twisting slowly at the end of a rope she is the perfect Zionist spy. I show enough of her face for the Americans to identify. My video is better than the Hezbollah's."

I felt a tremor of disgust and turned away from him in order not to show it. "Have you released the film yet?"

"No hurry. It is part of a broader plan. We do Munich in a few weeks, and I am thinking of releasing it just before."

"I don't understand."

"A two-kilo device in the Hofbrauhaus while a thousand fat Germans sit swigging their beer."

"But why the Germans?"

"Not only Germans. London too. Shock them on their Sunday as they pray and sing with their children at Westminster Abbey with a half-kilo device under the altar." He laughed at his wonderful joke. "Then we plan something for the American Zionists as well. You have heard of the Astrodome in Houston America?"

"A great stadium, I believe."

"But that must wait because of Belqair's betrayal. You carried explosives to Rome, Beida, which my brother was to take on a cruise ship to Port Miami. Now I must find another way."

"How can you be sure these attacks will succeed?"

"Because I have people like you I can trust."

"But how will you get the devices in undetected?"

His lip curled with pleasure as he savored his own genius. In the short space of a few minutes he had gone from hysterical rage to euphoric confidence and never missed a stroke. "Some are already in place," he confided. "Do you know the English holiday called Guy Fawkes Holiday?"

"Named for a rebel who tried to blow up their parliament."

"Now they will make a great holiday called Kahlil Malduum Holiday when their precious bloody church explodes to hell!" A childish giggle of delight escaped his lips.

"But the Hofbrauhaus?"

"The German bomb is already in Schwabing, and Najeeb will assemble the English bomb at a flat Bashir leased in Kensington.

Najeeb leaves for England on a university scholarship as soon as he has recovered." The cleverness of all this amused him greatly. "The English think he will study dead bones at the British Museum. But instead he will go to church to make his own."

"Are you planning to let anyone know in advance?"

"They would only tighten their security."

"Not if you didn't reveal the location? They cannot secure the whole world. And as you have said yourself, press coverage adds suspense and multiplies the terror."

"It is an interesting idea." He blew his nose with a great honk and nodded contentedly to himself as he savored the maiming and killing to come. "I'll think about it. You will not be left out," he added as an afterthought, "I promise."

"You are considerate as always, Khalil, but perhaps you were right. Maybe the police in Rome did recognize me."

"What are you saying?"

"They may have been watching Solange. I don't know. But I do believe I am more useful where I am less visible."

"As you wish."

On my way out, I congratulated Najeeb on winning his scholarship. For a moment he had no idea what I was talking about until I said, "To study archaeology."

"That was Khalil's idea. But it's legitimate, you know."

"You mean you really are interested in archaeology?"

He was a little offended by my question and probably thought I was patronizing him because he said quickly, "I studied in the antiquities department at Cairo University. My thesis was on first and second century Roman funerary portraits in Egypt."

"Oh?"

"Egypt is the only place one finds them in perfect condition because of the climate. Most were done on camphor wood with resin paints or tempera, and the colors are as vivid and true today as . . ." He caught himself and abruptly stopped speaking, embarrassed that he had revealed so much of himself to me.

I tried to look impressed, but it was impossible for me to reconcile the serious young scholar he claimed to have been with the murderous fanatic I had seen in action on the Egyptair flight. Almost as if he knew what I was thinking, he said, "I put my studies aside for more important work. After we have triumphed someday perhaps I will go back to them."

"I will introduce you to the old Italian prince who returned with me on the boat," I said. "He is a famous expert on Roman ruins in Africa."

"I have no time for that."

"How did they ever give you a student visa? The British must surely know about your connection with Khalil and the Front."

He looked at me as if I were a child with limited intelligence. "It is in the name of an Egyptian student, the same as the scholarship."

"And where is he?"

"Working hard in Egypt where he belongs."

"When will you be leaving?"

"Shortly. Did Khalil tell you what we've planned?"

"What he did not tell me is whether you will go through with the bombings if the other side agrees to a hostage trade."

Again he looked at me as if I were mentally deficient. "We will do what we must until Palestine is free."

Before I could get away from that cloud cuckoo land, Bashir cornered me and hissed into my ear, "Tell Preston that for a thousand dinar I can get his shit about the salt water factories printed in the newspapers."

"Why would he bother about that?"

"A bother, is it? You'll see what a bother it is when I tell Nagy that Preston is with the CIA and they arrest him!"

I went to see Nagy that same day at the *mukhabarat* headquarters in the old Karamanli Fortress and explained how important Preston's work was to Libya. I did not mention Bashir's absurd threat. To my surprise, Nagy agreed immediately to my temporary move from the bank. I suspected an ulterior motive behind such uncharacteristic generosity, but could not imagine what it was. On the other hand, I knew better than to underestimate Nagy. His hatred and suspicion of foreigners was greater than the average Libyan's, which is probably why he chose the security police as a career. He had learned English on a scholarship at some obscure American college and never forgave his benefactors.

"It will mean double work, Beida."

"And double money," I said, "which I can use now that I again have a wife to support."

"I'll arrange things with the bank, but make yourself indispensable. Worm your way into his confidence."

XVIII

◃ Nagy was as good as his word. In two days we had worked out an arrangement whereby I would assist Preston, with only occasional appearances at the bank. This pleased me but not the management because the computer section was still recovering from the electronic gridlock I had found on arrival. Herr Eidletraut, the manager, was worried that the whole operation would fall apart without my daily presence, but I assured him the new programs were working well, and I was only as far away as his telephone.

My days were spent assembling information for Preston about everything in Libya. The man's appetite for trivia was insatiable and he insisted on precise details which were always double checked. He wanted to know about security in the government, especially police and border guards, and all about the weather this time of year, winds, temperatures, rainfall.

"It is generally good, but when it is bad, it is very bad," I told him. "Remember the storm crossing from Naples? They are common in December and January. Very little rain except on the coast, but high winds and bitter cold and no sun for days."

"Get me tide tables, too."

"I beg your pardon?"

"Tides, Dahoud. The times they come in and out, and how high and how low."

"In the Mediterranean," I informed him, "tides are barely noticeable. No one pays any attention to them."

"Just the same, I want to know."

Likewise he had me doing time and motion studies of Tripoli traffic and assembling maps and photographs when we weren't surveying beaches, making protocol visits to the Development Ministry or the Secretariat of Disposable Resources, or checking driving times and distances between different inland towns. Our trips to the Development Ministry accomplished virtually nothing because the minister was a fool of an army major with no authority. He talked big about giving Libya a whole new water system, but then ignored Desal's bid.

Few people in the outside world know that Libya is a graveyard of stillborn social schemes. Token schools and hospitals were constructed by Qaddafi, but MIGs, rockets and tanks use up most of the oil money. Qaddafi's vision of the new Libyan state always derived more from his frustrated sense of power and the desolate emptiness of his diseased mind than from any desire to build from within. Like Saddam Hussein in Iraq, he's had twenty years to get it right but failed in everything except the futile squandering of his oil profits on arms. Libya's income is about five billion dollars a year, yet Qaddafi was spending eight billion, and for the first time running up a sizeable external debt.

Businesses languished, small factories and shops were closed down and spare parts unavailable everywhere while he embarked on one reckless military adventure after another. His reputation as a serious threat to peace and a world-class nutcase remained intact while foreign technicians pumped his country's oil, fixed his planes and ran his radar. After taking power, Qaddafi did not murder millions as Pol Pot did in Kampuchea or Idi Amin in Uganda. He only killed or imprisoned a few thousand. But the gloss of Libya's petroleum riches failed to mask the pathetic bitterness of his quirky personality or his grotesque posturing as friend to every terrorist who knocked on his door.

With Nagy and Khalil Malduum breathing down my neck I needed advice, and soon. There was no way I could communicate the information Malduum had given me to anyone without signing my own death warrant. Yet by remaining silent, I was condemning hundreds of innocent people to a violent, premature end.

When Preston noticed my anxiety and called me on it, I pretended concern about his Desal company getting the Libyan business. "Arab contracts are like the desert sands," I warned.

He laughed. "I understand what you're trying to tell me. But you don't have all the facts."

I assumed from his lighthearted attitude that he had some special access to Qaddafi. Otherwise funds seldom became available for domestic projects unless the Libyan dictator authorized them personally.

Life with Preston was one of daily surprises. A few days after our arrival, he leased a decrepit three-story Turkish tenement and put Hueblen in charge of renovating it. After our fruitless meetings at the Development Ministry, he liked to check on the renovation, but he always left me at the entrance while he inspected the premises alone with Hueblen.

Only an eccentric like Preston (and that is how I had begun to think of him) would have been attracted to such a place. To get there, one had to pass under the ancient Roman arch of Marcus Aurelius, cross the old *suq,* or market, and come out in front of the Bank of Libya. The building stood between the bank and the sprawling castle fortress where Nagy's security police were located, and where poor Rusty Kirshbaum and his friends languished.

"I love anomalies," Preston would say. "Here we are in the terrorist capital of the world, with a bank on one side of us and cops on the other. Is it true Qaddafi's got the American hostages in there?"

"It's true," I said, "though nobody's supposed to know."

"How did you find out?"

"Malduum told me."

"I forget. You two are buddies from hijacking days."

"I know you think that's funny, but believe me, Alan, it is not easy for a Palestinian to remain aloof in a place like this."

"I suppose not."

"I'm just trying to stay alive like everyone else."

"And doing an admirable job of it too, Dahoud. I admire your poise and equilibrium as much as your footwork."

"Footwork?"

"A term boxers use. Great footwork gets you close enough to tag your opponent without staying there long enough to let him tag you." He looked at the massive, windowless walls of the fortress for a few moments, as if measuring them, then shook his head sadly as we walked on. "Poor bastards. I wouldn't want to be shut up in there on a bet."

The ancient castle fortress which once housed the powerful Karamanli pashas was indeed a doleful monument. Only God knew how much cruelty, death, and torture those walls had witnessed during the centuries the Karamanlis were the pirate scourge of the Mediterranean. Although these legendary corsairs long ago ceased to prey on ships off the Barbary Coast, the tradition of terror endured with the likes of Qaddafi and the people he chose to accomodate.

That particular day, Preston cut short his inspection visit to the renovated building and told Hueblen to accompany us on a call I had suggested Preston make at the bank.

Apart from presenting him to the management, my real interest in going there that morning was to find out what was in safe deposit box 620-A. Since my return I had been frustrated because the regular vault guard was on holiday, and a sour-faced Libyan clerk was his temporary replacement. But my luck changed the day Preston and Hueblen went with me.

With Herr Eidletraut was Mr. Watanabe, a self-effacing Japanese hired to assist me in the computer section. He knew nothing about computers, but he was a cheerful soul who strived to be helpful.

The bank itself is a brick and tile monstrosity Preston described as "Mussolini moorish", erected by the Italians in the nineteen thirties. After the introductions we followed Eidletraut across travertine floors and up the wide staircase leading to the domed executive tower where Chairman Bahamy waited.

Walls of pea green marble ran to the second story gallery where a bust of some forgotten Caesar frowned at us, while the echoing din of a hundred impatient customers rang through the hall.

Bahamy was a tall, heavy-lidded Libyan in his sixties who knew nothing of banking and did not understand money. But he said his prayers five times a day and was distantly related to Qaddafi which is why he was picked to head the bank. "Libya's deposit bond regulation," Bahamy told Preston, "applies to all new construction. Fifteen percent of the total price must be deposited at least ten days before you begin. Unless, of course, you furnish a bank guaranty equal to the amount of the contract."

I had warned Preston about this but it did not seem to faze him. Nothing did, and I found new cause every day to admire the man's aplomb. The bid Preston submitted totalled eight million dollars, the pilot project to cost two of the eight million.

This meant Desal had to deposit at least $300,000 before turning the first spade. And if Bahamy insisted on observing the letter of the law, the company must put up a $1,200,000 completion bond or get an eight million dollar bank guaranty.

Preston said, "I suggest you check our New York bankers."

Bahamy said to Preston, "I am in favor of your waterworks. But I tell you my salary is small compared to your profit. If you and I come to a private agreement, maybe you get the contract in a hurry without the guaranty." Bahamy's heavy lips melted into a smile of such apparent innocence, I almost thought I had not heard him correctly. It was not an open demand for a bribe, but a casual observation on his depressed financial circumstances.

Preston said he would see what he could do.

Bahamy's smile became a hearty bray as he nodded agreeably to each of us and offered us tea. I assumed Preston could not get out of that madhouse fast enough, but to my surprise when Eidletraut asked if he'd like to tour the bank, he accepted.

As we passed the corridor guards and circled the tellers' cages in the main bay, Eidletraut babbled on about how foreign banks used to exploit the Libyan cash flow before he came along, delaying million dollar transfers and making unconscionable profits off the float. I had heard the tale often enough working under him.

We arrived at my old department where a dozen young Palestinian and Lebanese men worked at computer consoles.

"We move millions by computer," Eidletraut said proudly, "with coded systems known only to me and our corresponding banks. And of course Mr. El Beida," he nodded graciously in my direction, "who invented them for us."

Actually I had not invented anything, but just bought the right software and copied some systems from American manuals, keying them to a series of random numbers.

Hueblen said, "Isn't there a risk with your codes?"

"Herr Eidletraut keeps them locked safely in the vault," I said, "and they are only removed to be updated." I knew perfectly well the system could be penetrated by any high school hacker with time on his hands, but I could not admit it publicly.

We passed two more militia guards with automatic rifles before reaching the main vault where Eidletraut ushered us grandly through the gleaming door itself. This was a foot thick, weighed two tons, and opened on a time lock system whose combination was known only to him and the bank treasurer.

The main vault was twenty by thirty feet, and held over a billion dollars in marks, yen, francs, guilders, lire, pounds and metal bars, all behind an electrified barrier of wire mesh. Packs and bundles, bales and stacks of money were arranged on neat, numbered pallets one after the other in a kind of infinite still life of indescribable beauty, while gold and platinum ingots were piled around like fresh bread from an oven.

The vault contained one small table outside the money cage, and behind it sat the regular vault guard recently returned from his holiday. Not an armed tough like the rifle-toting militia patrolling the outer hallways, but the oldest of pensioners, a man with a fat belly, sleepy eyes and bunions. Beyond him the walls were lined with individual safe deposit boxes, each one with two locks, one for the bank's key which the old guard carried, and one for the key issued to the person renting the box. I lagged behind to greet the old fellow. Mistaking my intention he reached for his key. The other key in my pocket was obviously a counterpart to the one in his hand.

"Don't get up, *Haj*," I told him. "I am only accompanying these guests. Life treating you all right?"

"God is good, Beida. I have my health and my grandsons."

"And how many do you take care of?" I said, indicating the ranks of deposit boxes.

"Seven. The eldest is fourteen now."

"I meant these boxes."

"I don't know. Hundreds."

I flipped casually through his index file. Eight hundred and fifty boxes were listed alphabetically in English. A quick glance at the B's showed three Belqairs, none of them Khalid. But box 620-A was registered in the name of the United Palestinian Armed Resistance Front, and the only signature on the card was Khalid Belqair's. Although I was dying to open it, I dared not call attention to myself. Better to return alone another time.

Hueblen was dazed by the sight of so much money, open-mouthed like a small boy in a sweet shop. I had seen the look before on the faces of new employees and visiting officials.

"Libya used to have one of the largest per capita cash reserves in the world," Eidletraut was telling them, "but no longer. Colonel Qaddafi has been forced to spend too much on defense."

"Forced by what?" Preston said.

"His enemies," Eidletraut replied with a jerky smile.

As we ascended the stairs and made our way back through the crowded bank, Mr. Watanabe handed me a Fax response to the inquiry about Desal's credit. The instant I saw what it contained, I passed it to Eidletraut who blushed with embarrassment as he read it. "You never mentioned your firm had a revolving credit of fifty-four million dollars," he said to Preston. "In that case Mr. Bahamy will probably suspend the bond requirement."

"Without a private agreement?" Preston said.

The German fidgeted over the embarrassing question of the bribe. "That you would have to discuss directly with him."

On the walk back to the Desal building the usually morose Hueblen began to laugh. When Preston asked what the joke was, he said, "The old man on the take and Eidletraut checking you out like you were some fly-by-night drilling operation."

"You know how banks are," I said.

Hueblen shook his head in disbelief. "Imagine keeping a billion in cash out of circulation on their basement floor!"

"They keep it there on Qaddafi's orders," I said.

"And the vault?" Preston said. "That antique Chubb door!"

Heublen agreed. "Any halfway competent lock man could pop it with a thimbleful of plastique."

"Plastique?" I said, playing dumb.

"Explosive," Hueblen explained.

What an odd conversation for serious businessmen, I thought. They sounded more like two thieves. If I didn't know better, I might begin to doubt them. But did I know better? In effect, I assumed I did because of Preston's elaborate plans and the revelation of Desal's multi-million dollar credit line.

Yet the way Hueblen rattled on about how easy it would be to empty the vault made me wonder. "A billion dollars!" he said again and again. "It would be the biggest heist in history!"

XIX

⟨ The following day I was walking to the bank with the safe deposit keys in my pocket, when a big Mercedes nearly ran me down in Castle Square. I began to curse until I saw the driver was Captain Nagy. He was barely able to see over the dashboard, and all the pedals had wooden blocks so he could reach them with his little stubby legs. "Get in!" he snarled.

"This is very kind of you," I said. "You can drop me at the next corner if you don't mind."

"I'll drop you where I drop you." He gunned the Mercedes down Omar Mukhtar Boulevard toward the suburb of Giorgimpopoli, ignoring traffic signals and passing the fairgrounds police post doing a hundred. I gripped the handhold next to my head as he braked for a donkey cart, and when he turned off to the right at the old Underwater Club, we nearly skidded into the wadi.

At last we bumped to a stop in the sandy track, our dust cloud catching up and enveloping the car. The sun felt quite warm as I followed Nagy to the poolside terrace where he climbed into a chair, unbuttoned his tunic and pushed his cap to the back of his enormous head.

The Tunisian waiter brought us orange Mirindas while we watched a children's swimming race. The contestants and all the adult spectators were foreign employees of the Libyan state oil company. The little swimmers shivering by the poolside made a great deal of noise, and our table received its share of splashed water.

Nagy's raisin eyes regarded the scene malevolently. "A word from me," he gestured toward the squealing little ones, "and they are on the next plane out." He hated foreign children even more than he despised their parents, I suppose because of his size. "Well?" he said finally. "What do you have for me?"

I shrugged. "You know how it is."

"I know how you are, El Beida. A bit of a dreamer like all Palestinians. Have you figured out yet what he is up to?"

"Only what you know. That he hopes to build these purifying plants, taking the salt from sea water."

"Strictly business?"

"I'm sure of it."

Nagy smirked. "I have proof he is a foreign agent."

Bashir must have carried out his threat and gone to Nagy with some bull-and-cock story the Libyan would be only too ready to believe. "Do you realize how many CIA agents are in Tripoli?"

I shook my head, uneasy about the question and wishing I was safely back in the computer section at the Bank of Libya.

"They think because we don't arrest them, they are safe. They believe we are blind when we are really very clever."

"Bashir is deceiving you with lies and fantasies," I assured him.

"I'm convinced Preston is what he says he is."

Nagy regarded me with pity as he rapped his empty Mirinda bottle on the table until the waiter came running. "Beida, remember that no one can ignore Libya's importance. We are bigger than France, Italy, Spain and Germany put together! Eight times greater than England! They would all like to take us over if they could, but we are too smart for them! Now listen carefully and I will tell you how you can repay your debt to us and return one day to a liberated Palestine."

A liberated Palestine or any other kind was the last place I wished to return to, but I could not tell him that. I smiled and said, "It has always been my dream, as you know."

"You will never have it better than here, but I admire your spirit." He sighed and watched as a Yugoslav in white Bermuda shorts presented tiny medals to the winning children. Nagy's attention was so concentrated, so totally absorbed, I thought he might waddle over and demand one of the prizes for himself.

Finally he turned back to me and said, "I'm depending on you to come up with the goods."

"But I am no investigator!"

He held up one hand to silence any objection.

My heart sank. This monstrous little shit had the power to revoke my residence permit at anytime and arrest me or deport me, so I had to be very, very careful.

"Preston is a CIA agent," he said solemnly, "and I have reason to believe that he is planning to poison us."

"But I have seen his passport. He is Canadian."

Nagy fixed his evil little eyes on me. "Wake up, Beida! The man is CIA! Even my superiors failed to see it at first. Now, thanks to me, we are getting some place."

"I don't understand." The truth is I understood it all too well and wanted nothing to do with any of it. *En garde*, Beida, I said to myself. Listen up! Pay attention or you'll get caught in the crossfire.

Nagy snatched one of the fresh Mirindas from the waiter's tray, took a long swig and burped before he continued, "He will have secret papers and he will hold secret conversations with other secret agents. I must know about them all. If you duplicate my effort, it does not matter. Now that I have put you in the picture, drink up and we'll leave."

"I really believe you're mistaken."

"He is planning to poison our drinking water!"

"But that's insane," I blurted.

An angry frown clouded Nagy's face. "Exactly what they would have you believe! They bombed us, didn't they? Why should they not poison us too?"

Nagy's logic was impeccable even if his conclusions were absurd. The Americans had indeed bombed Tripoli and done considerable damage to the city, particularly around the compound where Qaddafi lived. The raid also confirmed the Libyan leader in his paranoia and hurt his reputation by demonstrating Libyan impotence in the face of American military force.

"But Preston is not a poisoner," I insisted.

"No? Read his technical folders carefully!"

I realized then what he was talking about. In the desalinating process, a tiny amount of prussic acid or hydrogen cyanide is introduced into the sea water where it binds chemically with the salt. The cyanide, of course, is a deadly poison, but it is later removed before the pure drinking water is pumped from the evaporators. I tried to explain the chemistry of this to Nagy but it was hopeless.

"Come, or we'll be late," he said looking at his watch.

"Late for what?" He did not answer me, but pushed himself away from the table and waddled off toward the parking area. The waiter did not dare follow with a check. I noticed that all the children were hushed as we passed, and did not begin to squeal and shout again until Nagy had entered his car and slammed the door.

On the breakneck ride into the city, he said, "We are late, but they will not proceed without me."

His own words struck him as very funny, but I did not know why until we arrived at Castle Square. A great, noisy crowd had gathered, and uniformed police were holding people back from a cordoned platform. At first I thought it was some sort of political rally, but I could not have been more mistaken.

"I'm betting on you," Nagy said, "even if you're not sure. Get me enough goods on this fellow Preston to hang him."

He was not speaking figuratively. The ceremony he wanted me to witness was the public hanging of two university students.

While the condemned awaited their fate, police and high-ranking government officials gossiped at the foot of the gallows, as relaxed as a theatre crowd before the curtain goes up.

Such displays were staged periodically in Tripoli as reminders of who was boss. I had seen them before, and knew that Qaddafi's justice was not only swift and vengeful, but mainly calculated to create maximum public impact.

If it were not so gruesome it would have been amusing. Qaddafi called this "People's Justice", although he was the only one who dispensed it. The "Great Thinker", as he liked to call himself, was a mystical socialist and Muslim fundamentalist who insisted that Libyans were the only people on earth who ruled themselves.

His thoughts are set forth in something called *The Little Green Book,* on sale everywhere, and required reading for every Libyan schoolchild. The slogans and aphorisms it contains are a jumble of Hitler and Mohammed as inspired by Karl Marx, but sounding more like Groucho. "Libya has no government," he says with a straight face, "because the People rule. Any power I have, the People give me."

This particular afternoon, signs of that power were everywhere. Guns and uniforms, chains and a public gallows, with huge colored photographs of Qaddafi on every column and lamp post in the square.

The condemned were dressed in white robes with signs around their necks listing their crimes, and they began reading their confessions over booming loudspeakers shortly after we arrived. In amplified voices trembling with fear, and prodded by the executioner to speak up, they recited their list of crimes including treason, disrespect, conspiracy, blasphemy, and espionage.

Then their hands were bound behind them, heavy chains hung about their ankles and the nooses placed around their necks. As the crowd applauded, the hangman hoisted them one by one on pulleys to the top of two posts where they slowly choked to death. Their bodies would then be left hanging for three or four days as a warning to others who dared trifle with the Libyan leader.

"Impressed, Beida?" Nagy asked as the two bodies jerked and twisted convulsively in their chains. He looked happily from them to me, searching my face for some reaction.

When I could speak at last without throwing up, or without fear or disgust causing my own voice to tremble, I said, "I am sure that when you understand the chemistry of Preston's work, you'll see that it is innocent, and designed to help Libya."

"But I understand it perfectly," he said with a tolerant smile. "You forget I have a trained mind. Preston is a fool to think I do not see through him, but that is to my advantage."

◇

All that night and most of the following day I twisted and turned in a limbo of my own making, uncertain but determined, fearful yet desperate to trust someone.

To add to my frustration I couldn't get at the damned safe deposit box because it was Friday and the bank was closed. So, call it instinct or call it foolhardiness, I made up my mind to play it straight with Preston, and to exploit his good will to throw my own chestnuts in the fire, as they say.

I found him with Hueblen in the half-finished Desal offices, among paint cans and drop cloths. When the German left us, I told Preston, "I can keep silent no longer. As your friend, I must warn you against Captain Nagy." I recounted Nagy's paranoid suspicions concerning the Desal operation, saying finally, "And the most preposterous thing is that he believes you are a CIA agent."

To my chagrin, Preston burst out laughing. "Duff Elliot will love it!" he said, ignoring the seriousness of the charge.

"For God's sake, not a word!" I cautioned. "Nagy is a warped, twisted, evil little man who has us all at his mercy. Didn't you see the two corpses dangling in the square today?"

"Corpses?"

"The students who were executed."

"Oh, is that what all the commotion was about?"

"One was hanged because he criticized Qaddafi to Nagy's agents. The other because he publicly agreed with the first one."

"There must have been more to it than that," Preston said. "Were they trying to spark a coup or what?"

"Bashir told me that one of them said Qaddafi liked to put on make-up and dress as a woman."

Preston began to laugh again. "Does he?"

"I've heard rumors," I admitted, "but one ignores them. As you see it's worth your life to speculate along such lines."

"You can't tell me he had college kids executed for something so silly. Qaddafi isn't that crazy."

"No? He thinks Margaret Thatcher is a weakling and Arafat a Zionist. If that isn't crazy, what is?"

"According to you, most Libyans are unbalanced."

"At last you are beginning to see the light."

Preston scoffed at this too. It was not the reaction I expected from a serious business executive, and I wondered if he fully appreciated the gravity of his circumstances.

"Nagy is very cunning," I said.

"I'm sure of it. But he's also blinded by suspicion and convinced he's right, which is in our favor. In fact you could almost call it a kind of guaranteed insurance in our line of work."

"I don't see how."

"You will. Meanwhile I'll do my best to live up to Captain Nagy's lurid expectations. Then when the time is ripe, we'll hoist him by his own petard."

"How do you propose to accomplish that?"

"He thinks he has us fooled, when he's actually outsmarting himself. I eat people like him for breakfast."

There was no point in mentioning that Nagy entertained precisely the same idea about him, and with the same blind confidence. I was caught in the middle, as they say, vulnerable and exposed, the tool of one and the confidant of the other, although by then I was not sure which role I was playing with whom.

XX

 I am an artist at heart. Who knows, if I had been born on the west bank of the Seine or the Hudson instead of the River Jordan, I might have become a poet or painter rather than just another scuffling refugee forced to live by his wits. I do my best with the means at hand. Although I have attacks of polyphagia and satyriasis from time to time, in general my health is good and I regard eating, drinking, and lovemaking as forms of artistic expression, something Solange finds vastly amusing. She might as well be blind and deaf for all the attention she gives anything creative unless there's a money connection.

From the moment she arrived in Libya, she was always sniffing around, hoping to learn how much I was making between the bank and Preston. But after the way she left me high and dry in Cairo, I have kept her on short shrift, as they say. In Tripoli she only bothered me when she wanted cash or some slap and tickle. Both were in her mind the day I returned from my disappointing talk with Preston, because she even cooked dinner before putting her hand on my crotch to get my attention.

"Beida, *habibi?* Look at this." She was fascinated by an article in the newspaper about some Japanese art dealer who paid eighty million dollars for a Van Gogh. Thus, even great art reached Solange only through a filter of the purest avarice.

Love, beauty, grace, symmetry, all the cherished aesthetics of classical Arab culture touched her not at all. Solange had the sensitivity of a street walker and the poetic vision of a gnat. Apart from her extraordinary beauty it was only her naked, shameless greed that made her interesting.

When I observed that her artistic appreciation was conditioned by all those zeros, she replied, "Look who's talking! According to you the greatest artist ever born was a cook."

"Escoffier?"

"No, the other one."

The 'other one' to which she referred was none other than the immortal Carême, architect of icing, sculptor in meringue. "I never called Carême a cook. I never even called him a great chef because he was so much more. He was the unchallenged spun-sugar king of France, Solange, the father of the immaculate confection!"

"Whatever."

"He stated quite rightly that the fine arts are five in number: music, poetry, painting, sculpture and confectionery, and he was the greatest confectioner the world has ever seen!"

"You're daft, Beida."

"Indeed! Who else could have turned out a perfect replica of the Winter Palace in *mille-feuille* for Czar Alexander? Who?"

"I said you're crazy."

". . . Or created an entire Venetian carnival with mocha and ginger gondolas floating on canals of blue marzipan?"

"Be serious."

"Carême was probably the most inspired genius ever to work in sugar! His creations were the cathedrals of cake!"

"Who cares, for God's sake?"

"I care, that's who!" And the truth was that I really *did* care. Carême had been a hero of mine since I first read about him as a boy in some cast-off book of my father's. Abandoned on the streets of Paris as a poor urchin of ten, by age sixteen he was a journeyman pastry chef, by twenty, *saucier;* and by twenty-five, *chef de cuisine* for no less discriminating a personage than Talleyrand.

I owned a copy of Carême's definitive five-volume history of nineteenth-century French cooking, and kept a journal of notes on sauces, savouries, icings and cakes. The notebook was a present from Udo Proksch, once a director of Demal's famous *konditorei* in Vienna, and a great amateur chef himself. Udo inscribed it, "To David Perpignon with thanks for his advice and counsel on my most fascinating, complex and dangerous of undertakings."

It was a joke of sorts, written with Udo's heavy humor after he hatched a brilliant scam to sink a freighter and collect the insurance. In spite of his expressed gratitude, Udo failed to take my advice, missed out on the insurance money, and was now a fugitive from justice, banned forever from the premises of his beloved Demal's.

Old Aboubakir Jeballah and his English pilot Jock Pringle were about the only friends lately who shared my keen interest in gourmet food. Pringle, twice divorced, was a splendid amateur cook when he wasn't flying, drinking, or playing poker.

And Jeballah was eternally grateful to me for once recommending a Lebanese chef in some difficulty with the Beirut police over a murder. The arrangement worked out well for everybody. The chef escaped, his guards picked up some extra cash from the old man, and Jeballah got the best cook in the Middle East.

Solange, on the other hand, wouldn't know a gingersnap from an *Apfelkuchen.* Furthermore, she had no patience with my hobby and never hesitated to say so.

"How you can be so interested in all that silly food stuff amazes me, Beida."

"Solange, anyone with your limited view of the world is bound to be amazed by a civilized taste for anything."

"Now you're trying to hurt my feelings."

"On the contrary. I was trying to raise your sights. Broaden your horizons. Open that clamshell of a mind."

"With what's-his-name's marzipan?"

"I would not expect you to understand, you silly twit, that the entire course of history was probably changed by the *blancmange* Carême made before the battle of Austerlitz! Not to mention all the meals he cooked for Talleyrand while Europe was being parceled out among the diners. What a pity I never had a chance to taste one of his sublime confections!"

"Always stuffing yourself."

"I live under tremendous tension and eating relaxes me."

"While Palestine bleeds. But what do you care?"

Solange's recent espousal of "The Cause" gave me a laugh. Her liberation philosophy came straight from Khalil Malduum's splenetic diatribes which regularly appeared in the local papers attacking anyone who disagreed with him. His hate list included practically all the leaders of the Arab world except his host Qaddafi, and Solange loved to quote from his articles.

The only Palestinian cause she ever took seriously was my bank account, and the only freedom she cared about was her own between the sheets. But violence turns some women on and Malduum's vicious streak held an appeal for Solange that was essentially sexual, although she would never admit it.

She liked it rough, and although I am by nature a gentle, romantic soul, I sometimes obliged her because of the anger she aroused in me. After our argument about the Great Carême, she goaded me for being weak and soft and self-indulgent. She ridiculed my ruddy French complexion, tweaked my cock disdainfully, and called me some of the more unflattering names she had picked up in the Cairo gutter. I finally slapped her and when she dared me to do it again, calling me a coward, I spread-eagled her across the bed.

She pulled me down on top of her, yelped like a scalded cat as I speared her hard, and raked her nails over my back with each heaving, writhing shudder of orgasm. When I climbed off I looked as if

I'd been attacked by a cheese grater, and I probably needed a tetanus shot. But Solange, with her usual misguided intentions, poured after-shave lotion over me so I wouldn't infect.

I was dancing around the bed in excruciating pain when the telephone rang. It was Preston saying that one of his engineers had arrived and would I mind dropping by the hotel? Cheeky as ever, Solange lifted my wallet as she handed me my pants.

"Hold it, right there, Solange!"

"Don't begrudge me my small pleasures," she said, plucking a thousand dinar note from among the smaller denominations with the dexterity of a Cairo cutpurse.

"All I begrudge is what you give that bastard Bashir."

"You should be happy to ease your conscience. He is not even Palestinian yet he gives everything he has to the cause."

"Which is zilch because he has nothing to give. The truth is he's a snitch, a deadbeat and a freeloader."

"When did you ever care about truth? The great Palestinian freedom fighter! If Khalil knew the truth about you, he'd shoot you straightaway. International shill is what you are! Small time scam artist and world-class bullshitter!"

I caught her roughly by the wrist and jerked her upright, angry enough to knock her across the bed. But when I saw her hungry eyes and heard the panting breath, I knew I'd almost been had. She wanted it again, rough and ready, and Preston was waiting. I left her kneeling on the pillows, screaming after me, "Come back, you faggot, and get it up like a man!"

XXI

◇ It was after ten when I reached the hotel and I was not prepared for Preston's surprise. He was having a coffee in the bar with another man, presumably one of the new engineers. But if this fellow was an engineer, I was an astronaut. In the years I had known him, the only things I ever saw him engineer had been at the point of a gun.

Retired M. Sgt. Ike Maxwell, pistolero, Delta Force veteran and survivor of a hundred raids, combats and alarums, saw me at the same time and crossed the lobby in three giant steps to deliver a bone-jarring backslap on the precise spot Solange had flayed with her nails. "Davey, you old monkeyduster!"

I looked at the towering figure, the familiar rough, reddened face beneath the broad-brimmed Stetson. "Some engineer," I said and he laughed as if I had told a very funny joke.

He removed his big hat and ran his fingers through thick white hair, grinning at me happily. "By Christian, it sure is good to see you again, Davey!" He was handsomely tailored as always, in a Texas-style gabardine suit the same off-white color as his Stetson. He wore a heavy turquoise-and-silver belt buckle I had often admired, and highly polished, hand-tooled cowboy boots easily worth a thousand dollars.

Ike said to Preston, "Me and Davey go back a ways."

"I'm using my Arab name here, Ike. Dahoud el Beida."

"Glad to hear that, Davey, but it'll take some getting used to. You'll always be Davey Perpi-non to me." He popped a tiny mint into his mouth. "When was the last time we worked together?"

I was sorry he had brought that up. "In Cannes," I said, hoping his memory was worse than mine.

"Right! I almost forgot that!"

How I wish he had. My last view of Ike Maxwell had been about five years before, at night on the beach in front of the Carleton Hotel, where he was trading gunfire with the French Sûreté.

We had just escorted a Turkish associate from Beirut to France. My responsibility was to arrange the necessary bribes and papers while Ike made sure the luggage—which had considerable value—was not lost or mislaid. We travelled on a Greek rustbucket to Ajaccio, then by Corsican "fishing" boat to the Côte d'Azure. When our crew tried to raise the fare, Ike wounded one and held the other at gunpoint until the wretch brought us safely into a dawn mooring at Juan-les-Pins. As soon as we disembarked, they betrayed us to the police, although we did not find that out until later. We delivered the Turk's luggage, collected our money, and ate a sumptuous bouillabaisse. Then I left Ike napping in our suite and adjourned to the casino to amuse myself. About three A.M., after I had met up with a charming English girl and was having a run of luck at *vingt-et-un,* the sacred hush of the inner rooms was broken by the sound of police sirens.

Some instinct of self-preservation propelled me out into the night air. It is the same response that works with birds and small animals when they sense danger and crave maneuvering space.

I had the girl telephone our room, and when she got a gruff-voiced stranger on the other end, I sensibly decided to head for the Nice airport and take the next plane out. I had eighteen thousand dollars in my pocket and the world to make good in if I could stay ahead of the Corsican Mafia and the French Sûreté.

In the taxi driving along the Croisette, I was putting away my David Perpignon passport and resuming my Dahoud el Beida identity when I saw an extraordinarily tall man dashing toward the beach. In the instant he was fully illuminated by the taxi headlights, I recognized Ike. That is when I heard gunfire and peered cautiously through the rear window as the driver ground the gears and hit the accelerator, muttering a prayer. I often wondered how my friend made it off that beach alive.

"It wasn't easy, Davey. You remember them pedal boats at the hotel? Well, I stole one of them and went to sea."

I wanted to ask, "Did you see me in the taxi?" but instead I said, "How did you ever get out of France?"

"A man with money never wants for friends, and one took me down to Malta on his yacht. Then I got me that work over in the Persian Gulf."

"So I heard. Blowing up Iraqi oil rigs."

Ike looked terribly hurt. "It was mostly advising these Iraqis, like in the Peace Corps. And I provided a little demolition service, too."

Preston asked me, "Where does the 'Davey' come from?"

"The French equivalent of Dahoud," I explained. "My father was a French diplomat posted to the Middle East when I was born."

"His name was Perpignon?

"Well, actually his name was Leblanc. Pierre Leblanc."

Trying hard to be helpful, Ike said, "Davey's old man got his last name off a champagne bottle. Right, Davey? Only he had a snootful and wrote it wrong."

Why had I ever told Ike Maxwell the truth about my origins?

"But you are Palestinian?" Preston said.

"On my mother's side. I was born and grew up there."

"I see. And where did you and Ike meet?"

"In jail," Ike said.

Preston looked skeptically from one to the other of us, expecting God knows what wild tale. Then he burst out laughing.

I explained, "I was translating for a Muslim militia group in Beirut who were holding Ike prisoner."

"Hostage, is what he means," Ike said, "and Davey saved my ass. When them clowns found nobody'd trade to get me back, they was going to use me for target practice."

"How did he manage it?" Preston asked.

"He got me a gun," Ike said.

"You mean you shot your way out?"

"Only part way," Ike said.

Preston turned to me. "Weren't your militia friends upset when they discovered you helped Ike escape?"

"There weren't enough of them left alive to care."

Preston said, "Boys, I'm going to leave you two to catch up. Dahoud, fill Ike in on what we've been doing. Ike, you know what to tell Dahoud. I'm very pleased to discover you're such good friends. It's a dividend I had not counted on."

Preston had hardly left the room when I started questioning Ike. "Whoa, Davey! Hold on! I don't know everything!"

"You know a lot more than I do. What's he up to?"

"What did he tell you?"

"God damn it, Ike, he told me he heads a company that's going to build desalinating plants for the Libyan government."

"What's wrong with that?"

"I don't quite believe him, that's what's wrong. Desal's a front for something else, isn't it?"

"Davey, let it go. I'm just trying to get a leg up in the world, same as you."

"Not the same as me, Ike. You hire out with guns."

"Do you like working for him, Davey?"

"I'll tell you better after I find out what the work is."

"Is that a complaint?"

"I like to know what I'm in for, that's all."

"You need patience with these fellers, Davey. They don't know who they can trust, which is why they're so security conscious."

"What about me, Ike? Who do I trust? Tell me what's going on or I'll only suspect the worst."

"You'll probably be right, too, smart as you are."

"That's a real comfort. Look, do you know why I'm worried?" I recounted Khalil Malduum's interest in me and the abortive mission with the Semtex suitcase. I described the shooting on the Naples pier, the strangled corpse in my cabin on the ship, and Preston's role. I only left out the safe-deposit key.

Ike said, "I can see how that might make a man cautious."

"Damn it, I'm more than cautious!"

"I can't tell you anything Preston ain't told you already. I got to keep my big mouth shut, drunk or sober, or by Christian, they'll toss me out on my ass. Davey, Preston's keeping quiet for your own good. Like what you don't know won't hurt you."

"Ike, what I don't know could get me killed."

"Sorry, Davey."

"If you can't help me, at least stop calling me Davey. Here, I'm Dahoud. If the Libyans ever found out about David Perpignon, I'd be out of business. Finished, kaput, terminated!"

"Sure, old buddy. Dowd. I'll remember that."

"Please do."

"Davey?"

"Christ!"

"Sorry. Tell me something before we drop it, okay?"

"On condition you drop it."

"What was the champagne your daddy named you after?"

◇

XXII

◇ There was no point in pushing Ike any further for information about Preston, so the following morning I did what I should have done in the beginning. I went to the bank to find out what I wanted to know. It was a Saturday, but Herr Eidletraut frequently came in on weekends, so the outer offices and my own computer section were accessible.

This always amused me. The vault, with a billion in cash, was locked and protected by inches of steel, time locks and an electric alarm system. But my computer section, which moved billions in Libyan funds worldwide, was open to any employee who expressed a desire to catch up on his work. Of course, only Eidletraut and I had the codes needed to transfer these foreign deposits. But if one of us was crooked, we could rob the Bank of Libya blind by just tapping out a few numbers.

I signed in with the guard, sat down at my computer, and tied into a London service we used. In seconds I had a wealth of confidential business information at my fingertips, as well as personal background about virtually anyone of consequence.

The service checked Desal with Dun & Bradstreet and Standard & Poor's, and found that the company was not listed. How, I asked myself, can a firm with a fifty-four million dollar credit line not be rated? Something was fishy. Yet Eidletraut was no fool, and if his sources said Desal had the credit in America, then Desal had the credit. Data bank "Who's Who" listings carried an entry for Duffield Elliot: "Born Shawsheen, Massachusetts, 1931; educated U.S. Naval Academy (B.S. 1952), M.I.T. (Ph.D., 1962), U.S. Navy, 1952–72, retired as Captain. Chairman, Brand Technologies. Directorships on the boards of several other institutions and corporations."

Desal, Ltd. finally popped on my screen as a Canadian subsidiary of Brand Technologies, itself described as one of the fastest growing hi-tech conglomerates in the U.S., a pioneer in micro-chip circuitry and inertial navigation systems. Asking for more detailed information, I discovered that Duff Elliot's industrial umbrella included something called the Defense Resources Institute whose New York address was the one Preston had been using for Desal. Nothing fishy there, but still . . . why would Alan Preston employ someone like Hueblen and the last of the great gunslingers, Ike Maxwell, to build a desalinating plant? I found the answer in the description of the Defense Resources Institute. It was a private, nonprofit center established for the "study and analysis of counterterrorist response, and to prepare covert action scenarios for low-intensity conflicts," precisely the kind of outfit to attract a Maxwell or a Hueblen. The description also implied the sort of front associated with the twilight activities of intelligence agencies. The Institute conducted on-site evaluation of unconventional equipment and weapons systems in collaboration with the *Grenzschutzgruppe* 9 (GSG–9) of the West German Border Guard, and at the Canadian facilities of Britain's Special Air Service (SAS) Regiment.

Bingo. The German connection and the Canadian connection in one bite. Pushing the data bank further, I turned up Hueblen's name and discovered he was an ex-sergeant in GSG–9, and an explosives expert. But the bottom line was what flipped my bright lights on. The executive director of the Institute was none other than Alan W. Preston, formerly major in the Canadian Army and instructor at the Hereford training center of the British SAS.

It would seem that Captain Nagy's paranoid fantasies about the CIA were not so far off after all.

When I had the last of the information, I dropped by the Suq al-Turk to reflect on it over a glass of tea. In the scented shadows of the ancient arched alley, I listened to the clack of dominoes and the bickering merchants. I ordered honeydrop biscuits to stimulate my thinking while loudspeakers called the faithful to prayer from the nearby minaret of the Karamanli Mosque.

The pungent, sweetish odors of an Arab teaship can bring tears of joy to my eyes. All my life I have loved this kind of place except when the Frenchman in me intrudes. Or is it the ambiguity every Palestinian feels from birth? We, who for half a century have been refugees on our own doorstep. I did not linger over my identity crisis however, because the main question was now more imperative than ever. Although I thought I was about to solve the riddle of Preston, my suspicions were so bizarre I could hardly credit them.

When I arrived in front of the Desal Building, Preston, Ike Maxwell and a man he introduced as Philipe Cardoni were standing next to an immense white Mercedes. Cardoni was a cadaverous fellow with lobster pink skin, piercing dark eyes and black hair brushed forward in bangs. He was dressed in a pricey polo shirt and cashmere slacks, and with his deeply scarred face he could easily pass for a professional fighter or a St. Tropez nightclub bouncer. A highly decorated officer in the French paratroops, his name was also familiar to me from newspapers years ago when he raced on the Formula One circuit. After a near fatal crash at Monaco, he entered his Corsican family's business and served time for throwing a Marseilles prostitute off a fifth floor balcony.

"Is that your Mercedes?" I asked him enviously.

Ike replied, "It's the car we drove from Tunis. Neat, ain't it? And we're going to put it straight in your garage."

I had decided to attack Preston directly that morning, but he got to me first. "I trust Ike Maxwell's judgment almost more than I trust my own," he said, ushering me into his unfinished office and closing the door, "and he's told me there's no one he'd rather work with than you."

I was on my guard, not knowing what else Ike had said.

As if he could read my mind, Preston let me have the worst first. "He mentioned you and he used to run drugs from Turkey."

I maintained my composure in spite of that bombshell, but I wondered what the devil Ike Maxwell was trying to do, painting me like a common criminal! I decided to stonewall it, so I said, "I don't know why Ike would concoct such a story."

"Dahoud, you've been holding out on me."

"I assure you, Alan . . ."

"It doesn't matter. Ike calls you brilliant, cool."

"I do my best."

"I respect that. It takes guts to hijack an airliner."

"You know I had nothing to do with that."

"Ike also said you knew your way around the Arab world."

"At least that part is true."

"Actually, he said the 'underworld.' "

"Look, Alan . . ."

"That machine gun scam in Egypt was brilliant. Not exactly ethical, but brilliant!"

"There was a misunderstanding."

"And the Japanese tourist racket in Greece? Whoever gave you the notion to learn Japanese?"

"I was only filling a need."

"A need?"

"Well, not too many Greeks speak it."

"The cops must have gone out of their minds! A Japanese-speaking Arab? No wonder they never caught you!"

"Look, I've had a few problems with the law, but . . ."

"Problems? You've been jailed in Damascus, Frankfurt, Helsinki and Cairo. You're wanted in Holland for questioning, and the Greek cops would love to get their hands on you. Not to mention the Italians, the Israelis, the Turks, the French and the Saudis."

Better to say nothing. The morning was not going at all as I planned. I had intended to challenge him, but now he sounded like the man from Interpol. Then I made the mistake of reminding him of my professional background, and he only laughed the more.

"That's what I mean! You never bat an eye! Who else could fool the management of the Bank of Libya, half the police forces in Europe, and some of the most dangerous terrorists alive? I don't think you know how good you are."

"But . . ."

"But me no buts, Dahoud. I know what I'm talking about." He seemed amused at my discomfort, but at least he did not hold my background against me. He nodded as if he had been reading my mind. "You guessed by now that Desal is a front."

"For the Defense Resources Institute?"

"You've been doing your homework, I see."

"What I found out, Nagy can find out as well."

"But we know it's unlikely that he will."

"But why go through this elaborate charade? The fifty-four million dollar credit? These quaint offices?"

"To establish credibility."

"I can't imagine what it's cost. Is it worth it?"

"Absolutely."

"What's the payoff?"

"I can't tell you about that yet."

"Then let me guess. We both know Maxwell's background." I began to pace the office as I talked and he listened. "And I've learned a few things about Hueblen."

"Such as?"

"That he knows demolition, explosives, that sort of thing." The vision of the choleric German turned loose with dynamite terrified me. "And now you're going to tell me your new Corsican playmate is not what he seems."

"I wasn't going to tell you anything."

"The underworld term is 'wheel man', Alan. Ike, the rod man, Hueblen the powder man, and Cardoni the wheel man. Colorful gangster-type job descriptions that add up to one thing."

He waited for me to go on.

"You're planning to rob the Bank of Libya, aren't you?"

"What an extraordinary conclusion!" Preston said.

"Not at all. And do you know how far you'd get?"

"I'm sure you're about to tell me."

"Qaddafi has two thousand tanks, MIGs, Mirages, radar! Hundreds of cannon! Thousands of missiles!"

"Suppose there was a sure-fire way into the bank."

"There is. It's called the front door. But you don't have a way out, because there is no way out."

"There's a billion dollars in there, Dahoud."

"As inaccessible as the stars. You couldn't physically carry more than half of it out of the place."

"Only five hundred million? That *would* be disappointing."

"All right, it's still a huge fortune. But all those banknotes are serially numbered and registered. Once Libya reported the theft, banks all over the world would be alerted."

Preston was amused. "Laundering five hundred million on world currency markets would not be easy, but with my connections it could be done."

"It still won't work."

"Actually, Dahoud, my guess is that it probably would work for the very reason that it is the last thing anyone in Libya would expect. But I'll tell you what I don't like about your idea."

"*My* idea! Since when is it *my* idea?"

"To sum up," Preston went on as if he had not heard what I just said, "the place is poorly guarded and their security is a joke. But one has the certainty of an immense cash haul even if there is a physical problem getting it out of the country."

"That's the understatement of all time, Alan."

"The real catch is that four or five hundred million is barely a month's oil revenues for Qaddafi. Stealing it wouldn't put him out of business or bankrupt the Bank of Libya."

"Nothing would, short of blowing up his pipelines."

"But the idea of humiliating Qaddafi intrigues me."

"Find a safer way. Poison his water like Nagy thinks you're going to do. Or kidnap him at the next OPEC meeting."

"I much prefer your alternative proposal, Dahoud."

"What are you talking about?"

"Remember after our visit to the bank, when Hueblen and I were joking about the world's biggest holdup."

"Joking is not what I'd call it."

"You said that a lot more could be stolen by computer."

"I wasn't being serious."

"Don't be modest. You said the worldwide deposits could be moved to private accounts by anyone with access to the bank codes. And you have that access."

"I was kidding. It would not be as easy as I pretended."

"But it could be done."

"They'd catch on the next day and know who did it."

"But then it would be too late."

"Steal twelve billion and you'd never live to spend it."

"Is that how much it would be?"

"More or less."

"Their oil revenues for a year and a half."

"That's about right, but it's impossible."

"Enough to bankrupt Qaddafi!"

"You're not listening."

"It's ingenious. I know you aren't equipped to attempt it alone, so you floated it by me to see how I'd react. I've given it careful thought, and although there's room for fine-tuning, it's basically brilliant. Your plan . . ."

"Stop saying my plan! It is *not* my plan! It was idle speculation between friends. And even that could get us hanged in a country like this."

But Preston ignored my protests as he warmed to his theme, "It has a symmetry I find appealing, Dahoud. I like the magnitude and audacity of the design! There's a kind of awesome majesty in the sheer size of the heist. Imagine, twelve billion dollars! Who was that famous French pastry cook you admire so much?"

"Carême?"

"Well, it's an artistic conception worthy of him, Dahoud!"

"Alan, I really believe you've lost your grip. Something's unhinged your mind. You've been too long in Libya."

"The eternal pessimist."

"It's called the survival instinct. And it tells me there is no way a handful of petty crooks can take down the Bank of Libya. As of today I'm looking for another job, Alan, preferably in some nice quiet place like Beirut."

"But that's out of the question," Preston said gently.

"Count me out. I never signed up for a bank robbery."

"Dahoud, you are already part of the team. You can't abandon us now, whatever it is you think we're up to."

"Your group insurance doesn't cover me, Alan."

"I'm afraid I must insist."

"Nothing you say would convince me."

"I'm not trying to convince you."

"Good, because it's a waste of time."

Preston rose and walked to the door. "Ike? Would you come in here for a moment? And Philipe, I'd like you and Heinz to join us too, please."

Cardoni and Hueblen entered scowling, while Ike followed with a cheerful grin, sucking on one of his eternal mints.

Preston was smiling. "Dahoud has come up with a brilliant suggestion which could make us all incredibly rich."

I said, "I wish I could find this as funny as you do."

"But," he added, ignoring me, "he wants out."

"It's not that I want out," I said. "I have never been in, and I'd rather not be included at this time, although I wish you all the luck in the world."

"Why not, Davey?" Ike said.

In desperation I finally said, "You're all so sure of this screwball mission, but you don't even know who you're working for."

Ike was the first to speak out. "Now Davey," he began in his most placating tone, "your nose may be a little crooked because Al didn't fill you in up front, but he's planned this operation down to the last pair of socks, and we're gonna bring it off."

"Why don't you all just quit and go home?" I said. "Or better yet, build the desalinating plants. Half of that eight million's got to be profit."

"Heinz, will you explain?" Preston asked.

"To leave now is not possible," Hueblen said.

"Philipe?"

"In is in. There is no way out except . . ."

"Ike?"

"Davey, you don't give a man much choice . . ."

"What do you mean?" I said in amazement. "Just carry on as you were. Don't mind me."

"Excuse me," Cardoni interjected, "but you are not hearing what this nice gentleman is telling you."

Preston sighed. "How many ways can we spell it out?"

Cardoni placed a scarred hand on my arm and whispered, *"Caro, mon vieux,* what your good friends here are saying is they will kill you if you leave now."

"I don't like to force anybody against his will," Preston said, "but everything would be jeopardized if you walked."

"I won't say anything."

"We can't take that chance." Hueblen said harshly.

I looked at them in disbelief.

Cardoni cracked his knuckles ominously as he smiled at me, and a picture flashed across my mind of his Marseilles girlfriend being flung from a fifth floor window.

"Ike," I pleaded, "Tell them I can be trusted."

"Davey, I'd like to do that, but they know better."

Preston said, "In view of what you know, Dahoud, this offer is good for a limited time only. Say the next five minutes."

"So, that's how it is?"

"Sorry," Preston said.

I was dizzy with apprehension. I only wanted to remain in one piece and not rob anybody's bank, but they weren't going to let me.

"In?" Preston said.

"What choice do I have?"

Cardoni extended his hand, saying, *"Auguri,"* with the same shifty smile he'd shown when he announced they would kill me.

"I'm not what you think I am," I protested.

"Look at it this way," Preston said, "none of us is."

An ignorant bystander might have assumed I was being received into some exclusive club when I bowed to the inevitable and joined them. Ike clapped me on the back and said, "Good boy, Davey. I always said we could count on you."

"Yeah, right."

"Sorry about the pressure," Preston said, shaking my hand, "but I can't tell you how relieved I am to have you aboard."

I glimpsed myself in the mirror grinning idiotically and saying, "Thank you, thank you," to my fellow club members. There I was, the cunning confidence man and eternal survivor smiling my life away without a care. Only I knew the smile for what it was, an insincere rictus born of fear and despair, masking my undiminished determination to get out from under the whole macabre affair.

There may not be much honor among thieves anymore, but there's still a certain degree of courtesy. After having just voted for the death penalty, Ike now tried to cover his embarrassment by persuading me I exaggerated the danger. The operation was so fantastically well planned, according to him, that they would be in and out before anybody even knew what had happened.

"In and out of that bank? No way," I said.

"In and out of Libya," Ike said.

Preston only smiled and said, "You never give up, do you?"

His threat to me was certain proof of his determination to carry through grand larceny. But it was not yet clear if he planned an armed assault on the vault, or expected me to cooperate in a more sophisticated sting, like manipulating the computer access codes to withdraw Libyan funds deposited around the world. Either way he was doomed to failure. A bank holdup would be simple suicide, as I had told him. One needed no special powers of imagination to visualize our broken, bullet-riddled bodies sprawled at the vault entrance.

On the other hand, an electronic swindle on the scale he envisioned would require days to prepare. Since joining Preston, I had not been present for the weekly changing of the access codes, but Mr. Watanabe had taken my place beside Eidletraut for this Thursday ceremony, running a printout later for me. I was not about to say anything to anyone, but in effect a folded paper in my pocket was the key to twelve billion dollars in Libyan deposits.

Ike said, "Stop worrying, Davey, and leave it to Preston."

"Ike, do me a favor."

"Anything you say."

"Shut up."

"Why sure, Davey. I was only trying to help as a friend."

"Some friend. Awhile ago you would have snuffed me."

"Aw, you know I wouldn't do that. We're buddies."

"Glad you reminded me, Ike."

"I knew all along you were the only man for the job."

"What are you talking about?"

"Without you, Davey, it can't work, don't you see?"

"No, I don't see."

"That's why we had to lean on you, to make sure."

"Because you need someone inside the bank."

"Because we need *you*, Davey, not just someone. I told Preston and Elliot they got to give you more money because there's only one man in the world smart enough, tough enough, and greedy enough to pull this off perfect, and that's you."

"Thanks, Ike. I appreciate your sentiments, but it's an endorsement I could have done without." The trouble was Ike Maxwell had me all wrong. Everybody did.

<><>

That night I had a nightmare in which I was being hanged before a jeering crowd in Castle Square while Nagy smirked and Solange said, "I told you it would all catch up with you!" I awoke in a cold sweat with the bedsheet twisted about my neck, crying out that I was innocent! And Solange wanted to know, "Of what?"

For the first hour after waking, I relived my execution in all its vivid horror. My hand trembled so badly I cut myself shaving and spilled my morning tea. Solange asked what I'd had to drink the night before. "You look like somebody put the fear of God up you, Beida. What happened?"

"Nothing happened."

"You've been spooked since Maxwell came. What is it?"

"Nothing."

"You're scared witless. What's the matter?"

"Solange, I've got enough on my mind without you nagging."

"I only want to help."

"Well, you're not helpful."

"I'm your wife, Beida."

"Don't remind me."

"They're on to something big, aren't they?"

"Right. An eight million dollar desalination contract."

"I mean something else."

"It's a new technology with a lot of problems."

"Bashir says Preston's CIA."

"Bashir is one of the problems."

"Is he?"

"He's a bloody nuisance, a sneaky, lying, corrupt little shit, and what you see in him I'll never understand."

"I mean Preston." Solange chewed noisily on some toast. "Is he CIA?"

"For God's sake, Solange!"

"Well, is he? You should know by now."

"By all means. Why else would he have come to Libya?"

"You joke while the world collapses around you."

I slammed my teacup down so hard it cracked the saucer. "I am not joking, Solange! Captain Nagy has me by the balls! Malduum wants my soul! Preston knows all about me, thanks to Ike Maxwell! Bashir drives me crazy with his rubbish about Preston. And now you're on my back . . ."

"I'm on my own back, whenever you're up to it."

"Solange, I'm in no mood for your Gaza strip humor. I'm speaking of life and death, in case you haven't noticed."

"Whose, Beida? Yours?"

"And, indirectly, yours."

"Oh, no you don't. If you're in some new trouble I don't know about, *habibi*, you're on your own."

"Nice to know where you stand."

"Where I always stood, Beida. What do you expect?"

"A moment ago, you were telling me you wanted to help because you're my wife."

"Bashir says . . ."

"Bashir again! I don't want to hear about bloody Bashir!"

"All right. I'll stop!" Her voice rises in pitch when she's offended, and she's offended now because I insulted her lover.

"Why don't you move in with him? Make it official."

"Oh, we'd never get along. He's not easygoing like you, and he doesn't make nearly enough money."

XXIII

▷ Israel was the price England and America were willing to pay for abandoning European Jewry to the Nazis during the Second World War. In the Middle East prior to that time there was seldom strife between Arab and Jew. But when the promised land became Israel and America became its patron, two million Palestinian Arabs were turned into embittered stateless persons. As such they regarded the Jewish state as a colony thrust upon them by foreigners, a restricted living space created at their expense to salve other people's consciences. Little did anyone dream how much the gesture would cost in thousands of lives and billions of dollars. But Israel had to be armed against hostile neighbors, and homeless Palestinian refugees had to be fed.

Americans grew so used to thinking of the tiny country as a brave island of freedom in a sea of Arab violence, that the Israeli army's harsh response to rock-throwing Palestinian youths of the *intifada* was especially disillusioning. It is hard to accept that a friend can sometimes behave in a cruel and unjust manner.

Israel has always been portrayed as the underdog, but recent American opinion polls reflect the new Israeli image of a bully, while the same polls show increased sympathy for Palestinians whose civil rights are routinely violated by rifle-toting troops. Gone forever, it seems, is the image of the Jew as victim.

Yet after half a century of conflict and suffering, Jews and Arabs still face the same precarious coexistence obsessed with each other now in a divided land too poor, too desolate and too small to hold them both.

Enter Khalil Malduum and those like him who vow to bury the Zionists. Their plans for genocide are so outrageous they would seem ridiculous to anyone unfamiliar with the history of Jewish persecution. But they are real and they are deadly. It is easy to dismiss men like Malduum as warped, demented criminal psychopaths who prey upon the innocent. But that is only half the story. The successful terrorist—from Abu Nidal to Saddam Hussein—is also intelligent and aggressive, with a special aptitude for political manipulation and timing, and an unerring ability to pick his victim.

The morning after my induction into his little band, Preston waved a copy of Tripoli's main daily newspaper at me. "Does this say what I think it says?"

"I didn't know you read Arabic," I told him.

"Old Prince Pozzogallo translated most of it for me over breakfast. I just want you to confirm what he told me."

The main front page article was indeed a surprise. It carried a picture of Qaddafi smiling, his modified Afro hairdo topped absurdly by his colonel's hat, shaking hands with a French diplomat. The headline read "Zionist Spies Turned Over to France". The article recounted how the Libyan People's Leader, in celebration of the Moslem feast of *Aid Al-Adha,* prevailed upon the gallant freedom fighters of the United Palestinian Armed Resistance Front to turn over four Zionist spies to the French government.

"The students from the Egyptair flight," Preston said.

"I heard through the grape arbor, as they say, that France stopped shipment on all Mirage spare parts to Qaddafi, as well as six new planes, after the hijacking."

"That's right," Preston said. "Paris cut the son of a bitch off cold. So in retaliation he suspended oil shipments to France. But then the French just increased imports of North Sea oil and told Qaddafi to go fuck himself."

"That's when he ordered Malduum to release the students."

"Apparently. But it's deeper than that, more complex."

"In what way?"

"For years Qaddafi has survived mainly by exploiting Soviet antagonism toward the West. Now Gorbachev's policy of disengagement leaves him in the cold. The minute Russians and Americans and Europeans all start dancing to the same music, his days are numbered. So he's got to rethink his relations with bastards like Malduum, Abu Nidal and the rest."

"Maybe," I said, not at all convinced. Preston's analysis was reasonable, but reason seldom governed the actions of any Arab leader, as the world learned from Saddam Hussein in Iraq. Most Libyans are paranoid and xenophobic, and Qaddafi was just a little more paranoid and xenophobic than the rest. And as long as Khalil Malduum acted against foreign "enemies", Qaddafi would support him.

"It's no accident that the Soviet Union has never dealt with one of these bastards," Preston continued. "Kidnap a Russian and you've got five minutes to give him back, or Moscow takes your guts and . . ."

"Just like the Americans," I said facetiously.

Preston laughed. "The United States is not so much the Great Satan as the Great Patsy," he said. "Every American life is negotiable, and every terrorist knows it."

"Then why don't they pressure Israel to get their people back. Can't they do what France did?"

"The American record on negotiations is terrible, and what Malduum wants, the Americans can't give him. Americans are so God-fearing. They tend to pray, wear yellow ribbons, and hope for the best."

"Will Israel yield anything without a *quid pro quo?*"

"Of course not."

"And Malduum won't give up something for nothing."

"It used to be called a Mexican standoff," Preston said. "But this time, Malduum went too far."

"He hasn't even started," I said.

"What do you mean by that?"

"Khalil Malduum is like the compulsive gambler who pretends a love for horses to justify his betting. He uses "The Cause" as a license to kill. He likes to inflict pain and enjoys killing. The same traits which make him anethema to a man like Arafat, endear him to Qaddafi." I mentioned the woman hostage dying of a heart attack and Malduum's glee over the fake execution on videotape, pretending he had hanged her."

"Jesus Christ, that's sick!" Preston said.

"It's macabre," I replied, "but not surprising."

"You know more than you're telling me, don't you?"

"Not really, I . . ."

"But you see him. He confides in you obviously."

"He confides in no one, but he does brag a lot, and anyone in my position has to stay on the right side of crazies like him."

"Another hijacking?"

"He has enough hostages for the time being."

"Then what?"

"Car bombs. Assassinations. You know how they are. They cook up things just to keep their hand in."

I was not yet ready to put a noose around my neck by revealing the elaborate schemes for mass death at Westminster Abbey, Munich's Hofbrauhaus or the Houston Astrodome. Time enough for that later. But Malduum would only take his bombs elsewhere, to St. Paul's Cathedral or Shea Stadium in New York, and most public places in democratic countries have woefully inadequate security.

I said, "Thirty lives, more or less, mean nothing to a man who has dedicated himself to ridding Palestine of its last Jew. It could be three or three million as far as he is concerned. And right now the Israeli army is his closest ally."

"Why do you say that?"

"The way they're cracking down on the *intifada*. Every time they kill another Palestinian kid, more people say Khalil is right. He's becoming a hero in spite of himself."

"Unfortunately, I must agree with you."

"You like the wisdom of the desert so much," I said sarcastically, "I have a Palestinian saying for you."

Preston smiled.

"It goes, 'Moderation is the quickest way to the grave. If your enemies don't kill you, your friends will.' "

"Yet Arafat is a Palestinian moderate," Preston said.

"And how many Palestinians have tried to kill him?"

"Good point."

"Try and crawl inside their minds for a moment," I said. "Like Malduum, Qaddafi believes everything bad stems from Zionists or Americans. And if he can't blame them, then some other devil has to be invoked, and he doesn't have one, except occasionally Egypt."

"You've given this a lot of thought," Preston said.

"When you're born Palestinian and forced to scuffle around the Middle East for a living, you think of very little else."

"But you have Arab friends everywhere."

"Syrian, Iraqi and Jordanian Muslims pity their Palestinian brothers," I told him, "but they are tired of the constant reproach implied by the existence of the Jewish state because it gives embarrassing and unwelcome substance to their own inadequacy. Officially they oppose Israel, but little love is lost on Palestinians."

"That's hard to believe," Preston said. "Do I detect a note of self-pity there? A touch of Palestinian paranoia perhaps?"

I shrugged. "Call it what you want, but there's something faintly disreputable about being born Palestinian. At best one is considered a poor relative or social embarrassment; at worst, a political orphan who is begging for handouts when he isn't running around stirring up trouble."

"But most of them couldn't wipe their asses without Palestinian professionals like you. They call you the Jews of the Arab world."

I smiled at that and thanked him for the compliment, but said I was the exception. "If a Palestinian is lucky like me, he becomes a never-quite-welcome guest drifting from place to place in an unfriendly world. If he's unlucky like most, he's stuck in the cruel poverty of a dusty village in the occupied zone or he subsists without hope in some squalid refugee camp."

I was wound up by that time and just kept talking. I told him that as a result of this peculiar status, a desperate population has grown up in and around Israel, two bitter generations nourished by strife and injustice in the camps and villages; rock throwers whose targets are Israeli soldiers, and who are in turn, targets themselves. "They say the Israelis have an atom bomb, Alan," I said, "but Palestinians have their secret weapon too: a birthrate four times that of Israeli Jews!"

"I didn't realize you could be so passionate," Preston said. "I don't agree with you, but I am impressed."

"I have spent my life trying to avoid the issue," I said. "I am not proud of this, but I am not a believer in causes, lost, just, or otherwise. Live and let live is my motto. Trust no one but get people to trust me. Sometimes they do, which would be flattering except it is almost always when they know me as David Perpignon."

"I see."

"I don't think you do because you don't see the prejudice in their eyes. They are suspicious of Dahoud el Beida. He can't be reliable because he's a member of a crafty, cunning, ruthless race who will smile while he steals your watch, then slit your throat as soon as your attention wanders. Look at Arafat, they say. That awful man with the heavy wet lips, the wens and scruffy beard, the bulging, hyperthyroid eyes. His cause might be just, but the Israelis should really be grateful for the image he projects. How could anyone as ugly as he is be up to any good?"

Preston laughed merrily. "You're so right," he said. "It wouldn't matter what he was selling, I'd never buy it."

"There you are. David Perpignon, on the other hand, is a French gentleman, son of a career diplomat and scion of an old family who is obviously forthright, dependable, cultivated and totally honest. He's a bit swarthy perhaps, even Jewish-looking, but definitely a man to be trusted and possibly admired."

Preston was still smiling. "You've made your point, Dahoud. Very well indeed. So why not live your life as Perpignon?"

"In Libya anyone who is neither Muslim, Arab, nor Libyan is automatically suspect," I told him. "Fortunately no one knows about Perpignon here, not even Solange. It's a secret I always kept from her. You wouldn't know about it either except for Ike Maxwell."

"It's safe with me," he said.

I assumed it probably was. What none of them realized was that Dahoud el Beida would sacrifice his very existence for David Perpignon, and that was my great advantage.

But Ike might inadvertently let the beans out of the bag with Solange, and she was a different story. A loose cannon, as they say, who already had been shooting off her mouth about my past, filling in the few disgraceful facts Ike Maxwell had not disclosed. If she ever let anything slip to Bashir, I was a dead duck, because he would surely flog it to Nagy or Malduum at my expense.

While she was in Rome, I wasn't worried. But now that she was underfoot all the time, if she really found out anything, she could tell me which way to jump and how far.

Meanwhile Malduum wanted to bomb the English, Preston wanted to rob the Libyans, Nagy wanted to hang Preston, and all their plans included me. The more I reviewed my peculiar circumstances, the angrier I became. They had all taken advantage of me to such an extent that everybody had a say about my destiny except me. I was a pawn, a victim, a catspaw, as they say, and like any man of spirit, I resented the role.

Okay, I told myself, I can play that game too. Nice guys finish last, they say. So, from now on, no more Mr. Nice Guy.

It wasn't easy. I could have dealt with Solange alone, or Nagy. But add Preston and Dick Diamond and Malduum to the mix and my defenses simply weren't up to a war on so many fronts. I needed money if I was to make a break for it. And I needed counsel, help, advice. I needed someone like Karen to inspire me, and a way to get safely away from the others without attracting too much attention.

The one who could help was old Aboubakir Jeballah, but before I had a chance to consult him, Preston took me completely by surprise, and got to the draw first, as they say.

"What can you tell me about the Jeballah brothers?" he asked. "In particular, the one named Aboubakir?"

"Where did you hear about him?"

"Friends recommended him."

"What did they say?"

"That he's rich and smart. That his construction firm is big, and that Qaddafi leaves him alone because he's too powerful."

"That's essentially correct."

"I have the feeling there's more."

"Aboubakir Jeballah was also a smuggler and bandit in his day, and is a leader of the Tibu tribe from the desert mountains of southwest Libya, which is one reason Qaddafi does not touch him."

"Can I do business with him?"

"The devil can do business with him, but even the devil is careful. Aboubakir uses sand instead of cement in his buildings."

"So do most crooked contractors," Preston said.

"Except he waters the sand."

Preston laughed.

"He is a black fellow, part Tibu, part Arab."

"Do you know him personally?"

"I am lucky to be his friend."

"What about his brother?"

"Fadlalah is a white Arab. Dangerous."

"Explain, please."

"Same father, different mothers. Fadlalah is younger, a thief and a cutthroat. Totally untrustworthy."

Preston smiled. "Remind me never to ask you for a character reference. I take it the black one's the boss."

"Correct. Old Aboubakir is fiendishly clever. He can be quite ruthless, while Fadlalah is fat and lazy."

"Can you arrange a meeting with him?"

"He'll want to know what it's all about."

"I need backup," Preston said with a smile. "Planes, trucks, men, supplies. I'm sure I can make him a proposition."

I did my best to talk him out of it because I still hoped to save old Jeballah for myself. But Preston is a stubborn fellow, and

Aboubakir had obviously come highly recommended.

"He'll never go for what you are planning," I said.

"But you don't know what it is, so how can you judge?"

When I returned home that evening, Solange was not yet there, but Nagy was, waiting in his Mercedes revving the motor. He insisted on driving me around for an hour while he fired questions about our visit to the bank that afternoon. Before he dropped me at my home he said, "Do not let this Preston out of your sight."

"He wants to visit Ghadames."

"Impossible!"

"To meet the Jeballah brothers."

"Those crooks!"

"What do you want me to do?"

He turned this over in his sick brain for a moment, picking at his acne and drumming his stubby fingers on the steering wheel. "Arrange it," he said, "and I will go with you."

"How do I explain your presence?"

"Let me worry about that. Call me as soon as you have booked the flight. Above all, he must not know I am wise to him."

"I still think you are mistaken," I said.

"Do not think, Beida. Just do as you're told."

XXIV

When I entered my apartment a note was on the kitchen counter saying Solange would return late and for me to go ahead and eat without her. Eat what? In the housekeeping department, she was a disaster, and as a cook she was close to a dead loss. I ransacked the kitchen in search of a snack, but found only Pupi's dog food.

Among her other misconceptions about me was a cherished belief that if she kept no food in the kitchen, I would eat less. She claimed that under stress I became a closet bulemic, and that's why her cupboard was usually bare. Living around her, Pupi did all right, while I felt like Mother Hubbard's dog.

Solange loved to quote the Duchess of Windsor's saying that a woman could never be too rich or too thin, and she refused even to store emergency rations in case I had a blood sugar blackout. But I did not care. Solange's days were numbered.

If I was a marked man, she was a doomed woman, condemned to a future without the disposable income of Dahoud el Beida, and beyond the consoling arms of David Perpignon. The moment I got myself out of this depressing fix she'd be on her own.

I took a bottle of mineral water from the fridge and dragged myself to the living room, cursing Solange, Nagy, Preston, the whole lot of them.

Preston's desire to do business with Aboubakir Jeballah once again confirmed my worst suspicions. No reputable person would ever employ Jeballah's construction firm because his fame preceded him. Libyan government ministers were the only ones who con-tracted the Jeballah brothers because throw-away buildings did not bother men with unlimited access to public money. The apartments owned in Rome by those same ministers, thanks to the Jeballahs, also guaranteed that life would go on for them no matter who ran things in Libya.

Now that Preston wanted to meet the great Aboubakir Jeballah and presumably enter into some kind of deal with him, my own request for assistance would have to wait. The old man would help me if he could, but he would also expect me to understand that friendship does not get in the way of business. So, patience, David, I told myself. Take it one day at a time. For the moment, my problem was how I was going to handle Preston and Nagy on the same plane when we went to visit Jeballah. The idea of the three of them together while I played referee almost made me physically sick.

Sagging into a sofa without looking, I sat on a book Solange had been reading called *Doctor Solar's Astral Secrets.* Although I had less belief in Doctor Solar than I did in the Easter Bunny, one is always curious. I thumbed the pages and found my sign, Sagitarius, and the forecast for December. Maybe he had some advice on how to get out of the elaborately crafted deathtrap Preston and the others were preparing.

"Mercury and Venus," I read, "are conjoined in the eighth house which governs crisis and change. Misgivings about dubious undertakings at this time are natural. Resist facile, get-rich-quick schemes. Easy money is not for you. Lucky numbers are three and thirteen. Take special care of your health until the change of the moon. Bundle up."

Bundle up?

That night I slept like a baby, as they say. I cried out in my sleep, woke up with colic, got the hiccups, went to the bathroom three or four times, then slept again. Like a baby.

In the morning Preston met at the Desal offices with Ike, Hueblen and Cardoni to discuss what he would need from Jeballah. My presence was not required for this logistical conference so I wandered over to the bank, looking very businesslike with my empty attaché case in one hand. I found Watanabe disturbed by a glitch in a new accounting program. I ran the numbers for him and fixed the error, earning his eternal gratitude for the hundredth time.

Watanabe loved to talk to me because I was the only person in Libya beside his wife who spoke some Japanese. Which meant he could vent his frustration in his native language, telling me over and over again what a hopeless lot the Libyans were.

After tea with him among the computers I casually wandered down to the vault, looking busy with a sheaf of accounting printouts in my hand. The guards in the corridor ignored me while the old man inside the vault dozed peacefully at his table.

I picked up his master key without waking him and went directly to box six-twenty-A, one of the larger boxes on the far wall. I had inserted the two keys into their respective locks when a familiar voice called out, "Ah-ha! Caught you in the act!"

I froze, and then slowly turned to see Eidletraut bearing down on me. While my expression remained calm, my mind thrashed desperately about for some explanation. I have this gift for looking unruffled, which people often mistake for ice in the veins, as they say. Actually, it's a kind of paralysis of the central nervous system brought on by abject terror, but it looks cool. How in God's name could I explain why I was opening a strong box not registered in my name?

As it developed, no explanation was necessary. Poor old Eidletraut always had a high opinion of me, but now that I was associated with

Preston's fifty-four million dollar line of credit, his warm regard verged on infatuation. He paid no attention whatsoever to what I had been doing, and barely noticed when I returned the master key to the old guard's table.

"Watanabe told me you were here. How much I enjoyed meeting Mr. Preston and his colleague. What a marvelous idea to make drinking water from the sea!"

The exquisite irony of his chatter was not lost on me. Once Preston carried out his plan and everybody had been killed or maimed, no one would believe that the German manager had not been involved. I mean he even invited the thieves to tour the bank!

Nagy would be the first to leap to the wrong conclusion, and I doubted Eidletraut could stand up to interrogation by the *mukhabarat*. Eidletraut rattled on while I was thinking, you poor fool, if they don't kill you when they shoot up the place, you'll wish they had after the Libyans get through with you.

The manager effervesced as he outlined the banking services he could offer Desal, as if I was not already familiar with all of them. "Watanabe told me Mr. Preston is interested in hiring safe-deposit boxes." That was the excuse I had given for wandering around in the vault unattended.

I said. "We'll need two or three large ones if they're available. That's what I was just checking."

"By all means, choose what you want," Eidletraut said agreeably. "And please impress upon Mr. Preston the efficiency of our foreign exchange department, and our agility in issuing and negotiating letters of credit."

After he left, I decided not to press my luck. Tomorrow or the next day I would rouse the guard to open the safe with me. I was about to leave when the old man awakened. "Ah, Beida, you have been waiting. Forgive me. You want your box? Here, take my key. You don't need me."

It was so simple I immediately decided to look into the box then and there. As far as he was concerned, I was a bank executive who could reasonably be expected to have a certain access.

This time 620-A seemed to stand out from all the other boxes, the biggest and most conspicuous of all. I inserted my key and then the bank key. Both turned easily, and the polished steel door swung open. When I slipped the metal drawer out, I staggered under the sudden weight. I carried it to one of the small cubicles designed to give boxholders privacy, wondering what rare treasure could possibly be this heavy. The drawer itself was padlocked but the second key in my hand fit the lock, as I assumed it would. For a moment I refrained from lifting the lid of the strong box, closing my eyes and calling on those capricious gods who determine the fate of us all. Let this be my way out of Libya, I said silently, let this be my lottery ticket, my big lucky draw.

But instead of gold coins or bars, I found the disassembled parts of an Ingram 9 mm. submachine gun, an M-10 as they are called, complete with silencer and four loaded magazines wrapped in oiled paper. My disappointment was palpable as I contemplated the weapon before dropping it into my attaché case.

I don't recall anymore why I decided to keep it, but the day would come when I was very glad I did. It is possibly the smallest of its class in the world, only a hair bigger than a Colt automatic pistol, but with a cyclic rate of fire exceeding a thousand rounds per minute; a great favorite among drug dealers and terrorists because of its small size and large killing power.

I silently cursed Khalid Belqair until I realized the box was deep, so I rummaged about to see what was underneath. I found several cardboard boxes of cartridges for the Ingram, and then another layer of oiled paper. Under the paper I finally struck paydirt, as they say: plastic wrapped packets of money, each with a paper band stamped "Crocker National Bank, San Francisco", and each containing ten thousand dollars in $100 bills. There were five layers of eight packets each, adding up to four hundred thousand dollars. I had found my ticket out!

One does not look a gift horse in the eye, as they say. If I entertained the least idea of taking the money—and that is precisely what I intended doing—I had to leave no link between me and the safe deposit box. Kahlil Malduum would kill anyone who touched his funds, which meant I had to recover the slip I had just signed before it entered permanent bank records. Then, if Malduum or any other member of the UPARF was ever able to open the box, at least they could not trace the missing money to me.

I was still in luck because the old man was paying me no attention. Further down the stainless steel wall of the vault, I sighted a row of doors with the boxholder keys still in place. These were the boxes Eidletraut said were available. I continued looking along the vault until I found one the same size as the one I had opened, and using the old guard's key, I removed the empty drawer from its niche and slipped in the full one, minus the padlock. The number was 313 oddly enough, according to Doctor Solar, lucky for me.

I closed the steel door, pocketed the boxholder's key, and took the empty drawer from 313 to the open niche of 620-A. I wiped it down with my handkerchief, slid it inside and closed the door, withdrawing the bank key and returning it to the old man, who barely looked up.

"Boxes three hundred twelve through sixteen are available," I said. "I'll sign for them now and take the keys."

"As you like," he replied amiably. "You must have many valuable things, Beida, to need so many safes."

I laughed. "Don't I wish. But they are for a foreign company doing business here, one that makes fresh drinking water from the sea."

"These foreigners!" he said admiringly. "What will they think of next! Here, I'll get you the signature cards."

"Don't bother." I withdrew the cards for 313, 314, 315, and the slip I had signed for six-twenty-A. The last I pocketed, so there was now no way to connect me to Malduum's safe-deposit box.

"I seem to have lost the visitor's slip you signed," the old man said, squinting through his spectacles at the floor around him. "Would you mind filling out another?"

I wrote in box 315 as the one I had visited and marked the time by the bank clock at quarter to twelve. On my way out I passed by the computer section again in better spirits than I'd been for weeks. Actually I was giddy with the sheer joy of sudden riches, light-headed over my newfound wealth. At the same time I was under no illusions about being able to spend the four hundred thousand dollars until I could get it safely out of Libya. The most obvious way, theoretically, was to take it out in an attaché case, but there was always the risk of a departure search at the airport. The alternative was to deposit it in a ghost account here and then surreptitiously transfer it abroad with other bank funds, but marked to my account in Vienna.

The danger was that a paper trail would exist unless I could delete my name and account number before the daily printout became a permanent bank record. To do that I would have to handle the transfer personally, removing the incriminating facts after the Vienna deposit was confirmed. Tricky, but it was the safest way to move the money without anyone knowing.

When I arrived at the Desal Building, Preston said, "You're looking especially cheerful today, Dahoud. Don't tell me. You won the lottery. No, better yet, you thought it over and decided we're a great bunch to work with after all. Right?"

"Alan, how did you ever guess?"

"Now what's the fastest way to put me together with your friend Jeballah? Ike tells me he's sunning himself out in the middle of the desert someplace . . ."

". . . Ghadames. It's an oasis."

". . . but he's got his own airline."

"If you want to call it that."

"I mean, can they take us to him?"

"It's a freight charter service, but I suppose they could fly you there. Otherwise it's a very long, dreary ride by land rover and Captain Nagy wants to go along."

Preston smiled. "By all means. The trip will give me a chance to tell the redoubtable captain all about the CIA."

"Don't joke, please. Captain Nagy has no sense of humor. He would just as soon kill you as look at you. In fact, I am sure he would rather kill you than look at you."

XXV

◇ Early the next morning I drove beyond the suburb of Gargaresh to see Jock Pringle about flying us to Ghadames. A Liverpool Irishman, Jock worked as chief pilot for Mabrouk Air, Jeballah's so-called airline whose headquarters was a decrepit sheet-iron hangar at the old municipal airport. The building dated from the Second World War and was hardly more than a rusty shell with holes stitched by wartime strafing runs half a century ago. A delightfully spicy aroma assailed my nose and awakened my appetite when I entered Jock's combination office and living areas where he cooked gourmet lunches and played endless games of poker when he wasn't flying. Mustafa, the Libyan mechanic, was raising his bet as Jock and two other pilots glumly concentrated on their cards. Nobody looked up until Jock leaped from the table to stop a pot from boiling over.

"Ghadames?" he said when I told him what I wanted. "You'll be going to see the old villain then. Well, himself is wintering there like a bloody migrant bird."

Jock scratched at his great shock of wild red hair, then shoved aside a pile of dirty dishes to find a scrap of paper and a pencil stub. "It's going to be pricey, mate. Two hours down and two back at four hundred quid the hour."

"My boss will pay it, Jock. The man likes his comfort."

"Then he should stay to hell out of Ghadames."

"Captain Nagy will be joining us as well."

"What did you do to deserve that, give him cancer?" He offered me a swig from a bottle of Jameson's, but I declined. Warm whiskey from the bottle at ten in the morning is not my cup of tea, as they say. "Any idea what day you want to go?"

"As soon as possible."

"By the way, old man, the other day you were telling me about a cream sauce for braised leeks that sounded like . . ."

"It's a *fondue* actually."

"Whatever you call it. Can you let me have the recipe?"

I loaned him the little leather agenda where all my sauces and other food notes were listed. "Here, Jock. Copy it yourself." As it turned out, I forgot to take the book back when I left, an oversight that was to have serious consequences for us both.

Preston was pleased with the Ghadames arrangement when I told him, and said, "Ike Maxwell and Prince Pozzogallo will be joining us, too." Many aspects of Preston's operation puzzled me, but none more than the part played by the octogenarian prince. If Desal, Ltd. was a front for a criminal enterprise employing people like Maxwell and the others, then why on earth was Preston financing Pozzogallo's archaeological investigations?

Yet I had seen the old gentleman nearly every day pouring over old maps and ancient street layouts in Preston's office. He always had time to chat, and was an authority on Libyan history.

Not just the ancient Roman and Greek periods, but the Turkish and Phoenician occupations, as well as the modern Italian chapter in which he himself had played an active part. But he was as close-mouthed as the rest of them when I questioned him about Preston, and all I got for my trouble was an occasional wink and a lot of double talk.

The day before going to Ghadames, Preston had me drive him and the old prince to Zavia, the modern Arab town near the ancient Roman ruins of Sabratha on the coast. We called on the *muhdir,* or mayor, whose only interest in the desalinating process was who would get the salt. We drank glasses of sweet green tea, fanning the flies away, while Preston complimented the *muhdir* on his squalid little town. I thought the day would be a waste of time, but as usual I underestimated Preston. He charmed the old *muhdir* to such an extent that we were invited to tour the local tuna canning factory owned by his sons. Then we proceeded to the Sabratha ruins to view the spectacular theatre, the Roman baths and the harbor with old Prince Pozzogallo as our guide. Then while Pozzogallo rested in the shade, Preston and I walked the beach with one of the *muhdir*'s sons until I had blisters on both heels.

"Lovely coastline," Preston said. "Great tourist potential, but the beach seems pretty steep here, doesn't it?"

"Are you thinking of opening a hotel?" I asked him.

"Sabratha could be a key location," he replied without elaborating further. When I looked at him he merely smiled.

We toured the small, rockbound harbor as well, bouncing around for an hour in an outboard skiff owned by the *muhdir.* "You're certainly thorough," I told Preston.

"One can't take anything on faith, Dahoud. You of all people should know that."

By the time we headed back to Tripoli the day was fading. We stopped briefly in Zavia again to thank the *muhdir.* Behind us the Sabratha ruins glowed with a warm roseate hue under the last dying rays of the sun. Moved by such stark splendor, I said to Preston, "You really should take time to see more of Libya's incomparable archeological sites. Leptis Magna is perhaps less beautiful but much more grand, and the Greek ruins at Cyrene are incomparable."

"I've offered him my exclusive guided tour to all of them," Prince

Pozzogallo said, "but he is always busy, busy, busy."

"It would be a shame to miss what Libya has to offer," I said, hoping he would tell me what he was up to.

"Don't worry," he replied with an infuriating smile, "I have no intention of missing what Libya has to offer."

As we left the ancient Roman port behind, he started to say something else, then stopped abruptly and just looked out the window, mute. I had the feeling he had been about to confide something of importance to me, but changed his mind.

I decided to push. "This survey, the beaches and all . . ."

"What about it?"

"Sabratha is not the best route out of Libya if that's what you're looking for, unless you're leaving by submarine."

Preston laughed. "Something like that," he said, "but not quite."

When we arrived at his hotel, the prince seemed worn out from the mild exertions of the day, and Preston asked, "Are you sure you want to come tomorrow? I can manage all right."

"I wouldn't miss it if it killed me."

"That's why I asked," Preston said.

The old man replied with great dignity, "I'll do what I can to oblige." A wink at me, and he entered the hotel with that cautious rocking gait of the elderly, like a sailor trying to keep his feet on a heaving deck.

Ike drove us to the airport early the next morning, and when he asked Preston if everything was on schedule, Preston nodded. "So far. I spoke to Elliot last night. He expects final approval today before the meeting."

I could only guess at the significance of the message, and Ike received it cheerfully enough. His smile faded however when he saw the aged DC-3 we were about to board.

"Christ, Davey, you don't expect me to get into that thing!"

I explained that Jock was a pilot of legendary skill.

"He'd have to be to get that crate off the ground."

"I believe it is war surplus," I said.

"Boer or Crimean?" Preston wanted to know.

Jock was nursing a hangover so I offered him a coffee from the thermos I had brought. He shook his head and made his way unsteadily up the aisle to the cockpit. When I joined Preston he did not ask the question I knew was foremost in his mind.

Old Prince Pozzogallo sat beside Ike Maxwell and looked apprehensively out the window. At the last minute Captain Nagy climbed aboard and settled sullenly into one of the bucket seats across the aisle.

One engine and then the other sputtered to life, and we bounced across the potholed apron and turned onto the runway without a pause. It was shake, rattle and roll as the ancient bird gathered speed. The old man clutched my arm until we were airborne.

"What does 'Mabrouk' mean in Arabic?" Preston asked me.

"Good luck. We're flying Good Luck Airlines."

He said, "At least that's in our favor. I must learn some Arabic."

"All you need to know is three words," Ike said. "I been all over the Arab world and never needed more than three words." Old Pozzogallo laughed and Preston was smiling. I had heard it before and I motioned Ike to go on.

"The words are *'enshallah'*, *'malesh'*, and *'mafeesh'*. *'Enshallah'* means 'God willing' or 'maybe,' " Ike said.

"I can remember that," Preston said.

"Just wrap your tongue around it, Al. *En-shaaaal-ah!*"

"*En-shaaaal-ah!*" Preston repeated perfectly. "Got it."

" *'Malesh'* means 'too bad', 'What the hell!' or 'tough shit!' "

Preston said, *"Malesh.* That's easy." Nagy scowled from across the aisle as he listened to their conversation. Apparently nothing was going to please him on this trip.

"And *'mafeesh'* means 'finished', 'finito', 'kaput,' " Ike explained. "With them three words, you can hack it any place they understand Arab."

"Let me see if I have it right," Preston said with enthusiasm. "If I see hope or promise in a situation, it is *'enshallah'.* Correct?"

"But if you want to cut your losses," I told him, "it is *'malesh.'* "

"And if you know in your heart that the game is over or the jig is up," old Prince Pozzogallo added, "it is *'mafeesh.'* "

The words were hardly out of his mouth when one of the engines began to sputter and cough, and the plane swerved to one side. We all tensed as the asthmatic engine rattled and wheezed a few more times, then suddenly quit.

"Mafeesh?" Preston asked uncertainly.

Mustafa, the Libyan mechanic, heard him and bobbed his head up and down in vigorous agreement. *"Mafeesh* motor!" he said, giggling hysterically. *"Mafeesh!* Ha, ha, ha! Ha, ha, ha, *mafeesh!"*

Through the open cockpit door I could see Jock desperately throwing switches to get the recalcitrant engine running again as he wrestled with the wayward airplane.

All Ike said was, "Shee-it! I knew it!"

Mustafa was smiling a reassuring smile that reassured no one. "Is nothing," he said, picking his way to the cockpit as the plane bucked and slewed across the sky. "Is perfectly nothing."

Pozzogallo had seized my arm in an iron grip as he muttered *"Sporcamiseria!"* I glanced across at Nagy and saw that he was fish-belly white, his evil little eyes wide with terror. It was small satisfaction, but it was all I could take from such a desperate moment. Pozzogallo shrugged when he saw me look in his direction. "What is it they say?" he asked me. "If God wanted me to fly, he'd have given me feathers?"

I was looking out to see how close we were to the ground when the second engine quit. There was no sputtering cough this time, no hiccupy transition from full roar to dead silence. As sudden as a slammed door, the ancient aircraft became a glider.

Jock's voice cut through the void, "Mustafa, you bloody fool! What have you done?"

Mustafa was squatting between the two pilots by then, a wrench in one hand, pulling up pieces of the flooring.

Finally Jock's voice came over the cabin loudspeaker: "This is your captain speaking. We have a little glitch here which is slowing us down, but we hope to solve it without divine intervention. So sit back, enjoy the scenery, and make sure your personal affairs are in order."

"Okay, crossfeed!" Mustafa shouted, his wrench gripping a nut on a piece of exposed aluminum tubing.

"What?" Jock demanded.

"Crossfeed!"

Jock's hand flew to a switch on the control panel as Mustafa nearly disappeared beneath the cockpit floor. For what seemed hours, we glided toward the empty desert, with only a faint current of air whistling through the cabin. Then suddenly one engine sputtered and came to life, followed almost immediately by the other. Mustafa reappeared, patted Jock's shoulder and turned grinning to face us in the main cabin as the pulsing engines recovered their smooth, reassuring roar.

Jock shouted at him, "When we get where we're going, Mustafa, I'm going to make fookin' couscous out of you!"

"Why is the pilot so angry?" Preston asked me. "It looks like that fellow just saved our lives."

"What the hell happened?" Ike asked Mustafa.

"*Mafeesh* gas," he said, giving him a thumbs down signal.

"Will we make it to Ghadames?" Pozzogallo asked plaintively.

"*Enshallah,*" Mustafa replied, grinning at Preston, "and if it pleases Allah that we don't make it, *malesh.*"

"I think my life was easier before I spoke your language," Preston said finally, and we all had a good laugh. During the rest of the flight old Prince Pozzogallo helped keep our minds off our precarious transport with stories about his youthful trips across this part of Libya by camel.

When we heard the sound of the motors change again everyone looked up in alarm, but Jock's voice came smoothly over the loudspeaker, "We are about to land in Ghadames, gentlemen, home of the Ghadames Gophers, desert ratbashing champions and four times winner of the Medfly Cup. Glaucoma capitol of the world and headquarters of Mabrouk Airlines. Please extinguish all seatbelts, put your cigarettes in an upright position and pray we make it."

The approach to the Ghadames escarpment is forbidding. Endless sandstone buttes and jagged rocky cliffs tower hundreds of feet above the winding desert tracks which lead to the oasis.

The town itself stands out like a wedding cake against this desolate landscape, its limewashed walls a shimmering white in the desert sun. Within those walls is a shuttered honeycomb of life, a maze of twisting streets and shadowy passages, hidden vaults and arches of mud brick decorated with crescent moons and the hand of Fatima in bas-relief.

Ghadames once lived off the slave trade, and Arab dealers bought and sold human flesh until the early years of the present century. Now, the town depends upon irrigated subsistance farming, the few goats, camels and sheep that graze in rocky pastures fenced off by camelthorn, and Aboubakir Jeballah's smuggling operations. Rows of lush date palms provide the only shade for leech-infested water holes dug beside the ancient wells.

Above it all, at the highest point, is the old Turkish fort, headquarters for the police assigned to this remote outpost. Rising out of the fort is a hundred-foot filigree of radio antennae, Ghadames' only communications link with the outside world.

As Jock circled I saw the dust plumes of two land rovers racing toward the airstrip, and noticed that a sleek business jet was already on the ground.

When we rolled to a stop, we descended into the bright dusty heat where a brace of Nagy's security police waited with Armand Gagnon, Jeballah's French radio operator. After the drafty comfort of the plane, Ghadames was an airless oven, a suffocating flytrap of a place, fit for no one.

Gagnon gave me a hug, greeted Preston, Ike, and the prince in his peculiar English, and saluted Captain Nagy respectfully. While Nagy climbed up into the government jeep with his officers, we piled in with Gagnon for the ride to the hotel.

As we passed the jet, Jock insisted on a closer look. "Whose is it?" he asked the Frenchman.

"Friends of Jeballah. Come to hunt gazelle."

"Germans?" Jock said.

"How do you know that?" I asked.

Jock pointed to the plane's registration. "Every country has a different letter prefix. The 'D' is Germany."

Ike Maxwell said, "Wherever it's from, it looks a damn sight safer than the one we came in."

"Sorry for the fright," Jock Pringle told him, "but that bloody fool Mustafa neglected to top our fuel tanks."

"Don't you have gauges?" Preston asked him.

"With the years they tend to stick a bit, you know?"

"How old is that antique of yours anyway?" Ike asked. "Thirty, forty years old?"

"It's closer to fifty," Jock admitted. "But it's a joy to fly when Mustafa isn't laying down on the job."

"*Enshallah*," Mustafa said grimly.

Ike clapped Preston on the shoulder and said, "That was a hell of a good Arab lesson, Al. One of them times when you had *mafeesh, malesh,* and *enshallah* all together."

XXVI

⟨⟩ Gagnon accompanied us to the town's only hotel, where we cooled off under a ceiling fan and awaited Captain Nagy. He staggered in at last, his uniform white with alkali dust and spongy with sweat after walking the mile uphill from the airstrip in hundred degree heat because the police landrover broke down. He resembled a dying blowfish with his dazed eyes and puffed-out cheeks, and I already pitied the policeman he would blame.

While Gagnon volunteered to show the old prince around the oasis, a turbaned Tibu tribesman was sent to escort us to Jeballah's house. Captain Nagy joined us without an invitation.

We followed a zigzag series of vaulted passages until we came to another Tibu crouched in the shade of a whitewashed arch which marked the entrance to Jeballah's house. These indigo black men present a fierce and sinister appearance, with their white turbans arranged to cover all of the face but the eyes which are hidden in deep shadow. At the man's waist was a curved dagger and in his hands a submachine gun.

The Tibu stopped before an ancient, massive wooden door, and pulled a bell rope. The door swung open and another turbaned guard appeared, a towering blue black man with veined hepatic eyes and a mouthful of gold teeth who smiled suddenly and threw his arms around Ike Maxwell. They clapped each other on the back like two bears. I recognized him as Jeballah's personal bodyguard, Mahmud.

Nagy knew him too, and gave him a wide berth as we entered. A year before, Mahmud had made a name for himself when a street Arab in Tripoli rudely jostled Aboubakir and failed to apologize. Mahmud's dagger flashed and opened the poor devil from belly to chin, leaving him with his guts tumbling over the sidewalk. There were twenty witnesses but no arrest.

We were in a large, low-ceilinged room whose earthen floor was layered with dozens of antique carpets. Squatting at the far end were several men, one of whom was Aboubakir Jeballah, small, black, and birdlike, his shrewd eyes missing nothing.

We embraced several times and inquired after each other's health as Jeballah led me aside before I could introduce Preston. Correct behavior in the desert is always a little long-winded, and I was careful of my manners around Aboubakir Jeballah.

"You like working for these men?" he asked.

"I'm not sure yet."

"But they pay you well?"

"That's part of the problem."

"Love, money and death are all you need care about," Jeballah said, "and when you reach my age, you can forget love."

"Don't misunderstand me. I am not complaining. I have nothing to complain about, but I do not know what will happen next."

"Do you think I know? You cannot order life to measure like a Savile Row suit. I am the most ignorant man in the world, and one of the richest. Make some sense out of that if you can."

"I am being pressed on all sides," I said. "By Malduum, by Nagy and by this man. A wrong step and I'm dead. I believe they want to rob the national bank."

"Good. I told you Libya would make your fortune."

"But . . ."

Jeballah smiled patiently as he patted my arm and we returned to the group. I introduced Preston, and then said to Jeballah in Arabic, "Can I talk to you when you have a free moment? To tell you what else I know and to ask your advice."

"Later I will make time for you. Now sit down and let him talk so I can find out what he wants from me."

Aboubakir's brother Fadlalah, a fat, expressionless Arab as white as Aboubakir was black, sucked noisily on a water pipe, studying Preston. Seated next to him were four tanned, muscular Germans in identical khaki shorts, socks and sandals, the so-called gazelle hunters, about whom Nagy was immediately curious.

Gagnon had said they were friends of Jeballah's, but the old man barely took any notice of them. Yet there was something deferential in their attitude toward Preston when they eventually rose to take their leave, and I got the impression they were standing by for orders, not gazelle.

After they left, I went into my usual pitch about Preston's plan to make the deserts green, and Aboubakir listened politely, his small bright eyes glancing from me to Preston and back again. I was speaking in Arabic for Fadlalah's benefit.

"Beida," Aboubakir said, "I congratulate you."

"Please. The credit is entirely Mister Preston's."

"And mine," Nagy piped up in Arabic. "It was my idea to put Beida with this fellow because he needs watching."

"Then you are to be congratulated, too," Aboubakir replied in Arabic. Without changing his tone, he switched to French, asking me, "Why is this cretinous little wart here?"

I replied, "With all respect, sir, he gave me no choice at all."

"He'll regret it," Aboubakir continued in his impeccable French, smiling at Nagy. "Won't you, you little grease spot?"

Nagy looked from one to the other. "What?"

Aboubakir raised both hands in mock apology, saying in Arabic, "Forgive me! I thought you understood French."

"I do," Nagy answered defensively, "but I prefer English."

"Let us talk in that language then," Aboubakir replied in English, "so we are also polite to our foreign guest."

According to legend, Qaddafi gave up persecuting Aboubakir Jeballah only after his man Mahmud crept past a score of guards late one night and entered the Libyan dictator's living quarters. He slit the throats of two servants, Qaddafi's military aide, and a Soviet adviser. From that day forward, they say, Jeballah has lived and worked undisturbed.

"Will you pipe the sea water like oil?" Fadlalah asked.

"That's the idea," Preston replied.

"Why not fly it in my brother's airplanes?"

I explained in Arabic that ten liters of sea water were required to make a liter of pure drinking water. Anything other than an aqua- duct would be prohibitively expensive.

Fadlalah said, "If the government's paying, who cares?"

Aboubakir chortled at that and patted his brother's arm in ap- proval. Nagy scowled at them, but said nothing.

Fadlalah nodded toward Preston. "Will he sell the water, etcet- era?"

"The plants will be owned by the government," I said, "and I suppose there will be some nominal charge."

"That won't do," Fadlalah said, sucking on his water pipe. "It is unfair competition to private business, etcetera."

Aboubakir explained, "My brother is the *muhdir* here and owns the water rights. People pay him for their water. Free water would hurt his business."

Preston said, "In that case, something would have to be done to compensate him. Perhaps a partnership with the government?"

"That's impossible," Nagy said.

Aboubakir's sharp monkey face showed mixed curiosity and irritation as he studied Nagy like some odd but annoying bug.

"It cannot be done," Nagy insisted.

Fadlalah glared at him and said, "Do not tell my brother what can or cannot be done. Only he decides that."

Nagy said furiously, "Don't forget you're both talking to an officer of the *mukhabarat!*" I watched Aboubakir's eyes narrow ominously, although his smile remained benign. No sane person had ever dared speak to him in that disrespectful way.

Aboubakir's thin high voice was soft, his tone sweet when he answered, "To be sure, captain, you have the people's revolution at heart, as we all do." If I had not known there was no craftier villain in the desert than this old pirate, I might have thought he was trying to ingratiate himself with Captain Nagy.

Fadlalah spoke from behind his water pipe again. "The security police, etcetera, will have to buy their water like everybody else."

Aboubakir continued, "My brother is against Communism."

"I said nothing about Communism," Nagy told them.

"You talk like a Communist," Fadlalah retorted.

Nagy grew red in the face as he sputtered, "Communism is not part of our revolution! Any fool knows that!"

"Don't call me a fool," Fadlalah said. "I am not a fool!"

"Nor is he a Communist," Aboubakir added serenely. "Communism is against the will of Allah, against the traditions of our bedouin society, and against common sense."

"Here, every man owns his own camel," Fadlalah said.

"I hope you are not a Communist," Aboubakir said to Nagy.

"You know perfectly well I am not!" he declared.

Fadlalah put on spectacles and peered closely at Nagy. "I have never seen a Communist before."

Nagy stood up angrily. "Why do you insist on calling me a Communist? I am not a Communist!" Standing, he was only a hair taller than Fadlalah seated.

"We are ignorant country people," Aboubakir said.

"I agree you are ignorant," Nagy said in English, "but that is no excuse. It is impossible to carry on a serious discussion here without being insulted!"

Fadlalah said, "If the Addida fits . . . etcetera."

Nagy was breathing heavily, but realized he had gone too far when he felt the glacial reaction to his words. He simply stood where he was, trying to get his quavering voice under control. "I must see about important police matters," he sputtered finally, and Aboubakir signaled Mahmud to show him out.

When the door had closed on Captain Nagy, Aboubakir Jeballah said, "Now to business."

Preston began immediately to outline for the Jeballah brothers what he needed and I translated everything for Fadlalah.

Mainly the conversation was about Preston's desire to bring equipment and supplies in or out of the country without government intervention. Aboubakir listened patiently, toying with his beads. Fadlalah said nothing.

"We can guarantee privacy and safe passage," Aboubakir said at last. "But our cooperation is not cheap."

"I will pay a fee of two hundred thousand dollars, plus expenses, for your services for the next forty days."

Aboubakir smiled. "That is far too little, Mr. Preston."

"Then perhaps I should be dealing with someone else."

"You can always bribe the police and take your chances."

"I cannot afford chances as you are probably aware. But how do I know I can count on you one hundred percent?"

"Mr. Jeballah keeps his word," I said.

"So I am told. But still . . ."

Aboubakir said. "If we agree on a price, you pay when you finish. That way, results are guaranteed."

"If we agree, I can live with that. But can you?"

"Why not?"

"What guaranty do you have that I'll pay?"

When I translated Preston's question, Fadlalah nearly choked on his water pipe with laughter. Then he pointed at Preston and drew his finger across his throat, still laughing.

"Quite a sense of humor," Preston said drily.

Aboubakir seemed scarcely to be paying attention. Finally Fadlalah said, "For normal wear and tear on his men and equipment, my brother will only charge a pitiful five hundred thousand dollars plus expenses, insurance, etcetera and etcetera."

"You have heard Fadlalah," Aboubakir said. "He is poor and he is ignorant. He cannot tell a Communist snake from a *mukhabarat* worm, but he is a good brother."

We all smiled at Aboubakir's joke and Preston played his part well. First he objected to the price so vigorously it seemed there was no chance of reaching an agreement. Then he looked pained, raised his hands in despair and eventually agreed to a fee of three hundred thousand dollars, with a hundred thousand dollar bonus if everything went smoothly.

Aboubakir would place his entire organization at Preston's disposal for forty days. This included trucks, land rovers and men, the rundown aircraft of Mabrouk Air, as well as a warehouse in Tripoli and a farm on the city's outskirts.

Preston asked if he wanted it in writing, but the old man only raised his hands at the thought. "What good is a paper between friends?" he said. "You need my help and I am pleased to offer it to get your business started."

"I'm glad it's settled," Preston said.

"You understand the fee is based on what you have told me. If the plan changes, like insurance, the premium changes too."

Preston nodded.

"You will inform me through Beida of any change in plan?"

"Immediately."

They shook hands and Aboubakir clapped for more tea when Mahmud entered, "Excuse me, *Haj*," he said to Aboubakir, "but there is trouble with the policeman."

"What is it?" Jeballah asked him.

"He arrested the old Italian for taking pictures at the radio station. When your other guests protested, he arrested them too."

Jeballah was amazed. "He did all this by himself?"

"No, sir. He ordered the local officers to assist. I did not want to kill them without your permission."

Jeballah excused himself and followed Mahmud out of the room with Fadlalah grumbling after him. Preston had not understood a word of the exchange, but as we hurried outside I told him what Mahmud had said.

In a small square near Jeballah's house, we found Captain Nagy and his officers holding the old prince, and the four gazelle hunters at gunpoint while three of Jeballah's men had their submachine guns leveled at the jittery policemen. But old Jeballah strode between the opposing forces, and with a wave of his arm like Moses parting the waters of the Red Sea, made them put up their weapons. The Tibu guards responded immediately and the policemen a little more slowly. But every gun except Nagy's was pointed away or returned to its holster within seconds of Aboubakir's arrival.

When Nagy realized his own men had obeyed Jeballah's orders, his face became a mask of such fury, I feared he might shoot someone just for spite. But Jeballah passed the old prince to me as neatly as if we were changing partners on a dance floor, and then led Nagy firmly aside, disarming him by saying, "If you don't mind, I need your advice."

"Are you all right?" I asked Pozzogallo.

"I could have handled Captain Nagy alone," he confided, "but after those German fellows came to help, suddenly everybody was pointing guns."

Preston joined us as we walked slowly back to the hotel where he asked me to book rooms for the night. One of Jeballah's men followed and squatted near the hotel entrance, submachine gun upright in his lap, alert as a desert animal.

Preston said, "Can I trust them?" indicating the Tibu.

"With your life," I replied sincerely, "as long as Jeballah tells them to obey you."

"And Jeballah? How far can I trust him?"

"Under ordinary circumstances I would say all the way. But now I don't know."

"Why not?"

"You didn't tell him the whole truth."

"I couldn't tell him everything quite yet. But I hope we have a firm deal anyway because I'm going to need him."

To show how firm the deal was, the Jeballah brothers put on an old-fashioned bedouin feast that night with male dancers who swooped and glided, daggers out, their faces darkly sinister behind the folds of their white turbans. An ancient nut brown man piped on a high-pitched flute while three heavily tatooed women beat intricate rhythms on homemade drums.

Neither Preston, Ike, nor Aboubakir appeared in time however, and Gagnon told me they were meeting privately and would join us later. The Frenchman entertained me and Fadlalah with tales of his past love life, while Jock Pringle got quietly smashed listening to

Prince Pozzogallo's stories. The four Germans insisted on clapping out of time to the drum beat which was maddening.

Although Nagy seemed to have forgiven old Pozzogallo, and even returned his camera minus the film, he did not seem more kindly disposed toward the rest of us. His normal ill humor returned the moment he discovered that Aboubakir and Preston were missing.

It was easy to see why Fadlalah was so fat. There were bowls of sherba, the piquant Arab soup of lamb, *fil-fil*, and mint. There was chicken *shish tawouk* and *jaj meshwi* and *fashafiche*—strips of lamb's liver cooked in cider—with lemon wedges and pots of wild honeycomb and heaping bowls of radishes. Only then did the main course of couscous arrive with succulent, steaming chunks of lamb and fresh pineapple, squash, peppers, chick peas, potatoes, carrots, onions, cucumbers and dates! To wash down the mountains of food we drank rivers of tea, Ben Gashir mineral water, Mirinda, and araq. By the time the candied pomegranates and almond-stuffed cherries were served, even I strained to make room. But not Aboubakir. His skinny little frame looked as if he never ate a square meal, yet his jaws never stopped. Prince Pozzogallo neither. Bony and dessicated as an old kite, his great hook nose accentuating the image, he put away twice what anyone except his host consumed. I have always envied the metabolism of people like that who can gorge themselves yet stay lean as scarecrows. Every bite of every meal I have ever eaten can be seen under my chin, around my middle, or across my beam.

The German "hunters" were taciturn and guarded, and refused to be drawn into all but the most superficial conversation. I asked one about gazelle hunting.

"Gazelle?" he said amazed, and the leader, a tatooed giant with close-cropped hair and steel-capped teeth, told him to shut up before he put his foot in it. Nagy, however, was less easily put off, and fired questions at them throughout the meal. He only gave up in angry frustration when Preston returned and took the tatooed German aside for half an hour.

When the party broke up at midnight I helped Jock Pringle to his room and I was heading for my own, key in hand, when I heard a voice. "Dahoud?" It was Preston beckoning me from the darkened patio. "Can you join us for a few minutes?"

It was impossible to see who was with him in the shadows until

I drew closer. Then I made out the tatooed German with the steel teeth, Ike Maxwell, and two other figures.

"You all know each other," Preston said amiably as I shook hands with Duff Elliot and Dick Diamond, the "archbishop" of Rome.

XXVII

⟨⟩ Dick Diamond blessed me with an exaggerated sign of the cross and said, "Greetings from the Pope, Beida."

"You're looking well, Dahoud," Duff Elliot told me.

"Sorry for springing this on you so suddenly," Preston said, "but we felt the time had come to know who your friends were."

I was so stunned to see them there, I no longer recall what I said in reply. Whatever it was, it must have been either awfully stupid or unintentionally funny because they all laughed except the German. I dropped into one of the creaking wicker chairs as Elliot began to pace briskly with hands clasped behind him. When I first saw him in Malta, I thought he looked rather professorial, but now with his hair clipped short, and dressed in military-style khakis he gave the impression of a combat commander briefing his men rather than a professor lecturing a class.

The biggest surprise of all was Dick Diamond, slouched in a chair opposite me, wearing a baggy navy windbreaker, flight suit and a blue baseball cap with "U.S.S. *Saratoga*" stitched in gold across the front. The significance of the cap was not lost on me. The American navy planes that had bombed Tripoli in 1986 had flown from the flight deck of the carrier *Saratoga.*

"How you been keeping, Beida?" he asked me.

"Getting by," I said. "Heard any good confessions lately?"

"None as good as yours," he replied with a smile. Then to Preston, "Did Beida ever tell you how we met?"

"I don't believe he did."

"He was looking for extreme unction, and found me."

Duff Elliot said, "Very amusing, Dick, but we've got damn little time for jokes. Horst has to be airborne in . . . how soon?"

"Two hours forty-two minutes," the German said after looking at his watch. "Or we're stuck here another day."

"Radar hole," Preston explained.

Elliot got his pipe going and blew impatient puffs of smoke as he said, "Now, can we get down to business?"

"It's your show, Duff," Preston said.

"When Alan mentioned you had misgivings," Elliot said to me, "I thought it was time to talk. If anything had gone wrong earlier, the less you knew, the better, but now in order to get the job done, you must know what we're up to. Is that clear?"

"I'm not sure."

"Then take it on faith, Beida," Dick Diamond said.

"Everyone's been telling me that lately."

He roused himself and leaned forward aggressively. "The other reason you haven't been told any more than necessary is that we're not all that sure of your loyalties."

"Dick," Preston said, "We know where Dahoud stands."

"Do we?" Diamond said, fixing me with hard eyes.

The others seemed a little embarrassed as Dick Diamond handed me a newspaper clipping. I had to move under the light to read it. At the top was scrawled "New York Times November 30". The headline said, "Terrorist Leader Identified" and the article described me, Dahoud el Beida, as Khalil Malduum's righthand man and the author of the Egyptair hijacking. It also speculated on the where-abouts of the thirty American hostages ("reliable reports indicate they are being held somewhere in Libya"), my involvement in the Lisbon bombing, and a power struggle among Palestinian leaders.

The picture of me that had appeared all over the world accompa-nied the article, the one where I'm standing in the door of the hijacked plane, holding the child.

"You know none of this about me is true," I said.

"Do we, Beida?" Dick Diamond said, "Or do we take it on faith like we expect you to do?"

"What I don't know," I said to him, "is where you stand. You gave me two numbers to call if I needed your help. Then you disappeared when I tried to reach you from Catania."

"Those telephones had been compromised. I couldn't take the chance of you giving yourself away over the line."

"So you left me out in the cold when I was in trouble."

"My guys in Naples watched you until you got on the boat. They scared off a punk who turned up in the port looking for you."

"Very efficient after he went for me with a knife."

"A scarface Arab, they said. Young and fast."

"Did they make him?"

"They think from APPL but he was no friend of yours."

"That I gathered when he tried to kill me."

"As long as Alan Preston was your babysitter, Beida, you were never in any real danger."

"Someone forgot to tell scarface that," I replied. "And none of you ever told me anything."

"Duff just got through telling you that you were given enough information to function, but not enough to do us any real damage if they nailed you."

"That way," Preston said, "if the wrong people asked the right questions, you wouldn't be left twisting in the breeze."

"Rather an inappropriate metaphor," Elliot said.

"You better tell me everything now," I said, "so I don't blurt out the wrong thing to those same wrong people later."

Dick Diamond's voice was heavy with menace when he said, "For your sake, Beida, that better not happen."

Duff Elliot intervened again. "If you two are finished, I've got a lot to cover tonight. Alan can explain the rest later."

Diamond told me, "Beida, this is for your ears only."

Elliot said impatiently, "Dahoud, we won't ask you to do anything you haven't done before, and you'll make top money."

"I've been paying him two thousand a week," Preston said.

Duff Elliot said, "There's no reason why he shouldn't have the same pay and terms as Maxwell and the others."

"That gets pricey," Dick Diamond said.

"Funding is not a problem on this op, Dick. Expertise is, however, and Dahoud has that." Elliot turned to me. "The contract is for three hundred thousand. Fifty up front and the rest upon successful completion. If the mission fails you still collect, and if you're killed your pay goes to whoever you designate."

"That's a comfort."

"If you have a bank account abroad, Dahoud, I'll deposit the fifty there immediately. The money may seem a lot but you'll earn it."

"That's what I'm afraid of."

Elliot smiled.

"Besides staying alive, what do I have to do to collect?"

"Keep Malduum's confidence, maintain good relations with your Libyan government contacts, and follow Preston's orders."

"It's the last part that worries me," I told him.

"Why?" Elliot said.

"Captain Nagy of the *mukhabarat*, or security police, believes the CIA sent Alan here to poison the water system."

"Jesus Christ!" Diamond said, laughing. "I knew they were stupid, but that's the most ridiculous thing I ever heard."

"I've spoken to Alan about this, but he doesn't take the captain seriously either."

"Who on earth could?" Preston said.

"Why do you think Nagy followed you here to Ghadames?"

"Point taken," Duff Elliot told him, sucking on his pipe. "Dahoud's already earning his money. This policeman may be dumb or paranoid or silly, but that doesn't make him less of a threat. He could gum up the works, and we can't afford that."

The German had been listening to every word and said, "I can take him out tonight, Duff, if he is a problem."

"No good," Duff Elliot said. "It would draw too much attention to Mr. Jeballah. No, we'll just have to put up with him awhile longer. But that is one of the reasons Dahoud is with us."

"I beg your pardon?" I said.

"To reassure Captain What's-his-name."

"When will I be told what's going on?"

"Don't worry. I'll get to that. But first, let's clear the air. Anything else you want to know?"

"Who told you I was carrying a suitcase full of explosives on that flight to Rome when I didn't even know it myself?"

"An informant, obviously," Dick Diamond said.

"Then you have someone inside Malduum's group?"

"Not exactly," Preston said.

"What then?"

Diamond looked inquiringly at Duff Elliot who nodded.

"Khalid Belqair was a Syrian shooter with Malduum's organization. He and Malduum's brother Ahmed were the ones who put the bomb on the jet that burned in Lisbon. The Italians had a tap on his phone. That's how we knew your flight number and the name on your fake diplomatic passport."

"What happened to him?"

"We missed him when we got Ahmed and rolled up the Rome crowd," Diamond said. "Smart son of a bitch, but not smart enough."

"He could have known about me working with you."

"He probably knew."

"If he talks, Malduum will know too."

"He didn't talk," Preston said.

"How do you know?"

Duff Elliot answered, "Malduum's never been bashful about showing his feelings. If Belqair had voiced any suspicions to him, Dahoud, he would have shot you on the spot. But he didn't, so we know he is ignorant of your involvement."

"But you did not know that when I first got back."

"No."

"So when I arrived, Malduum might have killed me."

"We considered that possibility, yes."

I looked from him to Preston. "Everybody knew but me?"

"What's the beef?" Dick Diamond said. "Nothing happened."

"No thanks to you people," I told him bitterly.

"We all run risks in this business," Duff Elliot said.

"But you weren't running that particular risk. I was! While you all just waited around to see if I'd survive it."

"You would have been no use otherwise," Preston said.

"Not dead I wouldn't."

"Actually," Elliot said, "since Belqair is no longer a problem, I think we can move on."

I said to Preston, "Belqair was the man on the boat, wasn't he?"

"He was."

"You thought he fingered me so Hueblen killed him."

"Hueblen didn't kill him," Preston said.

"Then who did?" I managed to ask. "You?"

It was hard to believe that this mild-mannered Canadian could strangle a man with his bare hands, coolly dispose of the body, and then join me for dinner! But his nod told me he had indeed.

"Your answers in the bar didn't satisfy Belqair," Preston said smoothly. "When Hueblen caught him tossing your cabin, I didn't know whether he was on to you or not, but too much was at stake to take the chance."

Elliot studied me over his pipe. "Does that bother you?"

"Of course it bothers him!" Diamond said. "He doesn't like murderers, do you Beida?"

"Belqair was a mass murderer," Elliot said. "More than a hundred passengers burned to death on that Lisbon jet."

"And who are you?" I asked angrily, "the World Court?"

"In a manner of speaking," Preston said, "yes."

Dick Diamond got up then, a contemptuous smile on his lips, fists clenched against his thighs. When he spoke to me, the voice was the one I remembered from the Rome airport. "You're some piece of work parading your phony fucking scruples around us. You're a small-time, two-bit, petty swindler and the Italians would have locked you up and thrown the key away if I hadn't spoken up for you. You know how bad they wanted your ass?"

"Settle down," Elliot said, "there's no call for insults."

But I had irritated Diamond. "I wasn't insulting him, Duff," he said, pointing a finger at me, "just describing him. You offered him a chance to fight on the side of the angels and get rich at the same time, and he comes back with cheap shit about running a little risk." He turned back to me. "Risk is what it's all about, Daisy Mae! Calculated fucking risks are what we do for a living!"

Duff Elliot said, "I've heard enough commentary on the obvious for one night," and Preston smiled.

I said, "You tell me nothing and then expect me to understand everything. But I'll manage. That's milk under the bridge, as they say. I'm prepared to go along, but you've got to take me into your confidence."

"Go along!" Diamond exclaimed indignantly.

"Shut up, Dick," Preston told him.

Oddly enough, of the three men, Preston, Elliot and Diamond, I had a hunch Diamond would be the most dependable in the clutch. Elliot's sense of destiny and high purpose would allow him to sacrifice anyone, including me, but Diamond was a realist.

"I was impressed with your idea of stealing the Bank of Libya's foreign deposits by computer . . ." Eliot was saying.

"That was not meant seriously . . ." I protested.

"A pity, because we like it. Now, from what Alan has told me, you know about the Defense Resources Institute, so I needn't go into any detail. Except to say that we occasionally provide services other than study and analysis."

"Like bank holdups?"

He gazed at me from behind a scrim of smoke, puzzled. Then he smiled. "Unfortunately we have a more important priority and won't have time to bankrupt Qaddafi. But whatever you want to take from him in your spare time is up to you."

"What is your other priority?"

Without answering Duff Elliot beckoned me to follow as he led the way to a room at the far end of the hotel where two of the Germans and one of Jeballah's men guarded the door. A powerful overhead lamp illuminated a large map of Libya spread over a pair of tables shoved together in the center of the room. We gathered around it like medical students at a dissection, while I waited to hear what Elliot had to say. He wasted no time.

"The rest of you have heard it all before but bear with me while I explain Dahoud's part." Elliot's eyes locked on mine. "The purpose of this mission is to release the thirty American hostages held in this country, and get them safely out of Libya."

"That's all?"

"I assume you're being facetious."

"I am. It's a pipe dream."

"People far more experienced than you," Elliot declared, "have decided it is the only way to go."

"Including the President," Dick Diamond emphasized.

"The last time one of your presidents made a decision like that," I told them, "was to get American hostages out of Iran. Ask Ike Maxwell about that. He was there. What a cock-up that was!"

"Dick was there, too," Ike Maxwell said.

Elliot said, "What happened on Desert One wasn't Dick Diamond's fault or anybody's at the operating level. It was a failure of organization and command at the top. That is the main reason we were contracted to go after these people now, over Pentagon objections. Although I would not undertake the mission if I was not certain of success, Washington has the option of total deniability if we fail."

"Convenient," I said.

"Your sarcasm is out of order here, Dahoud," Elliot said in his quarterdeck voice.

"Sorry. But I am interested to know why you think this will succeed where the Iran rescue attempt failed?"

"It is smaller, better contained, and not subject to inter-service bickering over priorities. "We also intend to eliminate Khalil Malduum and his intimate circle."

When I said nothing, Elliot added drily, "Good. I'm glad you're convinced we can pull it off."

XXVIII

<> There was a long silence when he had finished, and although I was facing away for a moment, I had the uncomfortable feeling they were all looking at me. They were, and Preston was the first to speak: "I doubt Dahoud much favors our chances of success."

"How many men will you have?"

"Enough," Elliot replied.

"How many is that? In Panama you needed thirty thousand elite combat troops. And you sent over a hundred thousand to fix Mr. Saddam Hussein."

"What's your point?" Diamond said.

"Panama was a joke country, a poor little banana republic with a joke army. Qaddafi's Libya is not a joke. It is a vast armed camp, like Iraq."

"This is not a military operation," Elliot said. "Think of it more as a break-in."

"As I remember from Watergate, you Americans aren't too clever at those either."

"We will be in and out almost before they know it."

"Almost?" I said.

"In before they know it," Elliot corrected himself.

"And out before they can react," Preston finished.

"Where do I enter the picture?"

"You'll be needed at every step."

"Starting?"

"To confirm where the hostages are," Elliot said.

"You know where they are, more or less."

"More or less isn't good enough," Diamond told me. "We've got to know exactly who is where and in what kind of shape. Some are older and may have special health problems."

"Are you planning to take them out in helicopters?"

"No."

"In what then?"

"We'll take the men off in launches. The women in Jeballah's trucks to where the planes will pick them up."

I nodded. Not in agreement. More in disbelief at their preposterous plan. They were all madder than I thought. Even Elliot, who was the brightest, was taken in by his own wishful thinking. We might as well have been speaking different but mutually unintelligible languages.

"Does Jeballah know what he's getting into?" I asked.

Preston and Elliot exchanged glances before Elliot said, "He'll have to be told the rest in time, of course, but he's being well paid not to ask too many questions up front."

"He may balk," I said. "If you want to be certain of his cooperation, I suggest you spell everything out now."

"We can't trust him that far," Elliot said.

"If you can't trust him that far you can't trust him at all," I reminded them. "If he thinks you haven't played straight, he could leave you stranded when you least expect it."

"Dahoud's right," Preston said.

"But if we lay everything out for him," Dick Diamond argued, "he might just change his mind and bug out now."

"What do you think?" Elliot asked me. "You know him."

"I can't speak for him," I said, "but Aboubakir likes the odds heavily weighted in his favor. And from what I've gathered so far, that isn't the case. He's still here after you clear out."

"But Qaddafi wouldn't touch him. Even you said that."

"He hasn't until now, Alan. But Qaddafi might have to move against him or risk trouble with his own security police and armed forces. And Jeballah's Tibu tribesmen couldn't stand up to tanks and rockets."

"Go without him," Diamond said, but Elliot shook his head.

Preston said, "Perhaps more money would make the difference," and Elliot looked inquiringly at me.

"Maybe," I said. "There's nothing the old man likes better. But I've never seen it obscure his common sense."

Elliot said, "I'm obliged to Dahoud for raising these questions." To me he added, "When you've heard it outlined, Dahoud, you'll agree our plan is sound."

Sound? It was the most unsound, insane, unlikely, preposterous, cockamamie scheme grown men could have cobbled up. Part Sheik of Araby and part Star Wars. On a scale of ten, it stood zero chance of succeeding, in spite of what Elliot's computers told him. When I assumed Preston was just interested in ripping off the Bank of Libya I thought that was ridiculous. But what Elliot described that night in Ghadames made a bank holdup sound smart.

About fifty men would take part, he explained, plus Jeballah's people. All of the imported elements were trained professionals recruited among former members of special commando groups and counterterrorist units. Several were veterans of the American army's Delta Force, and a few came from the navy SEALS which Elliot once commanded. Others had served with Preston in the British SAS, and some from the German Border Guard *Grenzschutzgruppe* 9, to which Hueblen and the Germans I met at Ghadames had belonged. But Elliot's biggest surprise were two Russians, former members of the Soviet Union's special combat Spetsnaz force. They were Afghanistan veterans and spoke Arabic.

The White House had decided against a military assault because no administration could afford a repeat of the Iran disaster when helicopters crashed, men died, and the mission had aborted without a single hostage rescued.

Under Elliot's plan, his team of professionals could be applauded if they succeeded and denied if they failed. There were four teams, in fact. One to keep the Libyans off guard with feints and disturbances, one each to go after hostages in Garian and Tripoli, and a command team directing the show from above.

The group also included air crews flying two MC-130 Combat Talon military transports with Surface To Air Recovery (STAR) systems capable of snatching six people at a time from the ground without landing. Elliot explained that one of these remarkable aircraft would in fact land to load the hostages, but would only employ the STAR system to take out team members if necessary.

The other C-130 Hercules carried an ALQ-8 Electronic Countermeasures pod to provide diversion on the night of the operation. This system would jam Libyan radar, Elliot explained, and send out a wide range of deceptive signals to convince the listener that all sorts of unknown or hostile aircraft were around.

This same Hercules would be loaded for bear, as they say. In case of groundfire or serious counterattack, it would carry batteries of 20mm., 40mm. and 105mm. cannon which can simultaneously track twenty ground targets using onboard computers.

The Talon's inertial navigation system included a terrain-following, precision ground-mapping radar made by Elliot's company which enabled the plane to fly blind in all weather as low as fifty feet. It also had a sophisticated, highly sensitive forward-looking infrared system which could pick up a pocket flashlight from a distance of five miles, and home in on it. As Duff Elliot described these extraordinary toys, his face flushed with pride and confidence. He was a firm believer in technology's triumph over everything, especially a bunch of insignificant desert Arabs who would scamper like hares the moment they faced serious opposition. He leaned over the map and indicated Garian, fifty miles inland from Tripoli, and then Mizda, a town on the Whadi Sofeggin, fifty miles further into the Sahara.

"The hostages rescued from the Garian caves will be taken by truck to the Whadi Sofeggin near Mizda. There, two Wizard rescue aircraft will be waiting. These are state-of-the-art STOL machines designed for night insertion and recovery of Special Forces. They can land and take off with fifteen passengers in less than five hundred feet over rocky, unprepared or ploughed terrain. They carry a Gatling defensive system and the same contour mapping capability as the Talon, but fly at a speed of 350 knots."

"Will they take out the fourteen women hostages?" I said.

"And the men who go in after them," Elliot replied.

Preston said, "All in all we'll be evacuating about eighty people. Thirty from Mizda and about fifty from the Tripoli area."

"So much for that," Elliot said. "Some of the men will fly in on the STOL aircraft. Others are already here, as you know. Some will parachute in and some others will arrive by sea."

"At night?"

"Naturally."

"Even at night, the parachutists won't stand a chance," I said. "And the frogmen won't find the beaches empty either."

Dick Diamond chuckled and Elliot said, "Tell him."

Diamond said, "We'll freefall from ten miles up before deploying what we call Controlled Aerial Delivery Systems, or CADS, which are computer linked parachutes programmed to home in on a pocket-size UHF beacon set wherever we want it. In this case, a field near the Garian caves."

"What about radar picking up the planes you bail out of?"

"We won't be dropping from planes," Diamond said.

"All right. Helicopters then. Same thing."

"Helium balloons," Dick Diamond said, "which don't paint on radar except like little cloud formations."

"Are you serious?"

"Never more so," Elliot replied.

"And the swimmers?"

"The men who come by sea," Elliot said, "will be ferried to within a short distance of the coast by Seafox Attack Craft which are small, highspeed, long-range vessels designed to bypass coastal radar and other defenses. Our guys will then disembark in SDV's, Swimmer Delivery Vehicles, four-man submersibles capable of depositing them undetected anywhere on the Libyan coast."

"The Libyan beaches are mined," I reminded him.

"Not around Sabratha," Preston said, "and not the rocky promontory bordering the west side of Tripoli harbor."

He was right. Only the immediate beach approaches to Tripoli were mined except for one rocky ridge that ran out into the sea like an accusing finger.

"I'm impressed." I said quite honestly, although I still believed that in spite of all their wonderful gadgets, they were biting off more than they could swallow, as they say.

"Besides weapons, communications gear and other essentials," Elliot said, "the men in the SDV's will bring in four Remote Controlled Undersea Vehicles."

"What do they do?"

"They're no larger than a child's toy," he said, warming to his subject, "about three feet long, like miniature submarines. They have a five-mile control range which is ample for Tripoli harbor, and they can move undetected or paint themselves on sonar as everything from a school of fish to a nuclear sub. They can attach mines, gather intelligence, misguide sensing devices, and in general wreak confusion where we send them."

"Remarkable."

"Indeed," Elliot agreed. "They also give off a stunning five-thousand volt jolt if anyone tries to interfere with them."

"Will these swimmers be the ones who free the Tripoli prisoners from the old Karamanli Castle Fortress?"

"With your help," Elliot said.

"I presume Alan has told you the same building houses the headquarters of the Libyan *mukhabarat,* or security police?"

"I'm aware of that."

"Your frogmen must gain entrance at night, overcome the guards, locate the prisoners and get everyone out safely."

"Correct."

"I just wanted to be sure there was no misunderstanding."

Preston laughed. "Dahoud finds that part hard to believe."

"No," I replied. "Not hard to believe. Impossible, a suicide mission. Five hundred policemen work in that building. They're all handpicked security specialists, armed and dangerous."

"Like that stunted clown who came with us?" Preston said.

"I know you don't take him seriously but you should. The Libyan security police are more paranoid and lethal than ordinary citizens. Believe it or not, Alan, Captain Nagy is bad news!"

"I know, I know," Preston said. "You tell me every day."

"But you still don't believe me."

"It doesn't matter," he said patiently. "The night shift numbers less than a hundred police."

"Still . . ."

"And they don't guard the hostages. Malduum's boys and girls do that in shifts, and we'll take them out easily."

"Alan, excuse me, but just going in the front door, you'll run into half of Nagy's men all armed to the teeth."

"No problem."

My patience with his stubborness was nearly at an end. "Of

course not," I said. "You'll be using flash-bang grenades, machine guns, and nerve gas or something."

"Dahoud, we won't be going in the front door."

"Over the rooftops then. You'll still be attacking one of the most heavily guarded buildings in the city. Why do you think Qaddafi allowed Malduum to put the hostages there?"

"Wrong," Preston said.

"Alan, you walk by there every day. The walls are thirty feet thick. The dungeons and tunnels below are hewn out of solid rock and could withstand a nuclear attack."

"I'm not finished," Elliot said, "and time is running out. Please pay attention."

For another half hour he talked, giving me more technical information than I could possibly assimilate, telling me how lucky we all were to be part of the finest rescue team ever assembled. Delusion piled on delusion until he had constructed such a dazzling, elaborate house of half-truths, dreams, and lies, that the others believed him as much as he believed himself.

When he finished he said proudly, "You see, Dahoud? After listening to what I've had to say have you revised your opinion?"

"I certainly have," I said, without correcting the impression he had of me. I now considered all of them certifiably mad.

Preston, who knew me better and suspected my true feelings, said, "but you're not entirely convinced yet, are you?"

"Getting inside the fortress bothers me," I said. "And hanging around Tripoli for an extra day after the hit."

"I'll explain that."

"So you said."

"Any other questions before we wrap?" Elliot asked me.

"One."

"Shoot."

"You said the Strategic Defense Resources Institute was contracted secretly for this mission."

"Correct."

"Because it had to be deniable if it failed."

"Mainly because the President felt that with our combined experience we could do it better than the Pentagon."

"But all this hardware, the Hercules Talons and the Wizards and the Seafoxes come from the American military."

"Some do. Some are from our own experimental programs. Others from friendly forces and some we buy on the open market."

"Where do you get the money?

"Special funds, public and private."

"Like the Iran-Contra arrangement?" I said.

"That was an entirely different situation," Elliot snapped. "Amateurishly conceived and ineptly managed."

"But the end result is the same. If we fail, the White House doesn't know us."

"No president in his right mind wants a can tied to his tail on an American hostage issue," Preston said.

"But if we succeed he takes the bows."

"That's just smart politics," Dick Diamond said.

"What's your question?" Elliot asked me irritably.

"Suppose it's a partial success or a partial failure?"

"It won't be if everyone does his job. Anything else?"

I nodded. "What happens to me?"

"We told you," Dick Diamond answered. "When it's all over you wind up rich and famous."

"Either way?"

And they all laughed.

XXIX

"Like any true artist, a thief needs a sense of proportion," Jeballah said. It was very late as we sat cross-legged before the small charcoal fire in his house, and he was in a philosophical mood. "Here, try one of these, Beida."

He selected a juicy morsel of broiled kid. How he could remain as wizened and drawn as he was, looking like a little brown nut, yet eat the amount of food he ate, I will never understand. Like old Pozzogallo. The disconcerting metabolism of the aged, I suppose.

Eat whatever they want and as much as they want and never gain an ounce. "After me," Jeballah said, "my cook is the world's greatest thief. He knows which bills to pad and how much."

"Why do you keep him?"

"Taste this and answer your question. His sense of proportion. He never takes more than I can afford or less than he needs. Clever fellow, Beida, very clever. Like you."

"You flatter me, *Haj*. I've been lucky."

"So far, yes. Now, what do these Americans want that they send you to ask instead of coming themselves?"

"To begin with, it's not a bank holdup."

"I know."

"Do you know what they're really after?"

"The American prisoners."

"And will you help them?"

"Do you think they can do it?"

"They can probably liberate the women in Garian. There is no regular garrison and by surprising the guards and overpowering them, they could get away with it."

"But?"

"They'll never get the men out of the Karamanli Fortress no matter how many commandos they use or what weapons they bring."

"Surely they would not attempt anything so foolish if they were not certain of success."

"Sir, they *are* certain of success. They have many wonderful weapons and planes and ships and electronic gadgets. But they underestimate the risk and danger of going up against the police guards in the fortress and Qaddafi's armed forces outside."

"You heard the money figure we agreed on."

"Yes." I also said that I had spoken with Preston and the others afterwards, and suggested they tell him everything.

"And they asked you to come and do it."

"Yes, sir."

"Did you say I would not cooperate?"

"I said you would not feel the same obligation if they did not inform you. They're concerned about security, but they agreed."

"So I am supposed to send you back to them with a new price list. Is that what they expect?"

"I also told them you might decide to decline their offer, once you knew the full extent of their intentions."

"There are only two questions to resolve, Beida. Can they afford me and can I afford them?"

I smiled.

"You have a great head for numbers. What do you think they are prepared to spend?"

"They said funds were not a problem."

"Good. Then they can afford me. But I can't compromise my men with that scum in Tripoli." "That scum in Tripoli" included everyone connected with the ruling clique around Qaddafi, and most especially Qaddafi himself.

"You know best, *Haj*." I said.

He was pensive for awhile, selecting and rejecting small bits of meat from the fire, cracking an occasional pistacchio nut and sipping from a small bowl of the fig syrup and araq mixture he favored before bedtime. "Tell them I understand everything," he said after many minutes, "but I must have two things. Here." Again he held up a choice bit of meat.

I chewed it, nodding my pleasure.

"First I thought of asking one hundred thousand dollars for each prisoner." He squinted at me to see how the number went down, but my face remained expressionless. "Then I thought, no, I am a foolish old man. They would never pay so much. As I said, a thief must have a sense of proportion." He cracked a pistacchio and studied it a moment before popping it into his mouth. "So I thought of other figures and decided I would accept fifty thousand dollars for each prisoner I help them release. Will they pay that?"

The truth was I had no idea, but I doubted it.

"It's up to them," he said indifferently.

"But that's a million and a half dollars!"

"I told you you had a head for numbers."

"They would probably call it blackmail."

"They can call it what they want. But never mind. The other thing I want from them is just as important."

"What is that?"

His crafty old eyes bored into me as he said, "Their solemn word that if they fail, they give me credit for catching them. And if they succeed, they make it clear to the press that my trucks were stolen and my men forced to help at gunpoint."

"Even if they agree to such a proposition," I said, "you have no way of holding them to it."

He shrugged. "If they agree," he said, "it is enough. I will worry about holding them to it when the time comes."

Upon my return to the hotel I heard a murmur of voices from the patio. In the moonlight I could make out Preston, Dick Diamond and Elliot with the tattooed German.

"Oh, there you are, Dahoud!" Elliot said when he saw me. He came forward quickly and drew me aside from the others. "Well?"

With no frills, I outlined what Jeballah had said while Elliot looked around him in exasperation, cursed the world in general and the Arab race in particular. "You don't bargain with people's lives!" he said angrily.

"Excuse me," I told him, "but it seems to me that under the circumstances that's all you can do."

The German gestured from the patio. "Duff! Five minutes!"

Then, to my astonishment, Elliot accepted both Jeballah's price and his conditions without a grimace. He further agreed to deposit four hundred thousand dollars in the old man's European bank, which would be discounted from the million and a half if everything went well, or forfeit if it didn't.

"There's something else," I said.

"Christ, not more money?"

"It's got nothing to do with Jeballah."

"What is it?"

I hesitated. "I'm dead if Malduum traces this to me."

"I'll respect your confidence. What is it?"

"He intends to carry out a series of bombings soon in London, Germany and the States."

"Do you know where?"

"Westminster Abbey, the Munich Hofbrauhaus and the Houston Astrodome. One bomb is already in Germany and the makings of another are waiting in a Kensington bed-sitter. Najeeb Hassan is going to London to set it off."

"When is he leaving?"

"Any day."

"Under what name?"

I told him.

As he climbed into the land rover with Diamond and the Germans, he said, "I know what it cost you to tell me, but you did the right thing. I appreciate that, Dahoud. And thanks."

A few minutes later I heard the jet roar off into the night and imagined Malduum's rage and frustration when they caught Hassan. It was shortly before dawn when I collapsed on my bed, but I had trouble closing my eyes. I tossed for an hour as the night faded to daylight, a thousand questions still coursing through my mind. By the time the sun was entirely up, so was I.

I no longer knew whether I was ahead of the game or behind, but I was more determined than ever to distance myself from Elliot's ambitious scheme to free the hostages. In one eventful evening I had discovered that my misgivings about a bank robbery were unwarranted, but I was no closer than before to a way out.

Gagnon arrived in the lobby at seven to take us to the airstrip. Nagy, Jock Pringle, Preston and the crew had gone on ahead, so only Pozzogallo and I were left. Once I had downed a light breakfast and filled a thermos with hot tea, I waited for the old man by the land rover. Gagnon said, "Beida, something has come to my attention which worries me."

"What is that, my friend."

"This deal with my boss. Don't get me wrong. I like to see everybody happy. But if that troll of a cop finds out what's going on, you could be in serious trouble."

"I am already in serious trouble."

"Jeballah will smell like a rose no matter what happens. But make sure you're in the same bouquet with him when it's over."

"Just call me the shrinking violet."

Gagnon laughed. "Take care, *mon vieux.*"

When we arrived at the airstrip, a number of Jeballah's Tibu guards were loading boxes aboard the old DC-3 from trucks backed up against the cargo door. Captain Nagy was shouting at Jock Pringle, and I thought, God help us, another attack of hysteria.

Jock said to Preston, "Mr. Jeballah asked me to tell you we'd be taking some freight back, if you have no objection."

"None," Preston answered, "as long as there's room."

Nagy pushed his way between the two men, saying, "It's not a question of room, it is a question of law!" Jock Pringle ignored him as the tall, blue black Tibu men continued to heft the boxes on board the plane. "He is smuggling whiskey to Tripoli," Nagy told us.

"No one's smuggling anything, mate," Jock said. "This is an internal domestic flight and we are just delivering Mr. Jeballah's private property. If you don't approve of my manifest, take it up with him."

But the little policeman was not to be put off so easily. "I demand you remove that cargo!" he cried. "I order it removed!" The whole time he was tugging furiously on Jock Pringle's trouser leg, and pointing at the men passing up the boxes.

"Now see here . . .!" Pringle's patience was running out.

Nagy shouted, "Enough! Take those boxes away!"

The tribesman in the doorway looked expectantly toward Jock. "Carry on," he said before turning to Captain Nagy. "I am the commander of this aircraft, sir, and Mr. Jeballah is the owner. I follow his orders only."

"But I am police!" Nagy raged. "Police ordering you!"

"Sorry, but you can't do that, old boy," Jock told him. "Not unless my boss, Mr. Aboubakir Jeballah, says you can."

I thought Nagy would have a stroke, but Jock finally brushed him away like a very small mosquito and mounted the steps to check the stowage of the boxes. I wondered if he realized Nagy's power back in Tripoli. He probably did. But he was also aware of Aboubakir Jeballah's power everywhere, and placed his faith in that. For his sake I hoped he was right.

Nagy searched angrily until his eyes rested on poor Gagnon. "You!" he cried, and climbed into Gagnon's land rover. "Take me to the radio!" The luckless Frenchman had no choice and they drove off in a cloud of dust.

"Is Nagy going to call Tripoli?" Pozzogallo asked me.

"Gagnon works for Jeballah so he probably won't succeed."

In a few minutes Mustafa had all the boxes securely strapped in place, and we waited in the shade of one wing for Nagy to return. I half expected him to reappear with a police patrol to prevent our departure, or failing that, have everyone taken away in chains.

"If he gets through," I said, "there'll be a reception."

"That we don't need," Preston replied gloomily.

As Mustafa beckoned us all aboard, Nagy returned triumphant, took a solitary seat in the rear of the plane and spoke to no one. His lips were pursed in a smug smile.

We had been in the air about twenty minutes when the cabin loudspeaker screeched on and Jock said, "This is your captain speaking. Welcome aboard Mabrouk Air's deluxe scenic flight to Tripoli, the pearl of the Barbary Coast, where our estimated arrival time will be ten thirty-five. On behalf of Mr. Jeballah and the cast . . . I mean crew, I would like to thank you for flying Mabrouk Air, and assure you there will be absolutely no difficulty whatever upon our arrival. So sit back, enjoy your flight, and let the good times roll."

Pozzogallo and I enjoyed Pringle's little speeches, but by the time Jock finished this one, Nagy was in a fury again. Preston tried to tell him it was only Pringle's idea of a joke, but Nagy's sense of humor was nil. He rose from his seat and waddled up the aisle toward the cockpit.

When he reached the door, he found it locked, which only infuriated him more. Although he pounded on it futilely for five minutes, shouting, "I know you're in there!" no answer came from the cockpit. He finally returned to his seat and sat in a tense fury.

Pozzogallo nudged me and said, "I make the score Pringle two, Nagy zero, but I fear the game's not over."

"That's what worries me," I replied.

Soon Preston was sound asleep, and even Nagy dozed off as the plane droned on through the Libyan morning. Our cabin was cold and drafty and Prince Pozzogallo produced a small silver flask from a side pocket. "Want some?" he offered. "Gets the heart started."

"No, thanks." He downed the stuff at a gulp and immediately began wheezing and choking so fiercely I thought he was having a seizure. "Here, have some tea!"

"It's all right" he gasped. "The Milk . . . of the Four Peppers . . . always . . . has . . . that effect before it . . . takes hold. Sure you won't have some?"

I shook my head, convinced he was as mad as the others. He sipped some tea from my thermos and was soon breathing normally again, a happy smile of gratitude lighting his face. Neither of us was sleepy, although God knows, I should have been. Finally the prince said, "Alan tells me you're worried."

"Oh?" What did this aging archaeologist know about what was going on. If Preston's security was any good at all, nothing. But the prince dashed my brilliant conclusion with his next words.

"Specifically he says you're skeptical about his access to the hostages in the Karamanli Fort."

I nearly choked on that. "I beg your pardon?"

We were speaking Italian but I glanced nervously at Nagy's sleeping figure anyway. There was no way he could hear our conversation above the engine sound, but still . . .

"Preston asked me to tell you something about the history of the building he leased in Tripoli," the old man said.

"The building? Yes, of course. I'm sure it's interesting," I said, wondering what the rundown of Desal offices had to do with Preston storming the Karamanli Fortress.

But the prince was content to take his time and launch into another romantic tale of his misspent youth in Libya. "The building was once the town house of Abdul Karamanli," he said, "the last pretender to the Karamanli Sultanate. At one time he and I were hunting companions . . . the closest of friends."

His fondest memories of Libya, he told me, were when he served as an officer in the Italian army during the thirties.

"That was when you met Abdul Karamanli?"

"Excellent chap," he mused. "Libya was great fun then. We had fine horses. Irish hunters. Arabs. Tripoli barbs."

"Were you in the cavalry?"

"Nothing so ordinary," the prince replied. "Il Duce appointed Marshal Balbo governor of Libya. My boss, Colonel Miani, became chief of staff. And I was his adjutant."

"You did very well for one so young."

"Not bad, not bad," he admitted. "But the truth is, family connections in Sicily had more to do with my success than talent."

"Tell me about Karamanli."

"Abdul was looking for a chance to regain his fortune under Italian rule. The Karamanlis had seen hard times during the hundred years since the American navy cut off their income. They were pirates, you see, like this chap Qaddafi. The Americans will have to fix his wagon just as they did Abdul's grandfather."

"You were saying . . ."

"It was nineteen thirty-seven and Abdul Karamanli invited me to a party at his home."

"The same building Preston leased? What a coincidence."

"No coincidence, my dear fellow. It was I who put him on to the place as soon as I knew his problem. Turkish, *fin de siècle.* Ideally suited to his needs, ha, ha!" His rheumy old eyes peered through the pince-nez as he sipped again from the tea thermos. "Abdul's party was very elegant, very stylish. European women, diplomats, a few Arab dignitaries and the army brass. I was in full kit and cut quite a figure then, if I do say so."

"I'm sure you did." I wasn't just saying that. The old man's jaw was still firm, while his height and thick mane of hair and dark, intelligent eyes gave him an austere distinction undiminished by age. I needed no special imagination to picture the dashing young officer of more than half a century ago.

"I was standing near the door," he said, "where Preston's office is now, listening to Colonel Miani, looking fashionably bored as dancers moved to the gramophone music. I remember it all as if it were yesterday. Ice tinkling in our glasses, the gay laughter of the guests as waiters passed with caviar and oyster canapés. Then the world suddenly danced before my eyes."

I thought he meant an earthquake or some other natural disaster had overtaken them, but he was not speaking literally. "Only a great poet, a Dante or a Boccaccio could describe her adequately," he said with a long sigh, as he savored the dulcet memories of fifty years like honey on the tongue.

"Hair," he said. "How can I tell you about the silky sheen of her hair? Or her breasts? Or the sweetness of her smile? A voice as soft as a mountain brook. Eyes like ice blue diamonds and skin flawless as a perfect dream. I fell very much in love."

"But who was she?"

"Fatima Karamanli."

"Abdul's daughter?"

"His wife."

<><

XXX

<> I imagined the young lieutenant's grand illicit love for the beautiful Fatima Karamanli, the sighs and soft caresses, secret trysts and surreptitious touchings, the impossible separations if only for a day, and above all the trembling thrill of danger in the presence of the husband. I asked, "Wasn't it rare in those days for an Arab woman to appear unveiled at a party?"

"Unprecedented. But she was not Arab, you see. No, *signore*, Fatima Karamanli was Berber. A Berber beauty married to that Ottoman Turk renegade, my good friend Abdul Karamanli."

"Indeed, Berber women can be very beautiful."

"Then you understand. I swore I would be content only to look at her, but my vow hardly outlasted the evening. Visions of the woman tortured me, and I sought Abdul out at home on any pretext. As she could not appear on the street unveiled, going to the house was the only way I could see her."

"So you suffered in silence?"

"Up to a point. It was only a matter of time before I put the horns on my friend Abdul Karamanli."

His confession of betrayal in the bedroom made me more than a trifle uncomfortable, accustomed as I was to being the victim, as well as the victor in these matters.

"Fatima's chamber was always cool and fresh, the floor thick with fine silk carpets, the low, inlaid bedstead shrouded with gossamer hangings. Like most women of her class, Fatima bathed every day, and except for the heavy red brown tresses which fell below her shoulders, there was not a hair on her body anywhere." He looked around him, ran a loving hand over the sofa cushion and heaved a long sigh. "And you see, she was not only a ravishing, breathtaking beauty, she was uncircumcised as well."

"I beg your pardon?"

"Most Berber women are infibulated at puberty. It ruins them for anything except childbearing."

"Infibulated?"

"The clitoris is cut off and both the inner and outer lips of the vagina are sliced away as well."

I winced.

"The cunt is then sewn up," he continued, "leaving only a hole the size of a matchstick to pass urine and menstrual fluid. Without the operation Berber girls were considered unmarriageable."

"But how did Fatima escape it?"

"Her father was European-educated and humane. She was lucky and, of course, so was I. A circumcised woman has no orgasms."

I had heard of the custom, I told him. It was still common enough among rural Arabs and Africans in a number of countries, but normally they only amputated the clitoris.

"Well, not the Berbers," he said. "The husband either opened his bride with a knife on their wedding night or else played with himself. Anyway, Fatima and I were spared all that, you understand. I loved her and I had to have her."

"Did she go away with you?" I could imagine the scandal of the dashing young officer running off with the wife of a prominent Turk in what was then an Italian colony. Romantic liaisons were absolutely forbidden, but they were impossible to prevent. Pozzogallo explained that any young officer who broke the rules, no matter what his family connections, could look forward to a blighted career in some bleak garrison town of the *Mezzogiorno.*

"So, did you?" I asked him again.

"I was intoxicated with her, drunk on her love, addicted worse than any opium user," he said, "while all the time behaving as friend to Abdul. As we know, all great dreams have short lives, and an idyll such as this could not last forever."

But as the plane droned on, the old man withdrew so far into his reverie that I had to prompt him several times to pick up the thread of the tale. "My billet at that time was in the old fortress," he said at last, "the castle of the Karamanli ancestors."

"How did you manage to see her alone?"

"I'll get to that. Suffice it to say that I did see her privately, intimately and carnally almost every night."

"But where was her husband?"

"Gambling and whoring usually. Abdul had interests in a string of racing camels and especially fancied a young jockey."

"While you made love to his beautiful wife!"

Pozzogallo shrugged and took his silver flask out again, looked at it for a moment and changed his mind. "My mornings were busy with Field Marshal Balbo's parades, reviews, and executions. Showing the flag, that sort of thing. There were insurrections almost constantly, especially in Cyrenaica, and Colonel Miani often sent me to coordinate troop movements. Hunts and races also took up most of my afternoons. And balls and receptions and dinners occupied the evenings. Then making love to Fatima Karamanli until the sun came up. Is there anything so soft to the touch," he asked me wistfully, "as the inside of a woman's thigh?"

"What happened then?" I said, to keep him on the subject.

"I was exhausted, of course. I seldom got more than three hours sleep, and the months of ceaseless activity took their toll. I became melancholy and neurasthenic. The quality of my work suffered. I grew forgetful, and permanent bags formed under my eyes. Colonel Miani sent me to the army surgeon, but I knew he had no prescription for my illness."

"So what did you do?"

"What could I do? I was a slave to love and there was no cure. There never is, you know. Only death releases one."

"And?"

"It was the only time in my life I ever actually contemplated suicide, double suicide in fact, but Fatima saw nothing romantic in taking her life with my help, so I was on my own. In my fatigue and confusion, I grew careless and the obvious happened."

"What was that?"

"Abdul Karamanli found us out."

"My God! His best friend in bed with his wife!"

"Yes," he said thoughtfully. "It's really sickening when you stop to think about it."

"What did he do?"

"The only thing he could. He issued a challenge."

"A challenge?"

"To a duel, you see. It was very awkward. I had no desire to kill him. He was such a good friend, you understand."

"Yes, of course."

"And I had even less desire to risk my life at his hands."

"What did you do?"

The old man sighed. "I recall the fragrance of her boudoir. Not the cloying French scents of today which only confuse a man, but myrtle, cloves, sweet marjoram and lavender, and always a copper bowl at the foot of her bed where rose petals floated in cool water."

He inhaled deeply through his long nose as if smelling them all again. "Musk and saffron," he said. "Anise and sweet cedar."

"Did you fight Abdul Karamanli?"

After a long moment he answered. "I had no choice. According to the local custom, if I refused, or if I lost, Abdul would have been obliged to cut off Fatima's nose before divorcing her. The only hope for my beloved lay in killing my friend."

"What a terrible choice!"

"My first impulse was naturally to look for a way to save Fatima without prejudicing my career or killing Abdul."

"And you succeeded!"

"No, I failed."

"I see. Then the duel was on."

"I'm afraid so. The Italian army at that time frowned on this kind of pastime, to say the least."

"Couldn't that have given you an out?"

"Perhaps. But it wouldn't have helped Fatima."

"So you had to fight Abdul."

"He and I were both superior horsemen, and Arab duels, as I'm sure you know, are always fought on horseback."

Never having fought one, I didn't know, but I nodded.

"Local custom called for swords and pistols. The place of our meeting was to be on the outskirts of Tripoli, at the Busetta race track near the Sidi Mesri oasis. At dawn."

"How did you answer him?"

"I sent word through my second that I would prefer to forget the whole affair, even at the risk of losing his friendship and his wife's. If he could not do that, then regretably, I would meet him on the field of honor."

"Then you denied there was anything between you and her?"

"I couldn't do that, old chap, because he had walked in on us, you see. No use denying what he had seen with his own eyes."

"I see what you mean."

"When I received no reply, I prepared for my ordeal."

I could imagine the dashing young Lieutenant Pozzogallo loading his revolver, buckling on his saber, and stroking the neck of his favorite mount to calm the beast before the fight.

"It was just breaking dawn when I arrived at Busetta with my second," he said. "Abdul Karamanli was already there, an awesome figure on his fine blooded stallion, his beard curled, pistols jammed in a red sash at his waist, and a scimitar laid across his jeweled saddle bow. I thought of all my noble Pozzogallo ancestors who had gone to the Crusades and perished at the hands of such infidels as this, and I trembled.''

"I don't know how you stood up to it," I said truthfully. "I would have been on a boat to Italy by that time.''

"There was no boat," Pozzogallo said. "There wasn't even a priest handy to hear my confession, just in case.''

"But you believed you would win.''

"I was young, wild, in love.''

I found myself truly caught up in the old man's story by then, and although he needed no encouragement to go on, I said excitedly, "You had to win for Fatima's sake!''

"And for my own," he replied. "It would have been very awkward to have lost. I had a brilliant career ahead of me.''

"Was Karamanli a good shot?''

"Excellent. And a fine cut-and-thrust man on horseback. I once saw him chop a goat in half at a full gallop.''

"Please continue," I urged.

"We faced each other in the cold dawn. Abdul was to the north, looking toward the oasis. I was to the south where I had a clear view of the sea at his back. Suddenly he reared his steed and let out a bloodcurdling war cry, the sort of sustained, high-pitched shriek the Saracens sounded against my Christian forebears under the walls of Jerusalem.''

"Terrifying!''

"In an instant he was bearing down upon me at a gallop.''

"You had your saber and pistol and you didn't flinch.''

"I was never a terribly good shot.''

"But you stood your ground!''

He shrugged. "I was as prepared as I would ever be. I calmed my horse as this juggernaut thundered toward me, his scimitar raised high. I tried to keep my courage up.''

"You are amazing. Most men would have turned and run.''

"When he was less than ten paces from me, when I was sure I could not miss, I let him have both barrels.''

"Both barrels?''

"My shotgun blew him out of the saddle and carried away half the horse's head. Pity. Splendid animal.''

"But you said the duel was with swords and pistols!"

"Those were the local Arab rules," Pozzogallo explained, "but in Sicily, where I am from, the shotgun, or *lupara,* is the weapon of choice. I felt quite within my rights."

"But didn't he see it?"

"Certainly not. It was sawed off and I naturally kept it under my jacket out of sight."

I experienced a genuine pang of sympathy for the defunct Abdul Karamanli who never knew what hit him. Suffice it to say I would never make his mistake. Solange could go to bed with the whole world before I would challenge one of her lovers to a duel. "I'm glad you survived," I told the old man.

"That was only the beginning," he confessed, a sadness coming into his eyes.

"But you did return to Fatima?"

"I allowed a decent interval. There was the funeral and the mourning to get through. Colonel Miani was very decent so my army position was not compromised. When things cooled down, I went to see Fatima's father and offered to marry her. He was rich, and anxious to see her settled again, now that she was an eligible widow, rather than an adulterous wife without a nose."

"And he refused?"

"He accepted. We were the new conquerors, after all, and he wanted to ingratiate himself with the military command. But my happiness was short-lived. I had to leave Fatima when Colonel Miani sent me campaigning against rebellious tribes in Cyrenaica."

"And . . .?"

"She put the horns on me."

I stared at the old man in disbelief, for I too had fallen in love with Fatima Karamanli listening to him tell her story more than fifty years after the events he described. "But how could she?" I demanded. "She was your one true love!"

"You could say that, yes. But she was a bit of a tart."

"You must have been in a great rage. Imagine killing your best friend over her, only to have her betray you with another man!"

"I don't have to imagine it," Pozzogallo said. "It happened. And I daresay it was not the first time in Berber or Italian history, or in Fatima's history either, for that matter. My precious Fatima liked spice in her life, change, variety, excitement. Especially in men."

So the ghost of Abdul Karamanli was avenged, I thought. "But tell

me something, did you kill the man who took her away from you?"
I expected to hear a harrowing account of a second dawn triumph
at the race track.

Instead, he said, "Oh, I couldn't do that."

"Why not, for God's sake? After all you risked?"

"It was Colonel Miani, and I couldn't very well take him on,
could I? That would really have blasted my army career."

"But what did you do then?"

"He had me transferred to Ethiopia where I was wounded by an
arrow . . . yes, an arrow . . . and then sent home to convalesce. When
the war in Europe began I was posted to Albania, then Greece, then
finally to Russia." He gave a faint shudder as he recalled the horrors
of the Russian front.

For awhile he sat gazing out the plane window at the empty lemon
sky, every so often giving off a wheezy sigh. "I never saw her again,"
he said, "but I never forgot her. There was a reason for telling you
all that, but I've forgotten what it was. No matter. If I concentrate
I'll come up with it again."

In spite of Jock's assurance about our being well received in Tripoli, I was a bundle of nerves when we landed because Nagy seemed
so confident. At the hangar two trucks waited on the tarmac near
the fuel pumps. No police were visible, but that did not mean much
in Libya. They can appear out of nowhere.

Jock shut down the engines while Mustafa opened the rear door
and put out the stairs. When we stepped down, there were still no
police, but a dozen of Jeballah's formidable Tibu toughs had materialized next to the trucks.

Nagy was nearly foaming at the mouth by the time his little legs
hit the tarmac. "Where are my men? Where is the customs?" he
demanded. The nearest Tibu responded with an empty smile like a
deaf mute. Apparently no one was obeying Nagy's orders anymore
even in Tripoli.

He hurled himself into the hangar in search of a telephone, muttering angrily. But he apparently failed to get through after several
tries and he emerged completely rabid in time to see Jock Pringle
breezily descend from the plane.

"Enjoy your flight?" Jock asked him pleasantly, and Nagy flung
himself at the pilot like a mad pekinese, pummeling Jock around the
thighs and kicking his ankles until one of the Tibu pulled him off.

"Very neat," Preston said to Jock as we watched the men begin to unload the cargo.

Jock merely smiled and brushed the place on his trousers where Nagy had tried to bite him. "With Mr. Jeballah, anything's possible," he said with a wink. I feared there would be a day of reckoning for Jock, and I did not want to be around when it came.

On the way into town, Pozzogallo suddenly announced to me, "Ah! Now I remember what it was Preston wanted me to explain to you."

I waited.

"I used a secret underground passage which ran between the fort and Abdul's house."

"Does it still exist?"

"Of course! That's how Preston intends to bring the prisoners out."

XXXI

◇ After dropping Preston and Prince Pozzogallo off at their hotel, I passed by my place for a shower and a fresh change of clothes. It was noon and I was not surprised to see the bedroom door closed because Solange often sleeps the morning away. But I was surprised to find it locked. As my clothes were in the bedroom, and I also suspected that Bashir might be skulking around in there, I banged on the door.

"Solange! Open up."

Immediately the dog set up a yappy racket and the sound of muffled, hurried scuffling came from the bedroom. I heard Solange whispering and then she called out, "Hold on, Beida!"

I really couldn't care less who she sleeps with, but I felt she could be a little more discreet about *where* she did it as long as I was paying her expenses. I shouted back angrily, "Open the door before

I kick it down, Solange! I know who's in there!"

I had every intention of dragging that damned Bashir out feet first from under the bed and punching him all the way to the garden. Not from any feelings of jealousy, but out of simple pique. No one respected my rights anymore, not Nagy or Malduum or Preston or any of them. But Solange had better learn to show some respect, by God, if she wanted to keep a roof over her head!

"Solange, I'm warning you!" I gave the door a kick.

But it was Hueblen who opened it and brushed past me without a glance before I could react. His belt and trousers were open and he was stripped to the waist, carrying his shirt. While I watched too stunned to speak, he pulled on the shirt as he strode out of the flat, dug for his car keys and never looked back.

"I don't believe this, Solange!"

She was naked under a filmy peignoir which she clutched to her throat, and the bed looked like World War Three. I noticed she also had welts around her arms and shoulders. "I wasn't expecting you at this hour, Beida," she said meekly.

"Weren't you indeed!"

"If I had been, I would have got rid of him sooner."

Always the logical one, Solange. "That creep Bashir is bad enough," I told her, "but Hueblen! Have you no shame at all? Under my roof, eating my food . . .!"

"We didn't eat a thing!"

"Because there isn't anything. If you spent half as much time shopping for groceries as you spend seducing . . .!"

"Beida, how boring can you be?"

"Let me make one thing clear, Solange . . .!"

"You already have. No need to go on."

"If I ever catch you again . . .!"

"But you won't, *habibi!* It was too careless of me."

"Don't *habibi* me! If you want to take on everything in pants, go ahead. Don't let me stop you. But give up this fiction of being my wife and find yourself another place to live!"

"I don't believe you care," she said, surprised.

"Do you know what the Moslem penalty for fornication is?"

"Oh, come off it, Beida. You sound like a total ass when you become self-righteous."

"You're in Libya, Solange, a country of puritan religious fundamentalists, starting with Qaddafi himself. They follow Islamic law which recommends cutting off a woman's nose as appropriate punishment for screwing somebody not her husband!"

"Really, you're too much."

"If the mullahs convicted you, they'd give you a face like the back of a baboon! With a future to match!"

"You don't scare me, Beida."

"Oh, no? You know what infibulation is?"

"No, and I don't care."

"You should because one day I'll by God do it to you!"

She lowered the peignoir and flicked it in front of her like a stripper's scarf, no longer meek and fearful, but as arrogant and cheeky as ever. She jiggled her tits enticingly as she caught me staring at her. "Well?" she said, hands on hips, cocking her head provocatively and running her tongue over her lips. "Want a little?"

The dog had retreated to a corner of the room growling.

I was tempted, to tell the truth. Tempted to knock her blocks off, as they say, and then put them to her before entering the shower. If I hadn't been so certain that it would give her more pleasure than it would me, I would have done it, too.

Instead I turned my back on her, stripped off my clothes and went into the bathroom. I had barely adjusted the water temperature when I heard the door open. She tossed the peignoir aside as she stepped into the shower, flicking her tongue like a hungry iguana, and began fondling my crotch.

"Get away, damn you!"

"Beida, don't be angry," she crooned.

"You're an insensitive, ungrateful bitch, Solange! And a fucking nymphomaniac into the bargain!"

"They're the best kind," she said sweetly, soaping my thighs and rubbing her body against mine, sliding gradually to her knees until she got her lips around what she wanted.

I hate myself when I give in like that, but I become a pudding when a beautiful, sexually determined woman like Solange takes the initiative. All my anger vanishes, my good intentions disappear and my self-esteem turns to so much sludge. Within seconds her educated tongue had converted me into the sexual object of her desire.

There was another aspect to our coupling that day which alarmed me about my own state of mind. I could not stand Hueblen and really didn't much like Solange in spite of our long haphazard relationship. But knowing she had been with him excited me more than I cared to admit, and kept me hard and going for so long that even Solange was breathless from exhaustion when I left her finally, limp and whimpering on the cold tiles of the bathroom floor. The shower action at least restored my confidence after the rude shock of Hueblen's exit from my bedroom. The more I thought about his interest in Solange, the more I saw it as inevitable, a natural attraction of opposites.

They must have been perfect together. Solange's idea of foreplay was to be beaten, slapped and reviled because it raised the sick sensibilities of her perverted libido and turned on all her juices. Hueblen, on the other hand, probably became aroused when he could do the beating and the slapping, which must have made their union as tender and cuddly as love between a pair of alligators. So far so good, Solange. You can make your choice between sneaky Bashir and slap-happy Hueblen while I bow out.

I shaved, dressed, and trundled myself out of the house, not even bothering to say goodbye or leave her any pocket money. Musing on the day's ironies, I got into my Volkswagen. How Libyan life had changed in sixty years, I thought. All morning old Pozzogallo had entertained me with tales of infidelity, duels and death at dawn. Then when I come home and find my wife in bed with a man I despise, all I do is tell her not to let it happen again, and ball her on the bathmat!

As I threaded my way through the jammed donkey carts and Mercedes Benzes of downtown Tripoli, my thoughts drifted to Karen whom I had not seen for so many months. I had written but received no answer, and my few attempts to call her were unsuccessful. But now that I knew exactly what Preston was doing, I was better prepared to make my move.

First I had to transfer Khalid Belqair's four hundred thousand dollars to my Austrian account and cover my tracks, and that I would begin to do today. David Perpignon could survive quite comfortably on half a million dollars, which would be about my net worth once I got Belqair's money out of Libya.

Today was December 12. Elliot had indicated they planned to take the hostages out during the last week of December, probably on the eve of the 24th which was Libyan Independence Day, because so many police and troops would be preparing for the parade. I planned to book my flight for the evening of the 20th, so if everything worked out, I would be long gone by the time they charged the cannon's mouth.

I needed at least a week to transfer the money and clear up a few other paltry affairs before shaking the dust of Libya from my feet forever. In eight days I would be a free man.

Nagy had to be notified because he would find out anyway when his men reviewed the outgoing passenger lists before departure. If I pretended I did not really want to go anywhere, but that Preston required it, Nagy would insist. But if I said nothing and then tried to explain at the airport, he might become suspicious, a luxury I had no time to deal with. As there was no direct communication between Elliot's rescue group and Nagy—except through me—I did not worry about Preston discovering what I had in mind. I would report daily, do as I was told, act normally, and lull them all until I was safely aboard that plane and out.

I felt sorry for poor Rusty Kirshbaum and the other hostages, but not so sorry I was willing to commit suicide on a harebrained mission with Preston and his hi-tech Rover Boys. The people who cared about me, like Jock Pringle, Gagnon and Jeballah, would understand and applaud my decision to depart while still alive. As Jeballah always said, "Luck favors the careful crook."

I had eased my conscience somewhat by giving Malduum's murderous bombing schedule to Duff Elliot, but Malduum might still suspect me when those plans were frustrated. And as far as that lunatic was concerned, suspicion was tantamount to proven guilt, so the sooner I was beyond his reach, the better.

The bank was closed to the public by the time I arrived the next day, and the tellers were checking out with the cashier. I did not see Eidletraut, and Watanabe as usual was tracking errors on one of the computer consoles. I went to the monitor in my office and called up Current Accounts on the screen. Then I inserted four fictitious accounts in the alphabetical list under "E" for Elliot, "H" for Hueblen, "C" for Cardoni, and "P" for Preston. I showed deposits of $85,000 in one, a hundred thousand in another, and so on to account for the entire $400,000. They would not show up on the bank's printout until the following day. Then I ran the foreign deposit list on the screen and ordered the $400,000 transferred in varying amounts over the next six days to Vienna. Once the deposits were confirmed, I would annul the transfer order, leaving no bank record.

Over the same six days I took the packets of money from the safe deposit box and slipped them on the morning cash trolley as it moved between the vault and the tellers' cages. The bank would not be short that way, although Eidletraut would eventually go crazy trying to discover how the cash turned up where it did.

On the sixteenth, just before the Alitalia office closed, I popped in to book my flight. The place was nearly empty, and I was in and out within ten minutes, clutching my ticket in one hand.

Arranging my departure with Captain Nagy was even simpler, but like everything else in this treacherous place, our conversation bristled with incipient danger. To give the matter less importance, I merely telephoned instead of going to see him personally. After greeting him, I made the mistake of asking if he had fully recovered from his tiring trip to Ghadames.

"I will have that bastard pilot in prison before the week is out!" he vowed. "You will see how many jokes he makes when he's shut in a cage!" I quickly apologized for disturbing him, and said I was only calling because there was something he should know.

"Shoot!"

"Preston would like me to fly to Rome."

"Why?"

"He wants me to bring back some kind of special electronic meters for his desalinating tanks."

"Electronic meters, ha! Why doesn't he go himself?"

"He feels I'll be able to handle the customs better."

"Sure he does! I'm busy now but I'll get back to you."

"Actually, I told him no, but I wanted to inform you."

"You refused before checking with me first?"

"I'm so busy here and it's not important, so . . ."

"I'll decide what's important, Beida! Tell him you changed your mind and you'll go. He's testing you, can't you see?"

"That hadn't occurred to me."

His sigh was audible over the line. "That is because you are not trained in these matters as I am. Report to me on who contacts you there, and when you bring these devices back through customs, our experts will examine them."

I raised one or two other mild objections until he reminded me sternly that I was under his orders and my trip was in the interests of Libyan national security.

But then he said, "One thing bothers me."

I tensed. "What is that?"

"If you travel as Beida the Italians might arrest you."

"All the more reason to stay put," I said cheerfully, "unless I use the Maltese passport Malduum gave me for the last trip."

"That is the solution," he said.

"But I don't know if he would approve."

"Leave Malduum to me. He will definitely agree."

So far, so good. I left the bank and crossed to the Desal Building, seeing it now from a different perspective. In spite of Preston's big sign and new paint, the place looked particularly sad and forlorn under the rays of a late afternoon sun. Why not? I thought. It was the last home on earth of Abdul Karamanli, and would soon become a shabby tomb for the hostages and the gallant but foolish men trying to set them free.

Inside, Pozzogallo was studying another one of his street plans under a plastic overlay while Ike Maxwell lip-read to himself from a technical manual, stopping every few seconds to jot notes and run calculations on a laptop computer.

Old Pozzogallo greeted me cheerfully while Ike barely looked up, which immediately made me wonder if something was wrong. Preston and the others were not around and I was glad not to confront Hueblen so soon after his hurried exit from my apartment.

". . . but you didn't hear me," the old man was saying.

"I beg your pardon?"

"Coming out of the Alitalia office! I called to you but you didn't hear. We're booked on the same flight to Rome!"

So that's what it was. Of all the rotten, idiotic, misbegotten luck! The old devil was half-blind without his pince-nez, but he had spotted me, probably picked me out of a crowd from a block away!

Ike just pretended to study his manual.

"But you're mistaken," I told Pozzogallo.

"Well, I certainly was surprised," he admitted, "because I understood you were going to be part of Preston's operation here. But I am not mistaken. It was you I saw."

"I'm not flying anywhere," I lied.

"But the ticket agent specifically said you had booked," the old fool insisted, "and I was there right after you."

Ike was looking at me now, gauging my reaction, waiting for the lie. "Did the prince see you in the ticket office, Davey?"

"Of course he saw me in the ticket office. Is there a law against going to a bloody ticket office?"

"No law, Davey," Ike said in a voice flat as a grave, "but it sets a feller thinking. If you ain't going anywhere, why bother to buy a ticket?"

"Why, indeed?" I said flippantly, not certain what I would say next, cool on the outside while I seemed to be flitting around inside my brain like a trapped bird. "Would you like to see the ticket I bought?"

"If you want to show it to me," Ike said.

"You think I'm trying to skip out on you, don't you?"

"I didn't say that."

"You didn't have to." I whipped out the ticket folder and passed it to Ike with a dramatic flourish. "After all the years we've known each other, for you to think something like that . . . well, I don't know what to say except that it hurts me deeply."

Old Pozzogallo simply looked from one to the other of us, wondering what he had started. "Open it." I said. "Read the ticket holder's name." I was gambling everything on the fact that the name I would be traveling under, Antoine Sicara, meant nothing to him. Thank God Dick Diamond or Preston wasn't there or I would not have been so lucky.

Ike read the ticket coupon and looked up.

"He's a friend of Malduum's," I said. "When Khalil Malduum asks a favor, I do it because I'm the one he's watching. Not you or Preston. Me! And I better keep him happy until this whole stupid business is over and he can't touch me."

Ike almost shamed me then. He handed the ticket back with a sad, contrite look, and, I swear, tears came into his eyes. "I feel like shit, Davey, for thinking what I did."

I tucked the folder safely back in my pocket with relief. "It's okay, Ike. Everybody's under a strain."

"I should have known you wouldn't run out on me! But you don't like the way we're humping this job, so it wouldn't exactly surprise me if you decided to split without saying anything. But I was wrong and I'm sorry, Davey."

"Forget it."

"I don't know what come over me there, I don't. If I can't trust you with my life, who can I trust?"

"Nobody," I said truthfully, feeling like a Judas.

I was suddenly so depressed that I did not want to stay a moment longer. It wasn't only my guilt that brought on the angst, it was everything together. I hated to deceive Ike because I liked him. But I liked life more, and still hoped to live the rest of mine in peace.

Prince Pozzogallo gave me the perfect excuse when he said, "You look terrible, old chap. Coming down with something, are you?"

"Just tired," I said. "A glass of tea will pick me up." Neither he nor Ike wished to join me so I walked alone to the Suq al-Turk.

The place was crowded with merchants and late-afternoon shoppers. The domino and backgammon players had started to take their usual places, but I found a table in the corner and got the waiter's attention. My tea and some almond puff pastry had barely arrived when I looked up and thought I was hallucinating.

In the entrance to the teashop stood Karen.

XXXII

◇ I nearly knocked the table over jumping to my feet, and just as I did so, Karen turned away without seeing me. I called her name, but by the time I had pushed my way through to the entrance of the teashop, she was no longer there. I stepped into the arched passageway of the *suq* and looked frantically in both directions, but she had been swallowed up by the noisy, jostling crowd.

I told myself not to panic. Tripoli was not that big a city. She would be registered at one of the six or seven hotels approved for foreigners. If I could not track her down myself, I could find her easily through Nagy's office. I was elated at the thought that she had returned. So much so that several minutes passed before I realized how her unexpected presence was going to complicate my own plans.

Najeeb Hassan and Malduum assumed my relationship with Karen was more intimate than it was because I had passed her off as my fiancée during the hijacking. Solange did not know about her, and probably wouldn't care, unless she saw Karen as a threat to her meal ticket. But Bashir would be sure to point that out. I returned to my table in the teashop thoroughly shaken. My dream of seeing Karen had come true sooner than I expected, only to become a nightmare. Malduum would never spare her once I ran out on him, and he could count on Nagy's official cooperation.

I had to find Karen and persuade her to leave immediately. But that presented still another dilemma. Would she do it if I did not tell her why? I saw myself trying to explain, "Look, Karen, Malduum thinks of me as part of his killer band. Meanwhile this crazy commando group is planning a raid to free the hostages with my help. But Captain Nagy of the security police thinks they are CIA agents plotting to poison the Libyan water system."

Karen might accept my explanation about Malduum's interest in me. And she would probably believe it about the planned raid on the prison. She might even laugh at Nagy's suspicions concerning Preston and the Desal water plot. But she would never in a thousand years swallow the whole pack of facts together. No one would.

It didn't take long to find her. She was registered at the Hotel Uaddan, but I left no message because I needed to think further about what to do before I saw her. There were too many traps she could blunder into if she came looking for me unprepared. Every step I took was perilous, but now that I had Karen's welfare to consider, the dangers multiplied. Had she come to find me, or was she on a photographic assignment? The Libyans had given her a visa and Nagy would know the details, but I did not wish to stir that kettle of worms unless I had to. Let sleeping fish lie, as they say.

An hour or so later I returned to the Desal offices where I hoped to be alone, but old Pozzogallo was there, eternally poring over his charts and street plan overlays. To my chagrin, he greeted me with, "I say, Beida! Just the man I want to see."

"Where are the others?"

"Mr. Preston and Mr. Cardoni have been at the port all day. But your wife called very upset about the German."

"Hueblen?"

"He got drunk and went to your flat. Maxwell went over there right away because she said he was breaking things."

Hueblen could start with her neck, I thought, but I didn't say so. "When was this?" I asked him.

"About an hour ago."

I hoped Ike could settle it. All I needed on top of my other problems was that drunken Hun careening around Tripoli.

Old Pozzogallo mistook my irritation for anxiety, however, and pushed the telephone across for me to call Solange at home.

Ike answered immediately. "She's resting, Davey, but she's okay. Mainly it's just friction burns from the ropes."

"What ropes?"

"You really want to know?"

"I know, Ike. I just wanted to be sure."

"A little S and M hanky-spanky got out of hand. Hueblen trashed some furniture and took off to get more booze. She panicked and called the cavalry. I'll wait for you if you want, Davey."

After I put down the receiver, Prince Pozzogallo said, "You look terrible. Are you feeling all right?"

"Apart from the fact that the stress and strain of simply staying alive has never been greater, I'm in fine shape, prince. Positively ripping, as they say. At the top of my peak!"

"I think you need help," the old man called after me as I slouched out the door. And no one ever said a truer thing.

Ike handed me a light bourbon and ice as I entered the kitchen. "Where is she?" I asked and he indicated the bedroom.

The place looked like an earthquake had struck. The bedstead itself had been broken, and sagged on one side. Some strands of cut rope were still tied to one of the corner posts, and the place reeked of cigarettes and alcohol. Solange was sound asleep so I closed the door and left her alone.

Ike and I sat at the small table in the kitchen and sipped our drinks. "I thought he ran out of whiskey?" I said.

"I had this in the Mercedes."

"Did you see him at all?"

Ike shook his head. "Only his tracks, Davey. He's a real ding-a-ling, ain't he?"

"Yet Preston swears by him as long as he stays sober." I told Ike about Hueblen's drinking on the ship and slapping Solange. And then catching them in bed after Ghadames.

"Some things in life are like that, Davey. Love at first bite, I reckon. Every Apple Lard has his Ella Louise, and old Hueblen must have found his. Too bad it's your wife."

"Who?"

"They were Eye-talian lovers. Apple Lard took a knife and cut his balls off when he couldn't have Ella Louise which shows you never know how a foreigner's going to react to a woman. I don't mean you, Davey. I don't consider you a foreigner and I'm glad you ironed out your differences with Preston."

"For the time being, anyway," I said. I preferred to avoid that theme, but Ike obviously wanted to talk about it.

He raised his glass and seemed to be studying the color of the whiskey. "You got to trust somebody on every job, Davey, besides each other. And I figure we got ourselves some right smart bosses this time out of the chute."

"You've been wrong before," I said drily. "Come to think of it, you've been wrong fairly often. But anybody who'd hang around with me can't be a very good judge of character."

That made Ike laugh, and he said I was as big a panic as ever and that was one of the reasons he liked working with me. "If I'm mistaken this time, it'll be the last!" he said finally. "Whoo-eee, if anything goes wrong, imagine!"

"I have and it's all bad."

Ike sipped at his drink. "You got to leave some things in the hands of the top management in the sky, Davey. You got to have a little faith in the Lord."

"Since when did you get religion?"

"Oh, I been saved two or three times. Down home in Lubbock it's something people do a lot. It's probably good for you if you don't take it too serious."

"Maybe you should take it seriously, because the job you signed on for will probably leave your carcass splattered all over some Libyan wall. You better hope God's on your side, you prairie nitwit, because you'll need all the help you can get!"

"Hold on a minute, old buddy," Ike said, raising his hand as if to ward off a blow.

"Did you know Nagy believes Preston is going to poison Libya's water? Did you know he plans to lock the whole lot of you up before that can happen?"

"Elliot know this?"

"Of course he knows it. I told him in Ghadames and I told Preston weeks ago. But no one takes me seriously."

"You mean that dinky little feller's gunning for us?"

"He thinks you're CIA. In my opinion, you'll be lucky if he gets you first. At least you won't be a corpse quite so soon!"

"How about that!" Ike said as his expression froze. For a moment I thought I had gone too far and made him angry because his look was suddenly all business. Seconds passed before I realized he was not focusing on me at all but on something over my shoulder. I turned to see Hueblen glaring drunkenly at us both, a whiskey bottle in one hand and a gun in the other. The gun was pointed unsteadily at my head.

"Where is she!" he demanded.

Ike sat still as a snake while I turned toward Hueblen and foolishly started to raise my hands. It seemed like the correct response under the circumstances.

He moved closer and rasped in German, "What have you done with her? Where is she? I'll kill you!" His reddened eyes were like an extension of the gun muzzle, and I could hear every hair on the back of my neck cry out for mercy. Meanwhile I said nothing, and probably looked cool, if not contemptuous, as I stared at the pistol and waited for him to shoot me dead.

The sharp crack of a shot sounded from behind me as the pistol flew from Hueblen's hand. He dropped the whiskey bottle and looked down to see his fingers slowly bathed in blood. Before he could react further, Ike Maxwell sprang across the room and delivered a stunning blow to the side of his head.

Ike picked up Hueblen's pistol and dropped his own back into his coat pocket. "By Christian, he was going to shoot," he said as he fingered the weapon expertly, ejected a shell from the chamber, uncocked it and emptied the clip.

I sank back into my chair as Ike got his breath and calmly filled our glasses. "Now, Davey, you were saying?"

"What about him?"

"He'll come around. I'm more interested in the point of view you were expressing when he interrupted us."

"I'm sorry I called you a dumb cowpoke. I didn't mean it."

"You think I'm acting like one so there's no need to apologize. Just call 'em as you see 'em, like you always do."

"The operation is foolhardy, Ike, and I like you. That's all. I think you're in the wrong army fighting the wrong battle."

"I'm just here for the money."

"It doesn't matter. You won't live to spend it."

"The odds ain't favorable, but they never are in my line of work. If I worry'd about odds I'd still be selling tractors."

"You? Sell tractors?"

"After I come out of the army. But there's no novelty. I need novelty, Davey, like you."

Hueblen stirred then and Ike went over to examine the injured hand. "Preston's going to be pissed if he can't work. You know a doctor who can sew him up?"

"They can take care of him at the Moassat Hospital but they'll ask questions. How do you explain what happened?"

"Caught his hand in a car door?"

"Ike, he's unconscious."

"Then we'll make it a garage door. One of them automatic kind that breaks your hand and hits you on the head."

Solange came into the kitchen, stepping over Hueblen's inert form as if it were an overturned chair. "Did you kill him?" she asked casually as she filled a glass with mineral water.

"Just a love tap," Ike said.

One side of her face was swollen and bruised where he had hit her, and her lower lip was cracked. As she sipped the water she pushed stray locks of hair aside and gingerly touched the injured lip with her tongue. When I said she was lucky the damage to her face wasn't permanent, she hugged herself inside her dressing gown, turned away from me, and sulked. There are few things as unattractive as a beautiful woman who hates the way she looks.

Hueblen finally woke up and yielded as easily as a sleepwalking child when Ike bundled him into the car. "Good luck," I said, and Ike replied, "Where do you think you're going?"

"Not with him. He's woozy now but as soon as he comes around, you know what he'll do and who he'll do it to."

"He's harmless, Davey. All the fight's gone out of him."

"For now. But tonight? Tomorrow? You want me killed?"

"If I wanted that, I'd have done it long ago." The cool authority of his tone conveyed more than the words. Ike Maxwell was undisputed boss at that moment so I drove them to the hospital.

The Spanish doctor at the emergency entrance accepted my story that Hueblen had been in a slight accident and suggested he remain overnight in the hospital to check for concussion. But I persuaded him the German would be calmer if he was restored to the bosom of his family.

We took him back to his hotel where Ike tucked him in while I waited in the lobby. When Ike returned, he said, "Let's wander out by the pool, Davey, and talk a little."

The hotel garden was deserted at that early evening hour and we sat in the dark under a palm-fringed umbrella while I waited for Ike to say what was on his mind. Finally he got around to it. "You ain't in favor of this operation, and nothing's going to change your mind."

"I wish I could talk you out of it."

"If anybody could, you could," he said, "because you're about the slickest talker I ever come across."

"Thanks for the compliment, if that's what it was."

Ike smiled. "I talked to the German."

"He's crazy, Ike."

"He ain't so crazy he don't listen. I told him the next time he steps out of line, even a little bit, I'd kill him."

"You think he believed you?"

"If he ever believed anybody, he believed me." The coldness had come back into Ike's voice. If he had said it like that to Hueblen, the man could not help but believe him.

He seemed to lapse into deep thought for awhile before he said, "Davey, I'm going to tell you something now and I want you to understand the spirit in which it's meant. No offense and no hard feelings, right? Just bizniz."

"Sure, Ike."

"I'm sure you ain't thinking of leaving no more, and I apologize in advance for even suggesting you might be."

"I understand, Ike."

"I ain't sure you do, but I'll just say it once. If you try to skip before we get them hostages out, I'll kill you, too."

His words hung in the dark night air like frost, and I felt the chill.

"You don't mean that Ike," I said hoarsely. But he was silent until I added, "You wouldn't kill a friend."

"That's what I want you to get real clear, old partner. If you cut out on me now, you wouldn't be a friend."

Neither of us said anything for some minutes after that. Then Ike grinned and slapped me on the knee. "Come on, cheer up. We'll both be rich by Christmas."

"Or dead," I said.

"You'll be okay, but I could go any minute. I ain't as young as I used to be and I can't do half what I used to do either."

"You look pretty fit to me."

"Maybe in some ways, but the body betrays you from inside, Davey. What I'm telling you now is in confidence, you understand? If Duff Elliot knew, he'd toss me out on my ass. You know them little things I chew all the time?"

"The mints?"

"Well, they ain't to keep my breath sweet, Davey, they're medicine. I got a bum ticker and I need 'em to keep going."

"You shouldn't even be here then!"

Ike smiled at me, and I thought he suddenly looked very old and sad, but it may have been the dim light reflected off the surface of the pool. "I got no choice, Davey."

"What do you mean?"

"There's a lot more you don't know about me."

"So?"

"Davey, I got Priscilla Pearl to think of."

"Who?"

"My daughter."

"You never told me you had a daughter, Ike."

"It ain't something I talk about much, Davey, because it's too painful. After that darling girl's mother died, it was hard taking care of her, handicapped like she was and all."

"She's a handicapped child?"

"Blind as a bat."

"But that's terrible, Ike! Why haven't you ever mentioned this before? All the time we spent together in Beirut and Turkey? The jobs in France? And I never even knew you had a child!"

"I don't like to burden my friends, old buddy."

"Ike, I don't know what to say."

"I only told you now so you'd know what I'm up against. I need the money desperate, Davey. It'll pay for my heart bypass and, God willing, if I can afford Priscilla Pearl's operation, they'll operate us together and my little girl will walk again."

"Walk again!"

"She's sort of crippled."

"My God, Ike!"

"Being blind an' all, she fell down a flight of stairs."

"How awful!"

"Let's change the subject, Davey. If you was to split on me before we get those people out, I couldn't hack it alone. But you wouldn't do that, would you?"

"Ike, I'm with you all the way."

"I mean, for Priscilla Pearl's sake."

"Ike, I told you."

"The Lord always gives a man at least one last chance, Davey, and this is mine. You, me, Preston, Cardoni and the rest, we're going to do it, you hear! We're going to free them poor people and make us some real fancy cash while we're doing it."

"Ike, let me ask you something."

"Anything at all, Davey."

"If I knew a way for you to get the money without sticking your neck out, would that change your mind?"

"You mean steal it?"

"Sort of."

"What about them poor hostages?"

"I'm not talking about them, I'm talking about money."

"Oh, I couldn't do that, Davey."

"Why not? What about your bypass and Priscilla Pearl?"

"But I ain't a thief. You know that."

"Yet you just said you'd kill me if I walked out on you!"

"Davey, that's different. That's between us."

◇

XXXIII

<> Between Solange's eccentric behavior, Hueblen's drunken appearance with the gun and Ike's menacing ultimatum, I was in no shape to deal with anything else by the time we parted. But the dilemma of what to do about Karen bothered me more than ever. I could not let another moment go by without warning her.

The concierge was a taciturn Italian who told me Karen occupied the hotel's second-best suite. I noticed her key was not in its box so I assumed she was in. Instead of calling first, I went up the stairs and knocked lightly on her door. A woman's voice answered, "Who is it?"

"Room service," I said, wanting to surprise her.

"There must be some mistake," she called back. "We didn't order anything from room service."

We?

The door opened and Karen stood there, her long blonde hair piled on top of her head, glasses perched on the tip of her nose, one hand holding closed a pink terrycloth robe. For an instant she gaped. Then letting the robe go, she threw both arms around me and cried, "David! Oh, David, you're here!"

No one had ever been so glad to see me as Karen was that night. Not in my whole life, and I was deeply touched. She clung to me for minutes in the doorway, laughing and sobbing and finally backing away, her robe nearly falling open on her nakedness, her eyes only on me. "Oh, David!" she said again with fresh sobs as she pulled me to her and I kicked the door closed behind me.

"You're pale," I said.

"From worry about you," she said.

"I left messages. You were never there."

"You did not say where I could reach you. I had no idea where you were, David. Then Mr. Diamond came to see me and that's how I knew you were still in Libya."

"Dick Diamond? What did he want?"

"He wanted to know all about you. Did you get the job?"

"What job?"

"He said you were being considered for a very sensitive, highly placed international position of great responsibility."

"And what did you tell him?"

"The truth. That you were one of the most fascinating men I'd ever met. That you were intelligent and brave and trustworthy."

I had to laugh and Karen immediately misunderstood. "But it's true," she said. "Every word. And I also told him many more lives would have been lost on that plane if it hadn't been for you."

Loves that kill, I thought. Karen had unknowingly condemned me with her praise, and convinced Diamond I was just the man to do their dirty work for them.

"Did I say the wrong thing?"

"No, my dear, of course not."

"I was weeks trying for a visa to come back," she continued, "but they are not easy to get for a woman alone. Thank God for Hanzi."

"Hanzi?"

A man came from the bedroom, naked to the waist with one of those monogrammed towel-sarongs wrapped around his middle. He extended his hand. "I am Hanzi," he said.

My first impression was that the bastard was extraordinarily, stupendously handsome! Blonde, wavy hair and smiling blue eyes. Clean, firm lines to his jaw and face. Dark eyebrows and a pleasant smile. Tall and muscular, with that perfectly symmetrical build of the trapeze artist or dancer.

I hated him on sight.

My face must have shown something of my disappointment. He and Karen were obviously sharing the suite. This grinning Adonis was her lover and I was her friend. Her dear, dear friend to be sure. She had certainly made that clear when she saw me. I was the friend from her awful hijacking experience, the friend she had worried about and been trying to find for months. But I was still only a friend while this Hanzi fellow . . .

"You are thin," she said to me. She was right. I usually carry twenty or thirty pounds of excess flesh as the price for small indulgences. But between my problems and Solange's cooking I had lost all of it and was actually svelte. Karen's smile reassured me that I was still attractive to women, however. She later told me she even found me handsome in a dashing, Continental sort of way.

But a glance at Hanzi confirmed we would never be in the same class, and I wondered what he was. Playboy? Broker? Oil magnate? The kind one sees in *Country Life* shooting grouse or leaning on the paddock gate while his thoroughbreds work out. The kind who can hang a ten dollar muffler around his neck and look like he just bought Canada, or stand windblown and saltsprayed at the helm of the America's Cup winner, checking his five thousand dollar watch and knowing he had the race in the bag from the start. Hanzi was just debonair enough to look at home in his private opera box, chateau or jet. He was not only handsome, he had that special grace that only breeding and success confer. I told myself it's no disgrace to lose to such a specimen. Most men place second behind the Hanzis of the world.

"I know what you're thinking," Karen said, which reminded me of how perceptive and outspoken she could be.

"I hope you don't."

"You're wondering about Hanzi and me."

Hanzi lit a long thin cigarette and held it in long thin fingers, smiling at Karen. Gloating, more likely.

"Karen, it doesn't matter about you and Hanzi," I lied. "I was a fool to entertain any ideas about us."

"But you really don't understand, David, darling. Hanzi and I work together. He's the top male model in Europe." Hanzi preened as she said that, pleased with himself. "And sometimes we room together," she added, "if it's convenient."

"It's all right," I said. "You don't have to explain. I'm glad he's with you because it makes things easier." I told Karen I had seen her that afternoon at the *suq* but could not reach her before she disappeared into the crowd. I also told her I had second thoughts about contacting her at all.

She looked hurt when I said that, so I added quickly, "I'll tell you why." I did not actually tell her why. I only hinted at the reasons because I began to sound preposterous even to my own ears. To make the tale more credible, I found myself leaving out important chunks of information. I did not mention, for example, the plan to free the hostages or Nagy's suspicions about Preston. Nor did I tell her about Hueblen, or Malduum's ideas for me, or Pozzogallo's work on the secret underground passage.

And the result was that although she believed what I said and wanted to humor me, she failed to see the gravity of our situation.

I could tell by her eyes that I had not convinced her. To make it worse, when I finished, Hanzi said, "But we can't possibly leave tomorrow. We just got here."

"Let me put it this way," I said. "I intend to be gone within a very few days. And the moment I'm gone, Karen will be in great danger because people will try to get back at me through her. And if she is in danger, so are you."

Hanzi looked anxiously at Karen, then reached out and took her hand in his. He said, "Maybe you feel threatened. But Karen and I are Austrian citizens. What can happen to us?"

"Karen was lucky once. She won't be lucky twice with these people. Karen, you remember Najeeb Hassan?"

She shuddered.

"He is a baby compared to the leader, Khalil Malduum."

"But they have nothing against me," she said. "I came to find you, David, but no one knows that except us. Officially Hanzi got our visas to shoot a men's fashion spread in the Sabratha ruins and the camel market."

"Go back to Vienna tomorrow, both of you."

Hanzi batted his eyes, waved his cigarette at me and said petulantly, "Darling boy, what you don't understand is that I have a contract with the most prestigious knitwear house in Italy!"

The exaggerated feminine gestures and the patronizing, affected tone of voice suddenly gave Hanzi away and made me feel much better. Karen might be stubborn and Hanzi might be the most beautiful hunk in the world, but Karen couldn't care about him as a man because he simply wasn't one in the usual sense. Nature was not as unjust as I had thought. Here at least I had an edge!

"I've brought my make-up and hairdresser," he complained, "and I have to pay them whether we shoot or not."

"I'll wrap in three days," Karen said. "I promise, and then we'll all go home." She looked at me and smiled.

"Karen, you are not a foolish woman."

"And you are not a hysterical man."

"Leave tomorrow." I took her by the hand and led her across the room from Hanzi. I put my arms around her, then held her away from me, my hands upon her frail shoulders. "Think," I said. "Remember Najeeb's rage and anger. Remember him walking that poor American soldier down the aisle of the aircraft and calmly shooting him in the head. Remember, Karen, the way he terrorized that child?"

"David, I could never forget any of it."

"Najeeb Hassan is the same animal he was then. They still hold hostages and they are plotting other outrages every day with Qaddafi's approval."

"I'll do what you want, David."

"There are several flights to Europe in the morning."

"What about me?" Hanzi said.

"We're both going," Karen replied. "David's right."

"In case you've completely lost your mind, we are under contract," Hanzi reminded her. "And I might add it was a contract you begged me to arrange, Karen. I could have gone to Tangier for the same money, but I came here to please you."

"Then leave here to please her as well," I said.

"Karen?" Hanzi pleaded.

"We'll do as David says."

"This will finish me with the Italians," Hanzi whined. "I lied through my teeth to persuade them Libya was the only place their stupid sweaters would look good. Roman ruins and all that."

"On you their sweaters will look good wherever we do the shoot," Karen assured him, and although he still flounced peevishly about the room, he was somewhat mollified by her compliment.

I told Karen I would not attempt to see her again. "Get out on the first flight you can tomorrow." My own plans would have to be changed now because I could not possibly leave at the same time as Pozzogallo. I would do it on the 21st, I decided, and not fly out of Tripoli at all, but drive to Tunis and take a plane from there. That way, neither Ike nor the Libyans would catch on. "Christmas in Vienna?" I said to Karen.

"Is that a promise?"

"It's a promise."

◇

XXXIV

◇ I returned to my apartment and poured a short nightcap from Ike's bottle to settle my frazzled nerves. Then, while Solange snored alone in the bedroom, I took a blanket and stretched out on a divan. I did not get much sleep. A wedding party in the neighborhood was no help, and every time I drifted off, bad dreams plagued me. The drumming and shrieking of the wedding guests went on until dawn, like a sound track accompanying my nightmares.

I dreamt Malduum and Najeeb Hassan were after me but old Pozzogallo showed me how to escape through the ancient passages under the Karamanli Castle. My torch went out, though, and I became lost stumbling around in the dark. I saw a light and ran toward it, but stopped in time to hear Nagy's voice say, "He's in there somewhere! Get him!"

I ran into the bank, but the corridor guards were stalking me too with their automatic rifles. I drove to the airport in time to see Jock Pringle take off without me, then went to the Roman ruins at Sabratha to warn Karen. She was taking pictures of Hanzi and I shouted at her. But my voice was a hoarse whisper and she could not hear me. Hueblen then heard, and I had to run again, dodging behind statues and ancient stone walls. Ike was with him and he was gunning for me too, calling, "Come on out, Davey, I won't hurt you!" But I could see the grim expression on his face and the enormous pistol in his hand.

Each time I found a new hiding place and thought I was safe, Solange or Bashir would find me and call out, "Here he is! Over here!"

At six I finally gave up and staggered into the kitchen in a stupor of fatigue and worry. I made tea and took some aspirin, then showered for half an hour. The wrecked apartment was even more depressing by daylight than it had been the night before. I couldn't get out fast enough.

At that early hour there was little traffic as I drove to the Desal Building. The air was cool but I was perspiring as I let myself in, probably coming down with something, but knowing perfectly well it was only panic. The entrance hall was filled by great wooden crates stencilled with Desal's name. I was wondering what the devil they could be when old Pozzogallo appeared. "Desalinating tubes and valves," he said, "and chemicals."

"What's the point? There is no desalinating planned."

"But the Libyans don't know that." He smiled. "For chemicals, read explosives. For tubes and valves read weapons."

"But how did Preston ever get them through customs?" What I really meant was how did he do it without my help?

"He had to leave some sizeable tips with the officials so they would not inconvenience him by opening anything."

"If they caught him, they'd hang him. No questions asked. He's a fool to take such a chance."

I sank into a chair, expecting him to leave me alone, but instead he said, "Are you ill, Beida? You look worse than you did last night, if that's possible. Forgive me for saying so, but you have no color."

In fact, I was beginning to think my heart might pack it in at any minute the way it fluttered like a bat against my ribs. My breath came in short gasps, clammy perspiration oozed through my shirt, and my pulse seemed to vacillate between fifty and a hundred beats a minute. Pozzogallo came closer and peered at me as if I had just crawled out from under a stone. He looked like a skinny puppet with his comical pince-nez and eternally rumpled white suit. But through the grey film that clouded my eyes, I could see that he was as full of energy and optimism as always, and seemed genuinely anxious to help. I felt my head swim as I loosened my tie. "You don't have a drink around, do you?" I asked him.

"Stay where you are and hold your head down to put a little blood in your brains," he said. He went to a battered plastic case I had seen him carry, opened it and produced a bottle of opaque amber liquid that looked like floor wax.

"Drink!" he commanded. He had the top unscrewed and was holding the bottle out to me.

"What is it?" I asked weakly as I swallowed some of the liquid. It had the consistency of kerosene and smelled heavily of cinnamon and eucalyptus oil. Whatever it was, I reasoned, it could not make me feel any worse than I did.

"Again!" he ordered as I tried to push his hand away. With the second swig I began to feel the stuff.

I started to cough and suddenly my throat was burning from my tonsils to my toes. I rose from the chair but his bony hand forced me back. In that instant I was sure he was trying to kill me with some terrible caustic lye solution. The burning sensation increased. My nose ran and my eyes watered. My throat closed so that I could neither breathe nor speak. I sat popeyed as fire stabbed my belly and ricocheted around my chest and down my arms to my fingertips. It had to be a heart attack! A stroke! My ears pounded and my lungs burst!

After a few minutes, the sensation receded and I felt only a fullness in the throat and a coppery aftertaste under my tongue. Then it went away almost as quickly as it had come, and to my astonishment, I felt much better. Indeed, my pulse was normal and my head as clear as ever.

Pozzogallo beamed over me with proprietary pride. "Does the trick, doesn't it?"

"What the devil is it?" I gasped.

"I have drunk a spoonful each morning for nearly sixty years and never been ill one day. I am eighty-two years old, nearly eighty-three, and expect to live past one hundred."

Fascinating, but I asked again what the stuff was.

"A gift from my friend Abdul Karamanli," he said, "before we had our little falling out. Do you realize the Karamanli dynasty flourished from 1711 to 1832, and the male line continued another hundred years until it ended with Abdul? Not a small part of their survival was due to what just helped you. It is called *Halib Arbah Filfil*, or, the Milk of the Four Peppers."

"It works," I said, rising from the chair and stretching, feeling rested and without a care in the world. "Amazing!"

"I prepare it myself," the old man said, "from the original formula passed down from Yusef Karamanli."

"You could make millions if you patented the secret. I feel better than I have for weeks. Months even."

"I'm satisfied if my friends profit from it in increased years and virility. It is, by the way, a great cock stiffener."

He made me a present of the bottle and jotted down the various ingredients and proportions. According to him, the four peppers were found wild only in the highlands of Anatolia and weren't peppers at all, but the pods of poppies.

"Take it as a preventive," he said, "and you will never need a cure."

"I'll be sure to take a shot for courage before we go after the hostages," I said.

The old man laughed. "You have nothing to worry about, Beida. In a few days you'll be a rich man."

"That's what Ike Maxwell keeps telling me."

"Never in history . . . have so few . . . done so little . . . for so much," he intoned, proud of himself for paraphrasing Churchill.

"You can afford to joke. You won't even be there."

"But my dear Beida. What can possibly go wrong?"

"Everything."

"Your pessimism is not justified. The Karamanlis are on our side. Here, let me show you." He beckoned me to the desk and began to display the drawings and overlays one by one. There were cutaways of the Karamanli Castle walls and several nearby buildings, including the one Preston had leased for Desal. A network of tunnels connected them, one of which seemed to reach all the way to the end of the rocky promontory jutting into the sea. I pointed to it and asked if it still existed.

"That's the way they come in," Pozzogallo said. "Brilliant, isn't it? Sailing right into the passage."

"If the Libyans aren't looking."

"But the Libyans will be far too busy elsewhere."

"How do you know?"

"Preston has it very cleverly worked out."

"I'll bet he does."

He indicated the passage that connected the Desal Building with the Castle Fortress. "This is the key to the whole operation," he explained. "The way to the prisoners."

"It's better than blasting your way in the front door, but it still looks like a dickey place to get out of alive."

"Faith and the sword," he said.

"I beg your pardon?"

"The motto of the Karamanlis. They believed you needed both to succeed in life. This maze of passages and dungeons was built by them to hold prisoners. But except for the few rooms used today, no one even suspects the existence of the rest."

"How do you know?"

"Because I had them sealed off fifty years ago, and not one had been discovered."

"Still . . ."

"Faith and the sword, Beida. You should have a little faith in things yourself. Follow Elliot's example."

"Sorry, but I am a skeptic and they know it."

"It doesn't matter if you are good at your job."

"Why did you seal off the passages?"

"To protect myself against people like me," he said slyly. "I was away so much and Fatima was alone. Or so I thought until I found out about Colonel Miani. At first I was only concerned about the passage I had used to put the horns on Abdul Karamanli. But then I discovered Yusef's dungeon with the bones of prisoners he had starved and tortured to death a hundred years before."

"But who cared, beside you?"

"My curiosity had me burrowing everywhere. I found the passage to the sea and the one that leads under the market. I discovered the secret buried history of the Karamanlis, a hundred and twenty years of piracy and lust, bloodshed and cruelty. It took American marines to bring them down."

He was as crazy as the rest, I decided. As woolly-minded and flawed as they come. Half-senile probably, although his brain seemed clear, but a real crackpot just the same.

"I envy you the excitement of the raid," he said.

"You can take my place."

He chuckled. "Faith, Beida, faith."

"When I'm dead faith won't help me."

"Naturally, you are nervous," Pozzogallo said.

"It doesn't matter. I'm committed anyway," I lied. "Unless they lose me in one of your secret passages."

"There are changes in the schedule. Preston talked with Mr. Elliot last night."

"Changes?"

"Don't quote me, but they've decided to go in sooner."

"They talked about this on the telephone?"

"Of course not. Preston records his messages on a microchip in a special Walkman Maxwell brought. He presses a button and in three seconds the whole thing reaches Elliot."

"That's a relief."

"Microburst radio, they call it. I thought you knew all about these modern technologies, Beida."

The old prince sat opposite me and tapped both index fingers against his temples. "There is nothing they haven't thought of. Nothing. Elliot is a great genius."

XXXV

◇ Whether it was Prince Pozzogallo's tonic or simply that I had decided to get out of Libya as soon as possible, I was feeling wonderful. In fact, I was probably a little stoned.

At any rate, I was thinking happy thoughts. Karen would be safely gone by noon and I only needed an hour later in the day to cover my tracks on the last of the money transfers. Then Dahoud el Beida would cross into Tunisia and vanish forever while David Perpignon surfaced on the next Europe-bound flight.

By the time Preston's meeting started, I was above it all, detached, removed from the fray, able to gaze upon this agreeable group with the kind of bemused tolerance the Milk of the Four Peppers conferred, knowing that nothing of what Preston had to say pertained to me.

Even Cardoni seemed friendlier than usual, flashing me a smile when he arrived. He was as natty as ever, his bangs brushed carefully forward above dark sunglasses, the sleeves of his loose cashmere pushed halfway up his sunburned, sinewy arms.

Hueblen attracted everyone's attention with his bandaged hand, but Ike's garage door story passed, even if no one really believed him. The German's reputation for drunken brawling and ill-tempered remarks was too well established to think he was ever a victim of anything other than his own bad character.

Pozzogallo looked pleased when Preston announced they would be going after the hostages sooner than planned, while Ike sat cracking his knuckles, his big Stetson on the back of his head and his glistening, handtooled boots resting on Preston's desk.

According to Preston, Duff Elliot had passed on some SIGINT indicating that Qaddafi feared an American military operation to free the hostages. SIGINT was the term they use among themselves for Signals Intelligence or satellite eavesdropping as opposed to HUMINT or human intelligence which refers to information gathered by agents on the spot.

In this case I was the only so-called agent on the spot, and Preston referred to me in his messages as HUMINT. "HUMINT says this" or "HUMINT indicates that". At first I considered the term slightly degrading until I realized it masked my identity if anyone from Captain Nagy's office was listening in. Dahoud el Beida or David Perpignon were eminently hangable, but HUMINT would go free.

"This is hard information," Preston was saying, "taken directly from Libyan government telephone conversations overheard by us. We know their fears are well-grounded," he added lightly, "but we also know Qaddafi's mistaken about who's after him."

Cardoni smirked. "It is so much better he thinks it's only the American navy. If he knew it was us he'd kill himself."

Ike tipped his Stetson to Cardoni before Preston continued. "Yesterday, he gave orders to step up coastal patrols, and to move four new batteries of ground-to-air missiles to Tripoli from Benghazi. The two Libyan fighter squadrons based here have also been upgraded to combat alert status."

"So the beach could be hairy." Ike said, "But their air force can't hurt us much. We ain't going to dogfight 'em."

Cardoni laughed and Preston said, "Maybe not, but something else came up that definitely affects us. Duff thinks they might be getting ready to move the hostages out of Libya."

Ike whistled. "What gave him that idea?"

"Malduum queried his people in Beirut about accommodating thirty guests if he flies them in."

"How'd we hear that?"

"Other SIGINT intercepts."

"When would he do it?"

"Probably within a few days."

Cardoni said, "I'd hate to hit that jail and find nobody."

"Don't even think it," Preston said. "So listen up, guys. It is essential you all know what, when and where everything will go down. Beginning today Sixth Fleet began conducting carrier operations less than fifty miles off the coast of Tripoli, and the Libyans are in a flat spin about it."

"Does that help us or hurt us?" Cardoni asked.

"Duff Elliot's idea is to force their thinking further in the direction of a military op, and the navy's cooperating. So while the Libyans are watching the skies we come out of the ground."

"And when do we do that?" Ike said.

"I don't know yet, because Elliot hasn't told me. All I can say is we'll move by the twentieth."

"Today's the seventeenth," Cardoni said. "Three days?"

"At the outside," Preston told him. "Probably sooner."

"Can we get it all together that quick?" Ike asked him.

"We can and we will. The two Russians are already here and we're meeting with them tonight. Everybody else is in place."

"Russians?" Pozzogallo said. "Communists?"

"I don't know what their politics are," Preston said, "but they are part of the team. They're Spetsnaz veterans, among the best qualified in the world for this kind of assignment."

"I wouldn't trust them," Prince Pozzogallo said.

"Do they speak English?" Cardoni asked.

"And Arabic," Preston replied.

"How do you know they won't give us away to the Libyans?" Pozzogallo said. "Russians have been helping Qaddafi for years."

"I don't know," Preston said with annoyance, "anymore than I know whether you would. But I have to take some chances."

"Has Jeballah been informed of the changes?" I asked.

"That will be up to you, Dahoud. Set up a meeting with him or his representative tonight or tomorrow. By then I should also know if we go tomorrow, the day after, or the day after that."

"Tomorrow?" Cardoni said.

"I doubt it," Preston replied. "But we've got to be ready if Duff gives the order, and we need Jeballah's full transport backup at the assigned places. I told Elliot we could do it on twenty-four hour's notice if everyone else was up to speed."

"We got a moon just past full," Ike said. "During the next three nights we'll have more light than we want on the beach."

"Live with it," Preston said harshly.

"Yeah, that and Qaddafi's patrols," Ike said.

"You'll be happy to know the PRC-three-nineteens arrived."

"What are three-nineteens?" Pozzogallo asked Preston.

"The latest and most reliable radio transmitter-receiver available," he replied. "It weighs about five pounds and is capable of microburst transmission. They're keyed to the same frequencies for everybody; the Hercules Talons, Wizards, the launches and the men on both sites."

"Well, shouldn't they be?" I said.

Ike laughed. "Ten years ago on Desert One, Davey, when we was trying to get them hostages out of Iran, there was three different kinds of radio and nobody could talk to one another. The Delta Force commander had to patch through Washington via satellite to talk to the helicopters only a few yards away."

"But that's incredible!" the old man said.

"That's why we were hired for this job," Preston said. "The President wants NMMFU's"

"Wants what?" Cardoni said.

"No More Military Fuck-Ups."

"I'll tell you this," Ike said. "We got a couple things in common with that Iran operation that worry me."

"Such as?" Cardoni asked.

"Unfamiliar conditions. Most of the guys coming in never been here before, don't know Libya, don't know each other."

"They're all handpicked," Preston said.

"I'd like it better if we'd rehearsed as a team. Elliot's got three different groups doing different things in different places. That could be a recipe for fuck-ups."

"Not if everyone does what he's supposed to do."

"You tell the Libyans that?" Ike said, and Cardoni laughed.

"Anyway, Ike, you knew the time frame was tight," Preston said. "And you're forgetting something else."

"What's that?"

"Everybody on our team is top drawer even if they haven't worked together before. Veterans all."

"I'm no veteran," I told him, and old Pozzogallo said, "That makes two of us."

"Dahoud, you'll always be with Ike or Cardoni, so not to worry. And Prince Pozzogallo will be back in Sicily."

"Not if you strike tomorrow," the old man grumbled.

Preston told Cardoni, "You and Hueblen get all those crates into the passage today. Prince Pozzogallo will show you where to put them."

"Ah-hah!" the old man said accusingly. "So I'm not finished! Squeeze the lemon to the last drop. I knew it!"

"Ike, you and I must test the homing devices," Preston continued. "I want them in place not later than tomorrow noon."

"How many are there?"

"Six for Tripoli, four for Garian and two for Sabratha. Cardoni and the Russians will take Tripoli. I'll do Sabratha, and Dahoud will go with Ike to the Whadi Sofeggin and Garian."

"Garian?" I said.

"First thing tomorrow morning," Preston said.

Ike shifted his long legs off the desk and flicked an imaginary dust mote from one mirror-bright boot. "The nickel-cad batteries on them homing devices are only reliable for about seventy-two hours," he said, "and you can't recharge 'em in the middle of nowhere."

"In three days," Preston told him, "we'll be a thousand miles from here. But first . . . pay attention, gentlemen."

For the next two hours he lectured, showing us Pozzogallo's drawings of the passages and dungeons where we assumed the male hostages were being held. He reviewed what I had been told by Elliot in Ghadames and said they now had satellite confirmation of the hostage presence in the Garian caves.

Americans love code names and they had called the hostage rescue operation "Big Stick". Ike explained to me that it came from one of the Roosevelt presidents who believed in showing force to small upstart nations like Libya.

Whichever night we went in, the schedule would be the same. Thanks to satellite photographs of Garian the team knew which of the troglodyte holes was being used.

One of the Hercules Talons would meanwhile be jamming radar and generally sowing confusion in the skies, and the navy carrier force would have planes continually in the air off the coast during the assault on the Tripoli fortress.

"People will try to stop you," Pozzogallo said reasonably.

"We will close the Karamanli passage behind us when we exit the prison," Preston said, indicating the exact place on one of the drawings. "We'll also place delayed charges in other parts of the Castle to keep them off balance.

Ike was sucking noisily on one of his "mints." "How long will we be inside the place where the hostages are?"

"Under ten minutes if we're on schedule," Preston said.

"Okay, so we're inside by ten and out by ten-fifteen," Ike said. "Then we bring the people through the passage . . ."

"Back up a little," Preston said. "As soon as Seaforce is ashore, the entrance will be resealed and other delayed charges set in shot holes Hueblen has already drilled in the rock."

"To blow what?" Cardoni asked.

"To let the sea flood the passages after we're gone. Prince Pozzogallo has calculated the exact point to set them.

"Suppose he's mistaken," Cardoni said.

"He won't be." Preston said.

"You mean everything depends on that old man's memory?"

"Look, Philipe," Preston told him, "this whole operation balances on the head of a pin. The old man's memory. His calculations. Our intelligence. The success of a hundred machines and electronic aids. Our weapons and our willingness to take a chance. If we wait until every contingency is covered, the hostages will die of old age."

"I hope he's right," Cardoni muttered.

"I'm right," Pozzogallo grumbled.

Preston said, "Seaforce will be led by Horst Halder, former captain in SSG 9 of the German Border Guard, who was with us in Ghadames. The rest of the group is comprised of five Brits, four Americans, two Egyptians and four Germans." As Preston spoke I recalled those Germans, and especially the tatooed giant with the steel teeth.

"Between you, Davey and me," Ike said, "and Hueblen, Cardoni and the Russians, that makes twenty-three on this end."

"Correct," Preston replied.

"Seems like an awful lot of bodies for what we're going to do," Ike said. "We'll be falling all over each other."

"Remember Phase Two," Preston said. "We're also hoping to take Malduum out once and for all."

Ike laughed. "In that case it don't seem like half enough. Davey says he's a walking machine gun nest. Takes an AK-47 to bed with him."

"When he's home," I said.

"What do you mean?" Preston asked me.

"What guarantee do you have he's going to be at home?"

"We have you," Preston said.

"Me?"

"You're going to set him up."

"I have no control over Malduum!"

"Your Austrian girlfriend turned up here yesterday."

"What does she have to do with Malduum?" I was surprised that Preston even knew about Karen at all, let alone that she was in Tripoli. Then I remembered that Dick Diamond had been in touch with her, so that was how he found out. But I could not imagine what her presence had to do with Malduum or my "setting him up", as Preston so quaintly put it.

"She's travelling with a man named Hans Christian Krebbs."

I waited. Where did Hanzi figure in Preston's plans?

"Hans Christian Krebbs is made to order, a gift from heaven," Preston said. "He once was runner-up for Mister Universe. He's a big time male model and also appeared in a couple of films."

"I don't see what that has to do with Malduum," I said.

"Khalil Malduum likes boys. Right?"

"How should I know, Alan? I never asked about his . . ."

"He likes boys and he likes men even better. And now you have access to Mr. Hans Universe, the glamorous movie queen . . ."

"I've met him but . . ."

". . . whom you will introduce to terrorist leader Malduum as soon as possible, hopefully today."

"There's still no guarantee . . ."

"Let love take its course, Dahoud, and we'll do the rest."

"Suppose . . . ?"

"Just do it," Preston said.

<>

XXXVI

▷ I think of Vienna whenever I am happy, and that's what I was thinking of as I sipped steaming sweet tea on Khalil Malduum's terrace. The late afternoon sun was warm because the garden is sheltered from wind by a high cement wall and a row of acacias. Two bored young UPARF guards in combat fatigues lounged near the water's edge, listening to Egyptian music on a small transistor radio.

Malduum had sent for me shortly after Preston's briefing broke up that afternoon, and now I waited to find out what he wanted. Not that it mattered. Karen should have landed in Rome by then and now there was nothing further to keep me in Libya.

As soon as I had seen Malduum, I would pass by the bank to delete the last transfer from the computer records, then head for the Tunisian border, leaving behind car, clothes, job, wife and Arab identity forever. The sense of relief was enormous.

In this frame of mind I sat woolgathering, as they say, gazing at the azure sea but thinking of food and Vienna and Carême. In a drab and dangerous world anything rich, safe and satisfying should be preserved at all costs. The French understand this. So do some Chinese, a few Hungarians, and the Viennese.

That is why I chose Vienna as the place I wished to settle. It is clean and cultured without being stuffy; old and staid, yet young at heart, a friendly city which welcomes strangers with just enough snobbish reserve to make them feel special.

It is also a gourmet's delight, a city of discriminating restaurants and a paradise for those, like me, who fancy sweets.

Karen would arrive in Vienna in time for tea if she made the right connection. As I gazed serenely at the blue winter glaze of the Mediterranean, my mind saw Vienna instead, perhaps with a light snow falling, people's breath in the cold air, oven warmth fogging the windows of Demal's Café-Konditorei, that enticing den of sweet debauchery.

I recalled the incredible aromas of *tortes* and *kuchens* and *strudels* that challenge the nerve of the toughest weight watcher. I daydreamed of currants and apples rolled in flaky crust, of rum-flavored truffles on pink iced chocolate cakes. Of raspberry tarts with poppyseeds and cream, and the famous Sacher *torte* of the Hotel Imperial! I like to think that if Carême lived today, he would forsake smoggy, sprawling Paris for warm and intimate Vienna. Ah, Carême! A man who drew inspiration from etchings in the *Bibliothèque National* and then created in his kitchens an Acropolis of marzipan marble or a Colosseum of chocolate fondue! He had that rarest of all gifts, the ability to transform food into art, and died at fifty, burnt out by the flame of his genius. Talleyrand told Napoleon, "He taught us how to eat!"

In his five-volume work *L'Art de la Cuisine au XIX Siècle* Carême listed 186 French sauces and 103 foreign ones he considered acceptable in the kitchen, and modern Viennese cooks know how to prepare most of them.

Like a bird watcher who records all the species he sights, I have noted in my private culinary notebook forty-one of these sauces that I have tried. This is barely scratching the surface, but having spent most of my time in countries not exactly famous for their cuisine, I would call it a respectable list. The pleasure I get from it is knowing I still have 248 sauces to go.

I sat up, suddenly remembering that Jock Pringle had borrowed the bloody notebook for the leek recipe, and I wanted it back before I left. I reached for the cordless telephone Malduum kept on the terrace and dialled the Mabrouk Airline hanger. Mustafa, the Libyan mechanic, came on the line.

"Hello, is Jock there?"

"No, who's this?"

"Beida."

"He's in jail."

"What!"

"Nagy's men took him away this morning."

I was shocked, but not really surprised. Jock had driven the little bastard round the bend by refusing to acknowledge his authority and by publicly humiliating him. If there was one thing Nagy would not tolerate it was lack of respect.

"Does Jeballah know?"

"Not yet, but when he finds out he'll fix it."

"How?"

"He'll send Mahmud, I guess. Mahmud can fix anything."

Indeed. No one was safe from Aboubakir Jeballah's private body-guard once the old man gave the order. If Nagy did not tremble in fear of old Aboubakir, it was because he was either ignorant or foolhardy. Mahmud would offer Nagy one simple option. Release Jock Pringle immediately or die.

Najeeb Hassan joined me saying, "Khalil will see you soon, Beida. He is anxious to talk but he has been up to here"—he touched his chin—"in policy discussions. Things are moving fast."

"Do you know what he wants?"

He shook his head. "Praise Allah for the new Zionists," he said, and for a moment I thought I had misheard him. "They sentenced a rabbi to only five months in jail for murdering an Arab shop-keeper! World opinion is outraged!"

Somehow I doubted the world cared much one way or the other, but the Israelis were becoming increasingly unpopular because of their harsh treatment of people involved in the *intifada*.

"That's not all," Najeeb proclaimed. "The Swedes have con-demned the Zionist thugs for killing our children. In the last year the bastards murdered seventy-four kids under fourteen!"

What he said was true and it saddened me. According to a Swed-ish relief agency more than a hundred and fifty Palestinian children had been killed by gunfire, beatings, tear gas, and other causes at the hands of Israeli soldiers since the uprising began, half of them within the year.

Every day there were new tales of gratuitous beatings and system-atic arrests. One pair of Israeli soldiers were given only the lightest suspended sentence for torturing an eleven-year-old child and put-ting a cigarette out on his back. All of this delighted Najeeb Hassan but he wished the numbers were greater. "Killing our children puts the world on our side!"

Mad as a hatter, of course, and like Malduum, completely unable to see his own crimes in the same perspective.

Palestinian terrorists had been rightly condemned by the press and politicians for years, but the Israelis had only recently come in for serious criticism by resorting to indiscriminate terror tactics to quell the *intifada*. This generation of soldiers seemed to be leaving their principles at home when they fought Arab kids, and the list of Palestinian martyrs grew daily.

"I'll tell you something in confidence, Beida, but don't mention it to Khalil unless he tells you himself." He took me by the shoulder and hissed into my ear even though there was no one within hearing. "We're moving the American Zionists to Lebanon."

"All of them?"

He nodded.

"Why?"

He looked both ways and clutched my arm before he said, "The situation in Iraq has upset Qaddafi. After what happened there, the Libyans are afraid the Americans will attack Tripoli again."

"Moving the hostages won't stop them."

"That's what Khalil told Qaddafi."

"So?"

"Qaddafi wants them out anyway."

"When?"

"Soon. They will be put on a secret Libyan Airlines flight to Lebanon. He is worried it will make negotiations harder, so say nothing unless he brings it up."

"Naturally."

"Except for that, things are really going our way."

"I can see they are."

"Did you know he had a message from that scum Arafat!"

"Really?"

"Begging for a truce between them. Wanting Kahlil to throw in with him and that bunch of cowardly traitors. Can you believe that? Renounce our aims and seek a peaceful solution? Arafat's crazy. Full of blah-blah in the UN when the only language the Zionists understand is the one we speak!"

"What did Kahlil tell him?"

"Nothing. No answer. Kahlil should kill him."

"I heard he tried that and missed."

Najeeb spat on the flagstone terrace and shook his fist at the sea. "I will answer Arafat in London! I leave in a few days, Beida."

"Right. Your scholarship."

"I'm glad to go into action again," he said. "I hate it here. I hate these ignorant, soft-bellied, backward Libyans who think they are so superior because they have money."

"This time you'll have the publicity all to yourself."

The broad open smile he showed me would have been engaging if I had not been so well acquainted with the vicious killer behind it. Then I remembered that when I first saw him in the Athens airport I had assumed he was a carefree university student, never a career terrorist. His smile was good cover. Maybe in another time, another life, I could have been a friend wishing him luck as he left to take up a real scholarship in England. But here I was his enemy, and the best I could wish him was a slow and agonizing death.

A beeper sounded on the belt of one of the guards who called to me, "You can go in now, *Essayed* Beida!" I had already been frisked and checked with the usual thoroughness on my arrival, so now I passed up the few steps and entered Malduum's enormous living room without being stopped again.

He was standing near the panoramic window overlooking the sea, a hunched, wizened figure, dressed in khaki pants and a baggy sweatshirt which concealed the automatic pistol he always wore. A man and a woman sat listening to him. They were facing away from me, backlighted in silhouette by the outdoor glare from the window. My first thought as I crossed the room was that terrorists certainly live well. Malduum's villa was one of the largest and most luxurious along the shore.

My second thought when I saw the faces of his guests was what in God's name was Karen doing here with Hanzi!

My third thought was that if either one of them addressed me as David Perpignon, I was a dead man.

"Dahoud, darling!" Karen said, rushing to where I stood gaping at her. "How wonderful to see you after so long!"

As she swept into my arms and buried her head against my shoulder, she whispered, "It's all right. I'll explain later, Hanzi won't give you away, so don't worry."

"Well . . . !" was all I could stammer as Malduum gave us his most benevolent sneer and raised one hand in a kind of benediction.

"You wondered why I sent for you, Beida?" he said, putting his arm around my shoulder. "A nice surprise, no?"

I nodded dumbly.

"And you didn't even know she was in Libya," he said.

"No, I didn't," I replied truthfully.

Karen said, "This is Hans Christian Krebbs, darling." Hanzi smiled and shook hands as if for the first time.

"Hans is a famous German actor, Beida," Malduum said, his eyes roaming hungrily over Hanzi's body, sheathed now in skintight jeans and a shirt that showed his muscles to advantage.

"Oh, I'm not so famous," Hanzi said coyly.

I don't remember what I said, if anything. All I knew at that moment was that I would not be on my way to Tunisia that evening. Karen would explain in time, but for whatever reason she had unwittingly trapped me and herself in a no-win situation, as they say. A houseboy brought tea as Malduum talked. He said that he had been thinking about my suggestion to allow some publicity of the UPARF and decided it was a good idea. Then when he heard Karen had arrived to take photographs, he sent for her immediately, knowing she was a professional journalist he could trust absolutely because of her relationship with me.

"And imagine my great pleasure," he said to me, "when she introduced her handsome and distinguished friend."

I did not have to imagine it. Malduum had been practically drooling since I entered, exchanging little knowing glances with Hanzi, and it was obvious what they would be up to as soon as Karen and I got out of there. I thought of Preston's suggestion about putting them together and letting romance take its course. This would please him. When I finished my tea, Malduum drew me aside. "You are preoccupied, Beida, worried and nervous. It is written all over you. But you can relax. I have taken care of everything."

"I beg your pardon?"

"I am sending Bashir to Germany tomorrow. Your wife has expressed a desire to accompany him. Does that please you?"

"Munich?"

"Yes, Munich. Those fat, complacent Germans. Bashir will make their Christmas. Najeeb, too, is leaving. Did he tell you?"

I nodded.

"To spend the Christian holiday with the English." Malduum's mad eyes danced. "He has the perfect present." He squeezed my shoulder happily. "I have not forgotten you, Beida. In fact I have selected you for the most delicate task of all, one that requires all your talent and tact."

He let the suspense build while I tried to imagine how much tact I needed to bomb a restaurant or shoot somebody, because I was sure something like that was in his mind. But I was wrong.

"Qaddafi wets his bed worrying about the American bombers," he said, "and insists I move the Zionists out of Libya. In two days you will take them to Beirut. It is all arranged."

When I did not react, he asked, "Aren't you pleased?"

"So much has happened," I said, looking toward Karen.

"Go now. I have work to do, but tomorrow she can take her pictures and ask questions while you arrange your departure."

He beckoned Karen to join me and walked us both to the door before he turned back to Hanzi.

XXXVII

In the car, Karen said, "I'm sorry, David, I really am."

"Why did you do it?" I said.

"Hanzi and I were checking out this morning when Hassan came by to say Khalil would give me the interview."

"You mean you asked him for one?"

"I had already done that before talking to you. I didn't expect he'd agree and when he did, I didn't know where to reach you. But it will be all right, you'll see."

"You should have been on a plane out of here."

"David, it's only one day more. I promise I'll leave the day after tomorrow." She squeezed my arm affectionately as she spoke, excitement animating her voice. "Do you realize he hasn't been photographed since 1978?"

"You don't know what you've done, Karen."

"But he said it was you who convinced him to do this."

I had no answer for that. I did not remember why I might have suggested the idea, but I should have kept my big mouth shut.

"He has agreed to let me shoot at the training camp and anywhere in the villa. The guards, the garden, everything. And he's willing to videotape the interview. David, I'll make a hundred thousand dollars easily. For one day's work!"

"I'd have given you that just to take the plane."

"Don't be cross with me, please. I swear I'll leave the moment I finish."

My plans were coming unglued because of Karen, yet I saw no way of cutting loose. I was in love and still hoped we'd both live long enough to do something about it. And I couldn't be angry, damn it, because it was my fault she didn't know all the facts.

"Where are we going? I don't want to go to the hotel."

"Then wait for me at the Desal offices, because first I must pass by the bank." If I did nothing else that afternoon, I had to finish my computer work or they would be able to trace my last cash transfer to the Vienna account.

I parked near Castle Square and we walked in the direction of the Desal Building, taking the short cut through the old arcade beside the *suq*. A scratchy voice hailed me and I saw Prince Pozzogallo waving his floppy Panama hat in our direction. He was at a table in one of the tea shops and invited us to join him. It was as good a place as any to park Karen while I finished up at the bank, so I agreed, pulling out the chair for Karen to sit, and helping her with her cameras.

"Any word yet?" the old man asked me, but I shook my head. "They've been calling you from the bank," he said. "Very urgent. Overdraw your account, did you? Ha, ha, ha!" The old rogue took an immediate fancy to Karen and I knew she would not be bored. When I left them he was already plying her with questions about her various lenses, being something of an amateur photographer himself.

At the bank, Watanabe was in a state. Apparently they had been searching all over town for me since noontime. Today was Dahoud el Beida day, it seemed, for better or for worse. "Beida, only you can save my life," he said.

I wanted to tell him I was too busy trying to save my own, but one must remember one's manners with the Japanese. "Why? Who's trying to kill you?" I asked gruffly.

He looked at me, a frown of perplexity creasing his face. "Nobody, but what happened here is my fault. If you cannot fix it, I must die of shame."

"Nobody ever died of shame, Watanabe. It's just a figure of speech. You know that."

"In Japan people die of shame all the time. It is called *sepuku.*" He bowed his head. "But I accept my fate."

"Stop talking rubbish and tell me what's going on." We were in the computer section by then, and I noticed that all the consoles were shut down except the one Watanabe normally used, and that one had been rejecting virtually everything he fed into it. The problem, as it turned out, was simple. The solution, on the other hand, was a little more complex.

What Watanabe fortunately did not realize, was that I was the cause of the trouble. Two days before I had been in a rush and neglected to limit my instructions to cancel only the records of the Viennese transfers. As a result the computer had simply eliminated all transfer records for the day.

These involved about forty million dollars, and although the deposits themselves had been made normally, only the client's original order existed. When asked for a confirmation, the computer refused to give it. I told Watanabe to leave me alone in my office with my own console and I would solve the problem. I also told him to begin the paper chase, and reconstruct the previous day's transfers from the order slips. That would easily take him and his assistants a week.

"You mean it's okay?" he said, disbelieving.

"Not yet, but it will be. You can forget *sepuku.*"

In ten minutes I had eliminated any trace of the last Vienna transfer and could have left the bank. Instead I sat there thinking. I had Khalid Belqair's four hundred thousand plus another hundred in my Austrian savings, and a clear conscience. And . . . I had an hour to steal a lot more. My conscience did not trouble me because I would be taking it from pirates and terrorists, so how much of a crime was that?

Watanabe's panic gave me the idea. Instead of trying to cover my tracks, I would mix them with hundreds of others. I called up the transfer program on my terminal again, and asked the computer to incorporate the data base of the Bank of Libya's overseas clients. I then fed a series of random numbers into this mucky stew, essentially infecting the entire system of transfer instructions with the binary equivalent of a virus.

It was not what Preston and Duff Elliot had hoped for, in the sense of hurting Qaddafi or bankrupting the Libyan financial system. But it was pretty good on such short notice, and I wondered why I had not thought of it before.

What I had sown in the bank's mainframe memory, because of

the random numbers, would be a kind of stop-and-go electronic chaos. Every time the computer system was keyed in, which meant every working day, millions of Qaddafi's oil dollars would be automatically siphoned to assorted foreign bank accounts around the world. Most of the lucky recipients would wonder where the money came from, but few would ever send it back.

A trickle would go to my account in Austria as well, although it was impossible to say how much. But there would be a steady, irrecoverable drain on Libyan resources which only a team of experts or an entirely new computer data base and accounting system could repair.

When Watanabe entered, I smiled. At least these few precious moments of satisfaction had partially redeemed my day.

"Telephone, Beida." He held out the instrument.

It was an inspector from Captain Nagy's office calling to say the little man wished to see me urgently. He was away from headquarters at that moment, but his aide said he would expect me there no later than seven o'clock.

I reassured Watanabe a little longer, telling him in Japanese not to worry, then returned to the teashop in the *suq*. As I entered, I heard Karen laughing at something Pozzogallo had told her, and saw her snapping his picture.

The old man rose when I approached the table, and signaled the waiter to bring us tea. "Charming, lovely," he said to me. "How I envy you, Beida." He kissed Karen's fingertips and was gone.

"Such a wonderful old man," she sighed. "So funny and warm. They don't make them like that anymore."

"No. They make them mostly like me these days."

"That's where you are wrong. You, too, are an extraordinary man." Her eyes became sad. "Will you ever forgive me, David?"

"It's done, Karen. And my motto is 'don't look back.' "

"I would not even be here except for you," she said, "and now I've made trouble by not leaving when you told me to. But it can't be as bad as you think, my dear. Say it isn't, please?".

"Right now we have very little time," I said.

"Then we must make the most of it . . ."

Her brown eyes were flecked with green like chips of emerald and her hand was warm as she placed it over mine. My heart dissolved as surely as the sugar in my sticky tea.

"Then let's do it," we both said simultaneously.

"May I tell you something?" Her voice was soft and breathy.

"Anything at all."

"I feel great peace with you."

"But I'm really no different . . ."

"That's just it," Karen said, squeezing my hand. "You are different, and so unassuming about it. Do you know how rare it is to find a strong man who is gentle? An intelligent man who is also capable of action and great courage?"

"You embarrass me."

"Is there some quiet place beside my hotel where we can go to be alone?"

"Come."

I could feel my loins stir as we hurried through the crowded *suq*. Our Desal office would be quite deserted at that hour.

Suddenly she gave a start and clutched my arm. I jumped too, half-expecting Nagy or Preston to materialize from the nearby crowd. Then I laughed as the thought grazed my mind, inspired more by desperation than lust. But the sight that alarmed Karen was one of the tiny donkey carts which clot the traffic in every street and alley. This one had been so shamelessly overloaded with cement blocks that the thin traces of the cart had given way, causing the blocks to shift forward, half-burying the poor donkey and crushing its hind quarters. The owner, typically, was beating the mortally injured beast about the head for causing him trouble.

"How can that awful man be so cruel," Karen said, turning her head away from the scene, "when it was his fault that the cart collapsed?"

"Oh, Karen, my sweet! If I knew the answer to that, I could solve all the problems of the world."

There was not a soul in the building as I ushered her in and double-locked the doors. She laid her cameras on my desk and turned into my arms. I held her shoulders for an instant and then brought her to me slowly, our eyes locked in common understanding and mutual consent. Our lips pressed together in a kiss as filled with hunger as it was with tenderness. Unlike Solange who was randy and indiscriminate, and never let love intrude upon her taste for sex, Karen's passion emerged as pure as the girl herself. She was as much in need of warmth and gentleness as I. I did not question the miracle of her interest in me. I was too intent on losing myself in the sweet rapture of her embrace, running my hands over every line and curve within reach as we moved to the long sofa beside my desk. Her small, knowing fingers were already exploring the bulge in my trousers as I lifted her skirts.

No descriptive powers of mine could ever limn my depth of feeling for her at that moment, or the softness of her body as we came together. The quickened pace of her breathing, the lubricity of her pudenda, and her small yelps of pure joy all filled me with pleasure as I pinned her to the cushions.

I have made love to women of many shapes and sizes, widths, thicknesses, and textures. But Karen was in a class apart. As we still lay thrusting and pushing, locked in love's last desperate spasms, I said, "Allah be merciful!"

"Oh, my prince," she sighed. "How well you know my needs."

"And you, mine."

She sat up suddenly saying, "Don't you feel it? The room? The past?" She rose gracefully, trailing her fingers over my chest, stunning in her nakedness, tilting her head as if she heard some secret music. She crossed the room and ran her hand lightly over the old fluted wooden door frame. "Wicked sheiks and nubile slave girls," she said, striking a seductive pose.

"You've been listening to too many tales of Prince Pozzogallo's thousand and one nights."

She laughed softly. "He's such a romantic old darling."

"According to him," I told her, "this room was, in fact, the boudoir of a Karamanli princess."

"I knew it! I have this special sensibility about places and the past. I can feel them on my skin as other people feel hot or cold. I sense things that happened years before I was born."

I did not say so, but the past is a trap for people like me whose histories are always in flux. Luckily, I am an orderly liar and can manage more than one autobiography at a time.

"It is so strange and mysterious," she said softly, "but love thrives on mystery, does it not?"

"How wise you are," I said.

"Not wise," she said, "just knowing, like all women." She returned to me and let me draw her down again to the sofa.

"*Habibi . . .*" I said.

"What does that mean?"

"Darling."

"Oh, yes, *habibi!*"

"You have just had your first lesson in Arabic," I teased.

"And from such a splendid professor." She ran her tongue around my ear. "Will you give me lessons like this often?"

"As often as you like, my little *Apfelkuchen.*" We fondled each other, nibbling, licking, sucking and kissing until we fused again in another violent, shuddering embrace. I am not a slave to sex, but I try to be its obedient servant. I could have whiled away the rest of that day with Karen easily enough, but people were not about to leave us in peace.

The telephone rang, telling me the world was closing in. "I must go," I said, rising and groping around in the dim shadows for my scattered clothes.

"You'll forgive me?"

I kissed her lightly. "There's nothing to forgive."

Whoever was calling wouldn't give up. The ringing went on and on. *"Addio,* my sweet," I said. *"Bis sala'am, habibi."*

"Oh, David! Is that Arabic for goodbye?" She flung herself one last time into my arms as I turned to pick up the receiver, whispering in her ear, "Only farewell, my darling."

"Beida!" Nagy snarled over the wire. "Is that you!"

"Speaking."

"You were supposed to be in my office an hour ago!"

I looked at my watch and saw it was past seven. "Sorry. The bank had some accounting problems and I got tied up."

"Beida, we have had a major breakthrough."

"On what?"

"Preston is not the top agent in place as I suspected. There's a much bigger fish to fry!"

I thought, my God, he's got poor Jock Pringle shut up in jail and now he's trying to turn him into some kind of master spy.

"His code name is Humint," Nagy said. I wanted to laugh out loud, but when he added, "Also known as David Perpignon," I didn't laugh at all. "Name mean anything to you, Beida?"

Only my life, I thought.

"Beida! Did you hear me?"

"No, nothing," I said, trying to keep the sense of utter hopelessness from my voice.

XXXVIII

◇ Nagy's headquarters was in the oldest part of the castle where pale blue paint peeled from scabrous walls, rubbish littered the halls, and stacks of dog-eared files lay everywhere. A uniformed aide escorted me past bored police clerks trying to look busy pecking at typewriters or dialling telephones.

The man motioned me into Nagy's private office and announced "Sir! *Essayed* Dahoud el Beida to see you, sir!" After a clumsy about-face, he stomped out and left me to my fate.

To my great relief the meeting did not take long. Nagy was so anxious to have me out hunting the elusive agent Humint, a.k.a. David Perpignon, that he did not notice my nerves were shot or that I was on the verge of throwing up.

A specially built platform and an enormous desk gave him an eye-level advantage over anyone in the visitor's chair opposite. In effect, he shed his dwarfishness when he climbed up behind his desk and showed the world who was boss. An expensive computer stood idle in one corner of the room next to a dust covered telex machine. A high window opened on the street behind Castle Square, but most of the light came from some flyspecked fluorescent tubes flickering uncertainly in the ceiling.

"I've got the Englishman Pringle locked up," he said, "and I'm finally getting to the bottom of things. An international ring of saboteurs directed by Humint and tied to the Jeballah brothers."

"Jock Pringle told you that?"

"No, no. They never talk without persuasion."

"Then how do you know?"

"Prima facie. Pringle had their code book. The rest came from the others when we tossed their hotel rooms."

"The others?" I said, wondering who else he had arrested.

"We went through all their papers. Preston and his men."

"But sabotage? Of what?"

"The cyanide in the water, Beida, the poison!" He kept cocking and uncocking one of those cigarette lighter replicas of an automatic pistol and pointing it at me. "I've known what Preston was up to from the start, and now I've almost got him."

"Oh? What did you find?"

"They think they are so clever," he sighed. "Did you see all the crates of machinery his Desal Company recently imported?"

"Yes, I did."

"He and the German spent thousands in bribes to pass everything through the port without customs inspection." He gave a wheezy laugh and his ugly, pocked complexion reddened slightly with the effort of his humor. "He didn't know I had already given the order to let it all come in without being opened."

"But why?"

"I want to lull them, Beida. Fuel their unjustified self-confidence. Let them hang themselves."

"Well done," I muttered more to myself than to him, grateful I was not about to be arrested.

"All in a day's work. If I happen to be better at my job than anyone else," he said in a voice of self-congratulation, "that's everyone's good luck." He bobbed his huge head and his little raisin eyes glowed with satisfaction.

"It looks as if you've got him then," I said.

"Almost," he replied happily. "In a week or two. I'm in no hurry. They're not going anywhere."

"What did you find among their papers?"

"I'll show you! The key that ties it all together. Impressions on notepads of messages written by Preston, in code naturally, about Humint."

He took a paper from his desk and read from it. *"Gratinée? Béarnaise? Béchamel?* Do those names mean anything to you?"

"Oh, for God's sake!" I blurted.

"Exactly! And these? *Chantilly? Meunière? Soubise?"*

"Well, they're all French names for . . ."

"How about *Mornay? Fouquet? Escoffier?"*

"French as well, but . . ."

"But that is only half the story, isn't it!" His voice rose. *"Poivrade! Tapenade! Marinade!* What about them?"

I began again, "They too are French . . ."

"I know what they are! I want to know *where* they are now! None of these places exists on my map! Not a single one!" He was almost shouting at me by then. "I have checked them all and they are not there! So what conclusions do you draw?''

I could only shake my head in dumb disbelief, thanking my stars for his blundering ignorance and knowing at last that he must have got my name from my cooking journal.

"Always look beneath the surface, Beida, because nothing is as it seems!" His eyes glinted with imagined cunning. "In Ghadames that old devil Jeballah asked if I spoke French."

"I seem to recall that, yes . . ."

"I'll show him how good my French is before I'm finished! You didn't know they speak it in Canada, did you, Beida? No, of course you didn't. And what is Preston? A Canadian! Jeballah's radioman is a French. Also Jeballah keeps a villa in France. Pringle's code book is French. It all fits. Do you know why?"

"Why?"

"Because Humint is a French! That's what threw me off." He climbed down from his chair and waddled around the room like a mechanical toy, his stubby arms punctuating every remark.

"I don't understand," I said.

"You see, I was convinced Preston was the leader. Wrong. I was certain they were CIA. Wrong again. Even I make mistakes," he said with a self-deprecating sigh. "But the minute I had Humint's real name and nationality, it all came together."

"How did you ever make the connection? I mean between Humint and this What's-his-name who owned the . . . ah . . . code book?"

"The first lesson in counterespionage, Beida, is thoroughness. I studied the book in great detail and discovered who Humint was because he was careless."

"Careless how?" I asked, anxious to find out in order not to make the same mistake again.

But Nagy wasn't giving it away easily. "We've intercepted their radio," he cried triumphantly. "I am breathing down this Perpignon person's neck and I'll soon have a noose around it!"

"What do you want me to do?"

"Visit Pringle in his cell. Pretend to be his friend. Tell him I have enough to hang him so it is no use playing games."

"Is that all?"

"Draw him out. He must know who David Perpignon is."

"Aboubakir will make trouble if you hold Pringle."

"I am *mukhabarat!*" he insisted. "No one in Libya is exempt from my arrest order. Jeballah would not dare challenge it!"

I agreed with him there. Jeballah wouldn't challenge any silly arrest order. He would simply ignore it and send Mahmud to call on Nagy. If the tales of Mahmud's various murders and intimidations had escaped Nagy's notice or failed to impress him, then that would be unfortunate. But I assumed I didn't have to worry much about Jock languishing long in prison.

Nagy said, "Tell Pringle he will be hanged in Castle Square next week unless he cooperates. He knows we have his code book and my experts will break it sooner or later. Once that happens I don't need him. But if he gives me David Perpignon now, I'll let him go. He may leave the country tomorrow."

"I doubt he'll tell me the name," I said.

"It is not a matter of life and death. Except for the Englishman." He chuckled at the thought. "The French owe me a favor for the release of those hostages Malduum was holding, so I also asked them for a description of this Perpignon fellow."

"But how would they know what he looks like?"

"If Perpignon holds a French passport, the French have his picture, and I . . . will have him!"

"Doesn't that take time?" I asked, knowing the Sûreté could find it and fax it to him in a couple of days.

"Only our public hangings take time, Beida. You have seen how painful and long drawn out they are. Describe them for Pringle. Convince him he will hang if he does not come clean."

One of Nagy's aides escorted me out of the main bay and down a broad flight of stone stairs to a barred gate. A small iron door in the gate was opened by a guard from inside, and I had to duck to pass through it. The sound of scraping bolts and crashing doors echoed around me as I was passed into the Castle prison.

Beyond the last guard was another iron door and beyond that more guards who frisked me and made me sign in to see Jock Pringle. Then down another flight of steps and a long, dimly lit passage with cells on both sides.

I could feel the eyes of silent prisoners follow me until the guard paused before one of the cells. He opened the door with a heavy key and motioned me inside. I was so paranoid by the time the door clanged shut behind me, that the idea even crossed my mind this was a trap or an elaborate joke on me.

"Christ, Beida, it's you!" Jock jumped up from the pallet which was the only furnishing in the cell beside a bucket. "Thanks for coming. Are they letting me go?"

"Not yet. How are you doing?"

"Under the circumstances, couldn't be better," Jock said. "But the circumstances leave a lot to be desired. I could do with a drink, if you happen to have one somewhere about."

"Sorry."

"I didn't really expect it. Jeballah send you?"

I told him who sent me.

"That little bugger had his men drag me out of bed this morning, but he never showed his ugly face. Afraid I'd smash it in probably." I noticed Jock had a black eye and several other bruises around his neck and jaw. "It's hard to believe he's so bloody stupid," he said. "If Mahmud comes after him, he's history. What is it I'm supposed to have done anyway?"

"Jock, Nagy's convinced that Preston and Jeballah are engaged in a conspiracy to poison Libya's drinking water."

Jock laughed. "That does sound like something he'd come up with, the bloody twit!"

"He also found my sauce book with the recipes and notes among your things when they arrested you."

"Sorry about that. I meant to get it back to you."

"But he thinks it's a code book."

"You're joking!" When I shook my head, Jock's laughter filled the drafty cell. "Oh, that's wonderful! That's bloody lovely, that is. Code book, indeed! That'll take him the rest of the way round the bend. He'll spend his declining years in a Libyan boobyhatch trying to break the code. Imagine the silly little bastard looking for the secret message in your leek *fondue?*"

"Nagy believes you're involved with a ring of saboteurs led by a secret French agent."

"That's rich!" Jock said. "Scarlet bloody Pimpernel!"

"Jock, this is serious. He claims he figured out the name of the agent from something written in the sauce book."

"What was the name?"

"David Perpignon."

"He didn't have to figure out damn-all. David Perpignon's name is scrawled across the title page."

"I mean how did he make the connection between Perpignon and

Humint, a code term Preston used in his radio messages?"

"That I couldn't tell you, old boy. Is this Perpignon a friend of yours? Is that why you're so worried about him?"

"Jock, Perpignon is me."

"Come again?"

Very briefly I explained the circumstances of my background, and pointed out that my life depended on keeping the whole business a secret. "Not even my wife knows," I told him.

"Nagy won't find out from me, old boy, but I have a feeling the sooner you put Libya behind you the better. I've been thinking of doing it myself, in fact. Beautiful country. Charming people. But everything has its season."

"I intend to get out as soon as I can."

"If I were you," he said cautiously, "I'd make it sooner."

"Do you know something I don't?"

"No, but if that mucky little midget has discovered your real name, it's only a matter of time before he puts the right face to it. Then Jeballah might or might not intervene, depending on how valuable he considers you."

"We're friends."

"Don't put it to the test, old boy. He's looking at this whole Preston project with a very jaundiced eye at the moment. Nice piece of change in it, but the risk factor's high."

"He's not thinking of pulling out, is he?"

"There's too much money involved to do that, but I'd never try to second-guess the old cock."

"Jock, can I do anything for you?"

"Very kind of you to offer, but Jeballah's in town at the moment so he'll have me out of here by morning. You take care of yourself and mind what I said." As I was leaving, he added, "By the way, there's talk they're going to be moving those poor bloody Yanks out of here soon."

"Thanks, Jock. I already heard."

"And Beida?"

"Yes."

"About your braised leek *fondue* . . ."

I waited.

"Don't misunderstand me, but I believe I improved on it by adding fenugreek and a little more cream at the end."

XXXIX

⬦ Nagy was no longer in his office when I returned, so I left him a note saying my meeting with Jock yielded nothing, and I was convinced he was only an innocent bystander. To whet his appetite I said I would follow up on some other suspicions I had concerning the real identity of Humint and get back to him.

I was covered at the bank, but my luck would run out the instant Nagy got my passport photo from the French. That should take two days at least, but I could not count on it. Karen and I had to flee *now*. She would certainly abandon the interview with Malduum and come with me when I told her everything.

First I hurried back to the Desal Building. I had been as guilty as Jock Pringle or Preston of underestimating Nagy until now. But I had to accept the fact that if he was searching hotel rooms and listening to clandestine radio transmissions, it was only a matter of hours before he started to ransack the Desal headquarters. Apart from warning Preston, I wanted to make sure nothing else was lying around that might incriminate me.

Preston was with two men I had never seen before, and I did an immediate about-face. But before I could escape he saw me.

"Dahoud, come in, come in!"

"Alan, I must see you alone."

Preston excused himself and stepped into the outer office with me. "I've been trying to reach you," he said. "What time do we meet with Jeballah this evening?"

"I've got to confirm," I lied, "but it's no problem. At the moment Jeballah's probably trying to spring Pringle."

"What happened to him?"

"He was arrested."

"For what?"

"Nothing much really. He ridiculed Nagy and the little man's showing his power. Jeballah will sort it out. But that's not the problem. Did you know Nagy searched your hotel rooms today?"

"Maxwell said he thought someone had been through our things, but there was nothing to find."

"According to Nagy there was. Notes, or impressions on a pad, he said. He's also monitoring your radio transmissions."

"Impossible!"

"I told you never to sell him short. He picked up on Humint as a code name for David Perpignon."

"You mean he knows about you?"

"Not yet. Fortunately he is still obsessed with the idea that you are planning to poison his drinking water."

As usual, Nagy's bizarre misinterpretation of the technical manuals made Preston smile. "Then what's to worry about?"

"Alan, listen to me! He's more dangerous than ever right now. He's even beginning to admit his mistakes."

"It doesn't matter, Dahoud."

"It matters to *me*, damn it! It's my life."

"Relax. The waiting is over. Come in and meet our Russian friends and I'll bring you up to date." He nudged me ahead of him into the office. "Dahoud this is Pietr," indicating a mustachioed giant taller than Ike Maxwell and at least a hundred pounds heavier, with a deep bass voice that seemed to come out of his boots.

"So you are the famous el Beida," Pietr said.

"And this is Boris," Preston said, pointing to the other one, a ferret-faced, wiry little man with no hair and only three fingers on his right hand.

Pietr and Boris, of course, were the two Russians Duff Elliot had promised, and they looked like what they were; men who had spent their lives making war. Pietr was hairy and muscled all over, coarse-featured and virile, the kind of supermacho who probably has testosterone for blood and makes normal men seem effeminate. Preston immediately dubbed him "Pietr the Great."

Boris, on the other hand, was thin and lithe as a monkey, with quick, intelligent eyes and a handshake like a clawhammer. Both men had seen Spetsnaz service with the Soviet Army in Ethiopia and Afghanistan, and had previously served in Libya as military advisers, so they knew their way around.

"Are you afraid he might try to arrest us tomorrow?"

"He won't move that fast. It will take him at least a couple of days to figure out the Humint connection."

"Then we're safe."

"I'm not. The instant he knows who I am, I'm dead."

"By the time he finds out it will be too late."

"For who? Me?"

"We're taking those people out tomorrow, Dahoud."

"But the beacons aren't in place. Suppose . . ."

"They will be."

"What if Jeballah isn't ready?"

"Then we'll hijack transport at the site."

"But . . ."

"Everything is go, Dahoud." He looked at his watch and smiled at the two Russians. "The countdown began when I got Duff's signal an hour ago. Now why don't you call Jeballah? We've got a lot to do before tonight."

As I turned away from them to go to the telephone, Pietr put his huge hand on my shoulder. "Is great fun, boy, fight all together now save ladies from bad Arab mens."

"Is great fun," I agreed, thinking if his Arabic was as bizarre as his English, we had a serious communication problem.

I rang the hotel first and asked for Karen's room. It was early evening but there was no answer and that bothered me. Hanzi was certain to be spending the night with Malduum, so where was Karen? A foreign woman alone in Tripoli has a limited choice of activities, and once the shops close, she is best advised to stay in her hotel. As soon as I could get away from Preston, I would go there and tell her what had happened. Then, God willing, we would streak for the Tunisian border.

When I called Jeballah's farm, Fadlalah answered. Aboubakir had not yet returned but if Preston wished to come after ten, he said, his brother was sure to be there.

"Any news of Pringle?" I asked him.

"My brother does not like such business," Fadlalah said.

"That's what I told Nagy."

"Such business is very naughty, etcetera," Fadlalah said.

"My feelings exactly."

"Such business offends my brother's spleen and saddens his heart," Fadlalah said, "It is business for Mahmud only."

"God bless Mahmud, etcetera," I said.

Preston explained that Hueblen and Cardoni would work late that night in the Karamanli passage with the Russians, preparing everything for Operation "Big Stick". Day-Glo tapes had to be laid down so the commandos could find their way, and gasoline pressure lamps left at critical junctions. Explosive charges also had to be set in place to blast into the prison, and to close the walls behind them once they got the hostages out.

I told Preston I would pick him up around ten-thirty to meet with Jeballah. He suggested I leave my humble Volkswagen and use his big Mercedes. That, of course, gave me another idea.

The Mercedes was sleek and powerful, and could outrun anything on the road. Unlike the Volkswagen, it was also sturdy enough to crash a road barrier if necessary.

The Tunisian frontier lay one hundred and seventy-two kilometers from the Desal Building. I could collect Karen and explain things to her on the way. In less than two hours we would be across the border and free. I felt bad about deserting Ike, but I also told myself that any friend who threatened to kill me had no right to call upon my loyalty. Of course, I was sorry for the hostages, too, but I was not so foolish as to think any action of mine could help them. I hoped Preston's mad scheme succeeded, but there were too many ifs to give it a serious chance.

Using the ancient Karamanli passage to reach the prisoners certainly favored the operation, and gave them the advantage of surprise. But virtually everything else was against them in spite of all their hi-tech toys. If they were lucky, they would be taken prisoner and eventually ransomed with the others. But more likely they would die like dogs in a hail of lead, or drown, or be blown to bits by one of Qaddafi's rockets, taking the unfortunate hostages with them.

Neither Preston nor Ike nor any of them could know how many fears compete for the attention of a man like me. Real or imaginary, it didn't matter. Six of one or dozens of the other, as they say. I feared Malduum, Nagy, Ike and even old Prince Pozzogallo conspiring with all those dead Karamanlis to get me from the grave. I am not a coward, but neither am I a fool. I was a corpse if I set foot inside that absurd Karamanli passage.

None of them could comprehend the priceless value I placed upon my own personal survival. It wasn't just common sense. David Perpignon was all I had. To keep him alive, I had to stay cool, think clearly, and move fast while they were each making their separate errors of judgement.

The temperature had dropped in the short time I was inside with Preston, and now a cold blustery wind blew off the sea. I took the Mercedes and drove slowly along the Sciara Giaddat toward the Uaddan Hotel, putting my thoughts in order, rehearsing exactly what I would say to Karen. I could not afford to pull any punches. I had to get her in the car and move. That way if anyone did come looking for either of us, they would think we had simply gone off somewhere to be alone, as lovers will. It was now eight o'clock and Preston wouldn't miss me until I failed to show at ten-thirty. By that time we'd be beyond everybody's reach.

Except that Karen was not there when I arrived and I had no idea where she could have gone. I was about to search the nearby tea shops and coffee houses when I spotted one of Malduum's young Palestinian guards hanging around the lobby. "Your friend has gone out, el Beida," he said. "She will not return until very late."

"Gone where?"

"To watch our night exercises at the Zavia training camp. Khalil suggested she could photograph them."

"Did he go with her?"

The boy smiled and shook his head. "He's much too busy tonight. Najeeb Hassan accompanied her."

Zavia! On the way to the Tunisian border.

"Beida, excuse me, could I ask a favor?"

"What is it?" My mind was running a mile a minute.

"I have never been to Beirut."

"You're lucky."

"But my sister is there, married to Osmar Farras who serves on the Hezbollah council. My name is Hussein Khabazy."

"Look, I'm in a hurry. What is it you want?"

"To go to Beirut."

"Ask Khalil, not me."

"But he has named you in charge of taking prisoners. If you speak up for me to go as a guard I could see my sister."

I said I would think about it, and went to sit behind the wheel of the car trying to make up my mind what to do next. I could wait for Karen to return in the early morning hours or I could leave now, collect her in Zavia and make a dash for it. Every instinct warned me to leave now.

Clothes did not matter, I could go with what I had on. But my David Perpignon passport was vital, and that I kept with a few thousand dollars cash in a secret place at home, a place not even Solange would ever have thought to look.

Ike Maxwell taught me that trick. "Most people think toilet bowls and bidets are cemented down," he once confided, "but there's only some bolts and a little grouting where the edges meet the floor. They're easy to move and they got big hollow spaces underneath, better than a safe-deposit box for anything small and valuable you don't need every day."

I put the Mercedes in gear and started for my place. If Solange was there it didn't make any difference. I needed three minutes in the bathroom with the door locked and I'd be gone.

The apartment was lit up like a penny arcade when I arrived, and the thought crossed my mind that she might be giving a party, although I couldn't imagine why or for whom. I let myself in through the kitchen and called, "Solange?", but no one answered, not even the dog. Through the dining room to the hall to our bedroom. All the lights turned on, the bedroom a mess, her drawers open and her lingerie and cosmetics missing. The closet door stood open too, and her winter dresses were gone.

At first I thought there had been a robbery, but then I saw her luggage was not on its usual shelf in the closet. Solange had blown the coop, as they say, taken a powder and her dog, and walked. I smiled and heaved a great sigh. Maybe my luck was changing after all.

I decided, as long as I was there, to throw a change of clothing into a small overnight bag anyway. That done I went into the bathroom and sat on the cold floor tiles where I began to unscrew the four bolts securing the bidet. As I was doing this I noticed that some of the grouting was gone, tiny bits of it powdered on the floor as if someone had tampered with my hiding place. But I immediately dismissed the idea. Solange would never have guessed my secret and it was probably just the sloppiness of the Tunisian houseboy who came in every day to clean. But when I got the last bolt out and slid the bidet off its base, there was no sign of the package I had left containing ten thousand dollars and David Perpignon's precious passport. My first crazy reaction was that I had been mistaken. I frantically started to loosen the bolts on the toilet bowl next to it, but stopped when I heard a sound behind me.

Standing in the open bathroom door was my friend Ike Maxwell. And in his hand, dangling between two fingers for me to see clearly, was David Perpignon's passport.

XL

◁▷ "Seems like everybody's in a hurry to go some place," Ike said. When he was sure I had seen the passport, he dropped it in his pocket, tossed me my packet of money, and withdrew to sit heavily on the sagging bed. I heard his voice as I slowly got to my feet and saw the haggard, desperate figure that was me in the bathroom mirror. "Your old lady was in such a hurry she even forgot her book," he called to me. "I been reading it while I was waiting for you."

"Look, Ike, I . . ."

"It's real interesting, Davey. 'The The-o-ree and Practice of Astral Projection'. You think that's what she's up to? Says here, 'Once mastered, astral projection technique can be used to escape from the physical body, move vast distances through space, penetrate solid matter, and experience strange encounters on the infinite inner planes.' "

"Ike, I can explain . . ."

"Or is that what you was up to?"

"Ike . . . ?"

"Davey, there's all kinds of stories. Long ones, short ones and tall ones. I think you're about to tell me a tall one."

"I wasn't going any . . ."

"Yes, you was, Davey."

"I think I need a drink."

Ike could not have been more polite. He produced a bottle of bourbon and some ice and a glass. My hand trembled so badly I could barely hold it, and I tossed the whiskey down in one gulp.

"Refill?"

I nodded. We still had not spoken about the matter at hand as he poured the bourbon. It must be like that before they walk you to the gas chamber or the gallows or pin the paper target over your heart. Always some friendly presence to lull you into a false sense of confidence when you're really falling apart. A reassuring hand to steady you when they say, "Time's up."

"Time's up, Davey," Ike said, looking at his watch. "We got to pick up Preston and go meet old Jeballah."

"Not until ten-thirty," I said. "I talked to Fadlalah."

"You want something to eat first?"

I shook my head. General anesthesia was what I wanted. Total oblivion. Then I remembered Prince Pozzogallo's awful formula and how well I felt after taking it.

"Where you going, Davey?"

"Just to get something." I brought back the bottle that looked like floor wax. "Here, you want some? It's called the Milk of the Four Peppers. Prince Pozzogallo's special drink to make you live a hundred years."

"I heard about it. Preston says it ain't peppers at all, but opium and hash mixed with a little jalapeña honey."

I took a swig and thought I would die. At that moment, in fact, I was sure my heart had stopped before it started up again and took on a whole new life. Ike was pounding me on the back while I gasped and coughed and shook, but once the initial paroxysm passed, I emerged on another level entirely. Between Ike's bourbon and the Milk of the Four Peppers I was a new man.

"You okay?" Ike said.

"Never better. I'm relaxed, confident, alert."

"You want to go easy on that stuff. It could addict you."

I laughed. "If you really cared about my health or your own, we wouldn't be sitting here having this conversation."

"We been all through that, Davey. It gets mighty damn tiresome trying to watch you all the time. But if I hold on to your passport from here on the problem's solved."

"It doesn't matter, Ike. I know when I'm licked."

"Wrong. You was licked the day you got hijacked. When Elliot started to put this bunch together, he said to me, 'If we only had an inside man,' and I said, 'You got one right here,' and showed him your picture in the papers. 'But he's one of the terrorists,' he said and I said, 'By Christian, Davey Perpi-non might be a lot of things, but he ain't no terrorist!' ''

Thanks to the Milk of the Four Peppers I was calm, almost amused as he told the story. "So I have you to thank," I said.

Ike shrugged with embarrassment. "You don't have to thank me, Davey. It was just a favor to a friend."

"You set me up."

"I just recommended you for the job is all."

"I already had a job."

"Not like this one. But I got to admit one thing. The reason I recommended you was selfish. I wanted you along because I knew Libya'd be real hairy and you always bring me luck."

"You're dumber than I thought."

"It's true Davey."

"You're a bloody imbecile."

"There's nobody I'd rather work a job with than you."

"Inside man! If you'd kept your mouth shut, Elliot never would have included me. All you're doing is getting me killed."

Ike looked genuinely contrite for a few seconds. His brow wrinkled and his whole expression deepened into a worried frown.

"After Cannes, why on earth would you want to work with somebody like me again anyway? I left you on the beach, you dumb son of a bitch. Don't you know that? I saw you shooting it out with the cops and took off like a rabbit! I ditched you!"

The frown passed like a cloud and the sun broke through in his sudden smile. "By Christian, that's just what I mean, Davey! You did the only smart thing that night. When you thought I was finished, you shifted for yourself. I admire that."

There is no defense against faith based on such monumental ignorance. No attack either. Hadn't he ever heard of cowardice? How could this great honest hulk really respect me for leaving him in the lurch? I was as appalled by his innocence as I was intimidated by his determination to keep me around.

I went into the living room, turned down the lights and stood looking out the window at the Mercedes parked in the drive. Freedom. I could try a run for the frontier without the passport. But I had no guaranty the Tunisians wouldn't send me back the minute the Libyans sounded the alarm. And there was the problem of Karen. Any plan had to include her.

I turned away from the window and contemplated my situation with equanimity. I sat in one of the sofas and closed my eyes. No sight, no touch, no taste, no smell; this then would be death. No music, no food, no sex. Dispatched before my time by rope or bullet into the eternal silence from whence I came. Would it hurt? Probably, but it no longer seemed important. A tear rolled over my fingers as I pressed them against my cheeks to feel the still living flesh. I was sorry about Dahoud el Beida, but he had always taken his chances and never looked back. It was my grief over that poor, innocent bastard David Perpignon that was insupportable.

"Ready, Davey?"

"What?"

"You dozed off there. It's nearly ten-thirty."

The wind had picked up some more by the time we left, and I put the heater on in the car. Preston was waiting anxiously when we picked him up. Hueblen, Cardoni and the Russians were at work inside the passage, he said, while old Prince Pozzogallo remained on guard in the Desal offices.

Ike drove while Preston tuned in some Arab music on the stereo and I sank into the upholstered comfort of the rear seat.

After passing through Garden City, an expensive, tree-lined suburb built by the Italians and now occupied by Libyan government bureaucrats, we turned onto the Homs road and headed for the outskirts of Tripoli. Grim rows of newly-built villas and apartment blocks marked the city limits, and beyond them clusters of squalid, dusty, tin-roofed huts occupied by the Libyan poor. These shanty towns were a sharp reminder of how Qaddafi's social revolution had paid the cost of his military ambitions in spite of Libya's oil billions.

The armed forces were everywhere that evening, confirming what Elliot had said about their rising fear of an American attack. We passed a long convoy of army trucks parked by the roadside, and every few hundred meters sinister-looking, mobile antiaircraft missile batteries surrounded by accordion barbed wire. I hoped Preston was taking it all in.

At one base beyond the Tarhuna gate a squadron of tanks ground across the highway in a great cloud of dust while civilian traffic was redirected by Qaddafi's green-uniformed militia. Made up primarily of high school and college students who owe their personal allegiance to the Libyan dictator, they were originally trained by Soviet advisers and all carried AK-47 assault rifles.

Beyond the university I directed Ike to a little-used dirt road leading past weed-choked pastures where goats and camels grazed. The farms which once had flourished under Italian hands were long abandoned or else had shrunk to grubby little subsistence patches of squash and chick peas. The few citrus groves still standing were dry and dead from lack of water, with here and there the glow of a charcoal fire where Libyan peasants squatted along the old, unused irrigation ditches brewing their evening tea.

Neat rows of gnarled, centuries-old olive trees bowed to the swift encroaching desert dunes. In its days as an Italian colony, Libya was agriculturally self-sufficient, and actually exported olive oil, fruit and dates to world markets. Since petroleum and Qaddafi, however, the country imports all its food.

After another four or five kilometers we reached the modest stone gate of Jeballah's farm.

"You sure this is it?" Preston asked as we parked. "It doesn't look as if anything's happened around here in years."

"Jeballah keeps it that way on purpose. No point in attracting unnecessary attention."

"Just like him," Ike agreed. "Old Aboo-baker never was a showoff except maybe with the ladies in France." I knocked, but when no one appeared, I tried the front door and found it unlocked.

For an instant after I entered I thought the building was burning, but it was only a cook fire in the middle of the main salon. The trapped smoke from the charcoal burned my eyes.

I wandered through the dimly lighted house, finding no one until I arrived at the rear patio off the kitchen. There, two women were preparing couscous, but they did not even look up. A lamb bleated on a tether while three or four psittacotic chickens pecked at gravel near the back door.

At the far end of the patio a storm lantern shed a flickering white light over a turbaned figure squatting at a grindstone. He put aside the huge knife he was sharpening and rose to ask my business, padding toward us on bare feet horny with calluses, a tattered army coat flaring behind him like a royal cape.

He was part Tibu like Jeballah, very tall, ancient and weathered, his face wrinkled as a walnut. *"Sabaah al-khair, Essayed,"* he said, touching his fingers to his mouth bedouin fashion. "Good evening, sir. *Keef-haaluk?"*

"Al-hammdu leelah," I answered. "I am well, praise God. And will *Haj* Jeballah be coming, grandfather? We have work to do."

"I am at your service. He and the others have not yet returned. They went to attend the business of Mahmud."

"What's he saying?" Preston asked. "Where's Jeballah?"

"That's what I'm trying to find out." I led the old man aside and gave him a hundred-dinar bill. "Allah pays the wages of the good," I told him. "I am Mahmud's devoted friend and Aboubakir Jeballah's faithful servant."

"Allah is bliss," he said, studying the banknote. "What do you wish of me?"

"Tell me about the business of Jeballah with Mahmud?"

"You didn't hear it from me," he said, his eyes narrowing confidentially, "But Mahmud's in jail."

"Impossible!"

"That is what *Haj* Jeballah said. His very words."

"How did this impossible thing happen?"

"When Mahmud went to the house of the small policeman, many other policemen were hiding. They threw a net over Mahmud and then tied him with ropes like a sheep."

Preston joined me. "Does he knew where Jeballah is?"

I explained what had happened.

"Of all the rotten luck! Now what? Does the show grind to a halt because they busted one of his men?"

"Not just one of his men, Alan. Mahmud is a Tibu legend. You met him in Ghadames tending the door at Jeballah's house."

"I remember him. The giant."

"He is like a son to the old man as well as his personal bodyguard. Anyone who touches Mahmud touches Jeballah."

"That's all wonderful, but you still haven't answered my question. What the hell happens now?"

"Unless Mahmud is released immediately, Jeballah will probably kill Nagy. He may kill him anyway."

"Just like that? I thought Nagy had a huge police force behind him. You've been trying to scare me with that every time we discuss the raid on the prison."

"I told you, Alan, Jeballah is a powerful leader of the Tibu. They are a warrior race who fought the Roman legions as well as Arab, Turk and Italian invaders over the centuries. And they always won, which is why everybody leaves them alone.''

"So much for the history lesson," Preston said. "But you still haven't told me what I want to know."

"Ethnic violence or civil war is the last thing Qaddafi needs in his own backyard right now, and that's what he'll get if he messes with Jeballah. There are forty or fifty thousand Tibu between the Sahara and the Tibesti Mountains and another ten thousand here in Tripoli. Nagy will have to let Mahmud go or else."

"Suppose he doesn't?"

"Alan, among the Tibu, even the women carry knives."

Jeballah showed up a little before midnight accompanied by a dozen armed Tibu in two pickup trucks. With them were an elderly Arab couple and two sobbing younger women whom the guards first herded to the patio off the kitchen.

On Jeballah's order the old caretaker seized the bleating lamb and held it up by its hind legs in front of the family. As one of the guards told them what would happen to them, the man's huge knife flashed in the glare of the storm lantern and cut the animal's throat. The old woman screamed as bright arterial blood spurted across the patio, staining her *baragan*, and one of the younger women swooned into the old man's arms.

Jeballah told the guards to take the old man where he could speak on the telephone to his son, and the terrified women were led away to another part of the house.

With no explanation of that extraordinary scene, Jeballah begged our forgiveness for his tardiness, but said it could not be helped. Preston was fretting and nervous, practically jumping out of his skin by then, and several times I had to tell him under my breath to please calm down.

"I'm not here for a lesson in Arab etiquette," he hissed into my ear, not caring if he insulted Jeballah. "We have no time!"

"Listen to Davey," Ike whispered. "Old Aboo-baker knows what he's doing. Bear with him."

Without another word, food was served as we squatted in a semicircle around the smoky fire in the main room. Only Jeballah and Ike Maxwell had much of an appetite. Eating around the bush, as they say, is just good manners to an Arab, so Jeballah helped himself liberally while he talked about the storm brewing outside before casually asking Preston, "Did Dahoud tell you what happened?"

"He said two of your men had been arrested."

Jeballah selected a steaming piece of carrot from the couscous bowl. "Fadlalah is waiting for them. They will be released soon, I think, or . . ." He nodded toward the other end of the house and drew a finger across his throat.

"You mean . . . ?" Preston said.

Jeballah continued, "A man with a wife, a mother, a father and a sister cannot afford serious mistakes. I explained to that little *mukhabarat* worm that it is a question of principle. If Nagy wants to play big shot he should choose his enemies more wisely. By now his father has told him to release Pringle and Mahmud or I'll kill the whole family." This was said in the same even, matter of fact tone he had used when discussing the weather.

After a very long silence, Preston said, "We are going in tomorrow night. Your trucks must be in place right after sundown to take the women hostages from Garian to . . ."

Jeballah shook his head, and Preston was as startled as I.

"But we agreed . . ." Preston began.

"There are no hostages in Garian," Jeballah said. "They have already been moved."

"Moved where?" Preston demanded.

"Probably Beirut," I said. "He wanted me to go with them."

"Jesus Christ!" Preston said angrily. "Who the hell are you working for! Them or us?"

Jeballah raised one hand for silence. "No one has gone to Beirut. The army brought them to Tripoli tonight."

Ike prodded me. "Remember the trucks, Davey? That must have been the convoy we saw on the road."

"Where in Tripoli?" Preston asked Jeballah.

The old man shrugged. "To the Karamanli Fortress."

"It means revising the whole scenario," Preston said, "and Diamond's para-force is already in Chad ready to take off."

"Go after the hostages another time," I said.

"We can't," Preston answered. "If they move those people to Lebanon, we'll never find them again."

"Either way," Ike said, "you got to abort Garian."

"I'll get on the radio. Cancel out. Christ!"

"We ain't equipped to snatch so many people out of Tripoli," Ike said, "unless we find a place nearby where the Wizards can land. The boats can't handle it."

"There are many places," Jeballah told them. "But your planes would be seen and shot down. There is no hidden place."

All the months of preparation had suddenly gone up in smoke and the cocky, calculated self-confidence I was used to seeing in Preston seemed to have gone with it. "There's not enough time to plan anything new," he said dejectedly. "We go with what we have."

Ike's next words stopped him. "We agreed at the start," he said, "if the odds ever went too high against us, we'd pack it in."

Jeballah told them, "Both attitudes are wrong. Maybe you cannot get everyone out with the men and equipment you have, but you cannot abandon the hostages."

"What can we do?" Preston said.

"I will tell you," Jeballah said.

XLI

⟨⟩ Much, much later that night at my place, Ike said, "That reminds me of something you told me once, Davey."

Ike was always being reminded of something I had told him once, as if I was some kind of oracle or sage. Yet I rarely remembered telling him all the things he claimed came from me. I suspect it was his shy way of getting his own ideas across by attributing them to me.

I asked him what it was this time.

"Remember telling me how all them people in Europe before Columbus believed the earth was flat, but the Arabs knew better?"

That I did remember.

"I'll never forget that," Ike said. "How'd it go again?"

"Ike, it's just to show that nobody's ever as smart as he thinks he is."

"Right! That's the one! How'd it go, Davey?"

"The great Arab mathematicians believed that the medieval Europeans were wrong, that the earth was not flat at all, and they could prove it through solid geometry."

"That's the one, Davey. That's the story, all right!"

"They established incontrovertibly . . ."

Ike echoed me happily, ". . . In-con-tro-vertibly."

". . . that the earth is a cube."

"I love it," he said.

"But what does it have to do with us?" I asked him. By that time my words were slurred between the booze and occasional shots of the Milk of the Four Peppers.

Ike was also fairly drunk as he said, "Davey, think about it, and you'll see what I mean. If Preston believes the earth is flat . . ."

"Yeah . . . ?"

". . . and Jeballah thinks it's a cube . . ."

"Uh-mmm . . . ?"

". . . then you and me are the only ones who know the truth about it being round, and we won't tell!" I remember thinking Ike was very clever to have come up with that one, and we both laughed heartily. "Davey, I owe you an apology," he said.

"No, you don't."

"Yes, I do, goddamnit."

"No, really, Ike. You don't owe me any apology."

"I do and you know it."

"It's okay Ike, forget it."

"Don't argue with me! When Ike Maxwell owes something, he pays it, and I owe you an apology!"

"What for?"

"Huh?"

"What do you owe me an apology for, Ike?"

"By Christian, I forgot."

Because I never wanted to be like my father who seldom drew a sober breath, and because I even feared there might be a random French gene somewhere which could mark me as an alcoholic, I have always been what people call a very light social drinker. But that night I overdid it. First to settle my nerves, and later to celebrate the release of Jock Pringle and Mahmud. My mind seemed to be functioning well enough, but by three A.M. I was having serious trouble with my motor reflexes. I never would have made it to bed without Ike's help. He was kindness itself, this man who only recently had threatened to kill me.

Before he put out the lights, he called from the living room, "Davey, you still awake?"

"I think so."

"Now I remember what it was."

"What what was?"

"Why I owe you that apology."

"Why?"

"You were right."

"About what?"

"About this whole crazy scheme being crazy. I didn't see how crazy it was until tonight."

"I'm glad you finally saw the light, Ike."

"You called it from the start. The whole damn plan was too iffy. I should have seen what we were getting into but I was dazzled by all of Elliot's bullshit. You listening?"

"Yes."

"And Dick Diamond dazzled me too. Gung-ho guy, but more guts than sense."

"I know."

"It never could have worked."

"Not the way they had it planned."

"I guess they couldn't do it any different."

"Maybe they couldn't, but I certainly could," I told him. What I said next I can only attribute to the remarkable effect of the Milk of the Four Peppers which removes inhibitions, emancipates the mind, and overexcites the imagination. "With a little bit of help from the American Navy, you could have had those people out of there in no time."

"How?" Ike asked me.

Now that I was sure the danger of anyone trying it was past, I spun out my own improbable scheme for liberating the hostages. I remember sounding quite lucid to myself as I said, "Qaddafi wants them out of Libya because he's afraid the Americans will bomb the place, right?"

"Right."

"So use that fear. Exploit his paranoia."

"We won't bomb Tripoli. Washington ruled it out."

"You and I know that, but who's going to tell Qaddafi?"

Ike laughed.

"Assuming Preston could break into the prison and free the Americans, his only problem would be getting them out of Libya."

"That's always been the clinker."

I heard myself say, "With the American fleet less than fifty miles offshore, it's got to be simple."

"They're only there as a diversionary force," Ike said.

"But Qaddafi doesn't know that."

Ike said. "Is this really you talking, Davey?"

"You've got helicopters in the Sixth Fleet. Use them."

"Qaddafi'd shoot them down."

"Not if he thought the sky would fall in."

"Explain."

"All Preston has to do once he has the Fortress secured," I blundered on, "is offer Qaddafi a choice. Either he lets the Navy helicopters in to pick up the hostages or you bomb Tripoli. With an hour to make up his mind, do you doubt how he'd answer?"

"I guess he'd go for the helicopters the same way he went for the Mirages when he made Malduum let those French kids go."

"Precisely," I said, quite proud of the whole idea, and not realizing how I had just pulled the sky down on myself.

"But suppose he didn't?" Ike said suddenly.

"Ike, the man's not a fool."

"You're the one's always saying Arabs think different. So suppose he didn't? Suppose he called our bluff?"

"Why would he risk an air raid? His adopted daughter was killed the last time you bombed Tripoli."

"That's true. It wouldn't be logical to turn us down."

"Qaddafi couldn't afford to say no. Do you imagine he'd sacrifice Libyan lives to save American hostages for Palestinians?"

"That reminds me of something you told me once, Davey."

"Oh, for God's sake, Ike! Not again."

"About the scorpion trying to hitch a ride across the Nile on the frog's back . . ."

"That was just a joke."

". . . and when the frog turns him down and the scorpion asks why, and he says, 'Because you're a scorpion and I'm a frog.' "

"Right."

"I forgot the rest. How's it go?"

"The scorpion finally convinces the frog to take him along, but out in the middle of the river he can't resist that slick green back one second more and he gives the frog a fatal sting."

"Now I remember. They're both drowning, and the frog says, ''Why did you do it when you knew you'd drown with me?' "

"That's right."

"And the scorpion says . . . What did the scorpion say?"

"He said, 'What did you expect? It's the Middle East.' "

XLII

At eight the next morning, as a cold December wind blew off the sea beyond my windows, Ike Maxwell was standing me on my feet and holding strong black coffee to my lips. My head was a factory of pain and I felt I could not face the day. But the coffee and a jolt of the Milk of the Four Peppers brought me slowly back to life as he began to tell me what I had to do before noon.

I said, "I thought we agreed last night that under the circumstances Preston's plan was unworkable. Even he admitted it."

"I already been on the horn with him and he don't admit nothing, Davey. He went for Jeballah's offer of extra manpower and he's been up all night reworking the plan."

"Don't tell me he's still going through with it!"

"Right the first time."

"Ike, you know . . ."

"He's also going to do what you suggested."

Inside my numb brain I was trying to remember what it was I had suggested. How could I have suggested anything last night?

"Anyway, we're going in," he said.

"We? I thought you agreed it wouldn't work."

"I did, but what the hell. If we can get the choppers in here, we'll get them people out." Digging in his pocket he produced David Perpignon's passport and handed it to me.

"I don't get it."

"I'm staying, but I can't force you to, Davey, knowing how you feel. If you want to split, now's your chance."

"I don't know what to say, Ike. I guess I owe you one."

"I'll collect, too, by Christian." He laid a big paw on my shoulder. "I'd go with you, but I got obligations, Davey."

I remembered Ike's bad heart and poor Priscilla Pearl, his blind, crippled daughter, and marvelled at his boundless optimism. But I was so relieved to be off the hook, I took full advantage of the moment to thank him for being such a sport about it.

"If Malduum moves those people to Lebanon," he said, "he'll never let 'em go. And Washington won't start a war over them. Either we get them out tonight or they're history."

"Take care, Ike."

"You too, Davey. I'll invite you to the ceremony in the White House rose garden when the president gives me a medal."

"Ike . . . ?"

"I told Preston your idea exactly as you explained to me. And I also said you was probably no longer in the picture."

"He agreed to that?"

"I didn't give him no choice. I said you'd probably want the Mercedes too. If we get airlifted out, we won't need it, and if we don't . . . well, we won't need it then either."

"All right," I said, "let's go. I've got to find Karen."

Ike said, "First we check in with Preston."

"But . . ."

"You owe him that. Then you're free to go."

Outside, the early morning sky was an ugly lemon color and the palms along the Lungomare bowed before the gusting seawind, their fronds thrashing angrily in the intermittent rain.

Except for Preston and Hueblen, the gang was gathered in the Desal Building where Pozzogallo was holding court, with Cardoni and the two Russians listening attentively.

"After that," the old man was saying, "I discovered Yusef Karamanli's dungeon and the remains of prisoners he had starved and tortured more than a hundred years before."

"You mean their bodies were still there?" Pietr asked him.

"Bones mainly with a little mummified skin, hair and cartilage still hanging in the chains. I sealed the passages forever and never once mentioned them in any government report."

"Not forever," I said. "You opened them again for Preston." I resented the old fool at moments like that for kindling my interest in spite of myself.

"In a good cause," Pozzogallo said, "and for money."

"But why did you keep silent before?" Cardoni asked him.

"Every man likes to save something out for himself," he said. "After my years here, that was all I had. It was not simply another archeological dig, you understand. It contained a piece of my own bitter history as well as the secrets of the Karamanlis. A hundred and twenty years of pillage and lust played out against a background of dazzling wealth, most of it taken in tribute. Protection money we call it in Sicily."

"What happened to the loot?" Cardoni wanted to know.

"A lot was squandered or lost over the years, but it was said that Yusef had hoarded gold and jewels which were never accounted for. I thought I might find some when I excavated the passages, but I never did."

Preston arrived then, accompanied by Hueblen. The German's hand was still bandaged and by now the bruises on the side of his face had turned an ugly shade of yellow. He sat like a killer dog, neutralized for the moment by the presence of his master, but potentially as dangerous as ever.

"Everything's set," Preston said. "Seaforce lands at nine and we blow the wall into the prison at ten. We're out before midnight. Mr. Jaballah has offered extra men to help move the hostages to the Mabrouk Air terminal where we hope to evacuate everyone by helicopter."

"Is that laid on firm with the navy?" Ike asked Preston.

"Duff Elliot is working the request through channels at this moment, but he doesn't think there will be any problem."

"Who talks to Qaddafi?"

"If Dahoud is no longer with us," Preston said, scowling in my direction, "I shall do it myself."

There was a loud banging on the door at that moment, and old Prince Pozzogallo went to look through one of the curtained windows of the reception hall. "It's the police," he said.

"Let Dahoud answer it," Preston told him, looking at me. He and Cardoni sat in suspended animation while Ike Maxwell drew a gun from his jacket and the Russians faded into the next room.

Both plainclothes policemen wore the mirror sunglasses fashionable among agents of the *mukhabarat,* and I saw four grotesque reflections of myself when I looked at their faces. Two more police waited by a land rover parked at the curb. "Dahoud el Beida?"

I nodded.

"Come with us."

"What is this about?"

"We'll ask the questions."

"Am I under arrest?"

"Move!"

They accompanied me to the land rover and drove the two blocks to the Karamanli Fortress where I was escorted up the long staircase and down endless littered corridors to the *mukhabarat*'s inner headquarters.

By then it was a little after nine o'clock, and I sat in an anteroom off Nagy's office until eleven-thirty, going slowly crazy under the eyes of a bored officer assigned to keep me company. If Nagy was around, he wasn't showing himself, and if he was deliberately trying to depress and disorient me, he succeeded.

I had no way of reaching Karen but it was probably just as well because the longer I waited, the more anxious I became. Perhaps the French had come through with a photograph of David Perpignon in record time and Nagy was just savoring the moment before he showed it to me.

They say the coward dies many times, the hero but once. That morning I was certainly a coward in my imagination. Physically, I was in no shape to face even a normal day, with the grandfather of all hangovers clanging around my head. Luckily the Milk of the Four Peppers had taken the edge off it, and allowed me to face my fate with the kind of numb equanimity which might just pass for courage.

If Nagy was on to me, he would make the most of it. Torture certainly, even though there was nothing I could tell them. Weeks shut away in a cell. Then a show trial and death by slow strangulation at the end of a rope in Castle Square.

Several of Malduum's Palestinian guards appeared in the outer corridor then, dressed in freshly laundered combat fatigues and carrying AK-47's slung from their shoulders. One of them called out to me, "El Beida, good morning! I wish to thank you."

When he came into the anteroom and shook my hand, I recalled that he was the one who had approached me at the hotel only the night before, asking to be assigned to the Beirut escort. "Is it true we're leaving today?" he said in a low voice. When I did not answer, he assured me, "We are ready whenever you are."

A uniformed policeman beckoned me into Nagy's office where the little man sat behind his enormous desk studying a file. Without looking up, he said in English, "Sit, Beida, and tell me what the bloody hell is going on!"

"I beg your pardon?"

"My headquarters was crawling with Palestinians this morning and I received word that you are off today for Beirut."

"I don't know who . . ."

"Malduum, that's who. I have just made it clear to him that you are not going anywhere because you are needed here. You work for me as well as Palestine. What's so funny?"

Without realizing it, I had begun to grin like a fool the moment I realized he wasn't wise to David Perpignon. "I'm just happy to avoid the trip, that's all." Happy? I was hysterical with joy. For two hours I had been sweating it out, as they say, waiting to hear my death sentence, and all he tells me now is that he needs me. "You say the hostages are being taken away today?"

"A military transport plane is standing by and good riddance. We didn't want them here in the first place. Qaddafi has been too patient, and American ships are now maneuvering off our coast. They may bomb us again. Do you have a family, Beida?"

"No, I have no one."

"I am recently married," he said, "and all my family is alive, thanks be to God. Mother, father, sister, everyone."

"You are lucky," I said.

"They are all alive."

"I envy you."

"They are safe at home where they belong."

"I'm glad to hear that."

"Alive and safe. Do you realize what that means?"

I realized from the way he spoke that he had probably cracked at last, gone bonkers, bananas, round the bend, as they say.

"It means . . . it means. Well, you understand," he said, and I saw that he was weeping. "It is wonderful to have them living."

"You sent for me this morning?"

He daubed at his eyes before he answered. "As an act of mercy I released the pilot Pringle last night. Once I had the code book, there was no point in holding him, but he must leave Libya."

"That was very wise," I said.

"We have nearly cracked the code. A matter of hours."

"Excellent."

"Stay with Preston now. I want you there when he meets with this Perpignon fellow."

"If he meets with him, I guarantee I'll be there."

As I was leaving headquarters Najeeb Hassan got out of a UPARF land rover and came angrily up the windswept stairs two steps at a time. Like the other Palestinians, he was dressed in combat fatigues, but instead of an AK-47, he carried a holstered pistol. When he saw me, he said, "Beida, what are you doing here?"

"Obeying a summons from Captain Nagy."

"Call Khalil. He must talk to you at once. Damned Libyans. Thanks to Nagy, I've got to go to Beirut."

"I heard."

"Your girl is with Khalil at the villa. Call him now!"

I headed back to the Desal Building to give Preston the news and telephone Karen. Things were moving far too quickly, but I was confident we could still make it if I kept a clear head. I had to get her away from Malduum on some pretext. Then we would head for the Tunisian border. All I needed was Karen by my side and two hours time.

"We've got no choice," Preston said when I gave him the news. "We go in now."

"Alan, there's no way six of you can carry it off."

He was very relaxed as he said, "It's a question of surprise, Dahoud. It always was. Once we get them out of the prison into the passage, we wait until our people land and Qaddafi is persuaded to let the choppers in."

"At the moment, beside Nagy's men and the regular guards in the building, there's a handpicked squad of armed Palestinians under Najeeb Hassan who will be escorting the hostages."

"But they're not expecting us, Dahoud."

"They and the Libyans will hit you with all they have."

Ike Maxwell had entered the room by then carrying the tube of an RPG antitank weapon. "Sight's bent," he said as he rummaged noisily in a drawer for a pair of pliers.

"Good luck," I said as I reached for my attaché case. "I've got to get Karen. Don't think it hasn't been fun, Alan."

I had opened the case and was checking the little Ingram submachine gun I had found in the safe-deposit box. I am not a gunman, and dislike even having them around. But I wasn't sure how easy it would be to talk my way past the Libyan border guards after the alarm was sounded. Better to have the Ingram as an option.

Preston put his hand over mine. "Take the Mercedes but do us one last favor before you go."

"What?" I said.

"Pass by Nagy's headquarters. Delay them. Get us an hour. Half an hour even."

"I'm sorry, Alan. But I want to be as far away from that place as possible when you rush in."

"Davey . . . ?"

"Don't you start."

"You can't let Hassan move those people," Ike said. He pointed to the telephone and I dialled Nagy's office.

The line was busy.

Preston said. "Fifteen minutes now could be critical."

"Run on over there, Davey."

"You'll get me killed!"

"Wasn't you the one just said you owed me? So why not do it?" He held the rocket tube to his eye, swung it in a slow arc around the room and squinted at me over the sight.

"Ike, God damn you!" I grabbed my case and streaked for the door. "I'll go," I called back, "but I don't guarantee anything."

◇

XLIII

◇ Many of life's most important decisions are taken out of a man's hands by fate, luck, or circumstance. But in my case, the gods throw them right back again with the same random disregard for my capacity to cope. If you ask me, it's the centrifugal force you've got to watch out for on the wheel of fortune!

They were mistaken if they thought I could affect the transfer, but I was too weary by then to argue. I knew there was no point in going back to the *mukhabarat* offices where I had no authority. Even if I spoke to Malduum, what reason could I give him to delay the move? Particularly with Qaddafi determined to see the hostages out of Libya as soon as possible. What no one—least of all me—realized at that moment, was that Libyan bureaucracy was already giving Alan Preston all the time he needed.

The storm front seemed to have passed when I reached the car, and although the day was still gray and blustery, it was no longer raining. I would go to Malduum's villa and get Karen away on some trumped-up excuse. If I thought of a way to delay the hostage move in the meanwhile, I would make the try.

A line of military trucks had parked in front of the castle entrance and I had to drive around them. That was when Najeeb saw me and waved me to a stop.

"Beida, come with me! These Libyans are impossible!"

I had rolled the window down as he arrived panting by the car.

"They're the ones want us out! Their damned air force is screaming because the plane was laid on for noon and we didn't show. But the prison administrator says he has no authority to release the Zionists to me. Can you believe it!"

"Have you talked to Nagy?"

"I can't find him."

"Call Malduum."

"I did and he said to get you."

"But they won't listen to me."

"Yes they will because your name is on the release."

"What?"

"Khalil's release order, countersigned by Qaddafi himself says the hostages are only to be turned over to Dahoud el Beida. When Nagy made Khalil replace you with me, no one thought to change this imbecile's orders."

Against my better judgement, I abandoned the relative safety of the Mercedes and accompanied him to the *mukhabarat* headquarters. The same policemen who earlier in the day had hustled me impolitely in for the meeting with Nagy, now saluted.

We walked the long corridors and descended the same steps I had gone down the day before to see Jock Pringle. Only this time I was taken to the officer of the guard, flanked by two uniformed turnkeys, a Humphry Dumpty of a man with a wide vacuous smile and pink, soft hands.

"This is Beida," Najeeb said without ceremony. "Now will you turn them over to us?"

The fat man rose to shake my hand. "I have read about you," he said. "You are the man who captured all these Jews."

That was exactly what Najeeb needed to blow his fuse, and I had to explain that he had been the actual leader of the hijack gang. But the fat man's smile remained fixed as he said, "I admire your modesty, Beida, but we older chaps know who are the heroes and who are the snotnoses." He looked meaningfully at Najeeb as he pushed a paper across the desk for me to sign.

Then he waved the two uniformed Libyan turnkeys and six of Najeeb's camouflage-clad Palestinians ahead of us down the passage. "I will accompany you personally," he said. "And give you what you signed for. Frankly I'll be glad to see the last of them. This is a prison, not a rest home for the elderly."

We walked past the cell Jock had occupied, the door now standing open. Two guards listening to a transistor radio rose lazily, took keys from hooks on the wall and opened a massive iron door onto another passage. We went down another flight of stairs and entered a long corridor. Here the walls were no longer stuccoed brick but bare stone, hewn from the rock beneath the castle. One could sense the prisoners stirring behind iron doors as we passed.

The accoustics were better, or worse, depending on your view. Gone was the crashing echo of every footstep and the scrape of every key turning in a lock. Here the world was muffled, hidden, secret. Here, anything could happen and no one would ever know.

Public buildings in the Arab world are generally lit by bluish, flickering fluorescent tubes, and Qaddafi's prison was no exception. More stairs awaited me, leading ever lower in the blue light, each successive landing like another level of hell. One was a shooting gallery with rows of silhouette targets, spent shells on the floor and earmuffs hung on hooks. When we reached the dungeon where the hostages were assembled, the sight appalled me.

None of the faces I saw bore any resemblance to the cheerful, overfed, middle-aged Americans I remembered with their Iliad Tour bags. This was a collection of spectres, ghosts, apparitions. The men were gaunt and ragged, unshaven and unwashed.

Although the women were cleaner and better nourished, having only just arrived from Garian, their unrouged faces were as devoid of expression as patients in a mental hospital. Pale, etiolated shadows of their former selves, their dirty gray hair hung in hanks over threadbare summer blouses and tattered pastel pantsuits now sizes too big for them.

"There are twenty-seven," Najeeb said.

"I thought only one woman died."

The fat officer said, "Also a diabetic and a suicide."

Najeeb ordered them all to gather whatever pitiful possessions they still had and form a double line. "You are being moved to better quarters," he said.

They shuffled into a semblance of order, their hollow eyes and cadaverous faces watching us in the eerie blue light like lost souls from hell. I saw no fear in their eyes, but rather a dull acceptance of the role they had been given to play, the passive connivance of the victim in his fate.

"All right, move!" Najeeb commanded, and the guards prodded the hostages toward the corridor. I don't recall what I was thinking exactly, but I was probably in the midst of a crisis of conscience after seeing the condition of these innocent people. Had I condemned them unknowingly through my lack of belief in Preston's plan? Who was I to judge anyway? Ike Maxwell was right. If they were moved to Lebanon, with the possible exception of a few lucky ones, the rest could remain hostages forever.

They deserved the chance Preston was offering them. Maybe his damn fool operation did have a prayer of success after all. God knows, he had managed to collect enough explosives and massed firepower in the passage behind the Desal Building to take on a small army. And he, Ike Maxwell and the others were all highly experienced in unorthodox warfare. If the other contingent landed by sea to back them up, they would be a formidable force indeed. It would take all of Malduum's might plus substantial Libyan help to dislodge them from behind the walls of the Karamanli Fortress.

If they could hold off any counterattack once they freed the hostages, and if Qaddafi agreed to allow navy helicopters to the rescue, they might just get these poor people out of here yet.

If . . .?

Was I kidding myself and falling into the same error of judgment Duff Elliot, Preston and the others? That was more than likely, but I was not as sure of their failure as I had been five minutes before seeing the hostages. Whatever the odds, something had to be done now to help them or they were doomed.

"Shouldn't you check the names on the list against the people you have here?" I asked Najeeb. "A roll call?"

"What for? We made a head count."

"I didn't just sign for twenty-seven prisoners," I said, looking at the fat officer. "I signed for twenty-seven individuals with names. Now you tell me three of the original group are dead and I'd like to be sure I haven't signed for dead bodies."

"You're quite right!" the officer agreed. "Let us check."

"We're late already!" Najeeb protested.

"A few more minutes won't matter," I said.

"What do these kids understand of the order that is needed in things?" the fat man declared, jerking his head toward Najeeb. "They are trigger-happy and always ready with a lot of talk, but then who has to clean up their paperwork afterwards?"

One of the guards sent for a clerk who had to return to the officer's desk for the roster of names. It took ten minutes and when the list appeared, Najeeb muttered, "Get it over with."

The fat officer called out, "Listen carefully and answer when you hear your name!" He squinted at the list, but before he could continue, the floor trembled and the wall shuddered and began to crumble before my eyes. Everyone watched as it caved in toward us to become a tilting slow-motion mass of rubble. The noise that exploded into the bay was deafening and the blast threw me against Najeeb with such force we were both bounced off the far wall.

The lights flickered and went out, then came on again in the choking smoke and dust which filled the passage. There were moans and cries from those who had been injured as shadowy figures appeared among us. I heard Preston's shout, "Throw down your weapons!" punctuated by three rounds from an Uzi slung at his shoulder. One of the Palestinian guards sprawled dead in front of me.

Najeeb was groggily getting to his knees when he was clubbed from behind by a rifle butt. It was too hazy at first to make out many faces but I heard Hueblen curse as he swung his good left arm high and hit another guard a vicious chop acros the face, staggering the man against the fat Libyan officer who was crying in Arabic, "Don't shoot! Don't shoot!"

I felt an arm around my shoulder then as Ike Maxwell helped me to my feet. "You okay, Davey? By Christian, you did it! I knew you would! I told Alan you'd never let us down and you came through!" He gave me a great juicy, mint-flavored kiss on the cheek and a pat on the back that knocked the wind out of me.

"Ike, behind you!" I shouted.

A guard was coming toward us, bringing his rifle level with Ike's chest at point-blank range. But Ike was faster and the boy was lifted off his feet by a bullet through the head.

The dust had settled slightly and I saw Cardoni pushing two more guards roughly against one wall, their hands on their heads and legs spread. Hueblen had subdued the others and was taping their hands behind them while Pietr and Boris were further up the passage.

The place exploded with noise again and I saw spurts of flame from a machine pistol on the stairs beyond the two Russians. Bullets ricocheted around us as I instinctively ducked. Two of Malduum's guards went down but so did the Russian Boris.

Preston was on the far side of the bay, calling to the stunned hostages, "Please! Stay where you are! Do not move until the area is secured! We are here to take you home!"

The hole they had blown through the prison wall was about four feet wide from floor to ceiling, and at that desperate moment an apparition appeared in the center of it. Like some theatrical ghost surrounded by a swirling cloud of blue-lit smoke, Prince Pozzogallo made his entrance. Dressed in his white linen suit, his floppy pan-ama hat jauntily in place, the old rogue peered through his pince-nez at the chaos his researches had made possible.

In ten minutes the dust had settled and Preston was reassuring the confused and skeptical hostages that they were indeed being rescued. Either the shock of the fire-fight or the prospect of their imminent liberation snapped them out of their torpor, for this shambling, silent crowd was suddenly transformed. They pressed around Preston asking, "Who are you? When can we leave? Did you bring food? Are we free to go?" while several of the women broke down and were softly crying in the background.

"Later, please!" he told them. "We will see to your needs as soon as we've mopped up here. Be patient!"

One of the bearded shaggy skeletons stepped forward to stand beside Preston, saying, "You heard the man! He's doing his best. Help him by shutting up!" I recognized the voice and saw then that the hair and beard were red. Rusty Kirshbaum was alive and well, and ready as always to help out.

Preston caught old Prince Pozzogallo by the arm, saying, "I'm not going to ask you what you're doing here, but as long as you are here, take charge of these people while we get on with what we have to do." Then he turned to me. "You okay?"

When I nodded, Ike Maxwell slapped an AK-47 into my hands. "Then let's get a move on, Davey, before they know we're here."

"You're crazy, Ike! I'm leaving." I tried to return the gun but he just laughed and gave me a gentle shove ahead of him.

"You can't leave now, Davey. They'll shoot you for sure."

He was right and I don't know what I was thinking. Beyond these dark passages lay the stairs to the street, the Mercedes, Karen and freedom. But I was not only committed, I was trapped.

Cardoni had turned over his prisoners to Hueblen and was gathering the captured weapons into a pile against the wall. Four Palestinians and one Libyan lay dead. Najeeb and one other Palestinian were unconscious. Hueblen manacled the remaining three with the fat Libyan officer.

Boris had a nasty chest wound but he was still conscious when his huge friend Pietr carried him back to lay him among the hostages. There, Boris himself began telling the women in Russian how to bandage him.

Ike and I had reached the second level before Preston, Pietr, Cardoni and Hueblen caught up. The long corridor was silent except for the scratchy music of the guard's radio from the top of the stairs at the far end.

Although I found it hard to believe, the explosion and shooting below had been so effectively muffled by the labyrinth of stairs and passages, that the guards here had heard nothing above the sound of their radio.

"Pozzogallo was right," Preston whispered. "He said no one would hear us. Is that gate at the top locked?"

"Yes. The guards are just on the other side of it."

"How many?"

"Two when we came in. But just beyond them is the whole *mukhabarat* force as well as the rest of Malduum's people."

"We've got to get them to open up," Preston said.

"I thought we were going out the way you came in?"

"We are. But I don't want any surprises. I want that gate locked from this side first."

"Alan, let it go. They'll never open for you."

"They'll open for you, Davey," Ike said.

And that is exactly what they did. While I went to the small spyhole in the door and showed my face, Preston and the others crouched against the walls out of sight.

"Where is the captain?" the guard asked before he opened.

"He sent me ahead."

The spyhole closed and after a moment the huge keys ground in ancient locks before the great iron mass began to move. Although it was on rollers, it took all the strength of both guards to open it. The instant a man could pass, Preston pushed me aside to rush through with Ike and the others.

The guards were too surprised to resist, and in seconds they lay disarmed and face down on the floor while Hueblen and Preston removed the keys and went to insert them on the inner side of the gate.

Preston cursed, then Hueblen angrily threw one of the monster keys clanging against the stone wall because it could not be inserted from the inside. There was no way of locking the gate as Preston wished.

Between us and the main *mukhabarat* headquarters was another flight of stairs and a corridor, and off the corridor was the main shower room and changing facility. From that room now came a file

of laughing, joking policemen in fatigue uniform, carrying an assort-
ment of automatic weapons, obviously on their way to the target
range in the lower passage.

A sergeant was telling them to make sure their weapons were on
safety just as they saw us. Ike Maxwell opened fire with his Uzi,
cutting down the ones at the head of the line.

The others, perhaps ten in all, reacted quickly enough, but in
different ways. Most of them sensibly fled back into the locker room
out of the line of fire. But two knelt where they were and opened
up point blank. Ike killed them both, but not before they riddled
Alan Preston. The slugs tore through him and around me, and why
I wasn't killed too I will never understand. He was dead, as they say,
before he hit the floor.

XLIV

⟨⟩ The air was thick with cordite fumes as we flattened ourselves
against the wall, ready to shoot anything that moved. For a moment
nothing did. Then a voice called out in Arabic, "Don't shoot! We
give up! Please, do not shoot!"

"Drop your weapons and come out with your hands on your
heads," Ike shouted, and I repeated the order in Arabic.

I expected to see at most a dozen men surrender. But to our
astonishment, the line never seemed to end. "Jesus!" Ike said under
his breath as we gave way before them to make room. Many were
half-dressed, either in uniform or civilian clothes which meant we
had probably caught them in the middle of changing shifts.

Hueblen meanwhile had been kneeling beside Preston, checking
for signs of life, but when he stood up he shook his head. He
retrieved Preston's Uzi, and turned to our collection of forty or fifty
police captives.

Others appeared at the far end of the corridor a moment later, armed and shouting, but a short burst from Ike Maxwell's Uzi sent them running for cover. Ike said, "God damn Preston anyway! What the hell do we do now without him?"

"Get them inside where they can't do any harm," I said. "And bring that fat Libyan officer up here. He's got the keys."

As fast as their hands could be taped, the captured police were hustled through the open iron gate and into the prison passage where Ike distributed them among the cells and stood by while they were locked in by the round-faced warder.

In front of Hueblen, Ike said to me, "Now what?"

"What are you asking me for?"

"Until Duff Elliot gets here, somebody's got to be in charge, Davey, and it might as well be you."

"Don't be ridiculous. You know more about what to do."

"All I know is we got twenty-seven hostages down there waiting to go home and forty-four cops locked in their own pokey."

"What was the last word on the helicopters?" I asked him.

"Standing by. With an all-clear from us tonight, they come into Air Mabrouk's terminal. If we can get the hostages there in Jeballah's trucks, then bye-bye Libya."

"And without the all-clear?"

"Jesus, Davey, you said . . . "

"I said Qaddafi will go for it. But I also want to know what options we have if he doesn't."

"Well, there's getting killed. We can always do that, I guess."

"Ike, you're not being helpful."

"There's five of us now. If Elliot makes it in to the beach tonight, we got a lot more chance, but I reckon he might not."

"Because of the Libyans?"

"Look at it this way. We just kicked over a hornet's nest. The original idea was to be in and out before they knew. Failing that, we got a small problem. But then there's your plan which calls for Qaddafi to let the choppers in. Failing that, we're in deep shit."

"Nagy has probably called in every cop in Libya by now."

"Plus the army, navy, marines and whatever else they got. My guess is they don't know what hit 'em yet and that's good. But the minute they cotton there's only a few of us, that's bad."

"We can't let them find out, Ike."

"Then tell us what we got to do, Davey, because they're going to be at our goddamn throats any minute. Now I can shoot and I can run, but I'm a lousy organizer so it's up to you."

I looked at Hueblen and Cardoni and they both nodded. "We agree with Ike," Cardoni said.

"Pietr?"

"We agree this time too much," the Russian said.

I gave them a few minutes to change their minds, but no one made a move. "All right," I said, "get on the radio to Elliot."

Hueblen surprised me when he said, "I can do that. I sent Preston's messages. And Elliot will be monitoring us all day."

"Tell them the mission has been accomplished and the hostages are safe. Tell them we have forty-four prisoners and are negotiating with Qaddafi for permission to bring in the helicopters. When we get that permission we'll give them the exact hour."

"We're in better shape than I thought," Ike said.

"Do you want to tell them about Preston?" Hueblen said.

"Not yet. The Libyans may be tuned in, so say as little as possible. Ike, do we have one of those portable loudspeakers?"

"Bullhorn," he said. "I'll get it."

"What about me?" Cardoni said.

"You will do the talking. Ask for Captain Nagy by name. He or Qaddafi in person are the only ones you negotiate with."

"*Me?*" Cardoni said. "You mean *we.*"

"And speak in French."

"But, *monsieur,* none of them understands French."

"They will find someone to translate."

"But that is absurd. You speak perfect Arabic."

I ignored him and told the big Russian, "While we're negotiating, can you prepare a charge to blow the passage so they can't follow us inside after we leave here?"

"It is ready, okay. Just to put."

"Then put, but don't blow."

"Only on good word of you," he said. I gave him a smile and a thumbs up and prayed we understood each other.

When Ike returned with the bullhorn I handed it to Cardoni. "Okay. Get their attention."

He called for Captain Nagy and every two minutes or so he repeated the message in French while we waited for a reply. At last, after about ten minutes, an electronically amplified voice boomed back in Arabic that Captain Nagy would arrive in a few minutes. Meanwhile, we would be treated leniently if we threw down our arms and surrendered. A few seconds later another voice translated this into French.

"So far, so good," I said, and Cardoni looked at me as if I was mad. "Now answer them that there is no question of surrender. Tell them we have fifty police prisoners in here."

Cardoni's amplified voice reverbrated through the building: *"Attention! Attention! Nous avons plus que cinquante agentes de la Sûreté comme prisonniers!"*

"Tell them no one can evacuate the premises now. All personnel must remain in the fortress."

After a delay they again demanded our surrender.

"Ike, pick out two frightened police prisoners."

"What are you up to, Davey?"

"A trick of persuasion I learned from Najeeb Hassan." I drew him aside and explained what I wanted him and Pietr to do.

I told Cardoni to announce that if the police refused to cooperate, we would have to begin killing the prisoners. Then I ordered Pietr to go into the passage out of sight, wait five minutes and fire half a dozen rounds from his Uzi into a mattress. After that he was to bring out the body of one of the Palestinian guards killed in the initial breakthrough.

After about three minutes, Ike brought the two police captives he had selected and shoved them roughly against the wall with me as if I was a prisoner too. "Do exactly as he says," I whispered to them in Arabic, "or they'll kill us all."

"Who are you?"

"Dahoud el Beida. If you get out alive, tell Captain Nagy you talked to me. He must cooperate. We cannot fight so many."

"But there are only a few," one of them said.

I nodded toward the heavy iron door. "The rest are in there preparing their assault. God knows how many."

"Who are they?" he asked in amazement. He was trembling so, he began to stutter.

"They look American," the first one said with a glance at Cardoni's scowling features and Ike Maxwell's broad back.

"French paras from Chad," I said, and their eyes went wide with fear. Libyan soldiers had been badly mauled by French Foreign Legion paratroops during Qaddafi's ill-advised invasion of that desert country. "Tell Captain Nagy this David Perpignon is a bastard who intends to blow up the whole place."

Pietr's burst of gunfire cut short our conversation and both captives went deathly pale. "Allah have mercy," one said. "They have started the killing."

Ike played his part well when Pietr dragged the body from the passage. He prodded the two prisoners forward as he pretended to give them orders through me. I said, "You are lucky. They are letting you take this unfortunate fellow out of here. Tell Captain Nagy they will kill everyone if he refuses to negotiate. Tell him they will start with me, Dahoud el Beida."

Not long after they disappeared down the corridor, Nagy's voice came over the loudspeaker. "Do you speak English?"

Cardoni looked inquiringly at me and I shook my head. Still not understanding my stubborness on this matter, he called back, *"Non! Pas d'anglais!"*

Nagy spoke again, this time in Arabic. "You are holding Dahoud el Beida. Let him translate. We will talk through him!"

Again I shook my head and told Cardoni what to say. He shouted in French, "We will kill another prisoner in five minutes if you do not obey orders. *Cinq minutes!"*

"Wait! Let us talk," Nagy called back. "Who is speaking?"

"I, David Perpignon!" Cardoni yelled.

After that the building emptied in a thrice, as they say. Police clerks rushed from their desks, officers from their telephones, and guards from their posts. They poured out of the main entrance and down the wide steps to the fortress courtyard and then to the street bordering Castle Square.

In ten minutes we had the place to ourselves. Ike did not believe it at first, until he and Pietr reconnoitered corridors and offices and found them all empty. They even walked the ramparts and looked down upon the streets where Qaddafi's green militia was beginning to arrive. Armored vans and personnel carriers were also being brought to the scene by that time. Ike said it was quite a show, especially with Nagy perched on the front of his Mercedes like some grotesque hood ornament.

"What the dickens did you tell them people that cleared them out the place so fast?" Ike asked.

When I repeated what I had said, he laughed. "If you'd ordered them out they would have dug in. It's all in knowing the mentality."

"Are the walls wide enough for helicopters to land?"

"Hell, they fly on and off them dinky little ships all the time so this should be a piece of cake."

"I don't want to wait until tonight. The longer we stay, the more time they have to think up ways of getting at us. If Qaddafi agrees to the helicopters . . ."

"If," Ike said.

I took Cardoni aside for a few minutes, outlining the speech I wanted him to make. "And remember," I told him. "Wait for the translator to catch up. You're David Perpignon. You have freed the foreign hostages and you are holding fifty Libyans you are prepared to kill if you don't get your way. You are also in control of the main prison and that's got to make them think."

I told the big Russian to pick up another one of the dead Palestinian guards and follow me to the top of the castle walls where we could work without being seen.

There I wrote out a message addressed to his excellency, Colonel Muhammar Qaddafi. I started by saying that the United States had no desire to bomb Libya, but it was determined to protect its citizens. I would release all Libyan prisoners if he allowed the U.S. Navy helicopters to evacuate those citizens. We would be gone by sundown and the incident would be closed.

I stressed that the American fleet offshore was awaiting word from me. If he refused permission for our helicopters to enter Libyan airspace on their mercy mission, an American fighter bomber strike force and airborne troops would be dispatched to neutralize Libyan defenses and provide the necessary air and ground cover for our evacuation from downtown Tripoli. It was now two in the afternoon. If I did not receive an affirmative reply by 1600 hours, I would order all prisoners shot and call in the air strike.

It was pure bluff, every word, because American naval orders were the exact opposite. On the spur of the moment, as they say, I had cobbled up an entirely new American foreign policy. No more backing down. No more namby-pamby, pussyfooting, soft-shoe dancing away from the terrorists. No more negotiating. This was hardball in my court, as they say, with David Perpignon, diplomat manqué, calling the shots. Preston might be dead, but Operation "Big Stick" was alive and well in my hands. Whether it had any better chance of working than it ever did was another story.

Washington had made it clear that no U.S. vessels were to initiate hostilities yet no Libyan believed that. As credulous as they were, they could never accept American good intentions and naïveté at face value. Their lack of faith in innocence I would use against them.

David Perpignon would take advantage of this blind side to exchange his Libyan prisoners for American lives, and if he was lucky, he would also exchange his old Arab identity for a quiet future as a peace-loving Frenchman. By nightfall it would all be decided.

I was smiling, but when Pietr asked me why, I couldn't explain my own presumption in any way he'd understand. I had just threatened the Libyan strongman with total destruction of his capital when I was not at all sure the American fleet commander would even send the choppers after us. I mean, suppose Qaddafi said yes and then the admiral said no?

I folded the note carefully and taped it to the dead man's chest. "When Cardoni finishes talking," I told Pietr, "fire a clip in the air where they can hear you but not see you."

The Russian grunted.

"They'll all duck down on the street. Count to ten then stand up in full view of the crowd and raise the body over your head so they can all see it. Got that?"

"You bet, okay, I know!"

"Can you hold him that long while you count to ten again?"

He snorted in contempt. "I hold him long time."

"Just count to ten. Then heave him so he clears the wall and lands near the green militia on the square."

My theatre for Nagy and the crowd was more effective than I dared hope. While Cardoni spoke there was silence. When he finished, there was a lot of milling around among the militia without any reply from Nagy. Pietr's burst of gunfire from the top of the wall sent them diving for cover. A minute later the huge Russian's appearance on the ramparts drew an audible gasp from the crowd. He followed my instructions to the letter, and the body seemed to fall a long time before it bounced off the lower slope of the wall and came to rest like a broken toy on the pavement.

At first no one approached it. Then two policemen in riot masks dashed forward and dragged the body behind one of the vans.

"You got a minute, Davey?" Ike had been roaming the rooms and corridors like a guard dog, checking to make sure there was no attempt to catch us by surprise. He told me Hueblen had set another charge in the wall between the prison and the Desal Building. "If they try to catch us from behind, they'll bring a hundred tons of rubble down on their heads."

"Did Hueblen get through on the radio?"

"He talked to Dick Diamond."

"And?"

"We got the choppers. Now it's up to the Libs."

"How are you feeling?"

"I'm okay, Davey, as long as I don't think too hard about the fix we're in if Qaddafi turns us down."

"Then don't think about it."

Ike laughed. "Jesus, four teams was supposed to carry out this operation. Fifty guys jumping out of the sky and landing from the sea while Duff Elliot's private air force circles overhead."

"It was always too complicated," I said.

"They must have spent millions on every God damn hi-tech thing Elliot could dream up. And look what happens. You, me, and a handful of guys with small arms do it alone!"

"We kept it simple."

That drew a bigger laugh. "You call seven guys and a eighty-year-old dope addict simple? I call it simple-minded. It only worked because you took over, Davey."

"As usual, you didn't give me much choice."

"Couldn't afford to. Why not tell me what's going on in that great brain now?"

"You'd never guess."

"You're thinkin' about food."

"You guessed."

Ike laughed. "You had that faraway look for a minute that always means food or women. I guessed food."

"Why not women?"

"I figure you're trying not to think about her right now."

"You're a mind reader, Ike."

"Tell me about the food. Steak? Smoked salmon? What?"

"I was thinking I missed my career."

"It happens."

"I should have been a chef."

"Never too late, Davey."

"Don't be so sure."

His laugh this time came from deep in his boots. "You're a caution. Jesus, a chef!"

"A pastry cook, actually."

"You're just hungry, Davey? Have a mint."

"There's nothing wrong with my heart, Ike."

"Oh, that. They say exercise is good for it, you know? Running up and down stairs and low cholesterol mints."

"Did you have a chance to check on our wounded Russian?"

"Boris ain't too good, but the hostages are looking after him. You didn't tell me they was all doctors and their wives."

"Dentists."

"Whatever. They know what they're doing."

"*Enshallah.*"

"Yeah. And if it ain't *enshallah,* it's *malesh.* Remember the Arab lesson we gave Preston?"

I nodded.

"Didn't help him much, did it? He could have quit this game years ago, but he was hooked like me. He rigged his own end, I guess. Ain't many of us get to do that."

"*Mafeesh* Preston," I said. "Now we wait on Qaddafi."

"If he don't come through," Ike said, "*mafeesh* all of us."

XLV

⟷ Patience is not one of my virtues and I have never been good at waiting. In that sense I am more French than Arab, tense and impetuous rather than calm and calculating. I checked my watch at

five-minute intervals expecting God knows what. Divine intervention? Qaddafi's immediate compliance? A sign from heaven? The
only sign I would welcome would be the sight of American helicopters winging in to save us.

Yet . . .

In this best of all possible worlds I was doing better than I had
any right to expect, but the irony made me laugh. For weeks I had
sneered at Preston because he insisted I accept so much on faith.
Now he was dead and I was telling myself the same lies. Not only
that; an hour ago I was only concerned with getting myself and
Karen out of here. Now I had the responsibility for saving the very
people I had been accused of abducting.

We were in control of the fortress prison, the passages below, and
the Security Police Headquarters. Yet with every passing minute the
likelihood increased that they might attempt to rush us. Without
a specific order from Qaddafi, I doubted Nagy's people would make
a move, but the same rules did not apply to Malduum's Palestinian
guards or to the young hotheads in Qaddafi's militia. They could
take us easily if they knew how few we were. But they believed fifty
of their comrades were being held prisoner by a great many heavily
armed men. They had also seen with their own eyes that we were
prepared to slaughter the lot, and they feared an American air strike.

Within three hours we would either be rescued or dead. After
another nip from the Milk of the Four Peppers I felt calm about the
whole situation. Not resigned by any means, but sanguinary, as they
say.

Once Cardoni realized how we had tricked the Libyans, he became such a ham he would have overacted the Perpignon part and
given the game away if I had not been firm about restricting his
appearances on the wall. Ike Maxwell was a rock. The Uzi looked
like a toy in his hand, but the laser-guided RPG slung on his back
was a formidable weapon with enough punch in one small rocket
to stop a tank—when it worked. But like many sophisticated gadgets, it had a tendency to become temperamental, particularly the
firing circuit. Ike grinned when he caught me watching him, and
said, "We're going to do it, Davey, just you wait and see!"

Prince Pozzogallo seemed to take years off his life as he hurried
about looking after the male hostages and flirting with their bewil-
dered wives. Most of the women barely had time to get used to the

idea of being reunited with their husbands before this threadbare geriatric Casanova was kissing their hands and telling them what beautiful eyes they had.

Even Hueblen surprised me. He might easily have given way to his natural ill nature without Preston around to civilize him. Instead Preston's death had sobered him in ways I would not have expected. He showed real grief, and when the others appointed me "scoutmaster", as they say, he apologized for his earlier conduct and said stiffly that I could count on him.

"Just do your job," I said.

He snapped to attention and gave me a jerky bow.

"Is your hand giving you much pain?"

He shrugged. Beside an M-16 slung over one shoulder, he carried a knapsack filled with plastique explosive, detonators, wire and other paraphernalia of his arcane trade. He and Ike had been talking about booby-trapping the Security Police Headquarters while they were waiting, but I suggested their time would be better spent ransacking the small safe Nagy used to keep "special" files which might be of interest to American intelligence.

I led them both down the corridor to show them where the safe was. Hueblen was in his element immediately, and now I understood why Preston tolerated his defects. He was an explosives technician without equal according to Ike. "Most of 'em are butchers, Davey, and got no finesse. But ole Hueblen now, he's as finicky as a brain surgeon."

Hueblen stripped off the armored vest he was wearing and began to take things from the pockets of his knapsack like Santa Claus. A roll of insulated wire, a miniature drill, alligator clips, files, picks and other tools I had never seen before.

He made me jump when he smashed an overhead fluorescent tube with his fist and clipped the cord of the drill to the bare wires. Within seconds silvery slivers of steel spiralled from the smoking bit as he bored a tiny hole next to the safe handle. When he had drilled three holes, he made tiny patties of plastique and worked them into each one, like a dentist filling teeth. He pressed detonators into the puttylike substance and waved us away as he backed out of the room, unreeling a fine copper wire. Once in the corridor again, he connected the wire to a pocket-size battery and the safe blew with an ear-splitting crack.

I checked the files we found, selecting those I thought might be of value. There was one confirming the security arrangements at the new highly secret poison gas plant under construction in Sebha, and others covering the various Palestinian terrorist groups and their leaders. A bulky file on Qaddafi himself took up most of the space. And of course there was one on Dahoud el Beida bearing the notation, "To be disposed of."

Whether Nagy meant to dispose of me or the file I would never know. While Ike and Hueblen began stuffing the ones I selected into plastic sacks I checked my watch for the hundredth time, trying to think of a way to get through to Karen and bring her here. The obvious did not occur to me until almost too late.

From Nagy's office I could look down upon the street where I had parked the Mercedes. No one had touched it. Behind me on his immense desk was a telephone. And next to it was a list of numbers which included the one at Khalil Malduum's villa.

One of the guards answered and I asked for Malduum.

"He is not here."

"Is this Ali?"

"No. I am Salhin."

"Salhin, this is Beida! It's important that I reach him."

"He has gone to the prison where there was a disturbance."

"Is the woman journalist with him?"

"She is here, Beida."

"I wish to speak with her. Put her on the telephone."

"David?" Karen said in a very small voice.

"Are you all right?"

"Just frightened. Where are you?"

"On my way. Who else is with you beside Salhin?"

"There is another man guarding the gate. Be careful, darling. Malduum said there was shooting in the square."

"Wait near the entrance. I'll be there as soon as I can."

Ike was behind me when I put down the phone. "If I didn't know better," he said, "I'd guess you're going after that girl."

"Ike . . ."

"I know you, Davey. You got no choice."

My name boomed over Castle Square and I froze. It was Nagy on the bullhorn: "Perpignon! Perpignon! David Perpignon!"

I took the steps two at a time until I came out on the top of the wall. Castle Square itself was almost empty, but I caught glimpses of militia and police moving under the old Italian arcade along the far side. Nagy was no longer astride his Mercedes where he had made such an attractive target. Ike hunched down behind me, and ahead Pietr and Cardoni crouched against the balustrade.

"What do I answer?" Cardoni asked when he saw me.

"Say you are fed up, losing patience."

"Wonderful!"

"In French."

"Mais oui, monsieur."

His angry voice was quite convincing as it carried over the square, and he added his own embellishments by telling them to stop wasting his time. I shut him up before he could spoil the effect. Just in time, too, because Nagy announced that he was sending a message for Perpignon, and not to shoot. One of Nagy's men stepped hesitantly out from the cover of the arcade, waving a white *baragan* the size of a bedsheet. He tripped over it as he approached the castle entrance.

Ike laughed. "He don't look too happy in his work."

"Get Hueblen up here to help cover the square. Then wait for that idiot and pray Qaddafi bought our story."

It took forever but finally the terrified man was inside the building where Ike relieved him of a large buff envelope and sent him running back across the square to Nagy. The envelope bore the seal of the Libyan Army General Staff, and when I didn't open it immediately, Ike said, "It ain't going to improve with age, Davey."

"If it's a no, we're dead, Ike."

Inside I found a copy of orders addressed to the commanders of the armed forces and police. All units were to stand down until twenty hundred hours to permit the evacuation by helicopter of personnel from the Karamanli Fortress. All ships were to remain on station, but no rocket was to be launched and no shell fired at any unidentified aircraft unless that aircraft shot first. No fighter plane was to take off, and no troops, tanks or police moved to the scene until further orders. It was signed by Muhammar Qaddafi in his capacity as commander in chief of the Libyan People's Defense Forces. Across the bottom under the words "Attention David Perpignon" were written the transponder code numbers the helicopters should use for identification.

We had two hours to get the choppers in and out.

When Ike saw the relief on my face, he seized me in an embrace that could have put me in traction. "You done it, Davey! I knew it! By Christian, you done it!"

Hueblen brought one of the PRC radios to the top of the wall and within minutes I was patched through to the Sixth Fleet communications net and Dick Diamond. True to form, he was suspicious when I said Qaddafi had given permission for the helicopters to enter Libyan airspace. "Can we trust the bastard? Where the hell is Preston?"

"Unavailable. How soon can the choppers be here?"

"Under an hour. Be ready to board immediately."

"We're ready now."

"Set a homing beacon on the wall and mark the landing point with a white cross. These pickups will be touch-and-go." After I indicated the transponder codes, Dick Diamond said, "I'm holding you personally responsible."

"Dick?"

"What?"

"That's exactly what I was about to tell *you.*"

He laughed and signed off.

Ike and I went below with Hueblen to move the hostages up to the stairwell just below the landing point on the wall. This was safer than having them wait on the wall itself, yet it was only a few meters from the pickup point Pietr marked for the choppers.

"Ike, I can't leave Karen here."

"Let's go get her then. But get a goddamn move on!"

He snatched a satchel containing two rounds for the RPG and we hurried down the stairs. At an empty guard post near the rear of the building he held me back as a squad of militia went pounding past toward the square. Then he cautiously slipped out the door before waving me forward with his Uzi. I could hear the amplified voice of a *muezzin* calling the faithful to prayer, but the street on this side of the castle was deserted.

While Ike tinkered with the firing circuit on the RPG and stayed out of sight in the rear of the Mercedes, I turned on to the coast road and headed for Malduum's villa, a ten minute drive. There was little traffic, and when I mentioned it, Ike said, "That's because they heard we was coming."

I parked the car a few feet beyond the gate and walked to a small pergola outside the wall where two guards were usually on duty. At first I thought no one was there, but then I saw a man stretched out on a bench sound asleep, his rifle and a walkie-talkie on the floor beside him. He was one of the older UPARF members, a cadaverous fellow who functioned as a kind of all-purpose clerk.

I gave him a shove in the ribs which sent him flying. As he stumbled to his feet and recovered his rifle, I said, "Is this how you protect your leader?"

"I got no sleep in Garian last night . . ."

"That is no excuse!"

"Or the night before at training exercises . . ."

"So now you sleep on guard!"

"But Khalil is not here."

"Lucky for you! Where is the girl?" I brushed past him into the garden where I saw Karen talking with Salhin. "Come," I called out to her, "we must go immediately."

Salhin said, "But Khalil said she cannot leave."

"It is Khalil who sent for her," I said as if my patience had run out. Salhin looked doubtfully from me to the girl as the other man watched us from the gate. "Get your cameras," I told Karen. "Quickly!"

Salhin followed us to the gate where his shamefaced colleague let us pass. So far so good, and my brashness would have worked all the way except that the guardhouse radio squawked at that moment and Salhin signalled me to wait while he answered. "It is Khalil," he said as he picked it up. Both Salhin and the thin man carried assault rifles, while I was unarmed. I knew the moment Salhin asked Khalil about me, the game was up, as they say, and we had fifty feet to cover between us and the car.

I said to Karen, "Walk toward the Mercedes. I'll be right behind you. And when I say go, run like hell." She did as she was told while I edged impatiently away from Salhin, ready to spring for my life and hoping Ike Maxwell was paying attention. Salhin was having trouble with the radio, but he kept signalling me to remain where I was. I pantomimed my hurry by pointing at my watch. His face was a mask of irritated concentration as he listened to whatever Khalil was telling him.

"Run, Karen," I said, and she ran. I saw the indecision on Salhin's face as he still held the radio to his ear. Then I ran too, and have never felt so naked in my life, expecting a stream of bullets to crash into my back long before I reached the car.

"Davey, God damn it, duck! You're in my line of fire!"

Ike was leaning across the broad hood of the Mercedes, with the Uzi aimed at me. I ducked. I swerved. I zigzagged. I did everything but go into orbit to get out of the way as an AK-47 drummed behind me and geysers of dirt erupted near my feet. I saw my running shadow cut in half as I made the backside of the Mercedes where Karen knelt calmly snapping pictures.

In the hands of a virtuoso like Ike Maxwell, the Uzi played impressive music. The bursts were sharp and brief until suddenly there was silence except for the scratchy voice still emanating from the radio. It lay where Salhin had dropped it when he fell dead against the guard shack. The thin man also lay on the ground just outside the gate, and when he tried to stand, Ike shot him again. As I helped Karen to her feet, Ike retrieved the radio, turned it off, and set it on the bench out of harm's way. He had great respect for gadgets.

The car was only slightly damaged by the fusillade, and the engine started immediately. Ike slid into the front passenger seat with the Uzi in his lap while Karen sat in the back next to the RPG, changing the film in her camera. When I told Ike about the Ingram M-10 in my attache case, he took it out, checked the mechanism, and laid it on the seat between us. We had the road to ourselves again as I barreled back toward town.

A few blocks from our destination Karen called out, "David, look! There they are!" and Ike said, "God bless them sailors!" Winging in over Tripoli harbor like giant blue dragonflies were three Navy helicopters. We were grinning as I rounded the last corner by the Bank of Libya, but our smiles vanished when we saw what was waiting near the rear entrance of the castle.

We should have expected it. Ike and I had been lucky leaving the fortress, but we weren't going to get back in so easily. Between us and the welcoming arms of the Navy stood a squad of Malduum's terrorists with a heavy machine gun mounted on an armored truck. And with them were some of Qaddafi's "green" militia, teenagers armed with assault rifles.

They saw us the instant I stopped the car. "Bluff 'em, Davey," Ike said in a low voice as he replaced the Ingram in my attache case and handed it to me. "You and the girl get a move on."

"What about you?"

The first of the helicopters passed overhead with a rush of noise, drowning his reply. Malduum's people and the militia watched as it hovered above the castle wall. Ike gave me a shove. "Go on, God damn it! The train's in the station!"

I took Karen's hand and we walked toward the building.

One of the green militia leveled his rifle at us when I raised my arm in greeting. But luckily a Palestinian recognized me. He wore a black kerchief around his head pirate fashion, but his beardless face gave him more the look of a child at play than a terrorist at work. "Beida! We heard you were a prisoner!"

I had to shout to be heard above the helicopters. "As you can see, I am only a prisoner of this charming lady."

"But you can't go in," he said as we approached the door.

"It's all right. There's no danger."

"We have our orders, Bieda. No one must go in or out."

"She is here to take pictures." More militia had gathered around us by then, some drawn by the presence of an attractive woman, but one or two openly suspicious of what we were up to.

"She can take pictures from the road," he said.

"Pictures of us," another added, striking a martial pose.

Meanwhile a militiaman was peering inside the Mercedes, his AK-47 held at the ready. I wondered where the devil Ike was.

"I will call Khalil," one of the UPARF troops said.

"Never mind. We will only be a minute."

"No! You cannot go in there!"

"Run for the stairs," I told Karen.

"But, David?"

"Run!"

She had barely turned away from me when another voice called, "Karen, darling! Isn't it exciting?" and Hanzi appeared from behind the truck dressed in skintight UPARF combat fatigues, a mincing parody of the others.

I shouted again, "Karen, run!"

But she hesitated, then remained where she was as Hanzi approached. I don't know how it would have ended if Khalil Malduum had not appeared behind him then and seen me. His rifle was raised, but he did not shoot. Yet I was sure he knew the truth because of the murderously purposeful way he was coming toward me, as if he wanted to kill me with his bare hands.

The world seemed to work in slow-motion, turning split seconds into hours as the lock on the damned attache case jammed when I tried to wrench it open. That is when Ike finally showed himself. A burst from his Uzi cut down the curious militiaman by the Mercedes before it stitched the wall a dozen feet from my head. One of the slugs caught Malduum and staggered him backward. It must only have grazed him however, because he broke into a run for the truck as Hanzi started screaming hysterically.

Karen still seemed rooted to the pavement until I pushed her so hard she stumbled through the door and nearly fell. "Run, Karen! Run!" And she ran as I fired point-blank at two of the UPARF guerillas nearest me before they could unsling their assault rifles. For a moment I could not tell who was shooting in the confusion. I saw Malduum crouched near the armored truck, his shirt bloody, with Hanzi behind him, hands over his ears. The pirate in the black kerchief unlimbered the heavy machine gun and another man jumped up to feed the belt. Ike was nowhere in sight as they opened up on the Mercedes, blowing out all the windows.

When I fired a burst from the Ingram it went high, but it got their attention so they swung the big gun in my direction. The weapon fired explosive bullets which could tear an ordinary wall apart, not to mention what it would do to flesh and bone. Malduum shouted at them to stay trained on the car, but it was too late.

They had traversed almost a hundred and eighty degrees to get me in their sights, and now they had to swing the gun back again because Ike had suddenly exposed himself from behind the car aiming the RPG at the truck.

But seconds ticked by and Ike didn't fire.

They would kill him, I was sure. I let off another burst and hit the second man. Still Ike didn't shoot. Then I saw that the firing circuit had malfunctioned, and he was hunched over the tube on the hood of the car, trying to fix it. Malduum shoved Hanzi out of his way and opened fire with his AK-47. I saw Ike sink to his knees. But he held on to the RPG and managed to keep it pointed at the truck. The pink flash of the laser blinked an instant before the thing went off.

I was inside the entrance to the castle and fifty feet away when the rocket hit. But still the blast knocked me down. I was dazed as I pushed myself to my feet and saw the carnage. Nothing was left of the vehicle except the rear axle assembly and some pieces of scorched iron and burning canvas. A severed forearm lay at my feet and bodies were scattered on both sides of the road, some still alive. One was Ike Maxwell who had collapsed next to the Mercedes. I slapped a new magazine on the Ingram and ran to help him. He was conscious but badly hurt, and I couldn't tell at first where he was hit. His shirt and trousers were wet with blood and he clutched his stomach in pain.

I pulled him to his feet and got one of his arms around my neck. He was weak as a baby, but gutsy as ever in spite of the pain. No one tried to stop us as I half-walked, half-carried him to the foot of the stairs inside the castle entrance.

"Go ahead, Davey. You ain't got much time."

"I'm not leaving you, Ike."

"Don't be a damn fool."

"You'll make it."

"Don't you ever learn?"

Another helicopter hovered above the wall waiting its turn to land, the last of the three. As we struggled up the steps, each one seemed steeper than the one before. The minutes passed. Ike was losing a lot of blood, but someone would come for us, I was sure. They wouldn't leave us behind.

One foot in front of the other. Then again. We reached the first landing, and the second. We made it the length of the corridor and I heard shouting above. I called out just as we were coming to the iron gate that led to the prison cells.

That was when the roof fell in. Literally. The charges Hueblen and Pietr had set did their job well, except they closed the passage directly in front of me as well as behind. I don't know whether we were lucky or unlucky. If we had been a hundred feet further, we would have been on the right side of the explosion and could have made the helicopters. But only fifty feet ahead or behind, and we would have been buried alive.

For several minutes I was too stunned to react. Ike kept fading out on me, and was very close to shock. When my own head cleared a little I realized that we were probably trapped. Ike's voice was weak, barely a whisper, and his breathing was labored. "Davey, I ain't going to make it this time."

"Sure you are, Ike."

"Don't argue. I know when I'm shit out of luck."

"Ike . . ."

"Now listen. All your enemies are dead and even Qaddafi thinks we took you prisoner."

"It doesn't matter, Ike . . ."

"Sure as hell does. You can walk out of here, now . . ." He struggled to reach his pocket, but the pain was too much. "Can you get it for me, Davey? My wallet?"

As gently as possible I managed to extricate the wallet from the torn and bloody pocket. That is when I saw the wound, a fist-size hole on the right just below his ribs.

"In one of them plastic windows there's a Swiss bank card. Red and white, looks like a credit card."

I found the card and gave it to him but he waved my hand away. "You keep it, Davey." I started to return the wallet to his pocket. "Wait a sec. That ain't everything. Look behind where the money is. Find it?"

"Yes."

He grimaced as he struggled to see the wallet better, then fell back, closed his eyes and tried to gather strength. The bleeding seemed to be less around the wound, but I could not be sure. "Look for a piece of paper with a number on it."

I held it up for him to see. It was a page from a pocket agenda with a number written in his childish scrawl.

"Read it to me."

I read the seven digit number.

"Now listen. You go to the Union Bank in Basel. Show that card and they take you into a client room. Write the number down for them, and you can draw whatever you want."

"But that money's yours, Ike."

"I want you to have it, Davey."

"But you'll need it."

"A fool can see I ain't going to make it, and you're no fool. Just be my partner like always and help me go easy."

"Ike . . ."

"I lied about that heart bypass so you wouldn't quit."

"Ike, your money still belongs to Priscilla Pearl."

"Who?"

"Your little daughter."

"I want you to have it."

"How can you say that when she's blind and crippled?"

"She is?"

"You told me she was."

"Davey, I was trying to con you a little . . ."

"She's not blind?"

"She prob'ly sees as good as you . . ."

"Or crippled . . . ?"

"Not that I know of . . ."

"Ike, it doesn't matter. The money still belongs to her."

"I guess it would, all right, if—"

"Then I'll see that she gets the bank card and the account number if you tell me where she lives."

"I kind of lost track of her."

"What was her last address? I'll find her."

"Davey?"

"Yes, Ike."

"I made that up."

"Made what up?"

"Priscilla Pearl."

"You mean you have no daughter? I don't believe you."

"Davey, even I wouldn't give a kid a name like that. I got some sense for what's right."

"What about all the stories you told me? About the Christmas you took her to visit Santa Claus when she said, 'I can see him, Daddy, with my own little fingers!' You made all that up?"

He nodded. "I'm a hell of a liar when I have to be."

His voice was so faint by then I had to lean close to hear him. "You wouldn't be in this fix if it wasn't for me, Davey . . . but I never thought . . . it would turn out this way." That little speech took all his strength and he drifted off, his eyelids fluttering closed.

He wore a lower denture which had slipped out of place and moved a little every time he drew a deep breath. He looked eighty years old lying there, yet I knew he wasn't much over fifty. Odd man out now, as they say, with his adolescent love of guns and old-fashioned code of honor. Yet without men like him no hostage could have been saved. And it was Ike Maxwell, not any government agent or policeman who finally put paid to Khalil Malduum.

I was not sure how many minutes had passed since we were cut off from the helicopters, but I was under no illusion about them waiting around for us. Ike was tough, but only immediate medical attention could save him. And now there was no hope of that, not even with the Libyans. They would reoccupy the fortress the moment the helicopters were gone, but they would take time to reach us through the rubble, and Ike could never last.

He was right about me. I might be safe until Nagy received David Perpignon's picture. But if anyone survived who had seen me in the shootout, I was a candidate for hanging.

I don't know how long I had been turning our fate over in my mind when I heard Ike call my name. He was propped against the wall, his eyes open, and I saw that he had thrown up blood. He tried to hold my hand as I took a handkerchief and cleaned his lips. I probably went on talking and trying to make him comfortable for some time after he died.

Then I closed his eyes and just sat.

XLVI

◇ It took time for the full effect of the catastrophe to sink in, but once it did, my depression followed like fog. Ike was dead, and I would soon join him if I didn't come up with some clever plan to save my neck. No matter how I looked at it, my predicament was grave, the odds against me astronomical, and my options so limited they were almost nonexistent.

The helicopters had taken off with Karen and the Americans, and I should have got some satisfaction from knowing I was the one responsible for their escape after all these months. Without the unexpected capture of Nagy's *mukhabarat* staff we would have had nothing to trade. Elliot's supersophisticated, "Big Stick" operation would never have worked. It was so brittle and unwieldy it fell apart the instant Malduum decided to move the hostages. And Dick Diamond's misguided enthusiasm for things like "Paraforce" and its exotic toys had been equally futile.

Like most important diplomatic breakthroughs, all it took in the end was imagination, a little muscle, and a lot of luck.

As I explored the immediate vicinity of my makeshift prison, I hoped that luck was still holding. I was in the center—the very bowels, in fact—of Tripoli. I had no food or water. I had the Ingram with two extra clips, half a pint of the Milk of the Four Peppers, and Ike's flashlight.

If I could find a way out, I would, but at first that did not seem likely. Moreover, the prospect of escape into the arms of people who might hang me was not appealing. Yet I'm a bit of a claustrophobe, and the idea of remaining underground one minute longer than necessary was so repugnant I had to do something.

To clear my head, I gulped a healthy jolt of the Milk of the Four Peppers, and after the shock of it wore off, I felt better. The demolition charge which cut me off from the helicopters had also opened a wide fissure in the far wall of the corridor. Shining the light through it, I looked upon another passage, musty and ancient, that ran under the prison. I was able to slip through the opening and dropped to a soft, cushioned floor. Above me were a thousand bats, and underfoot, a centuries-old carpet of guano.

So far so good. If bats lived here, there was an exit hole, and the quantity of them indicated it was probably a large one. I only hoped I didn't have to fly to reach it.

Every so often the passage would open out on a kind of room. I passed two or three of these before I noticed rings and chains embedded in the stone. Along one wall I found human bones and remembered what Pozzogallo had said about these tunnels being used by the old Karamanli pashas as dungeons and torture chambers.

The place had the feel of a tomb. Not dry, like virtually everything else in Libya, but damp and moldy. I flashed the light at something by my feet and saw a skull with a hank of reddish brown hair still attached. A little further on, scratched into the stone was a crude inscription. It read: "Roger Eastham, Surgeon, frigate Philadelphia, 1804. God have Mercy on my Soul!" Beyond it were other graffiti in different languages, and scattered on the carpet of bat dung, more bones.

I heard a soft rustle behind me and doused the light. Holding my breath I heard the sound again, or felt it, really. I swung the flashlight around and snapped it on hoping to surprise whoever or whatever it was in the sudden beam.

But I saw only a small ledge. I went closer. The ledge seemed to be moving, and I was certain I was hallucinating. It was solid rock, part of the fortress foundation. I took another step and froze where I was. The ledge was alive with vipers, a whole writhing, deadly colony of them, very agitated by my intrusion. I backed away, flashing the light around my feet, trying not to panic.

The Saharan pit viper, like the Barbary asp, is not large, but it is one of the deadliest snakes on earth. These could have been descended from the one Cleopatra held to her breast, but the painful death they cause is not at all romantic. I was half-hypnotized by their glistening, twisting shapes in the beam of the flashlight, but when a few dropped from the ledge and slithered in my direction, my cool deserted me and I broke into a run.

I didn't stop until I felt a stitch in my side, as they say. God only knew where the damned tunnel led. God and old Prince Pozzogallo, but neither was around to consult. I saw myself wandering lost in this maze for days without food or water, and finally when the batteries gave out, without light. Would I scratch my last plea on the wall like the unfortunate Surgeon Eastham, before lying down among the vipers and the bones to die? Would some other poor lost devil, two hundred years in the future, come across an inscription reading "David Perpignon, computer consultant?"

Suddenly the passage seemed to dead-end, and for a depressing instant I thought I might have to retrace all my steps. Then I realized I was not looking at a wall at all, but piles of boxes. I moved closer and saw cases and cases of beer, whiskey and champagne stacked to the ceiling. Crates of American coffee, instant iced tea, and breakfast cereal were piled high on pallets all around me.

My relief was almost palpable, and I laughed like a fool as I realized what I had found. Such a huge underground deposit implied a sizeable entrance somewhere. And the contraband nature of the goods meant they could only belong to one man, Jeballah.

I hurried on, cheerfully anticipating I would come to the end at any moment. Instead, to my dismay, I left the crates and boxes behind but with no sign yet of a way out. Only a Turk could build a thing like this. But I was being unfair. According to Pozzogallo, some of these passages had been here since the time of the ancient Romans.

I was cursing him and the Romans when I glimpsed a light. I walked more quickly, almost breaking into a run. The stone floor was no longer covered with bat droppings and my footsteps echoed eerily. Every so often I shone the beam of the flashlight on the walls in case of some obstruction. I was doing this when the floor ended abruptly and I stepped off into nothing.

I remember falling and great pain and being wet and cold. Beyond that, my mind is mercifully blank about those next few hours. Only much later was I able to reconstruct what happened.

The passage I had followed was one whose outside entrance was hidden by a great rocky outcropping on the backside of Tripoli harbor. Just inside the opening, the tunnel broadens, and on one side there is an ancient stone cistern about twenty feet deep. It was this I had fallen into.

All my luck was with me, however. There was accumulated refuse in the bottom which broke my fall, but not enough water, thank God, to drown in. I must have lain there unconscious for hours before one of Jeballah's Tibu discovered my inert form.

When I came to, dawn was breaking, and I found myself in the bottom of a small motor launch churning over the face of the sea. I was confused, in great pain, and with a terrible thirst. My head had been bound and it felt loose as a cracked egg under the dressing. I must have made some sound asking for water because a hand held a metal cup to my lips and I drank.

I vaguely recall being lifted from the boat in the bright sunlight and carried to a canvas-topped pickup truck which reeked of rotting vegetables. The slimy leaves of old cabbage and God knows what else were heaped around me and I slept again, aware only of the throbbing headache and a pain in my wrist from time to time. Then it was night again, and we were no longer moving.

The pain was still there, and sometime during the night I worked the flask of the Milk of the Four Peppers from my pocket and drank the last of it before drifting off to sleep again. I dreamt that Karen and I were together in Vienna about to make love when Jock Pringle interrupted us.

"Christ, mate! Too much of that stuff'll kill you. And I thought you never touched a drop."

"But I haven't even started," I protested, trying to hold on to the vision of Karen while he pulled the bottle rudely away. When I looked for her again, she was gone.

"Feeling better?"

"No."

"Hold on, then. We'll have you to a doctor soon."

The sun does not rise on the Libyan desert. Even in winter it slips above the horizon like a slowly opening furnace door. I was half awake and hungry when it appeared in the fading night sky just as we heard the plane. Against the sun it approached like a nesting crane, long legs and drooping wings, to touch down smoothly and roll to a stop nearby.

Dick Diamond materialized in the swirling dust like a dark apparition, but not in priest's garb or Navy flight suit this time. Even his face was blackened. He helped Pringle and the Tibu carry me aboard while the props were still turning. Then while Jock strapped me into a litter, Diamond banged the door shut, the engines whined, and after a short run we bounced back into the air.

"Why did you send Karen away?" I asked.

Dick Diamond was kneeling next to me. "You never pay attention. You never listen. She's okay. They're all okay."

"No, they're not. Ike Maxwell's dead."

"We know. You did a hell of a job, David."

I tried to sit up but the pain in my wrist was so severe I fainted. I later found out the arm was broken.

The American Navy couldn't have been more accommodating. They set the broken bone, took some stitches in my head, and for two days fed me aboard their ship. Before he left for England Jock Pringle dropped by the sickbay to return my leather-bound book of recipes and food notes.

"Where on earth did you get it?"

"As I often said, old boy, with Mr. Jeballah, all things are possible. I'm surprised your chaps missed it when they sacked Nagy's office. Anyway, God bless and Happy Christmas!"

Duff Elliot was there for the debriefing, as they call it, and so were Cardoni, the Russians, and Hueblen to fill in the details. Elliot said the files they had found in Nagy's safe were on their way to Washington. A cursory check of the one on Qaddafi indicated it had been compiled over the years by Nagy to protect himself. According to Elliot it would be invaluable for intelligence agencies.

That is when I learned that I owed my life to Aboubakir Jeballah and Diamond. When Ike Maxwell and I failed to show in time for the helicopter evacuation, Dick Diamond called Ghadames by radio, talked with Gagnon, and within the hour Jeballah's men in Tripoli had mounted a search for us. At first they assumed we had both been killed, but in checking out the underground passages around the castle, one of the Tibu spotted my flashlight beam and found me. I was taken in an old smuggling launch along the coast to Sabratha, then driven with Jock Pringle in a produce truck to a desert strip where Dick Diamond flew in and picked us up.

Meanwhile the released hostages had been flown to Wiesbaden for new clothes and a medical check, and then back to the United States where both the President and the French ambassador received them at Andrews Air Force Base. According to Duff Elliot, their arrival dominated the news and brightened the Christmas holidays for an entire nation.

I saw some of it on satellite television in the carrier sickbay. Rusty Kirshbaum was shown as he stepped off the plane, cleanshaven, with one arm raised in a victory sign, the other around his smiling wife. She was forty pounds lighter, she told the television reporter, and Rusty added, "But it's not a diet we recommend!"

Duff Elliot said to me as soon as I was up and about, "Everyone wants to interview you. I can ask the Naples public information officer to set up a press conference."

"But I'm not giving any interviews, and certainly no pictures."

"It's up to you . . . naturally." He was a little annoyed at my refusal, but still grateful that I'd saved his fat from the fire, as they say, so much so that he even offered me a job with the Defense Resources Institute. I said thanks, but no thanks. According to Dick Diamond, the success of the "Perpignon Exchange" could lead to a cabinet appointment for Duff Elliot.

I telephoned Karen in Vienna as soon as I was able, and told her I would be there for Christmas. Then I flew with Diamond as far as Rome, and we waited for separate connecting flights in the same VIP lounge where we had met.

"Looks like you've come full circle," he said.

"What will you do now?" I asked him.

"Go back to work."

"At the Institute?"

"Maybe, if Duff can arrange it. Otherwise I'll return to Tel Aviv. I was only on loan for this operation."

He had to be joking. "You're Israeli? But I thought . . ."

"That I was American?" He grinned at my discomfort.

"But Ike Maxwell said you were in Iran with him . . ."

"I was on loan then too, from the Israeli army."

"And who do you work for now?"

"When I'm not baby sitting crazies like you, I'm a cop." He stuck out his hand. "Inspector Ariel Diamond, counterterrorist section. My friends call me Dick."

Two men from the Israeli embassy brought him an enormous file of newspaper clippings which he scanned before turning them over to me. "Something to remember us by," he said. "In the end I'm happy to say it was a pleasure working with you, Dahoud, I mean, David. You'll get a kick out of some of these articles, I'm sure."

A kick indeed. The European and American newspapers had featured the story on their front pages for days, illustrated with Karen's dramatic photographs. When it was no longer hard news, many of them devoted columns to speculation on the whereabouts and background of the mysterious French hero, David Perpignon.

Paris always denied any official connection with the "Perpignon Affair," as they called it, and lamely explained that their ambassador was at Andrews Air Force Base only because the American president had invited him.

But no one believed these denials after a high-ranking French politician running for reelection said off the record that he had been kept fully informed regarding Agent Perpignon's undercover work for months prior to the rescue. "All covert operations must remain secret even after they become public," he explained, "or our agents would never be able to work in privacy."

Perpignon, he added, had only been assigned by his superiors to the hostage case following that same politician's demand for action. When negotiations broke down after the release of the French students, Perpignon led an international commando raid on the Libyan prison to force a further exchange of hostages.

The government insisted that no French troops were involved as had been reported, and a request by the Libyans to the Quai d'Orsay for a picture of Perpignon was denied.

The French president was publicly congratulated by world leaders for his government's stand against international terrorism, and the press noted that the list included the newly elected presidents or prime ministers of several former Communist nations as well as the head of the Soviet Union.

Meanwhile the reclusive Perpignon was not available for comment. After the dramatic rescue, one paper reported, he had skillfully dodged the press and retired to spend the holidays in Tahiti with his family. The same day that report was published, the mysterious agent was reported by the British tabloids to have been seen shopping in Harrods, dining at Simpson's on the Strand, and strolling in Hyde Park with his wife. A photograph of an unidentifiable man and woman trying to get a taxi in the rain accompanied this last article.

No one mentioned Vienna.

In an unrelated development, the German papers carried an item about an Iraqi identified only as Bashir who blew himself up together with a small dog in a Munich apartment. The accident was believed to have been caused while he was assembling a bomb. Bashir and a woman companion had been under surveillance by police for several days, the article stated, but the woman's whereabouts were unknown.

The Libyan press made no mention of any prisoners, hostages or captives of any kind in Libya. Instead, their front page stories and editorials were devoted to the brutal assassinations of the gallant Palestinian freedom fighter Dahoud el Beida and his political mentor Khalil Malduum. During a futile Zionist rocket attack against the Libyan People's Government offices in downtown Tripoli, both men, prominent in the struggle against Zionist colonialism, were killed.

Alert Libyan Green Militia and other members of the Peoples' Armed Forces under the command of Captain Abdulsalam Nagy repelled the Zionist terrorists. Beside the tragic deaths of Beida and Malduum, several members of the United Palestinian Armed Resistance Front also died. In reward for his distinguished conduct Captain Nagy was promoted by the people to become the Peoples' supreme *mukhabarat* supervisor.

The Illustrious Leader of the Libyan People, Colonel Muhammar Qaddafi, declared three days of national mourning and vowed revenge on the assassins of Beida and Malduum. The *Tarablus el*

Gharb newspaper carried a touching picture of Beida's distraught widow, recently returned from a diplomatic mission to Germany, weeping at her husband's state funeral. Solange must have enjoyed that moment. At last she had the status and attention she always craved. I wondered whose remains she was burying. Hanzi's?

Karen was waiting for me when I arrived in Vienna, and after much touching and holding and a few tears we went to her apartment and spent a lazy afternoon making love. Then we walked to Demal's for coffee with whipped cream and Sacher *torte* at sundown. The Austrian festive spirit was everywhere. Shop windows were gaily decorated and even the lamp posts in the narrow streets wore great red bows for Christmas. We stopped to listen to a brass choir playing on the steps of a church as it began to snow.

"Happy?" I asked as she snuggled into the crook of my arm.

She nodded, tears glistening in her pretty eyes. "You?"

"I miss Libya," I teased, "but I'll get over it."

"Oh, David!"

We bought sausages and wine and schnitzel, and got some currant and apple tarts from Demal's before returning to the apartment. There we had dinner, breakfast and lunch at all the wrong hours, and made love in between. We watched the snow falling outside against the streetlights and held hands when I reached the point where I couldn't do much else.

Shortly after the New Year celebrations the *Frankfurter Zeitung* featured an interview with Karlheinz Hueblen, former German border guard, who said that David Perpignon would never be found because he did not exist.

According to Hueblen, Alan Preston, a Canadian soldier of fortune killed in the raid on the Libyan prison, was the leader. After the second in command, an American named Isaac Maxwell, was also killed, Hueblen took charge. In the end, it was he who liberated the hostages and arranged their safe evacuation aboard Sixth Fleet helicopters. Asked to corroborate Herr Hueblen's version, both French and American authorities declined to comment.

Over the months that followed I heard a little about the others. Jock Pringle went to work for a flying service in the Falkland Islands while Jeballah returned to France where his business continued to prosper. Old Prince Pozzogallo paid off the mortgage on his ancestral estate in Sicily and took a holiday in Turkey.

Najeeb Hassan apparently decided to carry out the rest of the terrorist bombings after Malduum and Bashir were killed. Travelling under his assumed name, he was arrested by British police as he disembarked from a plane at Heathrow Airport.

I was rich, of course. Between what I had stolen, what I had earned, and what Ike left me, David Perpignon's net worth was well over a million dollars. I was so secure in fact, that I turned over my share of the reward money paid for Malduum to an international refugee organization.

An annual income would never be a problem thanks to my foresight before leaving Libya. Mr. Watanabe was promoted to head the Libyan bank's computer section after Beida was killed, but he never found any trace of the virus Beida left behind. So each year a few million dollars would be lost to an indeterminate list of random foreign accounts, and some would always find their way into mine.

Karen and I were married eventually because I saw no reason not to be. Dahoud el Beida was dead and his egregious widow was dining out everywhere on his martyrdom. David Perpignon, on the other hand was alive and well and in love with Karen Koenig.

But idleness is not for me and I soon began to cast around for a legitimate business occupation. I had not yet made up my mind whether to seek a computer distributorship or open a software boutique when one day Karen said, "Who was Carême, darling?"

"My dear, you don't know? Sit down and let me tell you."

That alas, was the beginning. Her eyes shone with pleasure as I recounted the great confectioner's magnificent career and described his astonishing creations. I talked for hours while she listened, and at four in the morning we made up our minds.

The place is called Carême's Café-Konditorei, and although it can't yet compete with the Imperial Hotel or Demal's, we are on our way. You'll find it just across the road from St. Stephen's cathedral, in the old part of Vienna. It is cheerful and cozy, with the most wonderful smells emanating from our kitchens. People come from all over to sample my secret specialty, a sweet, tangy cake made with jalapeña honey and four different kinds of imported Turkish poppyseed.